Anne McCaffrey

The Girl Who Heard Dragons

FIFTEEN SUPERB STORIES FROM THE CREATOR
OF THE DRAGONS OF PERN

ANNE McCAFFREY
&
ELIZABETH ANN SCARBOROUGH

Powers That Be

THE FIRST COLLABORATION BETWEEN TWO
OF SCIENCE FICTION'S MIGHTIEST NAMES

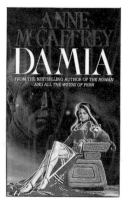

ANNE McCAFFREY
DAMIA

FROM THE BESTSELLING AUTHOR OF THE ROWAN
AND ALL THE WEYRS OF PERN

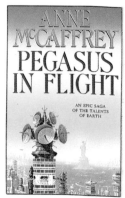

ANNE McCAFFREY
PEGASUS IN FLIGHT

AN EPIC SAGA
OF THE TALENTS
OF EARTH

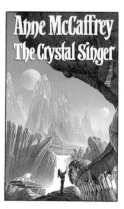

Anne McCaffrey
The Crystal Singer

Anne McCaffrey
Killashandra

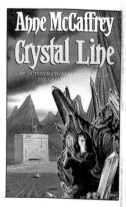

Anne McCaffrey
Crystal Line

AN OUTSTANDING NEW CHRONICLE OF
THE CRYSTAL SINGER

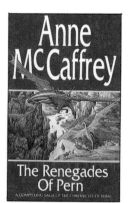

Anne McCaffrey

The Renegades
Of Pern

A COMPELLING SAGA OF THE CHRONICLES OF PERN

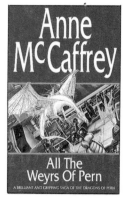

Anne McCaffrey

All The
Weyrs Of Pern

A BRILLIANT AND GRIPPING SAGA OF THE DRAGONS OF PERN

Anne McCaffrey
Get off the Unicorn

FOURTEEN WONDERFUL STORIES

Born on April 1st, Anne McCaffrey has tried to live up to her auspicious natal day. Her first novel was created in Latin class and might have brought her instant fame, as well as an A, had she written in that ancient language. Much chastened, she turned to the stage and became a character actress, appearing in the first successful summer music circus in Lambertsville, New Jersey. She studied music for nine years and, during that time, became intensely interested in the stage direction of opera and operetta, ending that phase of her experience with the stage direction of the American première of Carl Orff's *Ludus De Nato Infante Mirificus* in which she also played a witch.

By the time the three children of her marriage were comfortably in school most of the day, she had already achieved enough success with short stories to devote herself full time to writing. Her first novel, *Restoree*, was written as a protest against the absurd and unrealistic portrayals of women in the science fiction novels of the fifties. It is, however, in the handling of broader themes and the worlds of her imagination, particularly the two series (*Helva*, *The Ship Who Sang*, and the twelve novels about the Dragonriders of Pern) that Ms McCaffrey's talents as a storyteller are best displayed. One of the world's leading science fiction writers, she has won both the Hugo and Nebula Awards, the E.E. 'Doc' Smith, the Golden Pen, and has been seven times a winner of the Science Fiction Book Club Award.

Between her appearances in the States, England, Europe, Australia, New Zealand and Alaska as a lecturer in secondary schools and universities, and guest-of-honour at science fiction conventions, Ms McCaffrey lives in a house of her own design, Dragonhold-Underhill (because she had to dig out a hill on her farm to build it) in County Wicklow, Ireland. She runs a private livery stable and her three-day-event horses have been successful in international competitions. She does not do the competition riding, she hastens to add, but enjoys the success of horse and rider and the occasional canter on her favourite mount, a black and white mare named Pi.

Of herself, Ms McCaffrey warns: 'My eyes are green, my hair is silver and I freckle; the rest is still subject to change without notice.'

Ms McCaffrey graduated *cum laude* from Radcliffe College, majoring in the Slavonic Languages and Literatures.

Anne McCaffrey's books can be read individually or as series. However, for greatest enjoyment the following sequences are recommended:

The Dragon Books

DRAGONFLIGHT

DRAGONQUEST

DRAGONSONG

DRAGONSINGER: HARPER OF PERN

THE WHITE DRAGON

DRAGONDRUMS

MORETA: DRAGONLADY OF PERN

NERILKA'S STORY & THE COELURA

DRAGONSDAWN

THE RENEGADES OF PERN

ALL THE WEYRS OF PERN

THE CHRONICLES OF PERN: FIRST FALL

THE DOLPHINS OF PERN

RED STAR RISING: THE
SECOND CHRONICLES OF PERN*

Crystal Singer Books

THE CRYSTAL SINGER

KILLASHANDRA

CRYSTAL LINE

* to be published

THE GIRL WHO HEARD DRAGONS

Anne McCaffrey

CORGI BOOKS

THE GIRL WHO HEARD DRAGONS
A CORGI BOOK : 0 552 14436 3

First publication in Great Britain

PRINTING HISTORY
Corgi edition published 1996
Corgi edition reprinted 1996 (twice)
Corgi edition reprinted 1997

This book is set in 11/12½pt Linotron Plantin by
County Typesetters, Margate, Kent.

Corgi Books are published by Transworld Publishers Ltd,
61–63 Uxbridge Road, London W5 5SA,
in Australia by Transworld Publishers (Australia) Pty Ltd,
15–25 Helles Avenue, Moorebank, NSW 2170
and in New Zealand by Transworld Publishers (NZ) Ltd,
3 William Pickering Drive, Albany, Auckland.

Printed and bound in Great Britain by
Cox & Wyman Ltd, Reading, Berkshire.

CONTENTS

THE GIRL WHO
HEARD DRAGONS

SO, YOU'RE
ANNE McCAFFREY

I'm never sure what image readers construct of me from reading my books. But, generally, when I get a response of 'You're Anne McCaffrey?' I haven't had the nerve to ask what they were expecting. Tones range from skepticism to deep disappointment and incredulity. Yet I do describe myself: 'My hair is silver, my eyes are green, and I freckle. The rest is subject to change without notice' – the 'rest' being the unrepentant bulk of me.

Fortunately, the faces of authors are not as widely displayed as those of more public celebrities. Often the jacket flap or the back copy includes a photo, formal or informal, of the author, which very few people ever connect to the person sitting next to them on an airplane or walking in a mall.

Once, on the shuttle from New York to Boston, I was recognized: I'd been on a Boston TV talk show that noon. I remember the show vividly, because during a commercial break I was sitting in the audience, waiting my turn, when Ethel Merman suddenly swept in. She was there to promote her autobiography. She did, then swept out again. To my horror, I was beckoned to come on the set *then*.

I was still sort of in a trance (as I used to sing many of the songs that Ethel Merman had made popular) when the presenter asked me how I get such fantastic ideas.

'That's nowhere near as hard as following Ethel Merman's act on this show,' I replied, and got a laugh and applause.

About two hours later, as I was filing down the aisle of the shuttle, a girl tapped me on the shoulder and asked if I was Anne McCaffrey.

'Oh, are you a fan?' I asked, pleased.

'No, I just thought I recognized you from the show with Ethel Merman.'

Very early on in my career, I learned never to admit to seatmates on airplanes (particularly long-distance flights) that I write for a living.

That was a surefire way to be told in exhaustive detail their idea for a best-selling novel, invariably based on an autobiographical event. When asked directly what I do, I tend to vary between saying I'm 1) a potato farmer, 2) a horse breeder, and 3) going to visit my grandchildren. The latter generally silences all but the most garrulous. Who wants to be shown pictures or bored with tales of precocious offspring?

Twice, though, seatmates provided considerable gratification for me. In 1980, I was suffering from a heavy cold on a short hop from Melbourne to Sydney, Australia, and I had buried my head in the mammoth crossword puzzle I was doing. Having the window seat, I didn't pay much attention as the other two passengers filed into our row.

When I did come up for a look, I was amazed to see the man next to me – mid-thirties, attractive, very elegantly dressed in fine gray flannel with a silk shirt and Countess Mara tie – engrossed in a book with an extremely familiar cover: *To Ride Pegasus*. I waited until he was turning a page and then asked him in a sort of skeptical tone if the book was any good.

He looked up and replied that yes, it was good but then he enjoyed all this author's books.

'That's good,' said I, 'because you're sitting next to her!'

He introduced himself as David Ogilvy, the director of the Sydney Opera Company, on his way to direct Joan Sutherland in a concert version of *Lucia di Lammermoor*. We chatted quite amiably until the plane landed, but I count him as one of my more prestigious readers.

Every time I'm at Andromeda Book Shop in Birmingham, I'm asked to sign a book for Bob Monkhouse. 'We must stop meeting like this!'

In April 1984, on one of those remarkable zigzag air routes from New York to Alaska, I acquired two new seatmates in Dallas: a very pretty girl in the middle seat, and on the aisle a gangly guy, who immediately chatted her up. She was a beauty counselor on her way to Seattle, and he announced that he had just finished a first-aid course for helicopter pilots and was on his way back to Fairbanks, Alaska – my ultimate destination. I listened to their banter but didn't add anything.

When she left the plane at Seattle, I asked him about the weather in Fairbanks. He was quite civil, but he obviously wanted to get back to the book he was reading – which was an SF title. I asked him if he liked reading the genre, and he replied that he liked the hard science but fantasy bored him. Out of courtesy, he asked why I was on my way to Alaska, so I told him I was a potato farmer.

I spent a marvelous time as author in residence in Fairbanks, going dogsledding, eating moose-meat spaghetti, watching the aurora borealis, corrupting junior and senior high-school students and undergraduates at the University of Alaska – anyone I could get my hands on. I was there on my birthday, and the local bakery students whomped up an immense White Dragon cake – enough for everyone in the Fairbanks Arts buffet. On the final Saturday, I was doing an autograph session in one of the malls, when in comes my airplane friend, arms loaded down with books, wife and daughters trailing after him. He stopped in front of my table and plopped down every book I had written, including the three Dell romances.

'You didn't tell me you were famous,' he accused me.

'You didn't ask!'

Then there are those times at conventions when people don't yet realize that you're the Guest of Honor. I enjoy sitting at the registration table when my con schedule permits – and getting a charge out of reactions.

In Baltimore in 1977 (the year I discovered I had become a cult figure), I was sitting in the registration area when a woman, neatly dressed in a Villager shirtwaist dress, carrying two heavy Lord & Taylor shopping bags, advanced on the desk. She was not at all the type that you would expect would read SF. I thought she might have got into the wrong hotel. She wanted to know if Anne McCaffrey was really speaking that day. I replied that she was. The woman asked at what time, so I told her (all this with two of the registration staff trying to keep their faces straight).

'Are you sure she's going to speak?'

'Oh, yes, I can vouch for it. She's here and she'll be speaking at two o'clock.'

Only then would she pay for her day badge.

After my speech, the lady approached me again, still lugging her shopping bags. She gave me a sideways glance and then smiled.

'You fooled me.' She upended the shopping bags to display all my novels, including the romances, and the magazines that had published my short stories.

'And you fooled me,' I replied, pointing at the bags. We both had a chuckle.

I remember being asked if I knew Doris Pitkin Buck, who was in her seventies when I first met her at Milford,

Pennsylvania, but who could write tales with intense and horrific insights into human nature or gentle and restorative tales. When I admitted to knowing her, the boy asked me how old she was.

'How old do you think she is?' I asked.

'Oh, early twenties.' Obviously that was a considerable age to him.

'How ever did you guess?'

Well, why not? Doris wrote with a very young, romantic voice at times, and for the duration of those stories she *was* in her early twenties.

The identity dichotomy (the real versus the imaginary) started for me in the late 1960s, by the time of the Kent student massacre.

My son Alec, who started his career as a protestor at this point, asked permission to use the SFWA mimeograph machine to run off some flyers for a march to be held in Sea Cliff, Long Island, where we were living. Alec was bustling about my office, introducing his mother to the Columbia students who were joining in the march. One of them noticed the titles on the bookshelves.

'Hey, who reads science fiction?' one young man asked.

'My mother,' Alec replied, because he was not totally convinced that he wanted a science-fiction author as his mother.

'Hey, why does your mother have four and five copies of Anne McCaffrey's books?' the boy wanted to know.

'Because she *is* Anne McCaffrey,' Alec replied, exasperated.

'No shit!' was the admiring response.

I think that's when Alec realized that having an SF author as a mother was not altogether a bad hit.

Alec never has been much of a fiction reader anyhow, and certainly not as dedicated to science fiction as his brother, Todd. In fact, it wasn't until Alec was shamed by clients at the 100 Flowers Book Shop he managed in Cambridge that he finally read *Dragonflight*.

Now he takes great pride in my success and is diligent about reporting how my books are displayed at the local malls, and will always turn my titles out whenever he can.

A variant of that occurred the day I was looking for a copy of Todd's first published novel: *Slammers Down*, a Pathway adventure based on David Drake's military novels.

The B. Dalton store manager recognized me and came up proudly to point out their display of my titles.

'I'm looking for Todd Johnson's novel,' I told him, and saw his bafflement. 'He's my son, and it's his first!' I added, beaming like any fatuously proud mother. And I was.

'But you're Anne McCaffrey' was the manager's startled reply.

'That doesn't keep me from being Todd Johnson's mother!'

Todd also had encounters with the doubting: well, it's understandable, since I reverted to my maiden name after my divorce. When Todd was doorman one evening in Lehighs gymnasium, reading *The White Dragon*, which had just been published, one of the students noticed the title.

'Hey, is it any good?' he asked Todd.

'It's not bad,' and Todd has always been scrupulously honest, 'but there're a lot of typos.'

'There are? Going to tell the publisher?'

'No, I'll tell Anne McCaffrey.'

'How do you dare do that?'

'She's my mother.'

'I find that hard to believe,' the student replied, and stalked off.

As it happened, *Decision at Doona*, based on Todd's remarkable personality, was dedicated 'to Todd Johnson, of course.'

When I arrived at Lehigh in between conventions later that year, I signed all the copies of *Decision* in Lehigh's bookshop, adding 'Yes, I AM his mother!'

When Todd joined the U.S. Army to serve at Böblingen, West Germany, he would haunt the post bookshop for new titles. He was somewhat surprised to find his captain searching for new SF releases. So they fell to talking about authors and new titles, and the captain picked up a copy of *Moreta*, recommending it to Todd, who demurred.

'Thanks, sir, but I've read it.'

'It just came in.'

'I read it in manuscript.'

'How'd you do that, Johnson?'

'She's my mother!'

(Again) 'No shit!'

Having fans in useful places is a phenomenon that occurs when you least expect it, and most need it.

The best 'for instance' was during my arduous 1979 *White Dragon* promotional tour – twenty-two cities in thirty-two days. By Toledo, Kansas, I had been on such an adrenaline high that I hadn't slept in five nights. My escort managed to get a doctor to sit next to me at a press luncheon – he was also a reader – and he prescribed a tranquilizer, which, indeed, reduced my stress. But, sadly, it did not help me get to sleep. By evening I had to travel on to Minneapolis and at 3:30 had still not managed to get any rest. I called the desk clerk to ask what to do in a medical emergency. He recommended a cab to the nearest hospital.

I was the only patient entering the emergency facility, so I was seen immediately and explained to the nurse who took the usual pulse, temperature, and blood-pressure readings what my problem was, showing her my daunting schedule. She left me in the cubicle to speak to the duty doctor. I could just hear her whisper, 'Don't you know who she *is*?'

He may not have, but she did, and I got some sleeping pills – only, I suspect, because she knew I was 'who I was,' not just some middle-aged lady with travel fatigue. I went back to the hotel and had four hours of blessed unconsciousness.

Living in Ireland as I do has insulated me from having too many unexpected visitors, althought it's amazing how many people will go to the trouble to 'find' Dragonhold while touring Ireland. I prefer it when people phone me in advance – so at least I can pick up the comfortable clutter in the living room and be sure there are enough cookies to serve with coffee or tea.

I remember one young man who arrived just as a fractious mare had jumped out of the exercise paddock and was racing down to the road. He had the good sense to hold up both arms and scare her into turning. He'd arrived on a very 'Dragonhold' day – the sort when everything goes obliquely wrong!

It is a given that the visitors you'd like to have stay on and join you in a meal insist on leaving after an hour. The ones who bore you stupid are those who hang on and on and on. Fortunately my sister-in-law, Sara Brooks, who now lives with me, recognizes the symptoms and is always jane on the spot with an excuse for me.

I did have a very intense interview with a girl who insisted that there *had* to be religion on Pern. There was no way, in her lexicon, that the colony could have been established without religion. I told her in very certain tones and terms that Pern was my world and I could do with it what I wanted. I wanted it *not* to have religion, considering the crimes committed in the name of one deity or another.

There are some people you just don't argue with. On cue, Sis 'reminded' me that my accountant was arriving soon and I'd better assemble my files for him.

Then there are the earnest interviewers, some of them very young. Because there had recently been some bloopers in articles about me – the kind of mistakes and misrepresentations that are such a nuisance to correct when someone challenges them – I asked one nice, *young* interviewer to let me see her article before it was published. She agreed, with effusions of goodwill.

Now, she brought with her the two books that had prompted the interview, she had a tape recorder going, and she took notes. When she phoned me the next day to say that the issue was going to press immediately, so I wouldn't be able to see her interview but she just knew there would be no errors, I could only sigh in hopes.

They were daunted. She didn't spell my name correctly throughout; she mixed up the two titles; she described my sister-in-law as 'pottering' about in the kitchen – well, Sis has been a potter, but the correct term is 'putter.' To crown the confusion, she had my father dying in the Crimean War. When I phoned to ask for corrections, she didn't even realize the time scale between the two wars. They both started with a 'k' sound: Korea or Crimea, did it make that much difference? They were both wars, weren't they? As someone who tries to be positive about such blunders, I told everyone that I was really 134 years old and my mother had given birth to my younger brother posthumously. When I told Kevin about the mistake, he allowed as how that must explain why he'd had so much trouble all his life!

In Christmas '91, I visited the far-flung members of my family and agreed to do autograph sessions in Dayton, Ohio; St Louis, Missouri; Las Vegas, Nevada; and Los Angeles, returning favors done relatives.

I discovered that there are two new parameters in the readership: 1) that the kids who read the Harper Hall series are now grown-up enough to introduce the next crop to the books, and 2) that there are kids who've had to read either 'The Smallest Dragonboy' or one of the Harper Hall novels in class.

I've had very mixed feelings about having stories included in school textbooks or on required-reading lists. I generally loathed the books I had to read. So, in St Louis, when a trio of boys told me they'd read 'The Smallest Dragonboy' even as they asked me to personalize copies of *Dragondrums* for them, I got the nerve to ask if they liked it.

'Well, it wasn't that bad,' I was told by a Tom Sawyerish type. 'Not bad at all.'

'I liked it,' said another one of the group.

'D'you see that gentleman over there on the bench?' I said, pointing to my brother, Kevin, silver-haired like me and virtually unflappable. 'That's my brother and the model for Keevan' – the hero of 'The Smallest Dragonboy.' 'You should get his autograph, too.'

'Him?' asked the third boy, incredulous.

'He was young once, too, and very brave, just like Keevan.'

They did get Keve's autograph. Why should I do all the work?

I don't say that I adore autograph sessions: the last promotion trip has left me with tennis elbow. But they do provide me with the feedback that is invaluable to an author who spends a lot of solitary hours in front of a keyboard. It also answers some part of the question 'So, you're Anne McCaffrey?'

THE GIRL WHO
HEARD DRAGONS

Aramina was roused by the urgency of her parents' voices, Dowell's a fierce whisper of persuasion and her mother's a fearful rejoinder. She lay still, at first thinking that her mother had had another of her 'seeings,' but on such occasions Barla's voice was totally devoid of emotion. Straining her ears to pick up only her parents' words, Aramina ignored the myriad nocturnal noises of the enormous Igen cavern that sheltered some of the hundreds of holdless folk on Pern.

'It is pointless to assign blame at this juncture, Barla,' her father was whispering, 'or to moan about our pride in Aramina's ability. We must leave. Now. Tonight.'

'But winter comes,' Barla wailed. 'How will we survive?'

'I can't say that we survived all that well here last winter, with so many to share out what game was caught,' Dowell said as he rapidly stuffed oddments into the capacious pack. 'I've heard tell of caves in Lemos. And Lemos . . .'

'Has wood!' There was bitterness in Barla's voice. 'And none in Igen to suit you.'

'We may be holdless, woman, but we have not lost honor and dignity. I will not be party to Lady Holdless Thella's designs. I will not permit our daughter to be exploited in such a way. Gather your things. Now. I'll wake the children.'

When Dowell touched Aramina's shoulder, she

swallowed against her fear. She hadn't liked the self-styled Lady Holdless Thella when Thella had sought her out on the last few visits to the Igen caverns to recruit people to her roving bands. Aramina had been fascinated, and obliquely repelled by Giron, Thella's second-in-command, the dragonless man who had scrutinized her so intently that Aramina had been hard put not to squirm under his cold and empty eyes. A man who had been a dragonrider and lost his dragon was only half a man, or so everyone said. Thella had hinted at concessions for Aramina's family, perhaps even a hold, though Aramina was not so stupid as to contest that possibility, even as Thella offered the bait. Nor did Thella's argument that the holdless had to band together, sharing whatever possessions they had, hold any weight with a child who had early learned that no gift was free.

'I'm sorry, Father,' she murmured in fearful contrition.

'Sorry? For what, child? Oh, you heard? You are not at fault, 'Mina. Can you manage your sister? We must leave now.'

Aramina nodded. She rose and deftly twisted her blanket about her shoulders to make a sling for Nexa. She had carried her thus often as the small family had wandered eastward. Indeed, Nexa merely draped herself sleepily across Aramina's bony young shoulder and snuggled into the supporting blanket without rousing from her deep slumber.

Aramina glanced about, unconsciously checking to see that every one of their few belongings had been reclaimed.

'I've already packed the wagon with what we could take,' Dowell said.

'And Mother thought that that thieving Nerat family was pilfering things again.' Aramina was somewhat exasperated because she had been obliged to spend in the entire day surreptitiously near that noisome camp, trying to spot any of their belongings.

Barla had already gathered up her precious cooking pots, wrapping them in old clothes to prevent their banging. Another shawl held the rest of the family's portables, zealously guarded against the pilfering habits of the cavern's population.

'Hush now! Come. We must make the most of the full moons.'

For the first time Aramina regretted that her father's skill with woods had purchased for his family a partially secluded alcove toward the rear of the great Igen cavern. It had been much cooler during the blazing Igen summer, warmer and sheltered from the bitter winter winds, but now it seemed an interminable distance as they wended a cautious path among sleeping bodies to reach the entrance of the wind-sculpted sandstone cave.

Frequently Aramina had to shift Nexa in the journey down the sand to the river, sinking occasionally into old refuse holes and trying not to trip over debris. Having no hold to be proud of, the holdless residing in Igen cavern had no pride of place either, and any accommodation, transient or semipermanent, was marked by mute evidence of their occupancy.

The moons came out, bright Belior high and the smaller, dimmer Timor halfway down her arc, highlighting Igen River. Aramina wondered how long her father had planned this exodus, for not only did they have illumination but the river, dried by the summer's sun, was low enough to make crossing to the Lemos side relatively easy and safe. Very soon, when the fall rains began in the high mountains, no one would be able to cross the torrent that rampaged around the bend, flooding the now shallow ford. Aramina also remembered that Thella and Giron had been in the cavern that very afternoon, unlikely to return for several days, thus

23

giving the fleeing family some margin of escape. Neither had approached Aramina, for which she had been grateful, but perhaps Thella had alarmed Dowell. Whatever the reason, Aramina was grateful on many counts to be away from the brawling, odorous, over-crowded cavern. And she knew that Barla would be, too. Her brother Pell's tendency to brag about his family would now be limited to hill and forest, wherry and tunnel snake.

The dray beasts were already hitched to the family's wagon, a smallish one but adequate for four people. Since Aramina heard dragons and could give warning of the imminence of Threadfall, the family could travel with some impunity. It was this talent, until just recently considered the family's most valuable asset, that the Lady Holdless Thella wished to pervert to her unlawful ends.

Aramina shifted her sleeping sister once more, for both shoulders ached, and Nexa, like other inanimate objects, appeared to grow heavier. Pell had awakened; his initial outburst muffled by Dowell's large hand, he now trotted beside his father, burdened by the shawl bundle, and complained in a low undertone. Aramina came abreast of him.

'If you hadn't blabbed to show off, we wouldn't *be* running away,' she said to him in a tone for his ears only.

'We aren't running,' Pell snapped back, grunting as the shawl bundle cracked him on the right shin. 'We don't run away. We change camps!' He was taunting her now with her own words, used on previous occasions to ease the stigma of their holdlessness. 'But where can we go,' and his voice became a frightened wail, 'that Thella can't find us?'

'It's me she wants, and she won't find me. You'll be safe.'

'I don't want to be safe,' Pell replied stoutly, 'if you have to run because of me and my big mouth.'

'Hush!' said Dowell in a sharp voice. The children trudged the rest of the way in silence.

Their dray beasts, Nudge and Shove, turned their heads, lowing softly at the approach of familiar people; Dowell had left them with sufficient grain in their feed bags to content them. Barla climbed into the rear of the hide-covered wagon, took the sleeping Nexa from Aramina, the bundle from Pell, and gestured the children to the fore where Dowell was untying ring reins from the tether stone. Aramina and Pell reclaimed their goods from the wagon and took their positions, one on either side of the team, ready to encourage them into the river and up the bank on the far side. Dowell and Barla would walk behind to push should the wagon founder.

Despite the hour and the circumstances of their departure, Aramina felt a tremendous relief as they moved off. Two Turns ago she had been inexpressibly relieved not to have to plod at the pace of Nudge and Shove day after weary day. But now traveling was a far more palatable alternative to being part of Thella's vindictive schemes.

'We are not holdless by choice, Aramina,' Barla had often abjured her daughter, 'for your father held well under Lord Kale of Ruatha Hold. Oh,' and Barla would bow her head and press her hands to her mouth in anguish over terrible memories, 'the perfidy, the treachery of that terrible, ruthless man! To murder all Ruatha blood in one pitiless hour!' Barla would gather herself then, lifting her head proudly. 'Nor would your father serve Lord Fax of the High Reaches.' Barla was not an extravagant person in word or deed, retaining a quiet and unobtrusive dignity despite all the slights and pettiness that came the way of the holdless. Her acrimony was therefore the more memorable, and Aramina, as well as her surviving brother and sister, knew Fax as the villain, despoiler, and tyrant, possessed of no single redeeming virtue. 'We had pride enough to leave when he made his unspeakable order . . .' Barla would often color and then pale when reciting this part of their exodus. 'Your father had made this very wagon for us to attend gathers.' Barla would sigh. 'Attend gathers as respected holders, not as wanderers, holdless and friendless. For other Lord Holders did not wish to antagonize Fax just then, and though your father had been so certain of a welcome elsewhere, there was none. But we are *not* like the others, children. We chose to retain our honor and would not submit to the incarnate evil of Fax.'

Although Barla would never be specific about that, of late Aramina was beginning to get glimmerings, now that she had become a woman. For Barla, despite the depredations of fourteen Turns of nomadic life and endless pregnancies as tokens of Dowell's esteem, still retained a beautiful face and a slender figure. Aramina was old enough to realize that Barla was far more handsome than most holdless women and that, when they entered a new hold, Barla kept her lustrous hair hidden under a tattered head scarf and wore the many-layered garments of cold poverty.

Dowell had been a skilled wood joiner, holding a modest but profitable hold for Lord Kale in the forests of Ruatha. News of the treacherous massacre of the entire bloodline had reached the mountain fastness long after the event, when a contingent of Fax's rough troops had thundered into the hold's yard and informed the astounded Dowell of the change in Lord Holder. He had bowed his head – reluctantly but wisely – to that announcement and kept his resentment and horror masked, hoping that none of the troop realized that his wife, Barla, expecting her first child, also bore Ruathan blood in her veins.

If Dowell hoped that a meek acceptance and an isolated location would keep him from Fax's notice, he erred. The leader of the troop had eyes in his head; if he couldn't detect Barla's bloodline at a glance, one look was enough to tell him that here was a woman of interest to Lord Fax. Nor had the man's shrewd gleam escaped Dowell, and the woodcrafter had made contingency plans, which began with leaving the hold's gather wagon and two sturdy dray beasts in a blind valley on the Tillek side of the mountain. When half a Turn had passed with no further visitation, Dowell had begun to think his precautions foolish: that he had mistaken the man's reaction to Barla's beauty.

Then Lord Fax, followed by a score of his men, came galloping up the narrow trace to the woodland hold. His scowl had been frightening when he had seen Barla's gravid state.

'Well, the pump will be primed and ready. She'll whelp soon. Collect her in two months. See that she is waiting for her Lord Holder's summons!'

Without a backward look, Fax had cruelly spun his runner about and, clouting the lathered creature with his rawhide whip, clattered back the way he had come.

Dowell and Barla had left their hold within the hour. Seven days later, a boy had been prematurely born, and died. Nor did Dowell and Barla find a ready sanctuary in Tillek's hold.

'Not this close to Fax, man. Perhaps farther west,' their first host has suggested. 'I don't want him knocking on my hold door. Not that one!'

Dowell and Barla had traveled ever since, to the western reach of Tillek, where they had found brief respites in their journeyings while Dowell carved bowls and cups or joined cabinets, or crafted gather wagons. A few weeks here, a half Turn there; and Aramina was born on their way through the mountains of Fort, the first of

Barla's children to survive birth. The news of Fax's death caught up with them in the vast plains of Keroon, just after Nexa's birth.

'Ruatha Hold brought Fax nothing but disease and trouble,' the harper told Dowell and Barla in Keroon-beasthold, where Dowell was building stables.

'Then we could return and claim our hold again.'

'If there's anything to claim. But I'm told that Lytol is a fair man and he'll need good workers,' the harper had said, eyeing the notched timbers that Dowell had fitted.

'We'll return then,' Dowell had told Barla, 'when I've finished my bond with the mastercraftsman.'

More than a full Turn later, they did begin the long journey up the Keroon peninsula, with a sturdy daughter, a small son, and a tiny baby.

Then Thread began to fall on the innocent green land, raining destruction on a population that had denied the existence of their ancient enemy. Once again dragons filled the skies with their fiery breath, charring the dread menace in midair, saving the rich land from the devouring Thread.

Travel became more hazardous than ever for the holdless; people clung to the safety of stone walls and stout doors, and to the traditional leadership of their Lord Holders. Within those sanctuaries there was little room for those without legitimate claim on leadership, supplies, and refuge. A new terror was visited on the unfortunate, deprived for any number of reasons of their right to hold or craft affiliation.

For Dowell and Barla, the terror was slightly abated by Aramina's unexpected ability to hear dragons. When she first naively reported such conversations, she had been soundly spanked for telling lies. Then came the day when she persisted in warning them that her dragons said Threadfall was imminent. Threatened with a second thrashing and a supperless night, she had tearfully refused to retract her report. It was only when Dowell saw the leading edge of Thread, a silver smudging in the sky, dotted with the fiery blossoms of dragon breath, that he had apologized. As the family lay crouched under a rocky ledge just large enough to shelter them, they were grateful to her.

'The lords of Ruatha have always given dragonriders complete hospitality,' Barla had said, shielding the squalling Nexa against her shoulder. She had to stop to wipe grit from her lips. 'No one in my immediate family was ever taken on Search, but then, there haven't been that many Searches in my lifetime. Aramina comes by her talent as a right of blood.'

'And to think I ever complained that our firstborn was female,' Dowell had murmured, smiling at Aramina, tucked in the safest angle of the rock ledge. 'I wonder if Nexa will be able to hear dragons.'

'I'll bet I will when I'm older,' Pell had ventured, not wishing to let his sister take all the honors.

'It means we'll be safe traveling across Telgar Plains to Ruatha, for Aramina can always warn us about Thread-fall. We won't need to be beholden to any lord for shelter!'

To be without restraint or obligation meant a great deal to Dowell's pride. Since the advent of Threadfall, the holdless had suffered more than the usual indignities at the hands of holders, large and small. Having no right of affiliation, they could be cheated of the ordinary rights of hospitality; overcharged for any goods their infrequent marks could purchase; forced to work un-natural hours for the mere privilege of shelter from Thread; deprived of dignity and honor; and, above all else, required to express gratitude for even the least condescension shown by holders and crafters.

The elation of the small family was short-lived, for their dray beasts had run off in the panic of Threadfall.

Dowell was forced to return to Keroonbeasthold on foot, hire his skill at a hard-bargained price for the next Turn, then trudge all the way back with the new team to where his family had waited, fearful of marauding holdless men and women and Threadfall.

The indenture over, Dowell had once again turned team and wagon westward. A miscarriage and fever had forced them to take refuge in the huge Igen cave, and expediency had kept them there when Dowell's resolution had faltered under a series of misfortunes, all apparently designed to thwart his repatriation to Ruatha Hold.

Now they pushed on through the night, struggling to escape yet another threat to honor and resolve.

From somewhere Dowell had acquired a map of Lemos Hold, complete with road, track, and trace. Lemos had so many forests and mountains that rivers, Pern's other roadways, were unusable. Dowell elected to follow the faintest of tracks and was careful to remove any droppings. When he finally allowed them to rest, it was noontime. During the brief respite he allowed his family and team, Dowell crushed leaves and stained the wagon's leather cover with green to make it less visible to any searching eye.

'We'll be safe in the forests of Lemos,' he said, re-assuring himself as well as his family. 'There are caves there in the mountains which no one could find . . .'

'If no one can find them, how will we?' asked Pell reasonably.

'Because we'll be looking very hard, of course,' Aramina answered before her weary father's short temper flared.

'Oh!'

'And we'll live by ourselves and thrive on the prov-ender that woods naturally provide us,' Aramina went on, 'for we'll have all the wood we need to be warm, and nuts and roots because we know where to look for them, and berries and roast wherry . . .'

'Roast wherry?' Pell's eyes widened with delight at such a promise.

'Because you fashion such excellent snares . . .'

'I always caught more tunnel snakes than anyone else at Igen,' Pell began. Then, remembering that this helter-skelter trip was due to his boastfulness, he covered his mouth with his hand and huddled into a tight ball of remorse.

'Any of the forest caves ought to have lots of snakes, shouldn't they, Mother?' Aramina asked, wanting to lighten her mother's sad face as well as her brother's guilt.

'They should,' Barla agreed in the absent way of parents who have not really attended to their children's conversation.

Dowell called them to order, and they continued on their way until Nudge refused to go farther and, when Dowell took the stick to him, sank resolutely to his knees. Unhitching the recalcitrant brute, they forced Shove to haul the wagon into the brush at the side of the trace.

'Nudge has got sense,' Pell muttered to his sister as the weary children gathered enough branches to screen the wagon.

'Father has, too. I certainly didn't want to help Thella or,' and Aramina shivered with revulsion, 'that dragon-less man, Giron.'

'They're as bad as Fax.'

'Worse.'

Although Barla roused herself sufficiently to hand out dry rations, she found that Aramina and Pell had fallen asleep.

Only when they had put four mountains between themselves and Igen River did Dowell let up on the pace he had set. On the narrow traces, more logging tracks than proper trails, there were none to witness their passage as they climbed higher into the vast Lemos range.

They were not quite alone, for dragons passed overhead on daily sweeps and Aramina reveled in their conversations. She made her reports amusing, to liven evening campfire – for Dowell had conceded that a careful, smokeless fire would not be easily seen in the thick woods.

'It was green Path again today, with Heth and Monarth,' Aramina said on the tenth day after their exodus from Igen Cave. 'Lamanth, the queen, has clutched thirty fine eggs, but Monarth says that there are no queen eggs.'

'There aren't always queen eggs,' Dowell reminded Aramina, who sounded unhappy.

'That's what Path said. I don't know why Monarth was upset.'

'I didn't realize that dragons talked to each other,' Barla remarked, puzzled. 'I thought they only talked to their riders.'

'Oh, they do,' Aramina assured her. 'Heth talks constantly to K'van when they're doing the sweep alone.'

'Why are there three today then?' Pell asked.

'Because Threadfall is imminent.'

'Why didn't you say so?' Dowell wanted to know, exasperated with his daughter's diffidence.

'I was going to. They think Threadfall will come over Lemos tomorrow late afternoon.'

'How can we survive Threadfall out in these woods?' Dowell demanded, angry with apprehension.

'You said there were lots of caves here in Lemos,' Pell said, grimacing his face into a tearful expression.

'We'll need one!' Dowell said grimly. 'We'll start first light tomorrow. Aramina, you and Pell will search ahead.

On the upper slope. For there is bare cliff above us and somewhere there must be a cave for shelter.'

'And we'll need more roots and anything else you can find to eat,' Barla added, showing the empty stewpot as proof of the need. 'There's naught left of the dried meat and vegetables.'

'Why is it Thread always comes at times like these?' Pell asked, but expected no answer to his plaint.

He had occasion to repeat much the same expression the next morning when the off-rear wheel, sinking in a leaf-covered hole, cracked the cotter pin and lazily spun off. The team dragged the wagon on for several lengths, grinding the hub into the dirt before Dowell was able to halt them. Grimly he surveyed the damage. Then, with the sigh of long-suffering patience, he set to the job of repairing the wheel.

It was by no means the first time that wheels had come off, and Aramina and Pell needed no instructions to search out stout limbs, and to help roll a boulder into place for the lever. Indeed it was a well-drilled operation, and Aramina and Pell had wedged two blocks under the wagon bed as soon as Dowell and Barla had levered it up. They had the wheel back on the axle when Dowell discovered that there were no more cotter pins or kingpins in the wagon. He'd used the last on the journey to Igen Cave and had no reason to replace them in the long Turn.

'With the world and all of wood about us, Dowell?' Barla had remonstrated to cut short his flow of self-recriminations. 'There's a hardwood over there. It can't take much time to whittle new pegs. The children can forage ahead for food and a cave. Come.' She handed him the hatchet. 'I'll help. Aramina, take a sack and one of the hide buckets. Pell, make one of your snares and set it if you cross snake spoor. Nexa, you may carry the small shovel, but don't lose it in the woods.'

'If you hear more about Threadfall from the dragons, Aramina, you come back to me straightaway,' Dowell added as he made for the hardwood visible from the track. 'Don't dally.'

With a spirit of urgent adventure the three children ran up the track. For the first four switchbacks, there was nothing but forest on either side, though Pell insisted on inspecting several outcroppings of the gray rock that he felt looked promising.

Then the logging trace started a long, straight run, which finally disappeared around a rocky outthrust. To their right, up a steep bank, the trees were sparser as the native rock intruded.

'I'll go look up there, 'Mina!' Pell cried, and took off just as Nexa called Aramina's attention to the unmistakable if withered tops of redroots growing on the downside.

Aramina saw Pell scrambling for footing on the steep and slippery bank, and elected to forage with Nexa. They had been digging for only a short while when Aramina heard Pell's warbling, the family signal for an emergency. Fearful that he had injured himself climbing, Aramina raced back to the track.

'I found a cave, 'Mina! I found a cave.' Pell slithered back down the bank. 'A good deep one. Room for Nudge and Shove, too.' His voice reflected the jouncing his body took as he half walked, half slid the remaining distance to his sister.

'And lost your gathering,' she said sternly, pointing to the cluster of broken bulge-nut twigs he still clutched in his left hand.

'Oh, them.' Pell tossed the useless bits aside, stood up, and brushed the wet leaves from his leathern pants. 'There're plenty more where they . . .' He broke off, an uncertain look on his face as his hand hesitated.

'Hmm, sprung the seams again, too,' Aramina said

impatiently and, grabbing him, swung him about to see the damage the slide had done his trousers. She sighed, controlling her temper. Pell never considered risk and consequence.

'Only the seam. Not the leather. Mother can mend it! In the cave I just found. Plenty of space.' Grinning broadly to soothe the frown from his sister's face, he made exaggerated gestures with his arms, outlining the splendor of his discovery.

'How far up the slope?' Aramina regarded the steep incline with a thoughtful eye. 'I'm not sure Nudge and Shove could make it.'

'They'll make it 'cause there's grass and water . . .'

'The cave is damp?'

'Nah! Dry as far in as I went.' Pell cocked his head sideways. 'And I didn't go *all* the way in, just like you always warn me. Only far enough to see it was big and dry. And the tunnel-snake signs. Good eating.' He rolled his eyes and smacked his lips at the prospect. 'There's even a stream and – a cascade, too.'

Aramina hesitated, eyeing the steep bank and wondering if Pell's enthusiasm hadn't clouded his judgment. Pell would go through life seeing only what he hoped he was seeing, not what really was. But the need to get under shelter was critical. No matter if Pell had exaggerated: he had found a cave. Her father could decide on its suitability.

'How far up the slope is it?'

'Straight to the top of the ridge' – Pell pointed – 'down into the dip past the nut plantation. Turn to your right at the forked birch and you'll stare right at the entrance. Only it's to the left. A good overhang. C'mon, I'll show you.'

'No, you wait here. Nexa's down there digging roots' – Aramina pulled a face at her brother's sour expression – 'which we need nearly as much as the cave.' She hesitated once more. Maybe she ought to check the cave first, rather than raise false hopes.

'Ah, 'Mina, I wouldn't lie about shelter.'

Aramina scrutinized her brother's face, his features contorted into an expression of utter trustworthiness. No, Pell wouldn't lie about something that important. A ray of sunlight broke through the clouds, lancing past the soughing tree branches, reminding her that there was little time left if they were to be under cover when Thread fell.

'*Don't* wander off! You know how scared Nexa gets.' Aramina threw a deft twist of cord about the neck of her root sack and tossed it to the side of the logging track.

'I won't stir from her side. But I expect I'd do better gathering kindling.' Thus avoiding his most hated chore of rooting, Pell diligently collected branches.

Aramina started off down the track in a lope, her long plaits bouncing off her shoulders and buttocks. She was light on her feet, moving with an economy of movement that would have been envied by a hold runner.

The sunlight seemed to follow her, illuminating her way on the overgrown trace, the springiness underfoot making the going a pleasure. She shortened her stride as the track switched back on itself, and listened intently, over the thud of her footfalls, for the sound of the wagon. Surely it hadn't taken her father too long to whittle the necessary pins. Dowell and Barla should have made some distance up the logging road. Surely she ought to have heard the lumbering wagon, her father's voice urging Nudge and Shove to their task.

Peering through the thickly planted trees, Aramina looked for some glimpse of the covered wagon. Apprehension lent her impetus and down the trace she sped, every nerve anxiously alert for any reassuring sight or sound. Faster she ran, positive now in her mind that something had happened. Could Lady Holdless Thella have possibly caught up with them?

Taking a more direct line, she bypassed the next turn and pushed through the underbush, wriggling past trees. Then, as she discerned the bulk of the green-smeared wagon cover through the trees, she moved more circumspectly. The wagon had not shifted from the spot in which they had left it two hours past.

Trembling with fear, Aramina paused, listening now for the sound of voices, for the bass rumble of Giron or the crisp acid alto of Thella. Hearing nothing but the wind soughing through the leafless trees, she moved cautiously down until she was poised on the bank above where the wagon was still canted. Muffling a cry of fear, Aramina slid down the bank, recoiling in horror as she saw her father's head and shoulders protruding from under the wagon. Somehow the blocks had slipped and the wheel lay once again on its side. Horrified, Aramina was certain that her father had been crushed to death until she saw that one block had fallen directly under the wagon bed, preventing the complete collapse of the heavy load onto her father's chest.

Only then did Aramina hear the hoarse grunt and half sob, as she realized that her mother was attempting to lever the wagon bed off her stricken husband.

'Mother!'

'I cannot lift it, 'Mina!' Barla sobbed, leaning exhaustedly against the pole. 'I've been trying and trying.'

Wasting no words, Aramina threw her weight onto the lever, and though Barla gave every remaining ounce of her strength, the two women could not summon enough mass between them to shift the wagon more than a finger's breadth.

'Oh, 'Mina, what can we do? Even if we had Pell and Nexa, they couldn't help enough . . .' Defeated, Barla slumped onto the ground, weeping.

'*We* lifted it enough. If Pell and Nexa were here, they could pull him free . . .' Aramina swung 'round to her father, his tanned face pale with shock, the pulse in his neck beating slowly but reassuringly. 'Pell's found a cave. It's not too far up the track. I'll be right back.'

Giving Barla no chance to protest, Aramina started up the track again as fast as she could run. Pell and Nexa just *had* to be strong enough. She didn't dare believe anything else. And they must hurry. The sun glancing into her eyes warned her that time was very short if they were to rescue Dowell and get the wagon up the trail to the cave. She couldn't consider any other problems then, only the most immediate ones, and she almost ignored the sight of the dragon gliding overhead. She stopped so fast that she almost fell.

Dragon, dragon, hear me! Help me! HELP ME! Aramina had never attempted to communicate with the dragons, but a dragonrider would be strong enough to help her. Surely a dragonrider would not ignore her need.

Who calls a dragon?

She recognized the voice of Heth.

It is Aramina. Down on the logging trace, above the river in the forest. Please help me. My father is trapped beneath our wagon. And Thread will fall soon! She jumped up and down in the middle of the trace, waving frantically. *Oh, please help me!*

No need to shout. I heard you the first time. My rider wants to know who you are.

To her relief, Aramina saw the dragon change directions, circling down toward the track.

I told you, I'm Aramina.

May I tell him?

Such consideration rarely came Aramina's way.

Yes, yes, of course. Are you Heth?

I am Heth. My rider is K'van.

38

How do you do?

I'd do better if we could see you.

But I'm right here. In the middle of the trace. And the wagon is large . . . Oh, my father painted it green. If you'll just fly lower . . .

I'm a dragon, not a wherry . . . K'van sees the wagon.

Aramina crashed through the underbush to reach the wagon at the same time as dragon and rider. Barla looked about to faint with shock at their sudden appearance.

'It's all right, Mother. They'll help us. They're much stronger than Pell and Nexa would be.' Then Aramina realized that Shove and Nudge were taking great exception to the proximity of a dragon. She tied them tightly down by their nose rings to the tether stone, giving them more immediate pain to occupy their stupid brains.

Fortunately, the dragonrider directed Heth to land behind the wagon, out of the dray beasts' immediate sight.

To her dismay, Aramina realized that both dragon and rider were young. She'd always thought that bronze dragons must be big, and, indeed, Heth had seemed enormous, outlined in the sky. But now she could see that he wasn't fully grown and that his rider, K'van, was both undersized and younger than herself.

As if K'van sensed her disappointed appraisal, he straightened his shoulders and jerked his chin up. He walked forward, taking in the lever propped against the boulder and looking down at the prostrate Dowell.

'We may be weyrlings, but we can help you,' K'van said without ostentation. He turned to Heth. 'What I want you to do is to put heave on this, Heth, with your forearms. C'mon, Aramina.'

Aramina stopped staring at the bronze dragon, who waddled forward to place his five-clawed paws about the lever.

'Not until I say go, Heth,' K'van cautioned, grinning a

bit at Aramina as they knelt in the dust beside the unconscious Dowell, fastening their hands under the man's armpits. 'Heave, Heth! Heave!'

As quickly as they could, Aramina and K'van hauled Dowell's body from under the wagon. With a cry of incredulous relief, Barla rushed to her husband's side, opening his shirt to judge the extent of his injury. K'van had the presence of mind to replace the fallen block and prop the wagon up.

'You'll need the wheel back on,' he said to Aramina. 'That was fine, Heth.'

I am very strong, said the dragon with a trace of smugness, his great faceted eyes whirling bluey green as he maintained pressure on the lever.

'Oh, you are indeed, you beautiful beautiful creature,' cried Aramina.

'All right, Heth, ease it down,' said K'van, holding the block in place. 'Slowly now.'

The wagon settled, creaking as the block took its weight. K'van fumbled about in the grass and dust and triumphantly held up the pegs.

'Mother?' Aramina's trembling voice held a question as she turned to look at her father.

'I can't find anything broken,' Barla said in a low unsteady voice, 'but look . . .' Her hand indicated the terrible line of bruising already discoloring the skin. Carefully she smoothed the hair back from Dowell's brow, her expression of concerned tenderness causing the two young people to exchange embarrassed glances.

K'van touched Aramina's arm. 'Do you know how to set the wheel back on the axle?' He gave her a rueful glance as he proffered the pegs. 'I don't.'

'Whyever should you?' Aramina wanted to know as she took the pegs and noticed, with a pang, how carefully Dowell had made a cotter hole in the kingpin. 'You're a dragonrider.'

'Not all that long,' he said with a grin as he helped her lift the wheel and roll it into position. 'And weyrlings are taught a little bit of every craft needed by the Weyr. You never know when something will come in handy. Like now!' He said this on the end of a grunt as the two young people tried to force the wheel onto the axle.

'It's the dirt encrusted on the hub,' Aramina said as K'van paused uncertainly. With her belt knife, she scraped off the caked dirt, found a large rock, and, with a healthy knock, set the wheel firmly on. With another few taps of her rock, she rammed the kingpin through and then the cotter pin into its place.

'You're deft at that,' K'van said admiringly.

'Practice.'

With Heth's assistance, they removed the block from under the wagon.

'Have you far to go?' K'van asked then. 'Thread falls soon and, as I recall, the foresters' hold is a long ways up the track.'

Barla stifled a sound in her throat, but Aramina had an answer ready.

'I know,' Aramina lied calmly, 'but this accident delayed us. However, there's a cave not far up the track where we can wait out Threadfall.'

'Is it large?' asked K'van.

'Large enough. Why?' Aramina asked, suddenly wary.

'Well, just before you called us,' and K'van grinned ingenuously for her temerity, 'Heth spotted a band of runners beyond the river. Are they part of your group?'

'No,' Barla groaned aloud, looking wildly up at Aramina.

'There shouldn't be anyone else in this part of Lord Asgenar's forests,' Aramina said with all the indignation she could muster. 'We were warned that holdless raiders have been seen.'

'Holdless men?' K'van was instantly alert. 'If they are,

they'll disperse once they've seen me. Look, let me help you get your father into the wagon and see you safely on your way to the cave. I'll take care of the raiders. And warn Lord Asgenar, too.'

Aramina hadn't expected that, but she said what was appropriate, determined to play out her part in this charade. She unfastened the tailgate so that they could slide Dowell in. Then, while K'van watched beside Heth, she and Barla took up their positions and prodded Nudge and Shove into a walk, and then into a shambling trot up the trace.

Barla and Aramina had to keep hard at the dray beasts to maintain their trot. Nudge resented the pace, twisting his horned head and lowing piteously, but Aramina had no mercy on him. Women and beasts were sweating when they finally reached the bank. Pell cheering lustily until Aramina shouted at him to stop being so foolish and come help.

In a few terse words, Aramina explained what had happened, and Pell began shaking his head slowly from side to side.

'I don't know how we'll get Father up that bank,' he said, appraising the difficulty. 'You shouldn't've sent the dragonrider away.'

'It's not just Father being hurt, Pell. K'van saw a troop of riders on the other side of the river . . .'

Pell quailed, and his distress communicated itself to Nexa, who had been standing there, wide-eyed and perplexed. Now she burst into tears.

'So we must also get the wagon out of sight. And hide Nudge and Shove.'

'But Thread's coming. And we have to get Father up to the cave and . . .' Pell's words tripped over themselves in his anxiety.

'Somehow we'll do it,' Aramina said, peering up and down the trace to find a possible screen for the mass of the wagon. 'Maybe, if K'van has frightened them with Threadfall, they'll have to go back the way they came . . . Maybe if we rig a stretcher, we can haul Father up the bank . . .'

'Maybe, maybe, *maybe!*' Pell almost danced with frustration.

'I won't have you children fighting at a time like this,' Barla said tartly, appearing in the back of the wagon. 'We've got to rouse your father . . . How long before Thread falls, Aramina? Or didn't you ask the dragon-rider?'

Aramina bowed her head at her mother's rebuke. As she did so, her glance fell on a group of evergreens on the left-hand side of the roadway a few lengths farther up the track.

'There!' she cried dramatically, gesturing wildly. 'There! We can drive the wagon in there, behind the evergreens. They're just tall enough!'

With something constructive to do, even Nexa stopped her whingeing. Dowell was carefully lifted out of the wagon and covered by a sleeping fur. Then everyone concentrated on getting the wagon out of sight. Nexa was directed to brush away the tracks of the wagon as Aramina and Pell forced the dray beasts through the opening Barla parted into the copse. The artistic addition of extra branches completed the camouflage.

Then Barla sent Pell and Nexa on ahead to the cave with sleeping furs and Barla's precious stewpot, while Aramina and her mother tried to rouse Dowell. The usual aromatic had no effect, and the two women exchanged anxious glances, when suddenly Nudge and Shove, tethered by the trace, began to moan fearfully and pull at their ring ropes.

'Thread?' gasped Barla, bending protectively over her husband.

'No,' cried Aramina, 'Dragons! *Big* dragons!' Indeed

it seemed to her as if the sky was filled with them, their great wings causing the saplings to bend to their back-wind.

'Aramina, *how* did that dragonrider come to help us in the first place? You didn't *call* him, did you?' When Aramina mutely nodded, Barla gave a despairing cry. 'But the Weyrs will take you from us if they know you can hear and speak to dragons! And then what shall we do?'

'How else were we to save Father?' asked Aramina even as she, too, regretted her action.

I hear Aramina, said Heth's unmistakable voice.

Oh, please go away, Heth. Say you can't find me.

But I have! You must not fear. We won't harm you. Before Aramina could speak again, three dragons skimmed neatly down onto the track, making Nudge and Shove buck and strain to be free of their tether. As one, Barla and Aramina dashed forward to prevent the escape of the dray beasts, twisting the nose rings until pain paralyzed the stupid animals.

We will move down the track, Aramina heard Heth say as she coped with the frantic Nudge. When the dragons were far enough away not to be an immediate threat, Aramina and Barla relaxed their hold.

'I am T'gellan, bronze rider of Monarth, and this is Mirrim, who rides green Path,' said the oldest of the three riders who approached them. 'K'van wisely called for help to persuade those holdless raiders to absent themselves from this vicinity. So I thought we'd better make sure you had safely reached shelter before Threadfall.'

Barla hovered between her critical need for assistance and anxiety at the presence of dragonriders who might very easily depart with her daughter who could hear dragons.

Mirrim knelt beside Dowell and opened his shirt, then exhaled her breath on a long whistle.

44

'I can feel no broken bones, but he's not regained consciousness,' Barla told Mirrim, sensibly making her husband's needs her first priority.

'If he was under a wagon as K'van says, that doesn't surprise me,' Mirrim remarked. 'I've done considerable nursing at the Weyr. First let's get him to this cave.'

'We don't have much time to spare,' T'gellan added, squinting at the steep bank. 'And I don't fancy trying to haul an unconscious man up that!'

'Is there any sort of a clearing by your cave?' Mirrim asked Aramina.

'A small one,' she said, devoutly hoping that Pell's description bore some resemblance to fact.

'Path? Would you oblige us?' Mirrim asked the green dragon.

I see no reason why not. In a maneuver that Aramina couldn't believe she was seeing, the green dragon glided to the group without moving her wings or appearing to walk. *Silly beasts, aren't they?* Path added as Nudge and Shove began their terrified lowing again.

Aramina was obliged to go calm them; their perturbation abruptly ceased as Mirrim, Path, her father, and her mother disappeared.

'Well, it seemed easier to send your mother along, too, Aramina,' T'gellan said with a laugh for her astonishment. 'You'd best go the hard way. Thread will fall very shortly.'

'But I can't . . . Nudge and Shove . . .'

K'van grinned. 'Just get on one, get a good hold on the nose rein of the other. We'll supply the impulsion.' And he jerked his thumb at the two dragons watching with their jewel eyes whirling mildly.

It was perhaps the wildest ride Aramina had ever had. In the first place, dray beasts were not designed for comfortable riding, having straight backs, wide withers, short necks and low-held heads. However, the flapping of dragon wings behind Nudge and Shove was more than enough to have sent them plunging through fire. They took the bank, cloven hooves slipping on the wet footing in no more than four bucking jumps. Momentum carried them over the top and down the dip, almost right into the cliff wall, where they fetched up to a dead stop that sent Aramina onto Nudge's horns, and then to the ground with a force that jarred her from heel to headbones.

Pell appeared, eyes wide at her impetuous arrival.

'A girl on a green dragon brought Father and Mother. I didn't think girls were allowed to ride fighting dragons.'

'Help me get these inside the cave before they stampede again,' Aramina said, though she had been equally surprised by Mirrim and Path.

'Oh, look, they're going!' Pell's disappointment was patent, as he saw the dragons hover briefly in the sky. 'I'm forever missing the good parts,' he complained.

'Get Shove inside!' Aramina had no time to humor her brother, and she gave him such a hard prod that he sharply reminded her that he wasn't any old dray beast.

He hauled on the nose rein and, lowing, Shove followed his painful muzzle – then bellowed as his hindquarters scraped along the right wall of the narrow entry. Aramina pushed at his dappled flanks and set him right. She was careful to line Nudge squarely in the opening, and to prevent any further recalcitrance she twisted his nose ring. With an injured bellow, he, too, made the passage into the cave, running into Aramina, who stopped, amazed at what lay before her.

'Isn't this cave marvelous, 'Mina? Didn't I find a good one? Couldn't we get everything in here? Maybe we could even live here.' Pell dropped his voice to a hoarse whisper on the last sentence. 'For it's as big as a hold, isn't it, 'Mina?' The boy was all but dancing at the end of Shove's ring rein, momentarily oblivious of everything but his need for her approval.

In a sweeping glance, Aramina saw a solemn-faced Nexa cradling her father's head where he lay on the pile of sleeping furs, and her mother busy lighting a small fire within a ring of stones before she allowed herself to examine the cave in more detail.

'Why, it is truly big enough to be a hold,' she said in a voice awed enough to delight her brother.

'It's bigger than many holds we've been in, 'Mina,' Pell said with great satisfaction. 'Much bigger. It's nearly as big as any of the Igen caverns I ever was in.'

Aramina appraised the high ceiling, dry as far as she could see in the dim light filtering in from the entrance. She could sense rather than see clearly that the cave extended far beyond the immediate chamber in which they stood.

'There's even a sort of stall place where we can tether Nudge and Shove,' he went on, babbling happily, and pulled on Shove to lead the way.

The beasts settled, Aramina and Pell came back to the front of the cavern, where Barla was coaxing the flames on the small hearth. Then a soft moan broke the silence as Dowell rolled his head from side to side in Nexa's lap. She snatched her hands away from him, as if contact might somehow impede his recovery. With startled eyes she looked about for reassurance.

'There now, Nexa, I told you he'd come around,' said Barla, rising from the now healthy fire. 'Aramina, we'll need fresh water. As cold as you can draw it. We've nothing but cold compresses to ease the bruising. And hurry. Those dragonriders said that Threadfall was a matter of minutes away.'

''Mina,' and Pell caught the other side of the bucket, accompanying his sister out of the cavern, 'can you hear 'em yet?'

Aramina halted at the entrance, listening with every fiber in her ears, smiled at Pell, and walked quickly out.

'Show me where the water is,' she said, and Pell danced around in front of her and to their left.

'Right here! Right here!' he caroled, pointing and dancing about. 'Just like I said. You won't ever doubt me again, will you, 'Mina?'

'No, I won't,' she said, smiling as she extended her hand into the little cascade that leaped and fell down the side of the mountain. The water was ice cold, numbing her fingers in seconds. She filled the bucket. She was just at the entrance to the cave when Pell let out an excited whoop. At the same time she heard a multitude of voices, excited and anticipatory.

'They're here! I can see them! I saw them first!' His triumph found a lack in her talent.

'Well, I can hear them talking!'

'Can I watch the dragons fight Thread *this* time, 'Mina? This time can I watch?'

Aramina shushed him, examining the overhang of the cavern. Unless Thread should happen to fall at a tremendous velocity and at a slant, she couldn't see how any of the dreaded menace could score them. Turns of familiarity with Thread had dampened her fear of it.

'Yes, I think it's safe here for us to watch.' She placed a warning finger on her lips, and, slipping quickly inside to bring her mother the bucket of cold water, she rejoined him in the entrance.

To Pell's keen disappointment, there wasn't as much to watch as he'd anticipated. They could see the dragons in their ranks, suspended motionless in the clear mountain air, gleaming where wing and body reflected the sun briefly. Then the two watching children saw the sudden blurring of the sky, the silvery mist that was the leading edge of Thread.

Only then did the dragons break the temporary suspension, swooping up to meet the deadly rain, sending blossoms of fiery breath to char the parasitic Thread. Pell

48

didn't breathe with the wonder of the darting forays of the smaller dragons, exclaiming as he saw a long tongue of flame reach out to char a mass of Thread. Silver mist turned to black smoke and then dissipated lazily. Fire blooms traced the dragons' progress after their ancient enemy until the hills and trees covered the distant sight from the watchers' searching eyes.

'It didn't last long enough,' Pell said dejectedly.

'It'll last long enough for the dragonriders, I'm sure,' Aramina said with mild rebuke for his callousness. 'Did you remember to bring the roots with you?'

'Ah, who wants to eat roots. There are acres of nuts out there.'

'Then you'll have no trouble filling a sack, will you?' As Aramina turned back to the fire, she heard her father's querulous voice.

'I don't understand how you managed, with just Aramina.'

'Pell was a great help, too,' Barla said soothingly, wringing out another cold compress. She gave Aramina a quick stern glance.

'It was really very simple, Father. You keep telling us that if there was a lever long enough, we could even move Pern away from the Red Star,' Aramina said with a smile.

'This is no time for levity,' Barla said severely.

'Why ever not? Father's conscious, we've got this huge big cave all to ourselves, and Pell's gone out for more of these delicious nuts.' Expertly Aramina positioned two in her palm and cracked them. 'See?' She held out the meats to Barla.

After a supper of boiled roots and crisp nutmeats, Aramina and Pell used the last of the daylight to gather fodder for Nudge and Shove, and sufficient boughs and fragrant bracken for bedding.

Tired as she was, Aramina found that sleep eluded her. She had been brought up to honor truth, and today that

49

teaching had been disregarded for expediency. She had permitted K'van to think that they were proper holders, on their lord's business. She had avoided truth with her father, although at Barla's behest, so as not to worry him.

In each case the truth would confound her lies in very short order. But . . . K'van had chased off the Lady Holdless Thella and the band that had nearly caught up with her and her family. And . . . they had contrived to get Dowell safely into this cave refuge, hopefully without leaving an easy trail that Thella could follow. But . . . to achieve that end, she had revealed her ability to hear dragons to Benden Weyr riders. And . . . the dragon-riders now knew exactly where she was even if Lady Holdless Thella did not. She could not imagine what punishment would be meted out to her for that day-long imprudence.

Nexa, curled close against her sister's body, whimpered in a restless sleep. Aramina pulled the sleeping rug closely about her, stroking her arm, and Nexa subsided into sleep. For a while, she was distracted by Dowell's breathing, a light snore because he had to sleep on his back, but its soft thythm finally lulled Aramina to sleep.

It seemed all too short a time before Pell was urgently tugging at her shoulders and whispering excitedly in her ear.

''Mina! 'Mina! K'van is here! And so is the Weyr-leader! He wants to speak to you! And there are lots of strange men out there, too.'

'Here?' Frantically brushing sleep from her eyes, Aramina sat up, all too aware of yesterday's bruises and scrapes and the dull ache across her shoulders from abused muscles.

'No, on the track. The men are armed with bows and arrows and spears and I think the dragons brought them.' Pell's eyes were wide with excitement. K'van was just beyond him.

'It's all right, Aramina, really it is,' said K'van, softly so as not to disturb the other sleepers. 'It's the raiders, you see.'

Careful not to rouse Nexa, Aramina slipped out from under the fur and pressed it gently down about her sister.

'The raiders are coming?' Pell's voice slipped from whisper to harsh alarm, but Aramina quickly covered his mouth. Fear darkened his eyes as he stared at his sister.

The little one is suddenly afraid, said a surprised, richly mellow voice.

She has more to fear from the holdless. The second dragon voice was deep and dark, like a pool of the blackwater that Aramina had seen in Igen.

'I am *not* afraid of you.' Aramina spoke stoutly.

'Of me?' K'van asked in astonishment, his hand on his chest.

'Not you. Those dragons.' No, Aramina told herself, she was not afraid of the dragons, but of their riders and the impending justice that would be meted out for all the lies of yesterday. She hoped that K'van would not think too badly of her.

'I don't think badly of you,' K'van protested as they stepped out into the sunlight. 'Why should I? I think you were an absolute marvel yesterday, fixing that wheel and getting everyone safe inside the cave . . .'

'Oh, you don't understand,' said Aramina, trying to keep her voice from breaking.

'And neither does Heth but . . .'

It will come right, said Heth as if he meant it.

Then they were at the top of the bank and Aramina held on to a sapling to steady herself at the sight of masses of armed men, just as Pell had reported, and an incredible stream of dragons, taking off and landing in the track. Standing slightly apart with the enormous bronze dragon and a brown almost as big was the Weyrleader, F'lar, and his wingleader, F'nor, talking earnestly with two men dressed in gleaming mail. A fur-trimmed cape was slung negligently over the shoulders of the younger man.

'Are those who I think they are?' asked Pell in an awed whisper. His hands clasped in his sister's arm for reassurance. Then he stiffened, for F'nor had seen the three standing on the bank. He smiled and beckoned them down.

Aramina prayed earnestly that she wouldn't lose her footing and arrive in an ignominious heap at the bottom of the slope. Then she felt K'van's steadying hand. It was Pell who slipped, tumbling almost to the feet of the Weyrleader, who with an easy laugh, gave him a hand to his feet. Then Aramina and K'van reached the group.

'How is your father today?' F'lar asked with a sympathetic smile.

'Badly bruised but sleeping, Lord F'lar,' Aramina managed to stammer. That was the correct form of address for the Weyrleader of Pern, wasn't it? Aramina braced herself for the worst.

'We'll hope not to disturb him, but those holdless marauders did not disperse after Threadfall.' F'lar's slight frown indicated his annoyance with that intransigence.

'So,' F'nor took up the explanation, 'Lord Asgenar plans to disperse them.' He grinned as he gestured to the tall man.

It was all Aramina could do to stand straight as she stared, appalled to be in the company of the Lord Holder whose land had been invaded by impudent holdless raiders in pursuit of a trespassing holdless family. In a daze she heard Lord Asgenar wondering why the raiders were pressing so far into his forestry. She saw that men were marching down the track, quietly but in good array.

'I've foresters in the top camp, although I cannot see what profit raiders could make of sawn logs,' Lord Asgenar was saying.

Now the truth must out, to save good men from Lady Holdless Thella's brutal riders.

'It's me.'

Aramina's voice cracked so that her tentative admission was almost unheard. But the bronze dragon rumbled, and suddenly F'lar was regarding her with a sharp and penetrating gaze.

'You said that it was you, Aramina?'

The two men turned to gaze down at her. Pell's fingers tightened about her arm.

You do not need to fear, child.

'Mnementh's quite right, Aramina. Would you explain?'

'It's me. Because I can hear dragons. And the Lady Holdless Thella . . .'

'Thella, is it?' exclaimed Lord Asgenar, slapping his hand onto his sword hilt. 'By the first egg, I've been longing to meet that one.'

'Thella has been chasing you, child?'

It was such a relief to admit to the first truth that her confession was almost incoherent, except that between her words Aramina kept hearing the reassurances of three dragon voices in her head, calming her, bidding her speak more slowly and above all not to be worried about a thing.

'So, Thella thinks to Search for what is the Weyr's by right?' F'lar's amber eyes flashed with a fire no less frightening than dragon breath. 'And you and your family left Igen Cave only ten days ago? You have traveled hard to escape that woman. Where did you come from?'

'Last Turn my father bonded himself to Keroonbeast-master . . .'

'Then you are Keronese?'

'No, Lord F'lar. My father and mother had a small forest hold in Ruatha . . .'

Aramina stopped in midsentence, startled by the play of surprise and comprehension that flashed across the faces of the dragonriders.

'Lessa should have come, after all, F'lar,' F'nor said, grinning with some private amusement at the Weyrleader.

'So Fax made your family holdless, Aramina.' F'lar's voice was kind, though his eyes still sparkled.

Unable to speak, Aramina nodded.

'And your father was a forester?' Lord Asgenar's question was eager.

Again Aramina could only nod.

'He's the best wood joiner and carver in all Pern.' Pell spoke up, sensing a sympathy in their audience that Aramina, immersed in guilt, could not appreciate.

'Is he now? I thought as much.' F'lar took up the conversation, giving Aramina a chance to regain her poise. 'That's a very well made gather wagon you hide so neatly. We almost didn't spot it, did we, Asgenar?'

'Well hidden indeed. But I must go on, F'lar, F'nor. My men are assembled. I'm leaving men to guard your cave, Aramina, so you will have absolutely nothing to fear from our Lady Holdless Thella. Not now or again. We'll see to that.'

And, at his signal, two men ranged behind Aramina, K'van, and Pell. As Aramina watched the tall young Lord Holder stride down the track to join his men, she began to feel secure for the first time since her first encounter with Thella and Giron.

'We must leave, too,' F'lar said to F'nor. 'Can't let them sight dragons in the sky near this mountain. Aramina, K'van brings some medicines for your father from our healer.'

'We do not like to be beholden to anyone,' Aramina replied, as her parents had drilled her to say to any such well-meant offers. 'We have all we need with us.' She caught her lip to be telling yet another untruth.

'But we,' – and F'lar bowed slightly toward her – 'are beholden to you for luring that hellion Thella near enough to grab her.'

'Oh!'

'Take the medicines, child. Ease your father's injuries,' said F'nor, clasping Aramina's shoulders in his warm, gentle hands. He gave her a kindly little squeeze. 'And don't be afraid.'

'I'm not afraid,' Aramina replied, for she wasn't. Not of the weyrmen. But what would her proud father say of her actions over the past two days?

Then both dragonriders quickly vaulted to their waiting dragons, swinging nimbly up onto the neck ridges. With mighty leaps that sent dust, pebbles, and bruised leaves flying, the two beasts launched themselves upward. Suddenly the trace was empty of dragons and men, and only the two soldiers and the youngsters remained to hear the morning breeze sighing through the forest.

'I wonder if they'd have taken me along to see Thella get trounced,' Pell said, cocking his head around and beaming at the soldiers.

'Well now, lad, you should have asked, shouldn't you?' said the older guard. 'Now, young lady, if you'll just lead the way to this cave of yours . . .'

'K'van, where's Heth got to? You're here. Where's he?' Pell wanted to know, looking all about him as if the bronze dragon might be roosting in a nearby tree.

'He's up at the cave, Pell. Probably asleep in that small clearing . . . if it's big enough. Dragons like the sun and we had a very busy day yesterday.'

'And a busy one so far today, too,' Pell said amiably, digging his toes into the damp mulch of the bank.

'You could do with some steps cut in this bank,' said the younger soldier, who had just slipped as far as he had come.

'Oh, we couldn't do that,' Pell replied, horrified. 'We don't really live in that cave. Though I'd sure like to,' he added with such ingenuousness that the older guard chuckled. 'Can you make a good snare?' he asked him. ''Cause that cave is just crawling with tunnel snakes. They'd make mighty good eating after months and months of nothing but roots and fish.'

'I tie a pretty good snare,' K'van said, grabbing a sapling to pull himself onto the top of the ridge.

'You? But you're a dragonrider.'

'I wasn't always,' K'van admitted, grinning over Pell's head at Aramina. '*Before* I was a dragonrider I was a very lowly weyrboy, and small. Just the right size to set snares for tunnel snakes. My foster mother used to give an eighth of a mark for every fifty snakes we caught.'

'Really?' Pell was awed by the thought of riches beyond the eating. 'Well,' and Pell recovered from his awe, 'I'm bloody good at snake-snaring, too, aren't I, Aramina?'

'Not if you use the word "bloody" you aren't,' she said in reproof, not wishing the soldiers to think that the holdless were also mannerless.

They had reached the clearing – and there was Heth, curled in a tight ball that just fit in the available space. The soldiers grinned as Pell, eyes wide, carefully circled the sleeping bronze dragon.

'The cave is where, young lady?' asked the guard leader.

Aramina pointed. 'There!'

'There's water just to the right,' Pell said hospitably, 'and there's a whole grove of nuts just beyond the copse if you're hungry.'

'Thank'ee, lad, we've rations with us.' The guard patted a bulging pouch. 'Though a drink of cold water would be welcome. Traveling *between* sort of dries a man's mouth of spit. You go on in, tell your folks not to worry. We'll be out here on guard.'

'I'd rather stay with you,' Pell said confidentially.

Aramina caught the guard's expression and hastily vetoed that option.

'Aw, Aramina, you had all the fun yesterday.'

'Fun?' Aramina got a firm grip on his arm and pulled him ruthlessly toward the cave entrance.

'Later, perhaps, Pell,' K'van said in the role of conciliator, 'after you've eaten your breakfast, for I know I woke you out of a sound sleep. I've got enough *klah* here to serve everyone, and some bread, because Mende knew you wouldn't have had a chance to bake yesterday.' K'van's engaging grin dared Aramina to reject the treats.

'Bread? *Klah?* What else do you have in that sack, K'van?' Pell, displaying the manners of the worst Igen holdless riffraff, tried to pull open the neck of the sack for a glimpse of its contents.

'Pell!' Aramina's shocked whisper reminded her brother of their sleeping parents as well as his manners.

'But, 'Mina, do you know how long it is since we had *klah?*'

'I've promised to make it for the guards, 'Mina,' K'van said in a voice that had brought many around to indulge his whimsies. 'Surely a cup between friends . . .'

She relented, though she was sure to receive a scolding on that account as well as for her other errors. But a cup of *klah* would do much to ease the trembling in her stomach and knees, and give her the energy to bear whatever other shocks this day might hold for her.

The aroma, as it steeped, roused the sleepers, though Barla's first conscious act was to peer in her husband's face, reassured by the soft snores that emanated from his slightly open mouth. Only then did Barla react to the fragrance of the brewing *klah*.

'We had no *klah*,' she said, frowning at Aramina before she recognized K'van beside the little hearth.

'My foster mother, Mende, sent it along with fellis and numbweed salve to ease your husband's injury,' said K'van, rising to bring her a cup of the fresh brew. He smiled with a shy charm to which Barla was scarcely impervious.

Aramina regarded the young bronze rider with astonishment.

'My Wayrleaders insisted that I return to see if he is recovering from the accident.'

'That is kind of you, young K'van, but unnecessary. We do not care to be beholden to anyone.' Barla pretended not to see the cup he offered, but Aramina saw her mother's nostrils twitch in appreciation of the aromatic steam.

K'van gave her another of his charming smiles. 'I'm weyrbred, you know,' he said, undaunted, 'so I know how you feel about being under obligation.' When he saw Barla's incredulous expression, he went on. 'Before the Pass began, Benden Weyr was begrudged every jot and tittle . . . because' – and now his voice became querulous and his eyes took on a merry twinkle for his impersonation – 'everyone knows that Thread won't fall on Pern again!' He grinned impishly at Barla's astonishment and her sudden realization that Benden had indeed once been relegated to a state not much different from that of the holdless: tolerated when unavoidable, ignored when possible, and condemned on every occasion for uselessness. 'Drink, good lady, and enjoy it. Mende also sent along bread, knowing you'd've had no chance to bake yesterday.'

'Mother, could we not send Mende one of the wooden

spoons Father carved at Igen?' Aramina ventured to suggest to salve her mother's sensibility.

'Yes, an exchange is always permissible,' Barla replied and, inclining her head graciously, finally accepted the cup of *klah*.

Relieved by her mother's capitulation, Aramina carefully cut a thick slice of the round loaf, spreading it generously with the jam that K'van had also extracted from his sack of surprises. She bent a stern glance on Pell when he started to devour the treat ravenously.

Only when she had served the others did Aramina eat, savoring the *klah* and the thick, crunchy bread spread with the berry jam. Daintily she even rescued the crumbs from her lap with a moistened fingertip. When K'van and Pell went outside to serve the guards, Barla summoned Aramina to the sleeping furs, where she was delicately smearing numbweed salve on the livid bruises on Dowell's chest.

'Why is that rider still here?'

'He came back this morning, Mother.' Then Aramina took a deep breath, realizing that only the truth would serve. Evasion was as dishonest as lying, whatever her motive. The presence of the dragonriders and Lord Asgenar would insure the safety of everyone. With complete candor she accounted for her part in the events of the past day and this morning. 'And the Benden Weyrleader was just here with Lord Asgenar and his men because Lady Holdless Thella *has* followed us. Lord Asgenar is using this opportunity to ambush her and that horrid band of hers. So we'll be safe now because Lord Asgenar and Lord F'lar think Father built a fine gather wagon. And truly, they did call it a gather wagon just as if that's all it ever has been.'

'That's what it was made for,' said Dowell in a sad voice, slightly shaken by the pain of the shallow breaths he took to speak.

'Here, Dowell. Drink this fellis,' Barla said, raising the carved wooden cup to his lips.

'Fellis? We had no fellis!'

'We have it now, Dowell. Don't be so proud it hurts!' Barla said, suspending pride in the interests of healing her husband.

Thus abjured, Dowell swallowed the dose, closing his eyes at the pain even that minor movement caused his swollen flesh.

Barla saw Aramina's tender concern. 'The numbweed will be taking effect soon. I am truly grateful to this Mende. I think a spoon and one of the sandstone bowls. A woman can never have too many of them.' She sighed. 'I am truly grateful to her. And . . .' She turned to Dowell, who had closed his eyes in tacit accord. 'I think that we must be grateful to you, daughter . . . in spite of the fact that you seem to have forgotten all we have tried to instill in you of manners and conduct.'

Aramina bowed her head, assuming a contrite pose. Then she realized that although her mother's voice was sharp, there was no bite to her words. Discipline required a scolding, but this time it was only the form that was obeyed, not the spirit. Aramina looked up and tried not to smile at this unexpected absolution.

''Mina, if Lord Asgenar . . .' Dowell began in a voice no stronger than a whisper, speaking in short phrases between the shallow breaths he took, '. . . favors us . . . with his presence again . . . we must request . . . formal permission to stay . . . in this cave . . . until I am able . . . to continue our journey.'

'I'll tell him. And I'll mention it to the guard as well.'

Dowell nodded again, closing his eyes, his mouth beginning to relax a little as fellis and numbweed gave him surcease. Barla rose and, motioning Aramina to follow her, left his side.

'It is a good dry cave, 'Mina,' she said, as if this were

the first chance she had had to inspect it. 'There are guards? We must not fail in hospitality.'

'Pell remembered to offer, Mother, and they say they have their own rations.'

'That is not to the point, 'Mina, and you know it. Would there be more roots in the patch Nexa found yesterday? And nuts, too? For they make a tasty flat bread.'

Aramina schooled her features not to betray her dismay, for it took a great many nuts to make a decent quantity of nut flour, and the grinding took hours.

'I'll get nuts, and there may be some wild onions, too,' she said, aware of her narrow escape from punishment and determined to be dutiful today.

'Where's Pell? He ought to accompany you.'

'He's with K'van, Mother.' Aramina picked up her sack, cleaned her belt knife, and sheathed it. She glanced about in the habit of someone used to thinking ahead on chores before she left.

Pell was not with the guards, nor was K'van, although Heth's bronze hide was visible through the trees.

'The boys have gone off to set a wherry snare,' the older guard told Aramina with a grin for such youthful pastimes. 'There's roosts there.' He pointed over the rocky saddle leading to a farther dell.

'A roast wherry would be a real treat for all of us,' Aramina said, smiling to include both guards.

'Oh, aye, that it would, young lady.' When Aramina started toward the nut plantation, he caught her by the arm. 'It's you we're guarding. Where are you going?'

'Only over that ridge' – Aramina pointed to the south – 'for nuts.'

'I'll just have a look-see.' The guard strode along with her, past the sleeping Heth, and up the long slope.

He halted, catching her arm again, as he looked down into the peaceful grove. The nut trees, well grown, were so thick-branched that they had inhibited any under-growth that the acid of the nut mast had not killed. The approach of humans had sent the wood snakes scurrying, and only the last vestiges of the summer's insects flitted about. Nuts were visible in plenty.

'I'll give you a hand,' the guard said, seeing that it was a matter of scooping up the fallen tree fruits.

With two willing pairs of hands, Aramina's sack was filled in short order.

'How much do you need?' the man asked when Aramina began to make a carryall of her jerkin.

'Mother has a mind for nut bread.'

The man raised his eyes skyward. 'It do be tasty, and you might just need enough' – he winked broadly at her – 'to stuff that wherry your brother plans to snare. I'll just fetch these to your mother. Don't stray now.'

Aramina didn't stray, but in gathering she headed toward the far edge of the grove, wondering what other edibles might be found. She filled her jerkin as she moved, and had it stuffed to overflowing when she reached the boundary. There the land fell away into broken boulders. She looked up to the top of the mountain on whose flank she stood. She could see down to a twist of the river rushing through a gorge, just visible through the wintry forest. To be alone, after so many Turns of overcrowding, was a rare treat for Aramina. Maybe Lord Asgenar's gratitude would indeed extend to a longer stay for her family in the cave. It could be made quite tenable, she was sure, even in the coldest weather. Why, they could make stalls for Nudge and Shove, and if Lord Asgenar didn't object, maybe cut steps up the bank. From the fallen trees, they could fashion furniture. Her father could even season wood in the dry rear of the cave and have his own workshop. Her imagination embellished the dazzling possibilities. And then, being a practical girl, she sighed at her folly. She would be content enough to have a secure and private dwelling for as long as it took her father's chest to heal. She mustn't be greedy.

She listened then, as the breeze caressed her face, to what other sounds might be carried up from the river. She wondered if the ambush had been sprung and if she'd hear the sounds of battle. She shivered. Much as she feared Lady Holdless Thella and Giron, she wished only an end to their threat, not their lives.

She heard the faint sound of someone treading close and, thinking it was the guard returning, was taken completely by surprise as a rough hand covered her mouth and strong ones pinned her arms to her sides.

'It falls out well, after all, Giron,' said a harsh voice, and Aramina's head was pulled cruelly back by her hair so that she looked up into the stained, sweaty face of Lady Holdless Thella. 'We have snared the wild wherry after all, and the trap she laid is bare for Asgenar.'

Heth! Heth! Help me! Thella! Even if Giron's heavy hand had not covered her mouth, Aramina was completely paralyzed by fear. Her mind idiotically repeated the one syllable that meant rescue. *Heth! Heth! Heth!*

Giron growled at Aramina as he began to manhandle her across the grove. 'Don't struggle, girl, or I'll knock you senseless. Maybe I ought to, Thella,' he added, cocking his big fist in preparation. 'If she can hear dragons, they can hear her.'

'She's never been near a Weyr!' Thella's reply was contemptuous, but the notion, now Giron had planted it, gave her a moment's pause. Her face contorted with anger, she gave Aramina's hair another savage jerk. 'Don't even think of calling for a dragon.'

Aramina couldn't have stopped her mind's chant, but she frantically rolled her eyes as if complying with Thella's order. Anything to relieve the pain of her scalp.

'Too late!' Giron threw Aramina from him, a heave

that left a hunk of her hair and scalp in Thella's hand and Aramina teetering on the brink of a drop. A drop that was blocked by Heth, his eyes whirling red and orange in anger. He bellowed, sinuously weaving in among the trees, chasing Thella and Giron. From the other side of the grove came the two guards, Pell, and K'van, shouting imprecations. Aramina saw Giron and Thella disappear into the woods. The guards ran past in full pelt, but Heth had to stop at the edge of the grove, the forest being too dense for him to penetrate. He continued to bellow in fury, even after K'van reached him.

Shaking with reaction to her frightening experience, Aramina slumped against the nearest bulge-nut tree, clasping it for support and trying not to weep so childishly.

''Mina! What happened to you?' Pell knelt beside her, his hand hovering over the bleeding scalp wound. 'It was really Thella? Who else was with her?'

K'van was beside her, patting her shoulders.

'You did the right thing, 'Mina. Heth heard you and told me. We were setting snares. Heth's called for reinforcements. They won't get away. If there hadn't been so many trees, Heth would've caught 'em already!'

'Dragons,' she said in gasps, 'aren't built . . . to run in forests.' Sniffing, she pointed to Heth, who was retracing his way, weaving in and out of the trees, snarling as one wing caught on a protruding branch. He looked so funny; she oughtn't to laugh at the dear dragon who had saved her from Thella and Giron, but it *was* funny, and she began to giggle and then couldn't stop her laughing.

'What's so funny!' demanded Pell, outraged by his sister's laughter.

'I expect she's a bit hysterical. Not that I blame her. You take her other arm, Pell. We've got to get her back to the cave.'

'What about Heth?'

Heth rejoined them, his roars now reduced to belly rumbles.

I told her I was coming! I told her I heard her! Didn't you hear me, 'Mina? Heth curled his neck around K'van to peer anxiously up at Aramina.

Hiccuping somewhere between laughter and tears, Aramina speechlessly patted Heth's muzzle.

I was so scared . . . even her thought hiccuped . . . *I couldn't even hear myself.*

'Shards!' said K'van as a whoosh of wind signaled the arrival of a wing of dragons. Heth swiveled his head toward the display.

The guards chase them through the woods!

As the three youngsters watched, Aramina marveling at the snippets of conversation she caught in the confusion of orders given and received, the dragons began to peel off from the wing formation, going in all directions in a search for the renegades.

'T'gellan's leading the wing,' K'van informed them, deftly picking out of the stream the information that escaped Aramina. 'They'll search. We're to get back to the cave.'

'Oh, my sackful of nuts!' cried Aramina.

'Nuts, she worries about! At a time like this!' Pell was disgusted.

Aramina started to cry again, unable to stop the tears. 'Mother *needs* them for bread flour . . .'

'I'll come back for 'em,' exclaimed Pell at the top of his voice in frustration. 'I'll come back!'

Not completely reassured, since she knew her brother so well, Aramina was nonetheless willing to be helped back to the cave. Her mother, after her first startlement, bathed and salved Aramina's scalp and the other scratches she had received from the rough handling. If Barla did so with compressed lips and a decidedly pale face, she did not scold Aramina. Pell, under K'van's stern eye, had gone back for the nuts and Aramina's jerkin. K'van brewed more *klah*, a very welcome cup that infused Aramina's cold stomach with welcome heat.

Aramina, Lessa waits without, said Heth. *For your mother, too.*

'Mother, we're wanted outside,' Aramina said.

'By whom?'

'By Lessa, the Weyrwoman of Pern,' said K'van. 'Heth just relayed the message.'

Barla looked at her daughter as if she had never really seen her clearly before.

'You don't just hear dragons,' she said in a puzzled voice, 'they hear you, and they talk to you, and you can answer them?'

'A very useful knack,' K'van said with a grin; then he added, 'Lessa's waiting.'

'Is she angry with me?' Aramina asked timorously.

'Why would she be angry with you?' K'van asked, puzzled.

We could not be angry with you, Aramina, said the most beautiful dragon voice that Aramina had yet heard.

'C'mon.' K'van took Aramina firmly by the arm to haul her out of the cave. 'You don't keep Lessa waiting.'

Aramina's first impression of the slender figure standing in the clearing was surprise. The Weyrwoman of Benden was so small in stature: a full head shorter than Aramina. But, once Aramina confronted Lessa, the vivid eyes and the forceful personality made her forget about such a trivial detail as height. Nor had Heth mentioned that F'lar and Lord Asgenar also waited.

'My dear child, are you quite all right?' Lessa's expression turned anxious as her hand hovered over the ugly bare patch on Aramina's head.

'I don't know how that villain Thella eluded us,' said Asgenar, his teeth clenched with frustration. 'We have captured the rest of her band. Fewer to trouble you, and us. I am most chagrined, Aramina, that despite our precautions you were put at risk.'

'I'm fine, really, Lord Asgenar. Heth saved me. And Mother had the fellis and numbweed.'

'We are extremely grateful to you,' Barla put in, 'for those generous gifts.'

'Generous!' Lessa made a scathing remark. 'I would be a lot more generous, Lady Barla, if your stiff Ruathan pride would permit.'

Nothing could have startled Barla more, but, though she permitted a slight smile to curve her lips, to Aramina she seemed to be more prideful than ever.

'We Ruathans have reason to be proud, Lady Lessa.'

'But not stupid in that pride, Lady Barla. Lytol tells me that Dowell's hold is still vacant. Deserted, needing repairs, for no one under Fax's holding prospered. Would you prefer to return there? Lord Asgenar' – Asgenar bowed at his name – 'is also interested in anyone with wood mastery.'

Barla looked from one to the other. 'Ruatha is ours by right.'

'So be it, Lady Barla,' Lessa said, and, from the way her mouth twitched, Aramina was certain that she applauded the answer.

'However, Lord Asgenar, I am certain that my husband would be glad to build you a gather wagon . . . to acquit our lodging here.'

'Only if he also accepts the marks his Craft allots for the labor,' said Asgenar with a wide grin.

'Of course, Aramina is for Benden Weyr,' Lessa went on, her eyes now fixed on Barla's face.

'But I want to go home, to Ruatha!' cried Aramina, clinging to her mother now; clinging, too, to the dream on which she had been nourished from childhood, the return to the place of her birth, where her family belonged.

'A girl who hears dragons belongs to the Weyr,' said Barla, firmly taking Aramina's hands and pressing them hard.

'It's not as if you can't visit any time you want to,' Lessa said lightly. 'I do. Though we of Ruatha serve our Weyrs whenever we are called to.'

Please, 'Mina. Heth's tremulous whisper invaded her conflicting thoughts. *Please come to Brenden with me and K'van. We'd love to have you.*

You will be most welcome in Benden Weyr, said the dark black rich voice of Mnementh.

'There are eggs hardening on Benden Hatching Ground right now,' Lessa went on, her voice persuasive. 'Benden needs a girl who can hear dragons.'

'More than my family needs me?' asked Aramina perversely.

'Far more, as you'll discover,' said Lessa, holding her hand out to Aramina. 'Coming?'

'I don't have a choice, do I?' But Aramina smiled.

'Not when Lessa, and Benden's dragons, have made up your mind for you,' said F'lar with a laugh.

From the track, dragons bellowed an emphatic agreement.

VELVET FIELDS

Of course we moved into the cities of the planet we now know we must call Zobranoirundisi when Worlds Federated finally permitted a colony there. Although Survey had kept a watch on the planet for more than thirty years standard and the cities were obviously on a standby directive, the owners remained conspicuous by their absence. Since Resources and Supplies had agitated in council for another breadbasket planet in that sector of the galaxy and Zobranoirundisi was unoccupied, we were sent in, chartered to be self-sufficient in one sidereal year and to produce a surplus in two.

It would, therefore, have been a great misdirection of effort not to have inhabited the cities – we only moved into four – so patently suitable for humanoid life-forms. The murals that decorated a conspicuous wall in every dwelling unit gave only a vague idea of the physiology of our landlords, always depicted in an attitude of reverent obeisance toward a dominating Tree symbol so that only the backs, the rounded fuzz-covered craniums, and the suggestions of arms extended in front of the bodies were visible.

I suppose if we had not been so concerned with establishing the herds, generally breaking our necks to meet the colony charter requirements, we might have discovered sooner that there had been a gross error. The clues were there. For example, although we inhabited the cities, they could not be made fully 'operational' despite all the efforts of Dunlapil, the metropolitan engineer. Then, too, we could find no single example of the Tree anywhere on the lush planet. But, with R&S on our backs to produce, produce, produce, we didn't take time to delve into the perplexing anomalies.

Dunlapil, with his usual urbane contempt for the botanical, quipped to Martin Chavez, our ecologist, that the Tree was the Tree of Life and therefore mythical.

'Carry the analogy further,' he would tease Martin, 'and it explains why the Tree worshipers' – that's what we called them before we *knew* – 'aren't around anymore. Some dissident plucked the Apple and got 'em all kicked out of the Garden of Eden.'

Eden might well have been modeled on this planet, with its velvet fields, parklike forests, and rolling plains. Amid these sat lovely little cities constructed of pressed fibrous blocks tinted in pleasant colors during a manufacturing process whose nature frustrated Dunlapil as much as the absence of Trees perplexed Chavez.

So, suppressing our pervasive sense of trespassing, we moved into the abandoned dwellings, careful not to make any irreparable changes to accommodate our equipment. In fact, the only sophisticated nonindigenous equipment that I, as colony commissioner, permitted within any city was the plastisteel Comtower. I ordered the spaceport constructed beyond a low range of foothills on the rather scrubby plain at some distance from my headquarters city. An old riverbed proved an acceptable road for moving cargo to and from the port, and no one really objected to the distance. It would be far better not to offend our landlords with the dirt and chaos of outer-space commerce close to their pretty city.

We pastured the cattle in neatly separated velvet fields. Martin Chavez worried when close inspection disclosed that each velvet field was underpinned by its own ten-meter-thick foundation of ancient, rock-hard clay. Those same foundations housed what seemed to be a deep irrigation system.

I did ask Martin Chavez to investigate the curious absence of herbivores from a planet so perfectly suited to them. He had catalogued several types of omnivores, a wide variety of fowl, and a plethora of fishes. He did discover some fossil remains of herbivores, but nothing more recent than traces comparable to those of our Pleistocene epoch.

He therefore was forced to conclude – and submitted in a voluminous report with numerous comparisons to nearby galactic examples – that some catastrophes, perhaps the same that had wiped out the humanoids, had eliminated herbivores at an earlier stage.

Whatever the disaster had been – bacterial, viral, or something more esoteric – it did not recur to plague us. We thrived on the planet. The first children, conceived under the bluish alien sun, were born just after we had shipped our first year's surplus off-world. Life settled into a pleasant seasonal routine: the beef, sheep, horses, kine, even the windoers of Grace's World imported on an experimental basis, multiplied on the velvet fields. The centenarian crops from half a dozen worlds gave us abundant yields. We had some failures, of course, with inedible or grotesque ergotic mutations, but not enough to be worth more than a minor Chavezian thesis in the record and the shrug of the pioneering farmer. If a colonist is eating well, living comfortably, with leisure time for his kids and time off with his wife on the languid southern seas, he puts up with minor failures and irritations. Even with the omnipresent guilt of trespassing.

I was not the only one who never felt entirely at easy in the pretty cities. But, as I rationalized the intermittent twinges of conscience, it would have been ridiculous to build facilities when empty accommodations were already available, despite their obstinate refusal to work no matter how Dunlapil tried to energize them. Still, we managed fine and gradually came to ignore the anomalies we had never fully explored, settling down to make our gardens and our families grow.

The tenth year was just beginning, with surprising warmth, when Martin Chavez called a meeting with me and Dunlapil. Chavez had even convened it on a Rest-day, which was annoying as well as unusual.

'Just in case we have to call a meeting of the colony,' he told me when I protested. That statement, on top of his insistence on a meeting, was enough to make me feel apprehensive. Although Martin was a worrier he was no fool; he did not force his problems on any-one unnecessarily, nor was he one for calling useless meetings.

'I've an unusual report to make on a new plant growth discernible on the velvet fields, Commissioner Sarubbi,' he announced, addressing me formally. 'Such a manifestation is not generally associated with simple monocotyledonous plants. I've cross-checked both used and unused pastures, and the distortions of the growth in the used fields are distressing.'

'You mean, we've imported a virus that's mutating the indigenous grasses?' I asked. 'Or has the old virus that killed off the herbivorous life revived?'

'Nothing like this mutation has ever been classified and no, I don't think it's a return of a previous calamity.' Chavez frowned with worry.

'Ah, champion, martyr,' Dunlapil said with some disgust. 'Don't go calling for a planetary quarantine just when we're showing a nice credit balance.'

Chavez drew himself up indignantly.

'He hasn't suggested anything of the sort, Dun,' I said, wondering if the urban engineer was annoyed because Chavez might be closer to solving the enigma of the Tree than Dunlapil was the mechanics of the cities. 'Please explain, Specialist Chavez.'

'I've just recently become aware of a weird evolution from the family Graminaceae, which these plants have resembled until now.' He snapped on the handviewer and projected a slide onto the only wall in my office bare of the ubiquitous murals. 'The nodular extrusions now developing in the velvet fields show none of the characteristics of herbaceous plants. No joined stems or slender sheathing leaves.' He looked around to see if we had seen enough before he flashed on a slide of magnified cellular material. 'This cross section suggests genus *Helianthus*, an improbable mutation.' Chavez shrugged his helplessness in presenting such contradictory material. 'However, something new is under every sun and we have not yet determined how the usual blue light of this primary will affect growth after prolonged exposure. We might get a Bragae Two effect.'

'The next thing you'll be telling us, Martin,' Dunlapil said as if to forestall a discourse on galactic comparisons, 'is that these plants are the aliens who built these cities.' He shot me a grin.

'That ought to be obvious,' Chavez said with such a lack of rancor that the disbelief I had been entertaining disappeared. 'Commissioner' – Chavez's grave eyes met mine – 'can you give me another reason why every city has similarly fenced lots, all placed to catch full daily sun? Why the velvet fields with that central dominant Tree symbol appear to be the reverent focus of the aliens – excuse me – the indigenous species?'

'But they're humanoid,' Dunlapil said in protest.

'Their culture is agrarian. *And* there are no grazers. Nor a single example of that blasted Tree anywhere on the planet – yet!'

That was when I truly began to be afraid.

'There are no grazing beasts,' Chavez went on

inexorably, 'because they have been eliminated to protect the velvet fields and whatever is growing in them now.'

'You mean, when those fields bloom with whatever it is they bloom with, the aliens will return?' Dunlapil asked.

Chavez nodded. 'If we haven't irreparably altered the growth cycle.'

'But that's fantastic! An entire civilization can't be dependent on a crazy who-knows-how-long cycle of plant life!' Dunlapil was sputtering with indignation.

'Nothing is impossible,' replied Chavez at his most didactic.

'Your research has been sufficiently comprehensive?' I asked him, although I was sick with the sense of impending disaster.

'As comprehensive as my limited equipment and xeno-botanical experience allow. I would welcome a chance to submit my findings to a board of specialists with greater experience in esoteric plant-life forms. And I respectfully request that you have Colonial Central send us a team at once. I'm afraid that we've already done incalculable damage to the—' He paused and, with a grim smile, corrected himself. '—*indigenous* organism seeded in those fields.'

The semantic nicety jarred me. If Chavez was even remotely correct, we would require not only xenobotan-ists and xenobiologists but an entire investigation team from Worlds Federated to examine our intrusion into a domain that had not, after all, been abandoned by its occu-pants like a *Marie Celeste* but had simply been lying fallow – with the *indigenous* natives quiescently in residence.

As Chavez, Dunlapil, and I walked from my office toward the Comtower, I remember now that I felt a little foolish and very scared, like a child reluctant to report an accident to his parents but dutifully conscientious about admitting his misdemeanor. The plastisteel tower had never looked so out of place, so alien, so sacrilegious as it did now.

'Hey, wait a minute, you two,' Dulapil protested. 'You know what an investigation team means . . .'

'Anything and everything must be done to mitigate our offense as soon as possible,' Chavez said, interrupting nervously.

'Dammit!' Dunlapil stopped in his tracks. 'We've done nothing wrong.'

'Indeed we have! We may have crippled an entire generation.' Chavez spoke with an expression of ineffable sorrow.

'There are plenty of fields we never touched. The aliens – natives – can use them for food . . .'

Chavez's sad smile deepened and he gently removed Dunlapil's hand from his arm. '"From dust ye came, to dust ye shall return, and from dust shall ye spring again."'

It was than that Dunlapil understood the enormity of our crime.

'You mean, the plants are the *people*?'

'What else have I been saying? They are born from the Trees.'

We did what we could even as we waited for the specialists and investigation team to arrive.

First we cleared the animals and crops from every one of the velvet fields. We removed every sign of our colonial occupation from the cities. The team, composed of five nonhuman and three humanoid species, arrived with menacing expedition well before the initial flood of xenospecialists. The team members did not comment on our preliminary efforts to repair our error, nor did they protest their quarters in the hastily erected dwellings on the bare, dusty plain and the subsequent roaring activity of the spaceport close by. All they did was observe with portentous intensity.

75

Of course, except for vacating the cities – and occupying them was apparently the least of our cumulative crimes – everything we did to remedy our trespass proved horribly inept in the final analysis. We would have been less destructive had we kept the cattle on the velvet fields and not slaughtered them for food. We ought to have let the crops ripen, die, and return to the special soils that had nourished them. For the fields we stripped produced the worst horrors. But how were we to know?

Now, of course, we know all too fully. We are burdened to this very day with guilt and remorse for the wholesale dismemberment and dispersal of those irretrievable beings: eaten, digested, defecated upon by grazers. And again, eaten, digested, and eliminated by those who partook of the grazers' flesh. Of the countless disintegrated natives removed from their home soil by unwitting carriers, none can bear fruit on foreign soil. And on their own soil, to repeat, the fields we had stripped produced the worst horrors . . .

I remember when the last report had been turned in to the eight judges composing the investigation team. Its members wasted no further time in formulating their decree. I was called to their conference room to hear the verdict. As I entered, I saw the judges seated on a raised platform, several feet above my head. That in itself was warning that we had lost all status in Worlds Federated.

A flick of the wrist attracted my attention to one of three humans on the team. Humbly I craned my head back, but he refused to glance down at me.

'The investigation is complete,' he said in an emotionless tone. 'You have committed the worst act of genocide yet to be recorded in all galactic history.'

'Sir . . .' My protest was cut off by a second, peremptory gesture.

'Xenobiologists report that the growths in the velvet

fields have reached the third stage in their evolution. The parallel between this life-form in its second stage and that of the cellulose fauna of Brandon Two is inescapable.' Chavez had already told me of that parallel. 'Now the plants resemble the exorhizomorphs of Planariae Five and it is inevitable that this third stage will give way to the sentient life pictured in the murals of their cities.

'You came here as agrarians and agrarians you shall be, in the fields of those you have mutilated. What final reparations will be levied against you, one and all, cannot be known until the victims of your crimes pronounce the penance whereby you may redeem your species in the eyes of the Worlds Federated.'

He stopped speaking and waved me away. I withdrew to announce the verdict to my dazed fellow colonists. I would far rather that we had been summarily executed then and there, instead of being worn and torn apart by bits and pieces. But that was not the way of judgment for those who trespass in modern enlightened times.

We could not even make an appeal on the grounds that the planet had been released to us, for the colony in its charter took on all responsibility for its subsequent actions, having reaped benefits now so dearly to be paid for.

So we worked from that day until Budding Time late that heinous fall. We watched anxiously as the seedling exorhizomorphs grew at a phenomenal rate until they were ten, then twenty, finally twenty-five feet high, thick-trunked, branching out, lush with green triangular foliage. By midsummer we knew why it was that during our time on the planet we had never been able to find any examples of the Tree: such Trees grew once every hundred years. For they were the Trees of Life and bore the Fruit of Zobranoirundisi in the cellular wombs, two to a branch, three to eleven branches per Tree. In the good fields – that is, the unviolated fields.

In the others . . .

***

The galaxy knows we tried to atone for our crime. Every man, woman, and child was devoted to tending the twisted, stunted, deformed, half-branched Trees that grew so piteously in those desecrated fields. Every one of us watched with growing apprehension and horror as each new day showed further evidence of the extent of our sacrilege. Oh, the hideous difference between those straight, tall, fine Zobranoirundisi and – the Others. We were ready for any sacrifice as penance.

Then, the morning after the first good frost, when the cold had shriveled the stems, the first Zobranoirundisi tore through his vegetable placenta. He shook his tall willowy body, turned and made obeisance to his natal Tree of Life, ate of the soil at its roots, of its triangular foliage . . . and knew!

I can never retell the agony of that day, when all those Zobranoirundisi faced us, their maimers, and announced the form our expiation would take. We bowed our heads to the inevitable, for we knew the sentence to be just and of Hammurabian simplicity.

We had to give back to the soil what we had taken from it. The handless Zobranoirundisi, recognizing his missing member from the cells now incorporated into the fingers of a young colony child nurtured on milk from cattle fed in the velvet fields, had every right to reclaim what was undeniably his own flesh. The legless Zobranoirundisi could not be condemned to a crippled existence when the Terran child had used the same cells to run freely for seven years on land where previously only Zobranoirundisi had trod.

We rendered, all of us, unto the Zobranoirundisi that which was truly theirs – seed and soil of the velvet fields, part and particle of the originally fertilizing dust that would have been reconstituted during the cycle we had so impiously interrupted.

Nor were we permitted to evade the least segment of required reparation, for the galaxy watched. I will say this of us proudly, though I no longer have a tongue: Mankind will be able to live with its conscience. Not one of us, when required, failed to give his flesh to the Zobranoirundisi in atonement!

EUTERPE ON A FLING

Looking through old files for something else entirely, I chanced upon the notes I'd made during an interview with Madame Florence Foster Jenkins. Considering that the musical world had been far more concerned with the curious and brief career of one Peter Pelty, substitute tenor at the Metropolitan Opera House, I'd never transcribed the notes into an article. But reviewing them now – after nearly fifty years – I was amazed at how vividly I recalled the incident. Of course, Madame Florence Foster Jenkins had had her own niche in the recital world of New York. Having met and then heard her, I knew that she was eminently memorable.

I carefully unfolded the two yellowed and now fragile clippings attached to my scrawled sheets, and suddenly it was as if I were back in that dark corner of the gloomy old Seymour Lounge, where Madame Jenkins had agreed to meet me.

The first article, lamentably in only the last paragraph, described her Carnegie Hall debut, at age seventy-six. I'd been there: I didn't need further joggling. I grinned as I read,

> Her style, her artistry, her joy of singing, her technique remain one of the most refreshingly different pages in the annals of musical history. She was known as the mistress of the sliding scale, a skilled proponent

of altered tempi. Her ability to remain a quarter tone above or below the written note was truly inspired.

Her rendition of the Queen of the Night aria from *The Magic Flute* had, to my astonished ears, been certainly all that and more.

The second clipping mentioned the curious and unscheduled debut of the American tenor Peter Pelty, who remains far more of a controversial musical mystery than Madame Florence Foster Jenkins.

Or, I thought with sudden surprise, does he?

Pelty had substituted in the role of Radamès in a Saturday matinee at the Metropolitan Opera, the advertised tenor having been injured in a taxi accident on his way to the opera house. Those in the audience vowed they had never heard such a magnificent voice – an opinion substantiated by not only Milton Cross but also Mr Aaronsky, the director of the Met; Madame Neroni, who sang Aida; and Maestro Di Saltsa, the conductor. The radio audience, however, held a diametrically opposite opinion of Pelty's vocal accomplishments. The entire musical world was talking about the affair, so I had thought to set Madame Jenkins at ease by asking her opinion of the dichotomy, for she had been at the performance.

'Tenors are never so happy but when they are stage center,' Madame Jenkins told me, inclining her torso toward me, a habit she used to emphasize a point. Her voice, which, up to that point, had been genteel and refined, suddenly oozed with disdain. 'He had only himself to blame for overextending himself. Eighteen curtain calls is impolite: especially when he took most of them himself.'

'He won't do it again,' I said, remembering that he had expired before the curtain could be raised on the nineteenth demand of his audience to express their appreciation of that incredible performance.

'It shall remain as a lesson to others not to exceed operatic decorum.' Again that slight forward motion, but her lips were primly thin in disapproval.

She was, in herself, an astonishing figure: small, and so well corseted I thought I heard subtle creakings – but then many singers are tightly corseted during performances to assist breath support. Her rounded face displayed the jowls that often plague singers and mar an otherwise pretty face, but Madame Jenkins looked more Victorian, e.g. like the Queen. Her mousy hair was neatly marcelled in waves reminiscent of a prewar style, and her clothing, while well cut and an attractive cherry red that lent color to a rather pale complexion, also harked back to the pre-flapper era. But it suited her.

'Didn't you think it odd, Madame Jenkins, that a total unknown would be called upon to substitute at the Met?'

'Not at all,' she surprised me by saying. 'He was not only a dedicated subscriber to the Metropolitan Opera Society but he knew every libretto by heart.' An expression of mixed exasperation and then immediate remorse crossed her expressive little face. 'He sat near me, you see.'

'Sat near him, Madame Jenkins? I don't understand.'

She waved a graceful hand, preparatory to enlightening me. 'Ever since I have subscribed to my seat for the Saturday opera matinees, I have had *his* voice in my ear.'

'His voice in your ear?'

'It's quite simple, young man. *His* seat was diagonally *behind* mine in row H. I was in row G. I'm just a teensy bit nearsighted,' she added in a confidential tone. Then she drew herself up, reclasping her hands in her lap with Victorian precision. 'For twenty-four years, through every opera, he *hummed* every single tenor aria and chanted, mind you, *chanted* the recitatives. No one ever sat beside him, on either side, more than once but . . .' She shuddered delicately, eyes closed, her pale rounded face eloquently expressing her patient forbearance. '. . . he ought not to have done so.'

'That must have been frightfully irritating,' I said solicitously.

'Irritating?' One grateful hand rose in a gesture of dismay. 'It was ill-mannered in the extreme. My papa and my mama would have had words with the manager at the very first occurrence. Of course, Papa was not fond of opera although he attended when the troupe came to Philadelphia, where we lived. But a lone woman, with no escort, speaking to a man to whom she hasn't been introduced . . . No, simply not done.'

'But if he was interfering with your pleasure . . .'

Her eyes widened in surprise. 'The irritating thing, young man, was that he was often so much better a singer than the one on stage.'

I remember gawking in surprise.

'And when he took the stage as Radamès, I have never heard a more brilliant performance. He *lived* the role. He *suffered* it. He *sang* it.' Her voice wavered touchingly on the verb. 'We were totally under the spell of his magic voice.'

'Really?' It was hard to keep from laughing, either at her unexpected endorsement or my recollection of the cacophony I had heard issue from my radio – fortunately, for just the first act of *Aida*.

'Young man,' she said, waggling an admonishing beringed finger at me, 'I know whereof I speak. I was in that audience. You were not. I have seen *Aida* some . . .' She gazed heavenward, counting. '. . . some twenty times and I have never heard the role sung better. Furthermore, Mr Pelty did not, as some tenors would, depart from the tempi of Maestro Verdi's score, or put in those little embellishments that tenors seem so fond of.

83

Mr Pelty was in flawless voice throughout the entire performance. Now, the Amneris . . .'

'Oh, come now, Madame Jenkins,' I began, 'I heard the first scene. Madame Schezani's Amneris was on pitch whereas Pelty . . .'

'Radio is in its infancy, young man,' she said with a patronizing smile. 'We, in the audience, to the last one of us, heard exactly what we were supposed to hear – a superb, never-to-be-forgotten Radamès in full and glorious voice.'

'Madame, my cat with its tail caught in the icebox door was Nellie Melba in comparison.'

'Madame Melba, young man, was a soprano,' she said in a prim reprimand. 'Even Mr Cross,' and she smiled graciously at mentioning him, 'could not understand *why* the NBC was in such a tizzy over what appeared to all of us to be a unique experience. He said so to me several times – that is, *before* he refused to discuss the matter at all. He told *me* that his ears could not have so deceived him. After all, Mr Cross *is* Mr Opera. My poor opinion is as nothing next to his but, on this, we are in agreement!'

'Hmm, yes, but he won't, as you say, discuss the incident. I believe Mr Aaronsky has been on the carpet, too . . .'

'And so he should,' she confused me by saying, 'for not having assured himself of the availability of an understudy for the matinees as they invariably do for the evening performance.'

'You surely can't blame Mr Aaronsky for Mr Sostenuto's taxi accident?'

She gave me a stern look, her ample chin tucked down to her high bosom.

'Of course not. But, in my youth, *every* contingency was provided for. Consequently *our* society was very well ordered.'

'To be sure, to be sure.'

'At first,' she continued, nodding at my meek apology, 'when Mr Aaronsky stepped in front of the curtain to explain a delay of the performance, I presumed that he had sent for the first cover of the tenor role. Albeit, Mr Sostenuto had never missed a performance in his life – he resides on East Sixty-second Street during the season – still it was gross negligence of the director.'

I remember that I couldn't resist teasing her then.

'Even when you were treated to such a musical debut?'

'Sagacious provision against unexpected emergencies is another matter entirely. I fault him on that score, not on permitting Mr Pelty to sing Radamès.' A glow suffused her round face. '*That* was serendipitous.'

'What I don't understand, Madame, is how he got on the Met stage at all!' A question that had been asked over and over. If Madame Jenkins had the answer, I might have a scoop on my hands, not a fill-in article.

'Of course, when Mr Pelty rose from his seat behind me, I thought he was leaving, not going to offer to play the role.' She paused, drawing herself to an even more rigid position on the edge of the chair she occupied. 'You can imagine my surprise when, shortly thereafter, Mr Aaronsky reappeared to announce that Mr Pelty would sing the role.'

'But Mr Pelty was totally unknown . . .'

'He was known to me, though we had never been on more than nodding terms.'

'And the Met has an enviable reputation. Very few get past the initial auditions. I mean, someone out of the audience, saying that he *knows* an operatic role . . . I mean, anyone can *say* he knows an operatic role but . . .'

'Young man,' she said, interrupting me with an imperious gesture, 'I have already mentioned that he had been humming and chanting the tenor roles in my left ear for years . . .'

'I remember that, but his . . . voice?' I grimaced in

85

recollection of the tones that had assailed my ears from a usually trustworthy radio.

'Ah, but, as Mr Aaronsky said several times, quite forcefully at one point, I believe, Mr Pelty *did* have an audition. That is why Mr Aaronsky permitted him to go on.'

I must have looked my disbelief.

'Madame Neroni, who was singing Aida, as well as Maestro Di Saltsa,' she continued, compounding the evidence in Pelty's favor, 'were present. Madame Neroni declared herself delighted to sing Aida to his Radamès and the conductor was certainly willing. Then, too, singers go from opera house to opera house with rarely more than a walk-through of stage movements. Mr Cross said that Mr Pelty assured them he had seen the Met production of Aida often enough to need only occasional prompting. Which, under the circumstances, with the network demanding to proceed, was the most minor of the considerations.

'So, no matter what you may think, no matter what you *think* you heard on that radio – really, it is an abominable invention. I certainly shall never sing through its medium if that is how it distorts the human voice. What we in the audience were privileged to hear that day was a transcendent performance of *Grand Operah*!' Her eyes shone at the memory, her face lit with an inner warmth and dedication.

'Oh, no,' I said under my breath.

'Oh, yes,' she contradicted politely, not catching my facetious tone. 'As I'm sure you're aware,' she went on in a gently instructive manner, 'Radamès sings his big aria, the glorious "Celeste Aida," almost as soon as the curtain is raised.' She interrupted herself to tsck-tsck softly, sighing before she picked up her story. 'So often tenors will stint on the preperformance vocalizing. They appear on stage unprepared to do justice to the splendor of that magnificent Verdi aria. It has, you know, three B-flats and many a time I am forced to confess that I have heard the Radamès distinctly under pitch on the second B-flat. And twice, no, three times, the tenor has not held that final note its full count.'

'Inexcusable!'

'Of course, there are many tenors who, as the expression goes, "milk" that final B-flat beyond what Maestro Verdi wished. But Mr Pelty was in glorious voice.' Her eyes turned heavenward again, her hands lifted eloquently in the same direction. 'Each note, pure, spinning, magnificently supported.'

She and the bemused audience had been unanimous on that point despite the fact that everyone in radio range heard a cross between a gargling scream and a wailing animal in acute distress. Before Mr Pelty had finished the opening aria, there had been such a shocked wave of protest to NBC from radio listeners that the network – after tuning in to the opera – had peremptorily cut Mr Cross's microphones from the air and substituted a recorded but infinitely more acceptable performance of the opera. Mr Cross, when called to the phone by the frantic studio director, had insisted with vehemence that the performance was truly a memorable one, the tenor inspired, and that it must be the fault of the electronic equipment. In the early thirties the radio facilities at the Met were still makeshift. Mr Cross, however, would not credit the fact that only the tenor's voice seemed affected by the malfunction.

'His style,' Madame continued, 'his presence, his authority were . . . divinely inspired!' Her eyes returned to earthly horizons, still shining with remembered ecstasy. 'And it was, of course, a distinct relief to have him on-stage, *singing* the role instead of humming in my left ear.'

An air bubble or something caught in my windpipe and I began to choke helplessly.

'Waiter, a glass of water, please,' Madame directed thoughtfully.

'Oh, thank you, very good of you, Madame. My apologies,' I managed to gasp between sips. 'Would you join me? I mean, Madame, *do* you drink? Liquor, that is?'

She drew herself up with great dignity and said in measured syllables, 'Does a fish swim?'

The waiter resorted to pounding me vigorously on the back before the second paroxysm passed.

When he returned with the drinks, I was limp but functioning. I tried to get back to the subject of Peter Pelty's performance.

'We have wasted entirely enough time on tenors, young man,' she informed me. 'I believe you asked to interview *me*?' Her emphasis on the pronoun was genteelly delicate.

'Yes, do forgive me, Madame Jenkins.' I flipped to a fresh page. 'Yes, Carnegie Hall next week.'

She gave me a penetrating look before she retrieved her handbag from the floor beside her.

'You are, of course, attending?'

I hadn't planned to, but circumstances forced me to concur with a show of enthusiasm.

'Ticket agencies never make an exact accounting of their sales,' she said. Then, with a minimum of fumbling, she brought out of the copious black purse a package of tickets, secured with a heavy rubber band. She riffled through them expertly, extracting one, which she checked before handing it to me with a dainty flourish of her wrist.

'I am my own manager,' she said with a gracious smile. 'That will be two dollars, please. I've given you row H.'

I had no other option but to pull two dollars out of my wallet and complete the exchange with as good a grace as

I could muster. Briefly I wondered if she would have the consummate gall to charge the music critics, too.

'The demand for tickets to my concerts has been so great that I have been forced to move from the Sherry-Netherland to the Hall,' she said as she added my two crumpled bills to a huge roll, also confined by a rubber band. She returned money and tickets to the ancient black purse and it to its previous position.

'I've never trusted tenors, agents, or managers, and I find I do very well indeed without them,' she said without a trace of rancor. 'Now!' She folded her hands primly in her lap and cocked her head expectantly at me for my questions.

'Don't artistes usually start their careers somewhat earlier than you have, Madame?' I put it as diplomatically as possible. Not every seventy-year-old makes a debut in Carnegie Hall. I'd heard that her parents had kept her from singing while they were alive, and her husband during his life span. Unfortunately he had had a heart attack and died intestate, so she had inherited a considerable estate with no restrictions and immediately founded the Verdi Society, Giuseppe being her favorite opera composer.

'I have been a concert artiste, in my modest way, since 1924,' she told me demurely. 'I was taught, as all young girls' – which, in her enunciation, sounded more like 'gels' – 'in my day, to play the piano and accompany my vocal renditions evenings after dinner. I have always maintained that if you desire something badly enough, and work assiduously toward that goal, you will one day succeed. Papa and Mama were very strict, as indeed parents should be, and they felt that a stage career was not suitable for a young woman of my social standing. I approve of a certain amount of relaxation in such strictures these days. After all, these are modern times.'

'Indeed. Very true. Very liberal of you.'

'Of course, I would never dream of presenting myself in anything so lacking in taste as that dreadfully fast *Oklahoma*, which the public raves about.'

'The public' was patently not in the same social sphere as those who attended operatic performances. I nodded encouragingly. She didn't need much, for she was well launched now.

'But the concert stage has always been eminently respectable.'

'Indeed.'

'And when dear Mr Jenkins left me financially independent, I vowed to support my real love – Operah! – and to follow the career my parents felt constrained by the dictates of society to deny me.'

She consulted the watch pinned to her pleated lacy shirtwaist and rose to her feet. I found myself drawn up, as by strings, to my feet.

'Mr McMoon, my accompanist, is awaiting me. He is a jewel of patience and perseverance. So few pianists are gifted enough to follow me when I am inspired by the music I am performing. I have a *mattinata* tomorrow. The life of an artiste is rigorous and there are many demands on my time.'

'Yes, yes, you've been most gracious, Madame, but one last question?'

She smiled, the epitome of the gentle lost grace of another era.

'Mr Pelty,' I began, seizing my last opportunity awkwardly, unable to phrase my notion.

A look of penitent remorse crossed her face.

'I fear I might have sounded, not entirely charitable,' she said. 'Tenors are, you know, the cross we sopranos suffer for our art. I'm sure, however, I could have put any personal feelings aside to have sung Leonora to Pelty's Manrico.' She sighed expressively for the might-have-been. 'And he did deserve many curtain calls.

Perhaps not eighteen but what a glorious way for an artiste to pass to his reward!'

'Yes, glorious!' Fortunately she didn't catch the irony. 'But Madame, do you think it possible . . . It *would* explain why the radio listeners heard one thing and you in the audience another . . . Could he have been doing a reverse Trilby?'

She stiffened, her whole body rigid; her eyes lost their mildness and took on a piercing quality.

'What on earth do you mean to suggest?' she asked in the iciest of tones.

'That . . . he had the audience hypnotized into hearing . . . what they heard . . .' I stammered it out, slowing down with each word because of the awing, unnerving change in Madame Jenkins's face.

'The entire Metropolitan audience *and* Mr Cross? Hypnotized?' she demanded with regal and searing scorn.

'Well, it's a possibility, isn't it? After all, fifty thousand radios can't be wrong, can they?'

She drew in a deep breath, obviously controlling herself. 'And why not?' she intoned. 'Radio being a mechanical contrivance, crackling at best, with wavering transmissions of dubious quality. You would do well to forget such a preposterous theory, young man. There is a mystic bond between artiste and audience which some minds can never understand!'

'Yes, of course, Madame. Silly of me to suggest such a thing. Impertinent.'

'Indeed!'

After one more penetrating stare, she relaxed suddenly, smiling with more characteristic gentleness.

'Do not be late for my concert, now,' she said as she turned away. 'I can promise you an extraordinary musical experience. I know exactly where you'll be sitting and I shall throw blossoms at you during the lieder selections.'

Stunned at the prospect, I could only bob deferentially as she swept out of the lounge. But I am positive I heard her saying:

'Pelty? A Svengali? Impossible! He was *only* a tenor!'

Nothing could have kept me from that concert. Carnegie Hall was packed out. The rose blossoms she lavishly threw from the basket that completed her Dresden shepherdess's costume missed me entirely in row H. The concert was . . . unforgettable. But then, so was Madame Florence Foster Jenkins.

Over the years, there have been others who have tried to emulate her highly personal form of singing. Though there are recordings of her recitals, she never did perform on the radio and I wonder if it had something to do with Peter Pelty and his doubly ill-fated debut. Or perhaps it was the 'mystical bond between artiste and audience' that she felt she could count on. She could certainly hold an audience and, in her own way, she has remained unique: Euterpe on a fling!

DUTY CALLS

With the sort of bad luck that has dogged the Alliance lately, escort and convoy came back into normal space in the midst of space debris.

We came from the queer blankness of FTL drive into the incredible starscape of that sector, so tightly packed with sun systems that we had had to reenter far sooner than the admiral liked, considering nearby Khalian positions. But we had no choice. We had to leave the obscurity of FTL in relatively 'open' space. It would take nearly six months to reduce our reentry velocity of 93 percent C to one slow enough for us to make an orbit over the beleaguered world of Persuasion, our eventual destination. We also were constrained to reduce that tremendous velocity before nearing the gravity wells of such a profusion of stars; otherwise the fleet could be disrupted or, worse, scattered to be easily picked off by any roving Khalians. The admiral had plotted a brilliant two-step braking progress through the gravity wells of nearer star systems to 'lose' speed. So we emerged from FTL, nearly blinded by the blaze of brilliantly glowing stars which was, as suddenly, obscured. Then *wow!* Every alert on the dreadnought *Gormenghast* went spare.

Considering my position, attached to a landing pod, slightly forward of the main bridge section, I immediately went into action. Under the circumstances, the faster we could clear the junk the better, because 1) many of the supply pods towed by the freighters could be holed

93

by some of the bigger tidbits flying around at the speeds they were moving, and 2) we were awfuldamn close to a colony the Khalians had overrun three galactic years ago. If they had set up any peripheral scanners, they'd catch the Cerenkov radiations from our plasma weapons. So everything that could blast a target throughout the length of the convoy did!

Me, I always enjoy target practice, if I'm not *it* (which in my line of work as pilot of the admiral's gig is more frequently the case than the sane would wish). Against space debris I have no peer, and I was happily potting the stuff with for'ard and portside cannon when I received an urgent signal from the bridge.

'Hansing? Prepare to receive relevant charts and data for area ASD 800/900. Are you flight-ready?'

'Aye, aye, sir,' I said, for an admiral's gig is *always* ready or you're dropped onto garbage runs right smart. I recognized the voice as that of the admiral's aide, Commander Het Lee Wing, a frequent passenger of mine and a canny battle strategist who enjoys the full confidence of Admiral Ban Corrie Eberhard. Commander Het has planned, and frequently participated in, some of the more successful forays against Khalian forces that have overrun Alliance planets. Het doesn't have much sense of humor; I don't think I would if only half of me was human and the more useful parts no longer in working order. I think all his spare parts affected his brain. That's all that's left of me, but I got to keep an offbeat but workable humor. 'Data received.'

'Stand by, Bil,' he said. I stifled a groan. When Het gets friendly, I get worried. 'The admiral!'

'Mr Hansing' – the admiral's baritone voice was loud and clear, just a shade too jovial for my peace of mind – 'I have a mission for you. Need a recon on the third planet of ASD 836/929; its settlers call it Bethesda. It's coming up below us in a half a light-year. The one the pirates got a couple of years back. Need to be sure the Khalians don't know we've passed by. Don't want them charging up our ass end. We've got to get the convoy, intact, to the colony. They're counting on us.'

'Yes, sir!' I made me sound approving and willing.

'You'll have a brawn to make contact with our local agent, who is, fortunately, still alive. The colony surrendered to the Khalians, you know. Hadn't equipped themselves with anything larger than handguns.' The admiral's voice registered impatient disapproval of people unable to protect themselves from invasion. But then, a lot of the earliest colonies had been sponsored by nonaggressives long before the Alliance encountered the Khalians. Or had they encountered us? I can never remember now, for the intial contact had been several lifetimes ago, or so it seemed to me, who had fought Khalians all my adult life. However, it had been SOP to recruit a few 'observers' in every colonial contingent, equipped with implanted receivers for just such an emergency as had overtaken Bethesda. 'Het'll give you the agent's coordinates,' the admiral went on. 'Had to patch this trip up, Bil, but you're the best one to handle it. Space dust! Hah!' I could appreciate his disgust at our bad luck. 'You've got a special brawn partner for this, Bil. She'll brief you on the way.'

I didn't like the sound of that. But time was of the essence if the admiral had to prepare contingency plans to scramble this immense convoy to avoid a Khalian space attack. Somehow or other, despite modern technology, a fleet never managed to reassemble all the original convoy vessels and get them safely to their destination: some mothers got so lost or confused in the scramble, they never did find themselves again. Much less their original destination. Merchantmen could be worse than sheep to round up, and often about as smart. Yeah, I remember what sheep are.

'Aye, aye, sir,' I said crisply and with, I hoped, convincing enthusiasm for the job. I hate dealing with on-the-spots (OTS's): they're such a paranoid lot, terrified of exposure either to Khalian overlords or to their planetary colleagues who could be jeopardized by the agent's very existence. Khalian reprisals are exceptionally vicious. I was glad that a brawn had to contact the OTS.

Even as I accepted the assignment, I was also accessing the data received from the *Gormenghast*'s banks. The computers of an Ocelot Scout, even the Mark 18 that I drove, are programmed mainly for evasive tactics, maintenance, emergency repairs and stuff like that, with any memory limited to the immediate assignment. We don't *know* that the Khalians can break into our programs, but there's no sense in handing them, free, gratis, green, the whole nine meters, is there? Even in the very unlikely chance that they get their greasy paws on one of us.

The mortality and capture statistics for scouts like mine don't bear thinking about, so I don't think about them. Leaves most of my brain cells able to cope with immediate problems. Brawns have an even lower survival rate: being personalities that thrive on danger, risk, and uncertainty, and get large doses of all. I wondered what 'she' was. What ancient poet said, 'The female of the species is more deadly than the male'? Well, he had it right by all I've seen, in space or on the surface.

'Good luck, Bil!'

'Thank you, sir.'

Admiral Eberhard doesn't have to brief scout pilots like me, but I appreciate his courtesy. Like I said, the mortality for small ships is high, and that little extra personal touch makes a spaceman try that much harder to complete his mission successfully.

'Permission to come aboard.' The voice, rather deeper than I'd expected, issued from the air-lock com unit.

I took a look and damned near blew a mess of circuits. 'She' was a feline, an ironically suitable brawn for an Ocelot Scout like me, but she was the most amazing . . . colors, for her short thick fawn fur was splashed, dashed, and dotted by a crazy random pattern of different shades of brown, fawn, black, and a reddish tan. She was battle-lean, too, with a few thin patches of fur on forearm and the deep rib cage, which might or might not be scars. At her feet was a rolled-up mass of fabric, tightly tied with quick-release straps.

I'd seen Hrrubans before, of course: they're one of the few species in the Alliance who, like humans, are natural predators, and consequently make very good combat fighters. I'm not poor-mouthing our Allies, but, without naming types, some definitely have no fighting potential, though as battle support personnel they have no peer and, in their own specialties, are equally valuable in the Alliance war with the Khalians. 'A shacking goo,' as the man said.

This representative of the Hrruban species was not very large: some of their troops are *big* mothers. I'd say that this Hrruban was young – they're allowed to fight at a much earlier age than humans – for even the adult females are of a size with the best of us. This one had the usual oddly scrunched shoulder conformation. As she stood upright, her arms dangled at what looked like an awkward angle. It would be for the human body. She held herself in that curious, straight-backed, half-forward crouch from her pelvis that Hrrubans affected: the way she stood, the weight on the balls of her furred feet, thighs forward, calves on the slant, the knee ahead of the toe, indicated that she stood erect right now, by choice, but was still effective on all fours. Khalians had once been quadrupeds, too, but you rarely saw one drop to all fours, unless it was dying. And that was the only way I wanted to see Khalians.

'Permission . . .' she began again patiently, one foot nudging the folded bundle of fabric beside her. I opened the air lock and let her in.

'Sorry, but I've never seen an Hrruban quite like you before . . .'

I ended on an upward inflection, waiting for her to identify herself.

'B'ghra Hrrunalkharr,' she said, 'senior lieutenant, Combat Supply.'

And if survival is low for brawns, it's even lower for Combat Supply personnel. If she had made a senior lieutenancy, she was *good*.

'Hi, I'm Bil Hansing,' I replied cheerily. Ours might be a brief association but I preferred to make it as pleasant as possible.

She flung a quick salute with her 'hand' turned inward, for her wrist did not swivel for a proper Navy gesture. Then the corners of her very feline mouth lifted slightly, the lower jaw dropped in what I could readily identify as a smile.

'You can call me Ghra, easier than sputtering over the rest of it. You lot can never get your tongues around *r*'s.'

'Wanna bet?' And I rolled off her name as easily as she had.

'Well, I am impressed,' she said, giving the double *s* a sibilant emphasis. She had lugged her bundle aboard and looked around the tiny cabin of the Ocelot. 'Where can I stow this, Bil?'

'Under the for'ard couch. We are short on space, we Ocelots!'

I could see her fangs now as she really smiled, and the tip of a delicate pink tongue. She quickly stowed the bundle and turned around to survey me.

'Yeah, and the fastest ships in the galaxy,' she said with such a warm approval that my liking for her increased. 'Mr Hansing, please inform the bridge of my arrival. I take it you've got the data. I'm to share the rest of my briefing when we're under way.'

She was polite but firm about her eagerness to get on with what could only be a difficult assignment. And I liked that attitude in her. With an exceedingly graceful movement, she eased into the left-hand seat, and latched the safety harness, her amazing 'hands' (they weren't really paws – Khalians have paws – for the 'fingers' on her hands had evolved to digit status, with less webbing between them for better gripping) curving over the armrests. The end of her thickly furred tail twitched idly as the appendage jutted out beyond the back of the cushioned seat. I watched it in fascination. I'd never appreciated how eloquent such a tenable extremity could be.

Nevertheless, duty called and I alerted the bridge to our readiness. We received an instant departure okay, and I released the pressure grapples of the air lock, gave the starboard repellers a little jolt, and swung carefully away from the *Gormenghast*.

I enjoy piloting the Ocelot. She's a sweet ship, handles like a dream, can turn her thirty meters on her tail if she has to, and has, though not many believe me. I remind them that she's a Mark 18, the very latest off the fleet's research-and-development mother ship. Well, five years galactic standard ago. But I oversee all maintenance myself and she's in prime condition, save for the normal space wear and tear and the tip of one fin caught by a Khalian bolt the second year I commanded her, when Het and I ran a pirate blockade in FCD 122/785.

Of course, she's light on armament, can't waste maneuverability and speed on shielding, and I've only the four plasma cannons, bow and stern, and swivelers port and starboard. I'd rather rely on speed and zip: the ship's a fast minx and I'm a bloody good driver. I can say that because I've proved it. Five GS years in commission and still going.

I pumped us up to speed and the fleet was fast disappearing into the blackness of space, visible only as the slight halo of light where they were still firing to clear lanes through the damned dust, and that quickly dispersed – those telltale emissions, which could prove very dangerous. That is, if Khalians were looking our way. Space is big and the convoy was two light-years from its destination at Persuasion, slowing to move cautiously through the congested globular ASD cluster to make our ultimate orbit about ASD 836/934. Everywhere in this young cluster there was dust, which was a navigational hazard despite its small to minuscule size.

The reason the fleet was convoying such an unwieldly number of ships through this sector of space, adjacent to that known to be controlled by Khalians, was to reinforce the sizable and valuable mining colony on Persuasion 836/934 – and strengthen the defenses of two nearby Alliance planets: the water world of the Persepolis, whose oceans teemed with edible marine forms chockful of valuable protein for both humanoid and the weasel-like Khalians, and the fabulous woods of Poinsettia, which were more splendid and versatile in their uses than teak, mahogany, or redwood. In the ASD sector the Khalians had only three planets, none valuable except as stepping-stones, so that a takeover of the richer Alliance-held worlds had a high probability factor, which the Alliance was determined to reduce by the reinforcement of troops and material in this convoy. Or once again the great offensive strike planned for Target, the main Khalian base in Alliance space, would have to be set back.

As the tremendous entry speed was reduced, the convoy was, of course, vulnerable to any Khalian marauders during the six months that maneuver took. FTL is the fastest way to travel: it's the slowing down that takes so much time. (You got one, you got the other.

You live with it.) So Alliance High Command had created a few diversions in sectors BRE, BSF – attacks on two rather important Khalian-held planets – and had thrown great fleet strength into the repulsing maneuver at KSD: a strategy that was evidently working, to judge by the lack of visible traces of Khalian force hereabouts. In FTL, you have obscurity, Alliance or Khalian; but in normal space, the emissions of your normal drive make ever-expanding 'cones,' which *are* detectable in normal space. The large number of ships included in our convoy increased the detection factor – to any spaceship crossing the cone trail. Cones were, fortunately, not detectable from a planetary source, but the plasma bursts would be – that is, if Bethesda had the right equipment.

If we could be spared any further unforeseen incidents, the convoy had a good chance of relieving Persuasion and the other worlds before the piratic weasels could summon strike elements to the ASD area.

I had never actually been near a Khalian. Maybe my decorative brawn had. I intended to ask her as soon as I had locked us on course. Ghra's tail tip continued to twitch, just slightly, as we reached the Ocelot's cruising speed. I had now programmed in the data to reach Bethesda, and to reenter normal space at three planetary orbits away from it, on the dark side. I checked my calculations and then, warning Ghra, activated the FTL drive and we were off!

Ghra released the safety belt and stretched, her tail sticking straight out behind her. Good thing she couldn't see me gawping at it. Scout ships with a good pilot like me, and I'm not immodest to say so, could utilize the FTL drive between systems, where the fleet, if it wanted to keep its many vessels together in some form of order, could not.

'If you'll put what is now the spaceport area of Bethesda on the screen, Bil, I'll brief you,' she said, leaning forward to the terminal. I screened the relevant map. She extended one claw, using it to show me the landing site. 'We're to go in north of the spaceport, low, where they won't be looking for anything. Just here, there're a lot of canyons and ravines. And a lot of volcanic debris, some of it bigger than your Ocelot. So you can pretend you're an old mountain fragment while I mosey into the settlement to see the OTS.'

'And when the sun comes up and shines off my hull, it'll be bloody plain I'm no rock.'

She gave a rippling chuckle, more like a happy growl. 'Ah, but you'll be camouflaged by the time the sun rises,' she said, pointing her left hand toward the couch under which her bundle was stored.

'Camouflaged?'

She chuckled again, and dropped her lower jaw in her Hrruban smile. 'Just like me.'

'Huh? You'd stand out a klick away.'

'Not necessarily. D'you know why creatures evolved different exterior colors and patterns? Well, markings and colors help them become invisible to their natural enemies, or their equally natural victims. On your own homeworld, and I'll cite the big felines as an excellent example' – she twitched her dainty whisker hairs to indicate amusement, or was it condescension for us poorly endowed critters? – 'tigers have stripes because they're jungle inhabitants; lions wear fur that blends into the veldt or grasslands; panthers are mottled black to hide on tree limbs and shadows. Their favorite prey is also colored to be less easily detected, to confuse the eye of the beholder, if they stand still.

'A major breakthrough in Khalian biological research suggests that they are blind to certain colors and patterns.' She indicated her sploshed flanks. 'What I'm wearing should render me all but invisible to Khalians.'

'Ah, come on, Ghra, I can't buy that!'

'Hear me out.' She held her hand up, her lustrous big eyes sparkling with an expression that could be amusement, but certainly resulted in my obedience. 'We've also determined that, while Khalian night vision is excellent, dawn and dusk produce a twilight myopia. My present camouflage is blended for use on this planet. I can move with impunity at dawn and dusk, and quite possibly remain unseen during daylight hours, even by Khalians passing right by me. Provided I choose my ground cover correctly. That's part of early Hrruban training, anyhow. And we Hrrubans also know how to lie perfectly still for long hours.' She grinned at my skeptical snort.

'Add to that inherent ability the fact that Khalians have lost what olfactory acuteness they originally had as they've relied more and more on high tech, and I doubt they'll notice me.' Her own nostrils dilated slightly and her whiskers twitched in distaste. 'I can smell a Khalian more than five klicks away. And a Khalian wouldn't detect, much less recognize, my spoor. Stupid creatures. Ignored or lost most of their valuable natural assets. They can't even move as quadrupeds anymore. We had the wisdom to retain, and improve, on our inherited advantages. It could be something as simple and nontech as primitive ability that's going to tip the scale in this war. We've already proved that ancient ways make us valuable as fighters.'

'You Hrrubans have a bloody good reputation,' I agreed generously. 'You've had combat experience?' I asked tactfully, for generally speaking, seasoned fighters don't spout off the way she was. As Ghra didn't seem to be a fully adult Hrruban, maybe she was indulging herself in a bit of psyching up for this mission.

'Frequent.' The dry delivery of that single word assured me she was, indeed, a seasoned warrior. The fingers of her left hand clicked a rapid tattoo. 'Khalians are indeed formidable opponents. Very.' She spread her left hand, briefly exposing her lethal complement of claws. 'Deadly in hand-to-hand with that stumpy size a strange advantage. A fully developed adult Khalian comes up to my chest: it's those short Khalian arms, incredibly powerful, that you've got to watch out for.'

Some of the latest 'short arm' jokes are grisly by any standards: real sick humor! And somehow, despite your disgust, you find yourself avidly repeating the newest one.

'Khalians may prefer to use their technology against us in the air,' Ghra continued, 'but they're no slouches face-to-face. I've seen a Khalian grab a soldier by the knees, trip him up, and sever the hamstrings in three seconds. Sometimes they'll launch at the chest, compress the lungs in a fierce grip, and bite through the jugular vein. However,' Ghra added with understandable pride, 'we've noticed a marked tendency in their troops to avoid Hrrubans. Fortunately we don't mind fighting in mixed companies.'

I'd heard some incredible tales of the exploits of mixed companies and been rather proud that so many of the diverse species of the Alliance could forget minor differences for the main objective. I'd also heard some horror tales of what Khalians did to any prisoners of those mixed companies. (It had quickly become a general policy to dispatch any immobilized wounded.) Of course, such tales always permeate a fighting force. Sometimes, I think, not as much to encourage our own fighting men to fight that much more fiercely as to dull the edge of horror by the repetition of it.

'But it's not going to be brute force that'll overcome them: it'll be superior intelligence. We Hrrubans hope to be able to infiltrate their ground forces with our camouflages.' She ran both hands down her lean and muscled thighs. 'I'm going to prove we can.'

'More power to you,' I said, still skeptical if she was relying on body paint. While I was a space fighter pilot, I knew enough about warfare strategies to recognize that it was only battles that were won in space: wars are won when the planets involved are secured against the invader. 'There's just one thing. You may be able to fool those weasels' eyes, but what about the humans and such on Bethesda? You're going to be mighty visible to them, you know.'

Ghra chuckled. 'The Khalians enforce a strict dawn-to-dusk curfew on their captive planets. You'll be setting us down in an unpopulated area. None of the captured folk would venture there and all the Khalian air patrols would see is the camouflage net.'

I hoped so, not that I personally feared Khalians in the air or on the ground. For one thing, an Ocelot is faster than any atmosphere planes they operate, or spacecraft. Khalians prefer to fly large vehicles: as far as we know they don't have any small or single-crew craft. Which makes a certain amount of sense – with very short arms and legs, they wouldn't have the reach to make effective use of a multiple-function board. Their control rooms must be crowded. Unless Khalians had prehensile use of their toes?

'Yeah, but you have to contact the OTS and he lives in the human cantonment. How're you going to keep invisible there?'

She shrugged her narrow shoulders. 'By being cautious. After all, no humans will be expecting an Hrruban on Bethesda, will they?' She dropped her jaw again, and this time I knew it was amusement that brought a sparkle to those great brown eyes. 'People, especially captive people, tend to see only what they expect to see. And they don't want to see the unusual or the incredible. If they should spot me, they won't believe it nor are they likely to run off and tattle to Khalians.'

Then Ghra stretched, sinews and joints popping audibly. 'How long before reentry, Bil? Time enough for me to get a short nap?' Her jaw dropped in an Hrruban grin as she opened the lid of the deepsleep capsule.

'Depends on how long you want to sleep. One month, two?' Scout ships are fast but they also must obey the laws of FTL physics, and I had to slow down just as the convoy had to, only I could waste my speed faster by braking a lot of it in the gravity well of Bethesda's sun.

'Get us into the system. We'll have plenty of time to swap jokes without boring each other,' she said as she took two steps to the long cabinet that held the deepsleep tank. She pulled it out and observed while I set the mechanism to time and calibrated the gas dose. Nodding her approval, she lay down on the couch, attached the life-support cups suitable for her species with the ease of long practice. With a final wink, she closed the canopy and then her eyes, her lean camouflaged frame relaxing instantly as the gas flooded the compartment.

Ghra was perceptive about the inevitable grating of two personalities cooped up in necessarily cramped conditions for too long a time with little activity to defuse energy. We brain ships are accustomed to being by ourselves, though I'm the first to tell new members of our Elite Corps that the first few months ain't easy. There are benefits and we are conditioned to the encapsulation long before we're placed in any kind of large, dangerous equipment. The good thing about being human is our adaptability. Or maybe it's sheer necessity. If you'd rather not be dead, there is an alternative: and if we, who have had bodies and have known that kind of lifestyle, are not as completely the ship we drive as shell people are, we have our uses and I have come to like this new life, too.

The Ocelot plunged on down toward the unseen planet and its mission. I set external alarms and went into recall trance.

As the Ocelot neared my target, a mild-enough-looking space marble, dark blues and greens with thin cloud cover, it roused both Ghra and me. She came alert right smart, just as a well-trained fighter should.

Grabbing a container of the approved postsleep fortified drink, she resumed her seat and we both read the Ocelot's autoreports.

The detectors identified only the usual stuff – comsats, mining transfer gear, solar heater units – but nothing in orbit around Bethesda that could detect the convoy. The only way to be dead sure, or dead, was to check down below as well. Ghra agreed. Dawn was coming up over one of the water masses that punctuated the planet. They looked more like crater holes than natural subsidences, but there had once been a lot of volcanic activity on Bethesda.

'How're we going to make it in, Bil? Even with what the settlers put up, the Khalians could spot us.'

'No, I've lined the Ocelot up with the same trajectory as a convenient trail of meteoritic debris. You can see the planet is pocked with craters. Perfect for our purpose. Even if they have gear sensitive enough to track the Ocelot's faint trail, they'd more than likely figure it was just more of the debris that's already come in.'

'I had a look at Het's data on the planet,' Ghra said. 'Bethesda's spaceport facility had been ample enough to take the big colonial transport jobs. Last recorded flights in before the Khalian capture were for commercial freight lighters but the port could take the biggest Khalian cruisers and destroyers, not just those medium pursuit fighters.'

'What did Het say about Khalian update on the invasion?'

Ghra shrugged. 'That is unknown. We'll find out.' She grinned when I made one of those disgruntled noises I'm rather good at. 'Well, they could be busy elsewhere. You know how the Khalians are, mad keen on one thing one moment, and then forget about it for a decade.'

'Let's hope the decade doesn't end while we're in this sector. Well, we've got a day or so before we go in, did you hear the one about . . .'

Ghra told me some even *I* hadn't heard by the time I was ready to activate the trajectory I'd plotted. I matched speed with a group of pebbles while Ghra did a geology game with me. I thought I'd never see the last of the fregmekking marbles, or win the game even though we were getting down at a fair clip. Ghra was betting the pebbles would hit the northern wasteland before we flattened out for the last segment of our run. Whose side was she on?

Ducking under the light cloud cover, I made a low-altitude run over the nightside toward the spaceport and the small town that serviced it. The Khalians had enslaved the planet's small resident human population in their inimitable fashion, but there might just be some sort of a night patrol.

'Here's our objective, Ghra,' I told her as we closed in our landing site, and screened the picture.

She narrowed her eyes, mumbling or purring as she memorized landscape. The town had been built along the coastline, and there looked to be wharfs and piers but no sign of sea traffic or boats. Just beyond the town, on a plateau that had been badly resculptured to accommo-date large craft landings, was the respectably-sized spaceport, with towers, comdisks, quarters, and what looked like repair hangars. Infra scan showed two cooling earthen circles, but that didn't tell us enough. I got a quick glimpse of the snouts and fins of a few ships, none of them warm enough to have been flown in the past twenty-four hours, but I didn't have time to verify type and number before we were behind the coastal hill. I dropped the meteor ruse just in time to switch on the gravity drive and keep us from planting a new crater.

'And there' – I put an arrow on the screen – 'is where I make like a rock. You'll be only about five klicks from town.'

'Good.' She managed to make the *g* into a growl, narrowing her eyes as she regarded the picture. Her tail gave three sharp swings. 'May I have a replay of the spaceport facility?' I complied, screening the footage at a slower rate.

'Nothing fast enough to catch me, Ghra, either in the atmosphere or in space,' I replied nonchalantly. I made the usual copies of the tapes of our inbound trip for the Mayday capsule. Commander Het collects updates like water rations. 'Strap in, Ghra, I'm cutting the engines. Het found me a straight run through that gorge and I'm using it.'

That's another thing about the Ocelot, she'll glide. Mind you, I was ready to cut in the repellers at any moment, but Het had done me proud in choosing the site. We glided in with due regard for the Ocelot's skin, for we'd be slotted in among a lot of volcanic debris, some of which was, as Ghra had promised, as large as the Scout. No sooner had we landed than Ghra retrieved her bundle and was hefting it to the air lock, which I opened for her. Locked in my sealed chamber, I couldn't be of any assistance in spreading the camouflage net, but she was quick, deft, and very strong.

'Have you got a combutton, Bil?' she asked when she had returned, her breath only a little faster than normal. She walked past the console into the little galley and drew a ration of water. 'Good, then you'll get the gen one way or another.' She took a deep draught of the water. 'Good stuff. Import it?'

'Yeah, neither Het nor the admiral like it recycled.' I chuckled. 'Rank has some privileges, you know.'

Shamelessly, she took a second cupful. 'I need to stock

up if I have to lie still all day. It's summer here.' She ran a claw tip down the selection dial of the supply cupboard and finally pressed a button, wrinkling her nose. 'I hate field rations but they do stay with you.' She had ordered up several bars of compressed high-protein/high-carbohydrate mix. I watched as she stored them in what I had thought to be muscle but were carefully camouflaged inner forearm pockets.

'What else are you hiding?' Surprise overwhelmed tact.

She gave that inimitable chuckle of hers. 'A few useful weapons.' She picked up the button I had placed on the console. 'Neat! What's the range?'

'Fifteen klicks.'

'I can easy stay in that range, Bil.' She fastened the little nodule to the skull side of her left ear, its metallic surface invisible in the tufty fur. 'Thanks. How long till dawn?'

I gave her the times for false and real dawn. With a cheery salute she left the Ocelot, and I listened to the soft slip of her feet as long as the exterior sensors could pick up the noise before I closed the air lock. She had been moving on all fours. Remembering old teaching clips about ancient Earth felines, I could see her lithe body bounding across the uneven terrain. For a brief moment, I envied her. Then I began worrying for her.

I had known Ghra longer than I knew most of my random passengers and we hadn't bored each other after I roused her. In her quiet, wryly humorous way, her company had been quite a treat for me: If she'd been more humanoid, and I'd been more like my former self . . . ah well! That's one of the drawbacks for a gig like me; we do see the very best, but generally all too briefly.

Ghra had sounded real confident about this camouflage scheme of hers. Not talk-herself-into-believing-it confident, but certain sure-there'd-be-no-problem confident. Me, I'd prefer something more substantial than paint as protection. But then, I'm definitely the product of a high-tech civilization, while Ghra had faith in natural advantages and instinctive talents. Well, it was going to take every asset the Alliance had to counter the Khalian pirates!

Shortly before Bethesda's primary rose in the east, Ghra reported.

'I'm in place, Bil. I'll keep the combutton on so you'll know all I do. Our contact's asleep. I'm stretched out on the branch of a fairly substantial kind of a broad-leafed tree outside his window. I'll hope he isn't the nervous type.'

An hour and a half later, we both discovered that he was not the believing type either. But then, who would have expected to be contacted by what at first appeared to be a disembodied smile among the broad leaves shading your side window. It certainly wasn't what Fildin Escobat had anticipated when his implant had given him the warning *zing* of impending visitation.

'What are you?' he demanded after Ghra had pronounced the meeting code words.

'An Hrruban,' Ghra replied in a well-projected whisper. I could hear a rustle as she moved briefly.

'Arghle!'

There was a silence, broken by a few more throaty garglings.

'What's Hrruban?'

'Alliance felinoids.'

'Cat people?' Fildin had some basic civics education.

'I'm camouflaged.'

'Damned sure.'

'So I'm patently not Khalian . . .'

'Anyone can say they're Alliance. You could be Khalian, disguised.'

'Have you ever seen a Khalian going about on all fours? The size of me? With a face and teeth like mine? Or a tail?'

'No . . .' This was a reluctant admission.

'Speaking Galactic?'

'That's true enough,' Fildin replied sourly, for all captive species were forced to learn the spitting hissing Khalian language. Khalian nerve prods and acid whips effectively encouraged both understanding and vocabulary. 'So now what?'

'You tell me what I need to know.'

'I don't know anything. They keep it that way.' There was an unmistakable anger in the man's voice, which he lowered as he realized that he might be overheard.

'What were you before the invasion?'

'A mining engineer.' I could almost see the man draw himself up with remembered pride.

'Now?'

'Effing road sweeper. And I'm lucky to have that so I don't see what good I can do you or the Alliance.'

'Probably more than you think' was Ghra's soothing response. 'You have eyes and ears.'

'I intend keeping 'em.'

'You will. Can you move freely about the town?'

'The town, yes.'

'Near the spaceport, too?'

'Yeah.' And now Fildin's tone became suspicious and anxious.

'So you'd know if there had been any scrambles of their fighter craft.'

'Haven't been any.'

'None?'

'I tol' you. Though I did hear there's supposed to be s'more landing soon.'

'How soon?'

'I dunno. Didn't want to know.' Fildin was resigned.

'Do you work today?'

'We work every day, all day, for those fregmekking rodents.'

'Can you get near the spaceport? And do a count of what kind of space vehicles and how many of each are presently on the ground?'

'I could, but what good does that do if more are coming in?'

'Do you know that for sure?'

'Nobody knows anything for sure. Why? Are we going to be under attack? Is that what you need to know all this for?' Fildin was clearly dubious about the merits of helping a counterattack.

'The Alliance has no immediate plans for your planet.'

'No?' Fildin now sounded affronted. 'What's wrong? Aren't we important enough?'

'You certainly are, Fildin.' Ghra's voice was purringly smooth and reassuring. 'And if you can get that information for me, it'll be of major importance in our all-out effort to free your planet without any further bloodshed and unpleasantness.'

He gave a snort. 'I don't see how knowing what's on the ground now will help.'

'Neither do I,' Ghra said, allowing a tinge of resentment to creep into her silken tone. 'That's for my superiors to decide. But it is the information that is required, which I have risked my life to obtain, so it must be very important. Will you help the Alliance remove the yoke of the oppressor, help you return to your former prestige and comfort?'

There was a long pause during which I could almost hear the man's brain working.

'I just need to tell you what's on the ground now?'

'That's all, but I need to know the types of craft, scout, cruiser, destroyer, whatever, and how many of each. And would you know if there have been battleships here?'

'No battleships,' he said in a tone of disgust. 'They can't land.'

If colonial transports could land on Bethesda so could Khalian battle cruisers, but he didn't need to know that. What Ghra had to ascertain from him was if there were cruisers or destroyers that could be launched in pursuit of our convoy. Even a scout could blow the whistle on us and get enough of a head start to go FTL right back to Target and fetch in some real trouble. Only the fighters and cruisers escorting the convoy would be able to maneuver adequately to meet a Khalian attack. They would not be able to defend all the slowing bulky transports and most of the supply pods and drones that composed a large portion of the total. And if the supply pods bought it, the convoy could fail. Slowing takes a lot of fuel.

I took it as a small sliver of good luck that Fildin reported no recent activity. Perhaps this backwater hadn't been armed by its Khalian invaders.

'Cruisers, destroyers, and scouts,' Ghra repeated. 'How many of each, Fildin, and you will be giving us tremendously vital information.'

'When'll we be freed?'

'Soon. You won't have long to wait if all goes well.'

'If what goes well?'

'The less you know the better for you, Fildin.'

'Don't I get paid for risking my hide? Those nerve prods and acid whips ain't a bit funny, you know.'

'What is your monetary-exchange element?'

'A lot of good that would do me,' Fildin said disgustedly.

'What would constitute an adequate recompense for your risks?'

'Meat. Red meat. They keep us on short rations, and I'd love a decent meal of meat once in a while.'

I could almost see him salivating. Well, there's no accounting for some tastes. *A shacking goo!*

'I think something can be arranged,' Ghra said, purringly. 'I shall meet you here at dusk, good Fildin.'

'Don't let anyone see you come! Or go.'

'No one shall, I can assure you.'

'Hey, where . . . What the eff? Where did it go?'

I heard Fildin's astonished queries taper off. I also heard Ghra's sharply expelled breath and then a more even, but quickened, respiration. Then some thudding, as if she had landed on a hard surface. I heard the *shushing* of her feet on a soft surface and then, suddenly nothing.

'Ghra?' I spoke her name more as an extended *gr* sound than an audible word.

'Later' was her cryptic response.

With that I had to be content that whole day long. Occasionally I could hear her slow breathing. For a spate there in the heat of the afternoon, I could have sworn her breathing had slowed to a sleep rhythm. Suddenly, as the sun went down completely, the com unit erupted with a flurry of activity, bleatings, sounds of chase and struggle, a fierce crump and click as, quite likely, her teeth met in whatever she had been chasing. I heard dragging sounds, an explosive grunt from her, and then, for an unnervingly long period, only the slip-slide of her quiet feet as she returned to Fildin Escobat's dwelling.

'Fardles! How'd you get that? Where did you get that? Oh, fardles, let me grab it before someone sees the effing thing.'

'You asked for red meat, did you not?' Ghra's voice was smooth.

'Not a whole fardling beast. Where can I hide it?'

'I thought you wanted to eat it.'

'I can't eat a whole one.'

'Then I'll help!'

'*No!*' Fildin's desperate reply ended in a gasp as he realized that he had inadvertently raised his voice above the hoarse whisper in which most of his conversation had been conducted. 'We'll be heard by the neighbors. Can't we talk somewhere else?'

'After curfew? Stand back from the window.'

'No, no, no, ohhh.' The difference in the sound I now received told me that Ghra had probably jumped through the window, right into his quarters.

'Don't put it down. It'll bloody the floor. What am I going to do with all this meat.' There was both pleasure and dismay at such largesse.

'Cook what you need then.' Ghra was indifferent to his problems, having rendered the requested payment. 'Now, what can you report?'

'Huh? Oh, well . . .' This had patently been an easier task than accepting his reward, and he rolled off the quantities and types of spacecraft he had seen. I started taping his report at that juncture.

'No further indication of when the new craft are due in?' Ghra asked.

'No. Nothing. I did ask. Carefully, you know. I know a couple of guys who're menials in the port but all they knew was that something was due in.'

'Supply ships?'

'Nah! Don't you know that Khalians make their subject planets support 'em? They live well here, those fregmekking weasels. And we get sweetdamall.'

'You'll eat well tonight and for a time, Friend Fildin. And there's no chance that it's troop carriers?'

'How'd I know? There're already more Khalians on this planet than people.'

Bethesda was a large, virtually unpopulated planet, and Alliance High Command had never figured out why the Khalians had suddenly invaded it. Their assault on Bethesda had been as unexpected as it had been quick.

Then no more Khalian activity in the area, though there were several habitable but unoccupied planets in nearby systems. High Command was certain that the Khalians intended to increase their dominance in the ASD sector, eventually invading the three richly endowed Alliance planets: Persuasion for its supplies of copper, vanadium, and the now precious germanium; Persepolis for its inexhaustible marine protein. (Khalians consumed astonishing quantities of sea creatures, preferably raw, a fact that had made their invasion of Bethesda, a relatively 'dry' world, all the more unexpected.) To send a convoy of this size was unusual in every respect. High Command hoped that the Khalians would not believe the Alliance capable of risking so many ships, matériel, and personnel. Admiral Eberhard was staking his career on taking that risk, plus the very clever use of the gravity wells of the nearby star SD 836/932 and Persuasion to reduce velocity, cutting down the time in normal space when the convoy's 'light' ripple cone was so detectable.

Those fregmekking Khalians had been enjoying such a run of good luck! It'd better start going our way soon. Maybe Bethesda would come up on our side of the ledger. I had screened Het's sector map, trying to figure out from which direction Khalians might be sending in reinforcements or whatever. If they came through the ASD grid, they'd bisect the emission trail. That was all too likely, as they controlled a good portion of the space beyond. But I didn't have more charts, or any updated information on Khalian movements. The *Gormenghast* would. It was now imperative for the admiral to know about those incoming spacecraft. Ghra was as quick.

'It would be good to know where those ships were coming from,' Ghra told Fildin. 'Or why they were landing here at all? There seem to be enough ships on hand for immediate defense, and surveillance.'

'How the fardles would I know? And effing sure I can't find out, not a lowly sweeper like me. I done what I said I'd do, exactly what you asked. I can't do more.'

'No, I quite perceive that, Fildin Escobat, but you've been more than helpful. Enjoy your meat!'

'Hey, come back . . .'

Fildin's voice dropped away from the combutton, although I heard no sounds of Ghra's physical exertion. I waited until she would be out of hearing.

'Ghra? Can you safely talk?'

'Yes,' she replied, and then I could hear the slight noise of her feet and knew she was loping along.

'What're you up to?'

'What makes you think I'm up to anything?'

'Let's call it an educated guess.'

'Then guess.' Amusement rippled through her suggestion.

'To the spaceport to see if you can find out where those spaceships are coming from.'

'Got it in one.'

'Ghra? That's dangerous, foolhardy, and quite likely it's putting your life on the line.'

'One life is nothing if it saves the convoy.'

'Heroic of you, but it could also blow the game.'

'I don't think so. There's been a program of infiltrations on any Khalian base we could penetrate. Why make Bethesda an exception? Don't worry, Bil. It'll be simple if I can get into place now in the bad light.'

'Good theory but impractical,' I replied sourly. 'No trees, bushes, or vegetation around that spaceport.'

'But rather a lot of old craters . . .'

'You are not crater-colored.'

'Enticing mounds of supplies, and some unused repair hangars.'

'Or,' I began in a reasonable tone, 'we can get out of here, go into a lunar orbit, and keep our eyes peeled. All

I'd need is enough time to send a squeal and the admiral'll know.'

'Now who's heroic? And not very practical. We're not supposed to be sighted. And we're to try and keep the convoy from being discovered. I think I know how. Besides, Bil, this mission has several facets. One of them is proving that camouflaged Hrrubans can infiltrate Khalian positions and obtain valuable information without detection.'

'Ghra, get back here!'

'No!'

There wouldn't be much point of arguing with that particular, pleasant but unalterable brand of obstinacy, so I didn't try. Nor did I bother to threaten. Pulling rank on a free spirit like Ghra would be useless and a tactic I could scarcely support. Also, if she could find out whence came the expected flight, that would be vital information for the admiral. Crucial for the convoy's safety!

At least we were now reasonably sure that the Bethesda-based Khalians had not detected those plasma blasts to clear the debris. Now, if only we could also neutralize the threat posed by incoming craft crossing the light cone! We needed some luck!

'Where are you now, Ghra? Keep talking as long as it's safe and detail everything. Can you analyze what facilities the port has?'

'From what I can see, Bil, nothing more than the colonists brought with them.' Having won her point, Ghra did not sound smug. I hoped that she had as much caution as camouflage.

Dutifully she described her silent prowl around the perimeter of the space facility, which I taped. Finally she reached the far side of the immense plateau, where some of the foothills had been crudely gouged deep enough to extend the landing grid for the huge colony transports.

She had paused once to indulge herself in a long drink, murmuring briefly that the water on the Ocelot was much nicer.

'Ah,' she said suddenly and exhaled in a snort of disgust. 'Sensor rigs, which the colonists certainly did not bring with them.'

'You can't go through them without detection. Even if you could jump that high.'

'I know that!' She rumbled as she considered.

'Ghra. Come on. Pack it in and get back to me. We can still do a lunar watch. Under the circumstances, I'd even try a solar hide.' Which was one of the trickiest things a scout, even an Ocelot, could attempt. And the situation was just critical enough to make me try. Jockeying to keep just inside a sun's gravity well is a real challenge.

'You're a brave brain, Bil, but I think I've figured out how to get past the sensors. The natural way.'

'What?'

'They've even supplied me with the raw materials.'

'What are you talking about, Ghra? Explain!'

'I'm standing on an undercut ridge of dirt and stone, with some rather respectable boulders. Now, if this mass suddenly descended thru the sensor rings, it'd break the contact.'

'And bring every Khalian from the base, but not before they'd sprayed the area with whatever they have handy, plus launch that scout squadron they've got on the pads.'

'But when they see it is only sticks and stones . . .'

'Which could break your bones, and how're you going to start it all rolling?'

'Judiciously, because they really didn't shore this stuff up properly.'

I could hear her exerting herself now and felt obliged to remind her of her risks even though I could well visualize what she was trying to do. But if the Khalians entertained even the remotest thought of tampering by unnatural agencies, they'd fling out a search net . . . and catch us both. Full dark was settling, so the time of their twilight myopia was nearly past. If she counted on only that to prevent them seeing her . . .

I heard the roll, her grunt, and then the beginning of a mild roar.

'Rrrrrow' came from Ghra and she was running, running away from the sound. 'There! Told you so!'

I could also hear the whine of Khalian alert sirens and my external monitors reflected the sudden burst of light on the skyline.

'Ghra!'

'I'm okay, okay, Bil. I'm a large rock beside two smaller ones and I shan't move a muscle all night.'

I have spent the occasional fretful night now and again but this would be one of the more memorable ones. Just as I had predicted, the Khalians mounted an intensive air and land search. I willingly admit that the camouflage over me was effective. The Ocelot was overflown eight or nine times – those Khalians are nothing if not tenacious when threatened. It was nearly dawn before the search was called off and the brilliant spaceport lights were switched off.

'Ghra?' I kept my voice low.

A deep yawn preceded her response. 'Bil? You're there, too. Good.'

'Are you still a rock?'

'Yessss.' The slight sibilance warned me.

'But not the same rock. Right?'

'Got me in one.'

'Where are you, Ghra?'

'Part of the foundation of their command post.'

'Their command post?'

'Speak one decibel louder, Bil, and their audios will

pick you up. It's dawn and I'm not saying anything else all day. Catch you at sunset.'

I didn't have to wait all day for her next words, but it felt like a bloody Jovian year, and at that, I didn't realize that she was whispering to me for the first nanoseconds.

'They're coming in from the seven hundred quadrant, Bil. Straight from Target. As if they'd planned to intercept. And they'll be crossing the eight hundreds by noon tomorrow. By all that's holy, there'll be no way they'd miss the ripple cone. You've got to warn the admiral to scatter the convoy. Now. Get off now.' She gave a little chuckle. 'Keeping 'em up half the night was a good idea. Most of 'em are asleep. They won't see a thing if you keep it low and easy.'

'Are you daft, Ghra? I can't go now. You can't move until dusk.'

'Don't argue, Bil. There's no time. Even if they detect you, they can't catch you. Go now. You go FTL as soon as you're out of the gravity well and warn the fleet. Just think of the admiral's face when he gets a chance to go up Khalian asses for a change. You warn him in time, he can disperse the convoy and call for whatever fighters Persuasion has left. They can refuel from the convoy's pods. What a battle that will be. The admiral's career is made! And ours. Don't worry about me. After all, I was supposed to subject the camouflage to a real test, wasn't I?' Her low voice rippled slightly with droll amusement.

'But . . .'

'Go!' Her imperative was firm, almost angry. 'Or it's all over for that convoy. Go. Now. While they're sleeping.'

She was right. I knew it, but no brain ship leaves a brawn in an exposed and dangerous situation. The convoy was also in an exposed and dangerous situation. The greater duty called. The lives of many superseded the life of one, one who had willingly sacrificed herself.

I lifted slowly, using the minimum of power the Ocelot needed. She was good like that; you could almost lift her on a feather, and that was all I intended to use. I kept at ground level, which, considering the terrain, meant some tricky piloting, but I also didn't want to go so fast that I lost that camouflage net. If I had to set down suddenly, it might save my skin.

I'm not used to dawdling; neither is the Ocelot, and it needed finesse to do it, and every vestige of skill I possessed. I went back through the gap, over the water, heading toward the oncoming dusk. I'd use sunset to cover my upward thrust because I'd have to use power then. But I'd be far enough away from the big sensors at the spaceport to risk it. Maybe they'd still be snoozing. I willed those weaselly faces to have closed eyes and dulled senses, and, as I tilted my nose up to the clear dark night of deep space, the camouflage net rippled down, spread briefly on the water, and sank.

On my onward trajectory, I used Bethesda's two smaller moons as shields, boosting my speed out of the sun's gravity well before I turned on the FTL drive.

From the moment OTS had mentioned the possibility of an incoming squadron of Khalians, I had been computing a variety of courses from Target through the 700 quadrant to Bethesda's system. There was no way the Khalians would miss the convoy's emission trail entering from the 700s, and then they'd climb the tailpipes of the helpless, decelerating ships. I ran some calculations on the ETA at the first gravity well maneuver the admiral had planned, and they were almost there. I had to buy them just a bit more time. This Ocelot was going to have to pretend it was advance scout for ships from another direction entirely.

So I planned to reenter normal space on a course perpendicular to the logical one that the Khalians would take for Bethesda when they exited FTL space. Their ships would have sensors sensitive enough to pick up my light cone and I'd come in well in advance of any traces that the convoy had left. If I handled it right, they'd come after me. It's rare that the admiral's gig gets such an opportunity as this, to anticipate the enemy, to trigger a naval action that could have a tremendous effect on this everlasting war. It was too good to work out. It had to work out.

I did have several advantages in this mad scheme. The fleet was out of FTL, the enemy not yet. I needed only a moment to send my squirp of a message off to the admiral. The rest of it was up to him. The disadvantage was that I might not have the joy of seeing the fleet running up Khalian asses.

Once in FTL, I continued to check my calculations. Even if I came out right in the midst of the approaching Khalians, I could manage. I only needed two nano-seconds to transmit the message, and even Khalians need more than that to react. They hadn't yet broken the new codes.

They had to come out subspace near my reentry window. They were great ones for using gravity wells to reduce speed, and there were two suns lined up almost perfectly with Bethesda for that sort of maneuver, just far enough away to slow them down for the Bethesda landing. My risk was worth the gamble, and my confidence was bolstered by the courage of a camou-flaged Hrruban.

I had the message set and ready to transmit to the *Gormenghast* as I entered normal space. I toggled it just as the Khalian pirate ships emerged, a couple thousand klicks off my port bow, an emergence that made my brain reel. What luck!

I was spatially above them and should be quite visible on their sensors. I flipped the Ocelot, ostensibly heading back the way I had come. I sent an open Mayday in the old code, adding some jibber I had once whipped up by recording old Earth Thai backward, and sent a panic shot from the stern plasma cannon, just in case their detectors had not spotted me. I made as much 'light' as I could, wallowing my tail to broaden it, trying to pretend there were three of me. Well, trying is it.

The Ocelot is a speedy beast, speedier than I let them believe, hoping they'd mistake us for one of the larger, fully manned scouts, to make it worth their while to track and destroy me. The closer they got the faster they would be able to make a proper identification. I sent MAYDAY in several Alliance languages and again my Thai-gibber. Until they sent three of their real fast ones after me. It took them two days before their plasma bursts got close. I let them come in near enough for me to do some damage. I think I got one direct hit and a good cripple before I knew I was in their range. I hit the jettison moments before their cannon blew the Ocelot apart.

'Well, now, Mr Hansing, how does that feel?' The solicitous voice was preternaturally loud through my audio circuits as consciousness returned.

'Loud and clear,' I replied with considerable relief and adjusted the volume.

I'd made it after all. Sometimes we do. After all, the fleet would have engaged the pirates, and someone was sure to search the wreckage for the vital titanium capsule that contained Mayday tapes and what was left of Lieutenant Senior Grade Bil Hansing. Brains have been known to drift a considerable time before being retrieved with no harm done.

'What've I got this time?' I asked, flicking on visual monitors.

As I half suspected, I was in the capacious maintenance bay of the fleet's mother, surrounded by other vehicles being repaired and reserviced. And camouflaged with paint. I made a startled sound.

'The very latest thing, Lieutenant.'

I focused my visuals on the angular figure of Commander Davi Orbrinn, an officer well known to me. He still sported a trim black beard. His crews had put me back into commission half a dozen times. 'An Ocelot Mark 19, new improved and . . .' Commander Orbrinn sighed deeply. '. . . camouflaged. But really, Mr Hansing, can you not manage to get a shade more wear out of this one? Five years is not practical.'

'Did the convoy get in all right? Did the admiral destroy the Khalians? Did anyone rescue Ghra? How long have I been out of service?'

The commander might turn up stiff but he's an affable soul.

'Yes, yes, no, and six months. The admiral insisted that you have the best. You're due back on the *Gormenghast* at six hundred hours.'

'That's cutting it fine, Davi, but thanks for all you've done for me.'

He gave a pleased grunt and waggled an admonishing finger at me. 'Commander Het says they've saved something special for you for your recommission flight. Consider yourself checked out and ready to go. Duty calls!'

'What else?' I replied in a buoyant tone, happy to be able to answer, and rather hopeful that duty would send me to retrieve a certain camouflaged Hrruban.

And that was exactly what duty called for.

A SLEEPING HUMPTY
DUMPTY BEAUTY

'I don't know if we can do anything with what's left of Sleeping Beauty here,' Jessup said pityingly.

'What?' Bardie Makem looked up from the Jefferson militiaman who had bled to death. She wondered why the corpsmech couldn't read its own monitors. Except that it was supposed to return any remains. Families preferred to know their relatives had been duly buried – somewhere. Even space was more acceptable than MIA. With a sigh for him, she consigned the militiamen into the organ-removal slot of the triage area.

Then she craned her head over to Jessup's gurney and caught her breath. The face inside the helmet was of a very handsome man: tri-d handsome, though the strength of mouth and chin suggested character as well as looks. She rubbed muck and char off the helmet plate. Pilot, *Bonnie Parker*? Headhunter troop carrier?

'You know, Bard,' Nellie Jessup went on as she continued her evaluation, 'I think those new pressure suits actually work. This one's managed to control his bleeding, even if the limbs are mangled. The medikit is drained dry but I'll bet that's why he's still alive. Whaddaya know! Science triumphs over slaughter!'

Moving swiftly as she noted his vital signs, Bardie Makem fed his ID into the hospital ship's main banks. They must have fixed the glitch that last Khalian missile had caused in the internal system because the terminal printed up large and clear.

'O'Hara, Roger Elliott Christopher.' An O'Hara? She ignored the service garbage and scrolled down to the medical data she'd need, blood type and factors, latest jabs, previous injuries – and he had a fair number – good recovery from all repair jobs.

'Another thing, the genital cap worked, too, dented but the AI's all there. 'AI' being Nellie's abbreviation for 'all important' when dealing with male patients. 'Jeez! It's his own face,' Jessup remarked, amazed, as she noticed the medical log on Roger O'Hara. 'Only the one scar: gives his face a roguish look. But, Stitches, I don't think you can reassemble all the parts of him.'

'What're the cerebral functions like?' Bardie reviewed the medical data.

'Not bad,' Jessup said, scanning the gurney monitor. 'Must be a tough mother. Left arm is hanging on by a skin flap just below the elbow, but whatever it was missed the joint. Most of the left biceps is gone and the shoulder joint, left knee crushed, thigh broken in nine places, yeah, and his left foot's off. Left side of the rib cage is smashed, sternum cracked, lung puncture. Right fingers gone, right arm . . .'

'Damn.' Bardie, aka Stitches for her exquisite skill with the microsuturer and flesh glue-gel, grimaced with disgust at O'Hara's records. 'Clearly stated that he's not a brain donor, though he did sign a permit for organ use.'

'Hell,' Nellie said with vehemence, 'there's more of him still working outside than inside. Spleen's ruptured, pancreas sliced, punctured lung, one kidney, most of his liver's minced, guts are scrambled but they're easy. Eyes are okay!' Jessup liked to say something positive.

'We can replace those,' Bardie said, sighing heavily. 'But he wants out . . .'

'Shame to lose a guy looks like that. How come you just can't transfer the head?'

Bardie appreciated team support, but Nellie had a

ridiculous notion that her superior could do anything. She glowered at Jessup.

'You know the rules about that as well as I do, and even if we could, there hasn't been a whole body in here all day. His head is legally out of bounds.' She had been watching the vital-signs monitor now that the pressure suit had been hooked into it, thus saving any unnecessary manipulation of the injured man. Once again, Bardie shook her head in amazement. 'He's one tough fella. He should be dead from the trauma of such massive injuries.'

'The suit did it. That'll look good in the report.' Jessup smiled kindly down at the unconscious man: Bardie was surprised to see the tenderness on the woman's face. Nellie Jessup had developed the necessary tough and callous objectivity essential in triage.

'He's just not giving up without a fight.' His BP was low but steady, the heartbeat was weak but working.

'He deserves a chance, doesn't he?' Jessup was eager, her brown eyes imploring Bardie.

'I know I shouldn't listen to you, Nellie . . .'

'But you're going to!' Nellie Jessup's face radiated approval.

'Let's get to work.'

There were twenty teams of highly skilled surgeons and surgical nurses on this theater deck, one of five on the hospital ship *Elizabeth Blackwell*, though all the teams constantly bitched about being understaffed whenever a flood of wounded arrived from the latest assault on Khalian positions. At the team's disposal were the most advanced, and sometimes experimental, implements and procedures available to martial medicine.

Bardie Makem was serving her compulsory two-year term as a combat surgeon and was going to be very glad indeed when her stint was up in two weeks' time. She'd had enough of battle gore for the rest of her lifetime.

Nellie Jessup was on a ten-year contract – if she survived. She had already been wounded twice riding up the MASH courier shuttles.

Now Bardie and Jessup walked their patient to the stripper, a machine programmed to remove anything not flesh, bone, or sinew attached to a body. Its antigrav cushion managed mangled flesh as delicately as a spider weaves a web. Its sensors also examined hard and soft tissue, sending the results to the theater hood; weighed and measured the patient; retested blood, bone, and tissue type; and could color-dye the circulatory system to pinpoint punctures or embolisms. The speed with which the injured were prepared for surgery often made the difference between life, half life, and death. They walked him through the sterilization beams that sanitized surgeon and nurse as well. And on into the surgical unit, where Bardie began hooking up the heart-lung machines and the auxiliary anesthetizer while Nellie slipped a shunt into the relatively undamaged right arm to start the flow of supplements into his bloodstream and to service his bodily fluids. She kept up a flow of vital-sign information until the wrap screens in the theater hood took over. By then the pertinent damage was also visible.

'Not quite as bad as it looked,' Bardie remarked, assimilating information and making decisions as to what delicate repair to undertake first. It was her speed in assessment that made her the valuable surgeon she was. She seemed to have an uncanny instinct that had saved many almost irreparable bodies. She slipped her hands into the glove dispenser, for much of her work would involve the highly adhesive glue-gel, or GG. The joke was 'Adhere to proper procedures. Stick with the patient, not to him, her, or it.'

'Organ replacements?' She raised her voice to activate the theater wrap system.

'Ready,' said a disembodied voice. And it was, for the

intelligence that managed the organ bank had once been a senior surgeon.

'Red? Got a bad one here. Give me the whole nine yards. O'Hara, R. E. C., spleen, left lung, left kidney, liver, new left shoulder joint, left elbow, wrist, knee, ankle . . .'

'He belongs down here, not up there,' Red answered, but already the chill-chute signaled arrivals, sacks filled with the fluids that maintained the organs. Jessup began the antirejection procedures that would insure that each replacement adapted to the new environment. The catch-as-catch-can procedures of the late-twentieth century were considered barbaric, cruel, and inhumane. But it had taken the science of several species and several horrific space wars to perfect such repair for the humans who fought them.

'He didn't want his head on a plate!' Bardie said.

'What's so special about his head?'

'You're no longer in a position to appreciate it, Red.' Bardie shot a glance at O'Hara's classic profile.

Jessup had glued the thin face laceration shut while Bardie replaced the lung – his own heart would manage after the rest they'd give it – so the lung lay flaccid in the chest cavity. Well, this Sleeping Beauty was also Humpty Dumpty, so they'd better put the rest of him back together again. They both worked on the shoulder joint, the arm, and the battered sacrum and remolded the crushed ribs with bone-set gel. Liver and kidney, spleen, pancreas. He didn't need a new gall bladder. Now they both began reassembling the intestines, repaired the rip in the stomach wall, glued the skin back in place across the lacerated abdomen.

'Nicely hung,' Jessup remarked all too casually. 'Unusual in a tall man.'

Bardie merely grunted. It did not do to encourage Jessup's earthiness. She could go on quite irrepressibly, with endless variations on the theme.

'Me, I've already preferred short men.' Today Jessup was going to be incorrigible. 'BP picking up. Hey, he might make it yet. If one of those ET germs don't get him.'

'He might, at that,' Bardie said, then began to work on his left leg.

There were many servomechs, robotics, and other computer-assisted surgical machines, but, as every human being was slightly different from any other, even the most sophisticated machine could not duplicate the instinct of a human surgeon. Even the most gifted of the nonhumans didn't quite have the same knack with this species. Machines did what Jessup called the grunt work, but nothing replaced a human on the work at hand.

By the time they had finished putting Roger Elliott Christopher O'Hara back in one glued, stapled, renovated piece, they were both exhausted. The monitor told them in its implacable voice that they were to log off immediately. Their efficiency levels were dropping below permissible levels for surgical procedures. It had taken four intensive hours of flat-out surgical skill and decisions to effect the resurrection, and O'Hara had not been the first patient of the shift for Bardie and Nellie.

An orderly came forward to move O'Hara's gurney from the theater. Bardie and Jessup followed it, one on either side, through the sanitizing green-light bath and out into the broad corridor.

'Officer?' asked the orderly.

'Yup!' Bardie said, the adrenaline leaving her slightly lightheaded. She had to cling to the side of the cart.

'I can do it. Don't you goils trust me?'

Bardie grinned. 'No, Naffie, I don't. Not with this one.'

Naffie looked peevish because he had taken a very long look at the unconscious O'Hara.

'Oh, have it your own way. You always do. Not that he's any use to anyone for a while! Bay twenty-two, bed four.' The two weary women turned to starboard. 'Monitor says he's unattached. How can you be sure it's you who can attach him?'

'Naffie, you've had more than your share lately,' Bardie said firmly, and she and Nellie turned into ICU bay 22. Naffie was deft with the antigrav unit, slipping the unconscious patient onto the bed, which folded its sensitive wings around its new occupant with tender intensive care.

When Bardie reached her own cubicle, the first thing she did was program her screen for a ten-minute printout on O'Hara, Lt R. E. C. She took a fan-bath; even a cup of water could make you feel cleaner. She dialed for a hot high-protein meal, inserted herself into her bednet, and ate. The buzzer woke her and she had to blink hard to clear her eyes enough to see the screen. O'Hara was holding his own. She stayed awake until the next report but with great difficulty. She reprogrammed the screen to rouse her only if there was a significant relapse and was asleep almost before she lay back in the net.

To her surprise, she got a whole ten hours of sleep, waking up to feel guilty at the elapsed time. The screen was flashing a no-change and she had to think hard to remember why she would be monitoring a patient in her cabin. Then Humpty O'Hara's case came to mind and she tapped for a review.

He, too, had slept ten hours. His vital signs were strong, all along the line, with no hint of rejection from any of the new organs. But no signs of awareness, no return to consciousness. Which, Bardie thought, was kind. No one had discovered the universal pain suppressant. She didn't like to think of the pain, inevitable as it was in her profession.

She dressed, drinking the high-protein glop that was

supposed to be all she'd need for the day's efforts, and left her cubicle. The corridors were amazingly vacant, and the sounds of personalized snores furthered the thought that there had been no new assaults. A lull in a massacre was definitely welcome. She had only thirteen more days of this to endure before she was out of it. She alternated between wanting to be so occupied that the interminable thirteen days would be over and done with and wanting to have time to adjust her thinking to a civilian standard.

She stopped in the duty room and discovered that she and Nellie were in the next shift – if there was one. She had an hour's leeway. The information screen was scrolling through data on the last assault, but she had long since ceased trying to assimilate either victory or defeat – it all meant bodies to mend. She chided herself for letting that thought intrude. 'S'truth, but whatever victories were won against whatever enemy, she found no glory in it, no matter how necessary the action, how urgent the winning, or what odds and against what, whom, or why. She couldn't remember now what had prompted her to opt for a MASH assignment, apart from a momentary mental aberration. She had learned a great deal – maybe that's why she had come – but there was a large pit of nothingness that one day she would be required to look into, process, and put aside.

Bardie was somewhat surprised to find herself entering bay 22 of the ICU and stopping by bed 4. The vital signs were as strong as could be expected, the new organs still functioning normally. There was even a healthy tinge to O'Hara's skin.

'Can't raise so much as a groan from him,' Naffie said, slipping in to stand beside her, his bright eyes flicking from the screen to her face.

'Have you tried, Naffie?' Somehow Bardie Makem resented that.

'In the line of duty, of course.' Naffie grimaced. 'He really ought to come to long enough to know he's still alive. In gratitude, if nothing else.'

Bardie grinned at Naffie's disapproval. 'So you could hold his hand and reassure him?'

'I don't really think he's my type.' Naffie flounced off.

Bardie pulled back the thermal cover for a visual check. All the incisions and repairs looked good under their skinplas dressings. Of course, he hadn't been thrashing around with either delirium or pain. She laid her hand on his chest: the skin was warm under hers. She felt his forehead, smoothing back the crisp hair; it was unusually soft to the touch, not wiry as the curling suggested. He really had the most handsome face. Idly, she brought one finger lightly down his cheek, to the thin pink scar, and was surprised to see a faint smile appear on the sleeping face.

'O'Hara? O'Hara?' She spoke softly. 'Roger?' She spoke a little louder, for the smile was still there. 'Roger!' He took a deeper breath and then seemed to settle further into sleep, his head turning ever so slightly to the left on the pillow, toward her, the smile in place. 'Roger, lad. Wakey-wakey.' His brows pulled fractionally together in annoyance. 'Roger, I know you're in there. Open up!'

'You're having more success than anyone else,' said the ICU duty nurse at her elbow, startling her. 'And we've tried.'

'Since when is a grimace an indication of alertness?'

'Since it's the only reaction anyone's got out of Sleeping Beauty.'

'It's not a coma,' Bardie said, reviewing the signs.

'No, it's not. Normal sleep pattern. Doesn't even vary when the medication begins to wear off.'

'More should have that facility,' Bardie remarked as the patient in the next bed began to moan piteously. She walked as quickly as she could out of the ward.

Both she and Nellie stopped by bed 4 at the end of their shift, which had been relatively quiet. Mopping-up operations were rarely as hazardous to life and limb, though they'd had some minor repair work from the pong-stick land mines and some of the nasty heatseeking darts the Khalia deployed at such times.

At the top of the next shift, Bardie paused for another visit to bay 22, bed 4, where several colleagues had gathered, including the head psych.

'Ah, Surgeon Makem,' Brandeis said, his wide smile resembling nothing more than a trap for the unwary. 'I understand you did miracle surgery on this patient. Can you enlighten us in any way as to his current somnolent state?'

'He hasn't regained consciousness yet?' Bardie was surprised and saw concern and disbelief in the other medics at the bedside. 'Well, he did experience major bodily insults. Sufficient trauma there to keep from wanting to know.'

'Ah, then,' Brandeis said, leaping upon her suggestion, 'this could be psychosomatically induced?'

Bardie shrugged: she patched bodies, not minds. 'His pressure suit kept him alive, maybe even conscious, but he had to have known that he was badly injured. The suit doesn't record how long its inmate is conscious, merely his vital signs.'

'Good point!' Brandeis and the others turned back to regard the calm sleeping countenance. 'Could be! And his records to indicate "mercy" in preference to disembodiment.'

From his tone, Bardie thought Brandeis was annoyed that another 'subject' had slipped away from him. Brandeis did a lot of counseling to 'brains.'

'Dr Makem did get a response from Lieutenant O'Hara,' the duty nurse said. She'd been standing to one side and Bardie hadn't seen her. She could cheerfully have beheaded her.

'Ah, when? And what?' Brandeis wanted to know, his expression almost avid.

'Oh, I just felt his forehead.' Bardie felt silly: the hands-on was such an anachronism with so many sophisticated sensors to take accurate readings.

'And?' Brandeis encouraged her.

'Faint smile. Might have been reflex.' She could feel herself blushing.

'No doubt,' someone murmured in a droll voice. 'One would have thought that such a handsome man wouldn't have objected to brain duty.'

'Who'd see him?' The words were out of Bardie's mouth before she could think and she blushed even more furiously.

'A perfectly natural vanity,' Brandeis remarked with an equanimity not echoed in his hard eyes. Brandeis was a tolerably attractive fellow, in excellent trim, and according to wardroom gossip, had plenty of activity in the hetero relationships that were not all professional, so Bardie wondered at the subtle envy.

'Well, Dr Makem, if you would be so good as to repeat your gesture . . .' He stepped aside and indicated that Bardie should move to the patient. Bardie did not like his expression, his manner, or the suggestion.

Reluctantly she stepped forward, and feeling more ridiculous than she had since a lowly intern, she put her hand on O'Hara's broad forehead.

'Is that all you did?' Brandeis asked superciliously, with a tolerant smile to the others when there was no patient reaction.

Bardie fought a desire to turn and run. Grimly she replaced her hand and honestly duplicated the incident. 'Roger O'Hara! Roger!' She let her fingers drift back' ward from his forehead to his crisp, curly h~'

down the side of his face. When the faint smile again touched his lips, she didn't know if she was pleased or if she'd prefer the deck to open up and swallow her. But an experiment was an experiment. 'Roger, wakey-wakey, lad.' And once again the brows moved into the most imperceptible of frowns as his head inched away from her. 'I know you're in there. Open up!' Bardie paused, cleared her throat. 'At least, that's about what I said.'

There was a long and embarrassing pause as her colleagues absorbed action and reaction.

'And that's all you did?' Brandeis asked, frowning.

Bardie contented herself with a noncommittal nod, recovering her professional poise.

'That's more response than any one else has had,' the duty nurse said approvingly.

Bardie's collar alarm burred quietly. 'My shift, Doctors. Excuse me.' She was out of the bay as fast as was dignified.

Most of the casualties she and Jessup attended that shift were fairly routine: amputations, the savage lacerations of the latest Khalian mankind-mangler. There was satisfaction in saving all the lives, but Bardie suffered from a most insistent hallucination: O'Hara's smile on nearly every patient.

At the end of her shift, she went back to bay 22, bed 4 and read the latest chart entries. Technically Roger O'Hara had not regained consciousness. There was no one else in the bay. Feeling decidedly self-conscious, Bardie stroked his forehead, entangling his curls in her fingers, then let her finger ride down the side of his face. The faint smile appeared.

'Roger,' she said softly, caressingly, 'you're in there. Please don't keep hiding. It's all right to wake up. You're in your own body. We're not allowed to disembody you, you know. That's why you have the option. But you're all right. Really, you are! You're still in one piece and recovering far better than could be expected.'

She repeated the caress and he stirred, a deep 'mmmm' starting in his throat, and he licked his lips.

'Thataboy, Roger.' She dipped her finger in the water glass and passed it across his lips, which surprisingly were not as dry as they ought to be. 'C'mon, Roger. Wake up.' Again the frown. 'Don't want to wake up, do you? Well, it's okay to. You'll be just fine. Only wake up. I think Brandeis has some ideas about you, flyboy, that you wouldn't like at all. So I really do advise you to wake up.' The frown was deeper, Roger's head turned as if resisting the request. 'Do it for me, will you, Roger? Wake up for Bardie, will you?' She smoothed his hair back, fondling it, testing its softness and the way it curled tightly about her finger. 'You're some mother's son, Roger. C'mon, sweetheart, open your eyes!' She made her tone wheedlingly loving. The eyelids trembled and the muscles in his cheeks and temples moved. 'It's really okay to wake up, Roger.'

She chuckled. 'You sure don't like that word, do you?' The frown obediently appeared but it was deeper now. 'I wonder why. The call to duty, or merely back to life again. A guy who looks like you wouldn't have much trouble with life. And you'll be out of this war – that is, if you decide to . . . rouse!' She grinned as she substituted a synonym. Then, out of pure mischief, remembering what Jessup had originally called him, 'Roger, Sleeping Beauty,' she bent forward, and kissed him on the lips.

Simultaneously she heard movement just beyond her and saw his eyelids flutter open, blinking wildly to focus. She slipped from the bed and out of the bay before she could be hailed. Safely back in her cubicle, she dialed up bay 22, bed 4 and saw the alert readings of the alpha waves. Sleeping Beauty had awakened.

She got her wish to be so busy in the final days of her contract that she had no time to think be the moment's work. She woke that last morning on the *Elizabeth Blackwell* with a feeling of such intense relief that she had survived her two years that she was almost in tears. To restore her composure, she used her entire day's water ration in the shower and shampooed her hair, blowing it dry and attempting to style it as a going-home preparation. She dressed in the smart unitunic, tight-fitting pants, and boots, clothes she hadn't worn during her entire tour of duty. She even put on a touch of the scent that had lain unused on the shelf of her locker. Then she stuffed a clean shipsuit and briefs into her bag and the few personal things she'd been allowed to bring, and that was that.

'Hey, dress blues match your eyes. Nice!' Nellie said, widening her eyes appreciatively when she walked into the wardroom. Two of the other off-duty surgeons accorded her a long whistle before they served her the traditional farewell jigger of fleetjuice.

There were some letters consigned to her to bring home. Then Bardie left a good-bye message on the wardroom screen for the rest of her MASH friends before it was time to take the shuttle that would bring her on the first leg of her homeward journey. Nellie insisted on going with her to the air lock.

'Oh, Stitches, I'll never have another as good as you, I'm sure I won't,' Nellie said, unexpectedly sobbing in their farewell embrace.

Bardie held her off, rather chuffed that the case-hardened nurse had such a sentimental streak. 'How many surgeons have you survived so far, Nellie?'

'It doesn't matter,' Nellie said, gulping. 'It's you I'll miss.'

'Not if the next one is handsome!'

'Speaking of,' Nellie said, her sobs miraculously stanched as she looked down the ramp, 'here's Sleeping Beauty himself!'

Bardie cast a glance over her shoulder and saw, in the stream of wounded being evacuated on this shuttle, Lt Roger Elliott Christopher O'Hara on an antigrav seat being guided by Naffie, who was chatting affably to his charge. The pilot wore a pleasant enough expression but the slight furrow to his brows indicated more tolerance than interest. So he hadn't been one for Naffie after all. Awake, though still semirecumbent, and responding, Roger O'Hara was really too good-looking for anyone's peace of mind. And his hair curled outrageously over a still-pale face.

'Amazing recovery,' Nellie went on. 'Brandeis had hoped to make him a special study case. I heard he woke up the moment he found out.'

Bardie hurried the good-byes as much as she could, wanting somehow to get aboard the shuttle before Roger arrived at the air lock. She succeeded, wondering during the takeoff procedures why she had run like a startled virgin at the sight of him.

Her reaction puzzled her all through the long, boring run to the relief vessel. Then, just as the shuttle locked on to the mother hospital ship, she realized what had startled her: of all the men and women she had operated on, Lt Roger O'Hara was the only one whose face she recognized. And it hadn't that much to do with the Sleeping Beauty aspect of their patient-doctor relationship. She did ward rounds frequently enough, but the patients were bay and bed numbers, wound descriptions, severity categories that she forgot as soon as she moved on to the next wounded body. And it couldn't have anything to do with kissing the man, or his startling return to consciousness as a result of that method of resuscitation. It certainly couldn't have anything to do with him being a sleeping beauty, a frog prince, or a humpty-dumpty.

Fortunately the usual well-organized confusion as the

wounded were the first to be disembarked broke into that remarkable revelation. Bardie caught a brief glimpse of O'Hara being air-cushioned out, his eyes closed. She wondered briefly if he'd made the trip all right: two weeks was not long enough to mend his desperate wounds.

She had received her cabin assignment and was settling into quarters considerably larger than those she had enjoyed in the *Elizabeth Blackwell*: she had space to stand in and a pull-down desk surface and stool as well as her own sanitary cabinet. She had just turned on the screen to familiarize herself with the ship's facilities when the buzzer went off and the screen cleared to a duty station.

'Major Surgeon Makem, please report to desk C, ward station G.'

'What's the problem?'

The corpsman glanced down to his right. 'You're surgeon of record to a Lt R. E. C. O'Hara?'

'That's right. What's wrong?' Maybe he'd been evacuated too soon.

'He won't wake up.'

'What?'

'If you'd please come, Major?' Long-service corpsmen could develop a tone that was tantamount to an order.

Besides being worried about O'Hara, Bardie was curious. She had seen O'Hara leave the shuttle with his eyes closed, but for him to have slept? With the normal bucketing, creaking, and groaning on even the newest shuttle, much less the noise of its occupants, that was unlikely.

She keyed in the ship's deck plan and first located that antigrav shaft nearest her quarters on H deck, then ward G on C deck. When she got there, the officious corpsman was waiting for her with ill-concealed impatience. His expression said 'you took your time,' but he merely gave her a curt nod of his head and gestured for her to follow him.

'If you'll check him over, Major, since you're familiar with his case . . .' the corpsman said, stepping aside for her to enter the cabin. He shut the door immediately behind her and Bardie wondered if she should report his most unusual behaviour to the deck physician.

But there was Roger Elliott Christopher O'Hara, neatly cocooned in his sensor sheet, and the printout over his bunk gave her no cause for immediate alarm. Except that he looked rather more pale than he ought. She approached the berth, noting the light sheen of sweat on his brow. The sensor did not indicate any unusual amount of pain reaction, and according to his chart, he'd been given medication two hours before.

Without realizing her intention, she laid her hand against his forehead, moist and cool. Her fingers, of their own accord, strayed to the crisp, but soft, curls.

'Okay, mate, what's this all about? You were in good shape when Naffie wheeled you in.' Did she detect the faintest wrinkle of a frown? She stroked his forehead again. 'If you're not careful, you'll still end up in Brandeis's files, pulling this Sleeping Beauty act.'

'There's only one way to wake a sleeping beauty, you know,' he said, his eyes still closed. 'I liked it the first time. But I wasn't sure if you were real or not until I saw you ahead of me on the gangplank. Brandeis had me believing you didn't exist at all except as a wish-fulfillment dream.' Suddenly he opened his eyes, and they were a startling shade of clear green. He turned his head slowly to look at her. 'But you did kiss me then, didn't you? And I had to wake up because that's how the charm works, isn't it?'

She couldn't believe his ingenuousness: he couldn't have lived through three years' service and still believe in fairy tales, could he?

'You're no Sleeping Beauty, O'Hara. More Humpty Dumpty.'

'That's why I had to see you, Bardie Makem,' he said so earnestly that his rather rich baritone struck answering chords all down her spine. 'I knew how bad I was hurt before I finally passed out and I was terrified that . . .' His voice broke and he swallowed convulsively. No, Roger O'Hara hadn't believed in any fairy tales, but he had feared to end up in a personal horror story. 'I needed to know that you were real, Bardie Makem. And not a fairy tale.'

'Alice in Wonderland . . .'

His smile had an almost breathtaking charisma to it. 'Naffie told me it was wonders you did for me all right enough and no mistaking it, and not a king's horse in sight.'

'So, you played Sleeping Beauty again to entice me into your clutches?'

'I sure as hell can't come to you for a while yet.' He twisted his shoulders restlessly; then his smile became mischievous. 'Would you take as a given that I'm sweeping you off your feet, to plonk you on my white charger and carry you off into the sunset to live happily ever after together . . .' His face was merry with his smile but the intense look in his vivid green eyes affected Bardie far more than she had the right to anticipate. 'At least for the duration of this voyage . . . that'd give me a good reason to wake up again.' He closed his eyes, schooled his handsome face into repose, but a hopeful smile pulled at the corners of his mouth.

Laughing at his whimsy and more than willing to enjoy some happily-ever-after as an anodyne to the past two years, Bardie bent to bestow on O'Hara the favor he had requested.

The kiss became considerably more magical than Bardie Makem could ever have expected!

THE MANDALAY CURE

Her intercom screen blinked and Amalfi Trotter looked up from the frustration of her life-support-system reports, grateful for an interruption.

'Captain requests a meeting of all officers in the wardroom at sixteen-thirty.'

'Fardles, that's barely time enough to get there!' As a Life Support Systems officer, she was quartered on 9 deck, in the bowels of the troop carrier *Mandalay*.

With one hand, she toggled the acknowledgment switch as she began to strip off her coverall, stinking dirty from her latest wriggling tour of the air-conditioning systems. She'd been positive that she would find dead vermin to account for some of the pong that soured the *Mandalay*'s air. She was a conscientious officer and had done her best with filters, purifiers, and deodorizers to neutralize the pervasive reek.

She lay awake in her bunk night after night, trying to figure out what could be generating or perpetuating the odors, which, she was certain, were one of the chief reasons why she – and most of the complement of the *Mandalay* – didn't sleep well. It was that kind of a nightmare combination of stenches. Perversely enough, the heads on all decks were reasonably free of unpleasant odors.

In fact, Cookie had told her that it was getting to be a joke: go to the head for a cleaner breath of air. Cramming her fouled coverall into the reconditioner, she stepped into the jetter, turning swiftly in the thin mist allowed her for such ablutions. Thirty seconds for soaping and then the mist returned to rinse her body. It did her morale no good to realize that she had just added her sweat and ventilator dust to the pervading odor but one didn't appear before the captain in visible dirt.

Could he have called an emergency meeting about the air quality? She had done her utmost to improve it. She knew how depressing it was to breathe bad air, and morale on the *Mandalay* was low enough. But she *had* tried.

After the Khalian surrender (the official one, although many enemy units refused to accept their defeat and the ignominy of yielding), while the *Mandalay* was on the surface, undergoing minor repairs, Amalfi Trotter had scrupulously replanted the entire 'ponics garden, coaxing broad shiny oxygen-supportive leaves from her vines with careful dollops of fas-gro. She had crawled through all the major ventilating shafts on an inspection tour and used remotes to sweep those which were too narrow for even her slight frame – was that why a pint-sized person was invariably made life-support officer? – and replaced every one of 743 vent filters.

Despite her best efforts, once they lifted from the planet even the 'new' air had quickly taken on the taint of hot metals, acrid plastics, body odors too intense to neutralize, and the faint but throat-souring smell of Khalian weasel fur. Even after she had located and destroyed five badly preserved souvenir Khalian hides, she hadn't quite eradicated that taint. The residue was probably due to having to flush out the systems while they were still on a Khalian-occupied world, which had given the air its final touch of pollution.

Her only success was in eradicating the sickly sweet smell of blood and singed flesh. Perhaps, she thought grimly, there was simply no way to eradicate the rank odor of fear on a troop vessel. And why now? The Khalian War was over. They'd all be heading back to the Alliance ports and demob. Surely the fear contaminant should be fading.

The fighting men and women of the 202nd Regiment, the Montana Irregulars, on board the *Mandalay* had survived nineteen major engagements. The MIs were crack troops, a great point of pride to the naval crew that transported them to the various battle theaters. With the war over, why were these veterans still churning out the sour pheromones of fear? She could understand it if they were moving on to yet another battle area. But they weren't. They were in a holding orbit, and as soon as essential repairs were finished, the entire squadron would very shortly be leaving it on a course for an Alliance world.

She fastened the closings on her clean shipsuit, and grabbed up her clipboard of printouts on the air system. Complaints about the air, while justified right now, were analogous to complaints about weather on primitive planets. It was at least an impersonal, unemotive issue to bitch about. But she couldn't help feeling guilty when someone did. Clean air *was* her responsibility.

Maybe the captain had got the orders that would release them from orbit. Maybe that would reduce the stink. They'd been hanging about for a long time now, going nowhere in never-decreasing circles. Hope of that reprieve made her hurry down the narrow companion-way to the G grav well.

Once the troops knew they were going home, the air would clear up from the barracks decks, where it hung, an almost visible miasma of accumulated fear, stress, and pain. And when the old *Mandy* was back in a decent human port, she would scour the air system of this old bucket with good clean civilized air on a properly photosynthesizing planet.

Everything will improve, she assured herself, when we're on the way home. She scrambled off the null-grav lift onto the wardroom level. Her palms were sweating again. They always did when she anticipated criticism.

Her keen nostrils caught a new odor, a pleasant one, refreshing. She sniffed about her and realized that the smell was seeping from the wardroom. She identified the aroma with some astonishment. Lavender? In the wardroom? They *were* desperate.

She rapped the panel courteously and then entered, closing the door quickly behind her because she didn't want the outside air to dilute the fragrance inside. The odor came from a lighted candle on the wardroom table, around which ranged both naval and marine officers. She slipped into the only remaining seat, between the marine colonel, Jay Gruen, and Major Damia Pharr, head of the medical team. They gave her a nod, but something about their tenseness communicated itself to her. The clipboard slipped out of her sweaty hands and clattered to the tabletop.

She muttered apologies, which no one noticed. Then she, too, found herself trying not to stare at Captain August. His face was so expressionless that the flimsy that drooped from his fingers must contain bad news. The lavender was to soothe them all?

A sudden premonition shook Amalfi. They were *not* going home. She clutched the edge of the clipboard now as if she were squeezing the breath out of whoever issued such orders. Where in the Nine Pits of Hell could they be sent now? Not another pocket of Khalian resistance? Was that why there was such a stench of fear? Only how could the soldiers know the content of a message the captain could only have received within the past half hour? Scuttlebutt was quick but not *that* quick, and any important stuff came in code, which took longer to seep into general knowledge.

Captain August stood. He had been a lean man when she first joined the *Mandalay* seven long years ago. He was gaunt now, the flesh stretched across the bone of his skull, the skin under his eyes dark with sleeplessness and stress. He'd been in command of the *Mandalay* since the outbreak of hostilities with the Khalians. He spread the flimsy, its message bleeding black ink tracks across the dirty cream of the recycled paper

'In code, we have been given orders to proceed to a rendezvous in two weeks, GGMT, with the supply ship *Grampion*, which will have replacement personnel for you, Colonel Gruen, to bring the regiment up to full strength.'

'Replacement personnel?' Gruen demanded, his light, oddly flecked eyes bulging slightly as he challenged the captain. 'Full strength?'

'Yes, Colonel,' August said. He scowled as he glanced around the table, at the stunned expressions that ranged from horror through disbelief to despair. 'We are to reprovision to battle-readiness.'

'Battle-ready?' The words exploded from Hamish Argyll, the gunnery officer.

On both sides of Amalfi came the mutter of mutinous curses.

'But, Captain, who's left to battle with?' No sooner were the words out of young Ensign Badeley's mouth than he tried to melt under the table from embarrassment.

'That information is omitted from this communiqué!' Captain August let the flimsy fall from his fingers. He scrubbed his fingertips on his thumb as if he'd touched something unclean. The sheet drifted slowly to the tabletop, all eyes following it.

'Then the scuttlebutt is true?' Colonel Gruen asked in a hoarse voice.

Captain August turned his head slowly toward him. 'And you *believe* the scuttlebutt you hear, Colonel?'

'When it's affecting the morale of my soldiers, you bet your last tank of oxy I do.' Waggling a finger at the captain, Gruen went on. 'I got to tell you, Captain, the morale of my troops is so low, I shall withhold this information from them as long as it is humanly possible.'

'How can you keep it from 'em, Jay?' Major Pete Loftus, the adjutant, demanded, raising his hands in resignation. 'They know most things before I do. The air's full of fear stench.' He darted a quick glance at Amalfi, who tried to scrunch even smaller between the two larger bodies.

'How could they possibly know orders which were only issued thirty-five minutes ago?'

'They don't,' the colonel replied bluntly. 'They won't. They're sunk so low in battle fatigue right now, such orders would result in a rash of suicide attempts, brawls, and possibly even a mutiny attempt . . .'

'Not on my ship . . .' August began.

'You're exaggerating . . .' Brace, the naval science officer, protested.

'We can't cope with that,' added Major Pharr.

Colonel Gruen eyed everyone dispassionately. 'I've been the regimental commander now since we were mobilized to fight the Khalians and there's no fight left in my soldiers. I'll tell you this, I stay awake nights trying—' His fist came down on the table. '—trying to figure out some way to revive their morale. Right now, I doubt they'd even suit up. There've been wars before where there weren't no soldiers to fight.'

'How can you have a war if there're no fighters?' Ensign Badeley piped up.

'You have been apprised of my orders.' Captain August rose to his feet. 'We break orbit at twelve hundred hours tomorrow. If it's any consolation, the entire squadron is headed in the same direction, not just the *Mandalay*.'

'It is no end of consolation, Captain,' Gruen replied with bitter sarcasm, 'to know that High Command isn't picking on us alone. I'd like permission to make a private call on the secure band, sir.'

Captain August gave a curt nod and strode quickly out of the wardroom.

'Wait here for me,' Gruen said, pointing a commanding finger at the others as he rose to follow.

'You bet!' Loftus replied, glancing about the table to see if anyone would be fool enough to leave.

Gruen's wife served on the flagship, and had often been able to discreetly reassure those aboard the *Mandalay* to their advantage.

'There is no way that I, as chief medic,' Damia Pharr began in her gravelly voice, 'would certify these troops as battle-ready. They can dress 'em up and kit 'em out and load 'em up but they won't fight!'

'Surely they'll follow orders?' Badeley asked, his round, youthful face screwed up in droll surprise.

He was alternately a headache, a laugh, and a raving bore. It was the universal opinion that he was likely to remain an ensign. Two years on a troop ship that had made four landings on hostile planets – and in which he had had to defend the *Mandalay* from vicious attacks by would-be boarders – had not shaken the down from his cheeks or given him any significant insights into Life and the Real World. He could be counted on to ask just such a stupid question as he had.

'No, laddie' – Hamish's accent became thickly ethnic when emotional – 'they wouldn't. And I, for one, would not lay a feather of blame on them.'

'But . . . that would be tantamount to mutiny!' His eyes bulged.

'Wouldn't it!' Argyll agreed too amiably.

'It's inhuman to ask any soldier in their current depressed states to trundle off and fight another war.'

Loftus brought both fists down on the table, his expression deeply troubled. 'They've got to have some R and R on a decent planet, not one with the stench of weasel and blood and death. They need sleep and unprocessed food and rest . . . Plague take it, Trotter, can't you do *something* about the air?'

Amalfi tried to hide behind Damia Pharr, who was looking down at her with a slightly quizzical expression on her face.

'Yeah, Malf, isn't there something you can do? Who can sleep easy with tainted air in their lungs all night long?'

'I've done everything I can,' Amalfi said, her voice just one note away from a whinge. She brandished her clipboard. 'I changed every plant in 'ponics when we were grounded. I've cleaned every duct, refitted every filter . . .'

'Had my gun crew jumping out of their skins when they heard her sweeping out the shafts above us,' Hamish said, grinning encouragingly at her. 'They thought the captain had found the still.'

'Which reminds me,' Damia said, 'I'll need four liters tonight if I'm to get my patients to sleep.'

'Has Farmeris come out of his coma yet?' Loftus asked.

'No, and I've done nothing to wake him up. He's better off asleep in that babbling bedlam I used to call my infirmary,' Pharr replied, her wistful tone intimating envy of the man's condition. 'He's okay apart from staying asleep. He's got the right idea. Sleeping it out till better days.'

A tinny voice filtered through from Major Loftus's com unit. 'Major, fight broke out in D barracks: tranked nine combatants, but infirmary says they've no room for 'em.'

'That's right,' Damia replied cheerfully. 'Any injuries?' she added as an afterthought.

'No, sir. We had warning of the mood and arrived in time to restore order.'

'List their IDs for report, Sergeant Norly, then dump 'em in their bunks with wrist and ankle restraints. There's no more room in the brig anyhow.' Loftus swore as the crackling of the intercom ceased.

'Do you think they feel safer fighting among themselves?' Pharr asked rhetorically, glancing about the room.

Amalfi saw Badeley open his mouth, and she glared so fiercely at him that he subsided. A depressed silence fell on those waiting at the table. Two of the marine captains who had listened intently to their commanders' remarks were now obviously trying to get a few winks of sleep in the lavender-scented air. Amalfi was only too relieved that no one started in on her again. The sound of boots clomping on the metal decking alerted them all. As one, they looked toward the door, anticipating Gruen's return and whatever hope he might have gleaned from his wife.

The blank expression on Jay Gruen's face as he entered was sufficient to depress all hope. He closed the door behind him with meticulous care and then leaned against it with the weariness of total dejection.

'The truth is so bad,' and he paused, 'that not even High Command has the balls to put it in the orders.'

'Well?' demanded Damia Pharr when Gruen let an atrocious span of time go by without enlightenment.

'I agree.' He pushed himself off the door and toward the table. Loftus and Argyll made room for him as he folded, like a decrepit aged man, into the chair. 'It would appear that the Khalians are not the primary enemies of the Alliance.'

'Say what?' demanded Loftus.

Gruen clasped his hands before him, one thumb massaging the other. He didn't lift his eyes once as he continued to speak.

'The Khalians appear to have been the first line of defense of an oligarchy of merchant families – of human or humanoid stock – known as the Syndicate. The Khalians questioned named them the Givers.'

'They give war?' asked Damia softly.

'There are a lot of gaps about the Syndicate but one thing is sure: they subjugate any useful entities and massacre any that defy them.' Gruen's voice mirrored the defeat in his expression. 'The Khalian War, the one we just finished, is apparently only the prelude to the Big One. And the Alliance has got to win it or expect that every single planet and star system in the Alliance could, and would be, destroyed by the Syndicate.'

'But surely in a large group, a Syndicate, there would be an outcry against wholesale destruction?' Brace asked. 'It's just not economical to obliterate whole planets and star systems . . .'

'The Syndicate doesn't think the way we do. They may be technologically superior, but not sociologically,' Gruen said, massaging his thumbs with such force the blood suffused the tips. 'They're prime bigots – hate any alien race and enslave or exploit them. And we thought the Khalians were bad . . .'

'They were,' Loftus muttered respectfully. 'But surely if the Alliance sticks to our sphere of influence . . .'

'That would work with anyone but the Syndicate. And the Syndicate doesn't tolerate powerful neighbors . . .'

'The Alliance isn't hostile,' Bradley began. 'We live in peace with lots of other species and civilizations.'

'We blew the peaceful image by fighting the Khalians . . .'

'But, Colonel, they began the hostilities,' Badeley replied belligerently; 'we were only defending ourselves.'

'Oh, plug it up, Badeley,' Argyll said. 'Jay, what about other regiments? Can they take another all-out offensive?'

'I don't have to worry about other regiments,' Jay Gruen said, slapping both hands palm down on the table, his eyes averted. 'I have to worry about mine. And mine are not ready to hear the score.'

'We can't keep them in the dark for long,' Loftus protested. 'And if we don't level with them, whatever faith they have in us as commanders flushes right down the tubes!'

'You're right there. So,' and Jay Gruen glanced around at the others, 'we've got approximately twenty hours to come up with a way to restore morale – which news of fighting a brand-new war is not going to do – before leaving orbit.'

'But we won't be making the rendezvous for two weeks . . .' Badeley began.

'If someone,' Loftus said, pinning Badeley with a hard glare, 'isn't smart enough to figure out that we're *not* heading back to Alliance territory, there's nothing we could do to resurrect our once-proud regiment. And I'll just bite the bad tooth and get my discharge.'

Badeley looked even more shocked but he shut his mouth.

'I'd sleep on that notion, were I you, Lofty,' Damia Pharr said kindly. 'Oh, Great Gods and Other Lesser Deities!' She slapped her forehead and expressions of amazement, anxiety, incredulity, and dawning hope flitted across her broad homely face. 'Why didn't I think of that before!'

'Think of what?' Gruen asked with acid impatience.

'Sleep therapy! We could all use a really good sleep. I read about the therapy in the *Space Medicine Journal*. The Surgeon General . . . someone named Haldeman . . . recommended dream sleep therapy for troops being transported from one theater of war to another. I don't see that much difference in this application. It could work. It should work. It sure won't hurt and it'll cut out all the brawling, that is . . . Arvid.' She spoke sharply because the supply officer was quietly napping in his corner. 'You still have all those barrels of hibernation gas, don't you?'

Startled, the j.g. had to have the query repeated. 'Sure, yeah, hey, that stuff's probably the only thing we haven't used in this campaign.'

'Deep sleep will not solve a morale problem,' Gruen said. 'It'll only defer it.'

'Used as a hibernant, yes, but used to induce a deep and restful slumber, now, that's another thing. We can't give the men an R and R but we can give 'em S and D. Sleep and dreams.' Damia was so positive that some of her enthusiasm began to infect the others with hope. 'What your troops need is restful, REM sleep, to help relieve the backup of willie-horrors . . .'

'And how in hell are you going to tend close to four thousand sleeping troopers? They've got to be fed, evacuated, and . . .' Gruen stopped and Damia, grinning broadly now, waved her hands, encouraging him to talk himself into the next step. He stared at her with dawning comprehension.

'Yup, that's right. Battle dress drill. I know you made 'em all service their suits on the surface. There's enough nutrient fluid to keep every single one of them going for ten days. And the suits do bodily functions as well as monitoring. Why must such expensive equipment be used only in war?'

The others around the table, even those who had remained silent, began to talk.

'Malf' – Damia turned to the life-support officer – 'can you block off the barracks decks from Operations? You guys still have to run the ship even if your passengers are all asleep.'

'Ah, yes, I think so, except I thought sleep gas is skin-permeable. Wouldn't the suits . . .'

'Seal all the air locks from the troop decks, and penetrating as that hibernation gas is, it won't affect the ship's crew,' Damia went on, sort of running roughshod over objections.

'Now, just a minute, Dame,' Gruen began.

'Shit, Jay, you need the rest more than your men. I promise you, at the concentration we'll pour into the troop quarters, everyone will go beddie-byes and dream sweet. Dream themselves right back into rested, resilient minds quite willing to take on this new challenge. Hell, if they're deeply asleep, we can even do some sleep training, and they'll be fit as fiddles when we rendezvous with *Grampion*.'

'You're sure it'll work?'

Amalfi had to look away from Colonel Gruen's face: the beseeching look of hope revived was almost more than she could bear seeing.

Damia put her hand on Gruen's shoulder. 'I don't know anything else to try. And sleep's not going to hurt anyone aboard this ol' tub . . .' She shot an apologetic grin at Brace and Argyll. 'If the entire regiment is suited save the medical staff, and with a little help from the *Mandalay* personnel, we can check you all out.'

'Is there enough protective garb, Arvid?' Loftus asked. 'You gotta have the right gear or you'll end up asleep at the switch.'

'Yeah, yeah, sure. Plenty,' Arvid replied. Amalfi thought he hadn't taken in exactly what was being planned.

'Malf, can you handle your end of it? Blocking the vents?'

'I'd only need to block off at three deck. But I'll have to bunk in with someone else,' Amalfi said. 'I wouldn't mind sleeping through it all but I haven't got a battle suit,' she added, responding to the lightening of mood.

'Good girl, Trotter,' Gruen said, his eyes alive again in

his face. 'Now, Brace, how d'you think the captain will take this?'

The science officer and nominally the second-in-command to the captain gave the colonel a slow smile. 'I don't think he'll quibble, Jay, it's not exactly a naval decision. *Mandalay*'s proud to ferry the Montana Irregulars. We want to help. After all, if this Syndicate is half as bloodthirsty as rumor makes 'em, we've got to have at least one regiment fighting-fit.'

'Good. I'll just stop up to his quarters and give him the word. Let's get cracking. The faster we can suit 'em all up, the quicker we avoid problems.' The colonel nearly bounced out of the wardroom, followed by a cheerful Loftus and their captains, looking remarkably bright-eyed.

'Arvid,' Damia Pharr said, 'I'll just get the specs on that sleepy-time gas so I get the dose calibrated correctly. Can't have our beauties oblivious to wake-up time . . .' She had the supply officer by the arm and was hauling him away.

'How many hands will you need, Miss Trotter, to effect the seal-off?' Brace asked her. Amalfi was running the figures in her head, but Brace waved her to the wardroom console. 'If this works, I might try a little compulsory shut-eye myself on the next leg of this voyage.'

At 2302, following Captain August's devious advice, every alarm system on the *Mandalay* howled, hooted, and shrieked. Troopers on every deck, even those in the brig and infirmary, were ordered into their battle suits until the 'break in the skin of the *Mandalay*' could be mended.

As the seasoned troops, cursing vehemently, struggled into their protective battle armor, complaints were rife but not a breath of suspicion. If some thought it very odd that they hadn't been ordered to close and seal their helmets against loss of oxygen, battle-weary troops don't do more than they're told to. The first insidious flow of the diluted hibernation gas spread across every deck simultaneously. Not one trooper noticed – and every one of them fell asleep, held upright in parade readiness by his stout battle suit.

The crew in their protective gear muttered about it being bloody unnatural to move through the rank and file, lowering each to the horizontal mode. To relieve the tedium of their caretaking duties, there was a spritely competition about who had the most outrageous snore, the longest, the most involved, the funniest. There was considerable controversy in the *Mandalay*'s wardroom about the competition: they didn't want the results to affect the Navy-Marine relationships when the troops were finally awakened. Captain August had been heard to chuckle as some of the snore tapes were replayed.

'You'll notice, Captain,' Damia Pharr said shortly before they had reached the rendezvous, 'that crew morale has also improved.'

'Noted, Major. We can only hope that the improvement also includes our sleeping beauties.'

'It will, sir, it will,' Pharr replied so devoutly that the captain entertained no further doubts.

By the time the *Mandalay* eased into position in a docking bay at the gigantic supply ship *Grampion*, even the air aboard had improved from barely breathable to quite pleasant.

The officers were the first roused, for orders had come for them to attend a briefing on the flagship. If the sparkle in the eyes of Colonel Gruen and Major Loftus was any indication, Pharr's therapy had indeed worked its magic.

'We'll wait till our return, Pharr, to effect a full-scale revival,' Gruen told his medical officer, ignoring her smug grin. 'We just might have some good news to relay with the bad by then. Won't hurt. It's been so peaceful I almost hate to wake 'em up.'

Damia Pharr responded with a huge, jaw-popping yawn. 'I get a chance for some S and D first, Jay!'

'S and D?'

'No R and R? Try S and D. Makes a difference. You will see.'

Formally piped on board the flagship, the colonel found an anxious wife waiting at the air lock for sight of him. Her amazement at his rejuvenation was heartening.

'I can't believe my eyes, Jay,' she said, giving him a quick but ardent kiss under the eyes of the grinning officer and ratings who were in the portal. 'Two weeks ago, you looked ghastly . . .' She broke off without further detail of that clandestine contact and pulled him down the companionway out of sight. 'And it's not just you. Hello, Pete, you look rested and raring to go, too. How ever did you do it?'

'You can't keep a good regiment down, you know,' Pete Loftus replied, grinning. Then a yawn escaped him and, chagrined, he belatedly covered his mouth.

'There was nothing wrong with any man in the Montana Irregulars, Pamela,' Jay Gruen told his astonished wife, 'that a good long sleep couldn't set right. A little S and D would do you no harm either. I'll tell you all about it on our way to beard the general in his lair.'

And he did. Nor was any of the *Mandalay*'s complement surprised to find a reference to S&D, aka 'The *Mandalay* Cure,' in the next General Orders. Damia Pharr was given a double jump to bird colonel and celebrated the occasion with M&M as the *Mandalay* joined the first Syndicate Expeditionary Force. But that's another story.

A FLOCK OF GEESE

The time storm shifted and that resettlement was enough to rouse Chloe, attuned as she was to the distortion phenomenon. Awareness returned to her. She fumbled for light, uncertain in her sleepiness what she was reaching for until her hand found the slim metal cylinder. She had to focus her thoughts to remember how to flick on this sort of beam. Then she angled it to shine on her left wrist as her fingers sought the digital switch. The display informed her that the relative elapsed time of the latest shift was four days, fourteen hours, thirty-two minutes, and ten seconds. Time in Issaro's society had been exceedingly complex. In her natal eighteenth century, she had been accustomed to judging the relative time of day accurately by the sun's position. But the sun was no longer a reliable timepiece.

From the stone shelf above her pallet Chloe took the clipboard and the incredible pen that never needed to be dipped in ink. When she had added the elapsed time to the neat columns of figures of time-storm duration and intervals between the phenomena, no sudden insight revealed to her the secret of the records she had assiduously kept for the past three years elapsed time. Chloe sighed. If only she could discern the relationship between time storm and interval, she would be as much in control of her continued existence as she was of the cave and anyone who resided in it.

'Damnation take thee, Issaro,' she said, ironically

aware that Issaro probably had met damnation when he had been caught too far from the cave at the onset of that time storm. She hadn't meant to lose him until he had unlocked the rhythm of the shifts. If, indeed, there was one, as he had constantly averred. 'Be that as it may,' she added on a philosophical note.

At some future time, future at least in the sense of her own continuous occupation of the cave, she would probably encounter another man from Issaro's computer-oriented society and, with his help, delve the message of the columns.

Now she prudently turned off the light. It was a useful device, less dangerous than candles or sparks from flint and tinder, and brighter than any lantern. Judicious use would extend the beam's life. One day, when her records had divulged their secret configuration, she might know when she would touch again in or near the time that had produced the compact hand light.

The cold of the time storm was gone and Chloe was feeling distinctly warm under her layers of quilts, which she preferred to the lighter-weight blankets and thermal covers the others used. In the earliest days in this cave refuge, there had been freezes of such shocking intensity that her people had bundled together under every available covering to generate enough warmth to keep them alive. Determined never to suffer from such temperatures again, Chloe sewed one patchwork after another from whatever scraps came to hand. The cave had escaped such extremes of weather for a long time, and Chloe had a fleeting moment's anxiety that the balance for such clemency would soon fall due. She folded back her quilts carefully, catching a slight odor from the body-warmed fabric. If it was a good day, an airing would freshen them. Should the river be running clear, and the sun shining, she would have Dorcas launder one or two.

She rose from the thick air mattress. That, like Issaro's digital watch, had been an unexpected treasure, the remnant of camping paraphernalia found discarded by the river. She chided herself for coveting the elegancies when she could not, in all conscience, approve the societies that had produced them. In truth, the fripperies did make life more endurable in the cave. The disadvantage was that luxuries, such as the light beam of the stonecutters, inevitably lost their power. Then one had, perforce, to resume the more primitive ways of accomplishing the same tasks. The tedious if reliable methods caused her people to grumble and be dissatisfied, forcing her to be unnecessarily stern in order to achieve her desired ends.

Chloe let her eyes become accustomed to the stygian darkness of her little alcove. If the stonecutters had not depleted their power packs, it would have been a proper room, instead of a niche opposite the stores. She listened intently but heard nothing more than the muted breathing of the sleepers in the main room of the cavern. She inhaled deeply. The air was still good, though slightly tainted with the stench of fearful sweat. Chloe thought of those asleep there: Michael, Destry, elderly Edward, the Indian Fensu, moaning Rayda, the timorous Malenda, and stolid Dorcas. Pregnant Dorcas.

Chloe did not dwell on that problem. She pulled her skirts straight, the fine-textured and durable cloth a product of yet another culture. She had never been able to bring herself to wear the more practical but immodest unmentionables favored by many societies. The sweep of her skirts added a subtle authority to her slender, erect frame. To have pranced about in trousers would have been to demean herself. Chloe moved toward the front of the cave complex, one hand on the wall to steady herself, for the floor of the cavern was uneven. One day she would have paving stones placed in the worst dips. She knew the contours of her refuge well and lowered her head where the ceiling slanted downward. When she acquired more of the stonecutters, she would lop off the bumps. Then she was in the small entrance, an arm's length from the massive door.

With an involuntary supplication to a God she knew no longer existed, she hesitated before she put her hands flat against the wood. She could feel no vibration, pressure, or extreme of temperature through the wood. She inhaled, smelling neither the acridity of a foul atmosphere nor the dampness of rain or snow, aware only of the preservative in which the wood had been soaked. How well she recalled the jubilation following the discovery of the railroad ties. It had been the work of most of that interval to transport the bulky pieces of wood to the cave.

'They'll make the best door in the world and we've found bolts and iron enough to make a frame,' Douglas had cried triumphantly. 'No more cowering in the back of the cave, praying the elements won't devour us. Nothing in the world, any world, will get through that door when I've hung it!'

Douglas was long gone, but his door remained as a tribute to his ingenuity and workmanship. She had rather regretted his exigent departure, but those in the cave must owe their allegiance only to her, not to a jumped-up ne'er-do-well. She was the only person who could discern the ripples that preceded a time shift.

She felt for Douglas's bolts and eased them back in their well-oiled slots. She tilted the heavy safety bar and drew the latch. She paused once more, though she knew in her bones that this had been a good shift and terror did not lie on the other side. She braced herself to heave open the heavy door.

Spring again! Not a false spring with the mutated horrors growing on the strangely altered ground of three shifts ago. Midafternoon, unless this time shift had changed the sun as well. The fragrances borne on the air were sweetly familiar. Chloe stepped out and turned as she always did, to look up at the mountains, to the everlasting hills. They were all right! The right shape. No help might be forthcoming from their crags and slopes, as the psalmist had once intimated, but their unchanging aspect formed the one constant from which Chloe could take any reassurance. She feasted her eyes now on their blessedly familiar outlines. Through all the foul and fair forms the land outside the cave assumed after time shifts, the outline of the hills endured.

'You chose well, good citizen,' Douglas had told her his first night in the cave so many years ago. 'This is basement rock, solid basalt.' He had affectionately slapped the stony bulwarks beside him. 'Part of the bones of this tormented earth, established millennia ago and not likely to change no matter how these time storms shift. Until old Earth bounces all the way back to the Archeozoic Age, these rocks will endure. Mark my words!'

She had, until Douglas had tried to turn the then residents against her, and gain dominion over her cave. Ruthlessly she had left him, and them, behind in the next shift. She had missed him sorely for his many skills and his logical solutions to the practical problems of their curious existence. She chose to believe that his theoretical assessments of their condition, such as the durability of the hills, were as accurate as his practical applications.

Once more the hills gave her comfort and assurance. Serenely now, she could turn to see what had transpired around her and in the valley. The rivers, seen through a thin or young forest, were in residence and their banks unmarred by buildings of any description. Those rivers had watered her father's prosperous holding, obtained from the governor of the colony, rich farmlands, coveted by his neighbors. Well, she was no longer chattel-goods, unable to guide her own destiny and manage her inheritance. She wondered how those gentlemen, her ardent suitors, had fared the night of the first time storm, when they had chased her into these hills. And fortuitously into the cave, which had proved the one sure shelter in this time-heaved world.

A faint breeze ruffled her hair, a breeze wet and clean of unfamiliar taints. She saw no stunted or exceptional trees. In this young forest, she recognized elm, birch, chestnut, oak, ash, and, further down the hills, beeches and willows. A comforting undercurrent of noise drifted to her ears, the conversations of birds, animals, and insects. Into what era Earth had passed, Chloe could not guess, for the mountain forests of the American eastern coast had stood undisturbed for centuries before England had established her colonies there. This particular section had been alternately called Upper New York State, Lesser Metropolis, Eastern Sector, and Red Region and had been relatively unscathed by urban development, Douglas had said, until the late twenty-fifth century.

Twenty-five centuries seemed incredible to Chloe, a woman of the eighteenth. Yet, in some society future to the twenty-fifth, the fabric of time itself had been ruptured, causing the great distortion shift storms during which the planet was flung from one point to another along the fifth dimension. Or so Issaro had asserted. The storm-bedraggled Chloe of the eighteenth century might not have comprehended such a theory, but the Chloe who assessed this new period of relative stability could accept that interpretation after all the marvels she had seen during her twelve years of time-faring.

Chloe moved from the cave's overhang. This would be a welcome stop, though autumn would have been more beneficial in terms of replenishing supplies of herbs, grains, fruits, and nuts. Automatically she bunched her skirt in one hand and began to gather dead branches from the clearing. Firing was always in short supply in the cave, and she despised idleness in anyone above any other flaw and would not tolerate it in herself, either. It took her no time to gather the first load, which she took back to the cave, stacking it quietly and quickly in the bins. No one was disturbed by her slight noises. They were all exhausted by the rigors of the last shift, though it hadn't been a bad one, and they would sleep until she woke them. That was all to the good. Chloe valued this time of solitude to collect her thoughts and plan how best to use a new shift.

She went back to her alcove and gathered up her quilts. As she spread the patchworks on convenient branches, she hoped there would be game abroad this time. Meat was the most urgent requirement. She would have the able men set snares and hunt. The women could fish and look for spring berries. She had the feeling that they might be here for a goodly while. Time enough to explore and see what other benefits might be derived.

She took a pail from the supply shelves, noting that some of the precious implements had not been stored properly. She'd have a word with Rayda. Born in a high-technology society and loath to dirty her hands or stretch her muscles in honest labour, Rayda had few skills to recommend her to Chloe. She had been in the cave now for five shifts and could be sloughed off as unsuitable. Chloe did not believe in undue benevolence with respect to castaways. She exploited whatever talents they had and generally managed to retain the artifacts with which they came encumbered. Bitter experience had taught her to be ruthless in maintaining her authority and domination. Wisely she had remained silent on the score that she always experienced a warning of the onset of a time storm. With that unique faculty, she had been able to decide which of her companions of the moment passed the storm in the safety of the cave. Fortunately she had never touched in the same time twice, a mercy of which she was entirely sensible.

So, she would dispense with Rayda at the conclusion of this interval. A simple ruse at the appropriate time would suffice. The woman had no orientation skill at all.

Would it ever be possible to have a stable complement in the cave, Chloe wondered, each occupant possessing skills useful in their transitions and valuable in various of the civilizations in which the time storms deposited them? Harmonious personalities with no sudden inexplicable ambitions to usurp her prerogatives: a decent assembly of folk all dedicated to surviving decently in this one refuge on a planet utterly abandoned by time's order? The best of all possible worlds?

As Chloe wound her way through the trees in search of early berries, she smiled at her conceit. Issaro had suggested, on several occasions, that there had to be other refuges on the planet, other stable areas on the Earth's crust or under it. Chloe had scoffed at the notion of trying to contact other survivors, though occasionally the technological equipment to do so had been available to her. Speaking to people she had never met across vast leagues of continent or ocean seemed a futile effort to her. What value would such contact have? How could one possibly pit mere scores of men against this ultimate disaster? She could not envisage that the combined effort of even the most substantial numbers of folk could affect or alter the cataclysm that had overtaken the world. If, as Issaro had maintained, some future scientific experimentation had ruptured time, then all the efforts of the past could not mend that fracture. The wiser course was to endure the phenomenon in reasonable safety and comfort.

Chloe broke from the thin forest into a clearing. Gooseberries grew in profusion on the bushes. Chloe ate greedily of the yellow-green ovals, letting the juices moisten tissues dried by the uncertainties of the time shift.

She had nearly filled her pail when a sudden heavy rustling in the undergrowth alerted her to the presence of some animal. She crouched behind the screen of bushes, observing that she was upwind of the creature. For several fearful moments, she wondered what horrible denizen might emerge. Her relief was double as she recognized the distinctive snout and furry bulk of a bear – not a large one and, judging by the way it gobbled berries, recently awakened from its hibernation.

Any bear could be dangerous, so Chloe eased her way out of the bushes and walked swiftly back to the cave. Would she rouse the men to chase the bear? No, a thin one with winter-mangy fur would be of little value. And a large predator would provide Michael and Destry with an excuse to use firearms. Still, the presence of a bear augured the likelihood of other familiar, and useful, species. Again, she stifled the wish that the season were more advanced and the bear fat enough to be worth hunting. Perhaps they would remain here through the entire summer and be able to garner the autumn's harvest.

The sunlight and fresh air streaming in through the open door had not roused the sleepers. She regarded them with a distaste bordering on contempt. The only really useful one was Fensu, and she could not countenance sharing the cave with the Iroquois, for only the presence of the other three men had inhibited his savage appetites.

Chloe set the pail on the stone floor, the slight grating noise disturbing no one. Michael slept next to Malenda but under separate coverings. Fensu was beyond them, rolled in his lynx furs. Rayda was curled close to the pregnant Dorcas, while Edward and Destry, with some curious vestige of chivalry, lay across the entrance to the inner chamber.

Yes, thought Chloe coolly, she would dispense with the pack of them. She had long since gleaned from each what information and skill could be of use to her. She was bored with their tales and their long faces. Wasn't it enough to *live* through the time storms? With enough to eat and decent water to drink? Clothes to warm their hides? They had no courage, no real fortitude, no furnishings in their minds at all. She had sloughed off far better companions than these. Indeed, she wondered at her charity in sustaining such a collection of lazy louts.

'Wake up, you vagrants, you idlers,' she cried, prodding indiscriminately at the sleeping bodies. 'Wake up! 'Tis well past time to be about the business of the day. Fresh meat must be caught for I wish to eat a warm meal at supper. Michael, thee and Destry will help Fensu set traps and snares . . .'

'We can use the rifles?' Michael threw off sleep quickly in his excitement.

'What? And drive the game away with unnecessary noise? I do not have unlimited supplies of powder and shot . . .' She paused, seeing the tightening of his face muscles. 'Ammo' was what Michael called powder and shot. 'Snares and traps will be sufficient for our needs.'

'Then we are lodged here for a time?' asked Edward, and silence fell for her answer.

'Long enough to profit more by industry and application than needless questions. Edward, the brook is in full spate. Fill the big kettle first and then replenish the water butts.' It amused Chloe to make a water boy out of a learned man. 'Dorcas, start the fire. A goodly blaze will rid this chamber of the chill of time . . . and fear.' She glanced around to see if her jibe rankled. Edward and Destry looked quickly away and began to fold up their sleeping bags. 'Nay, slovens. Take the bedding out to be aired. Faugh! Malenda! Rayda! There are ripe gooseberries a short step from here. Strip the bushes . . .'

'Then we may not be here long?' asked Michael, catching an inference she hadn't meant.

She gave him a long stare for his impertinent query.

'Why leave ripe berries for birds when they would sweeten our dry mouths?'

Michael shrugged and moved out of the cave with his sleeping roll.

'Come! I've given you your orders. Do not dally!'

Fensu glided past Chloe, brushing so close that she caught the musky smell of him. Yes, despite his woodcrafts, he was expendable. Rutting animals such as he had forced her from her father's fine farm and into this tenuous existence.

'Days in the dark, and no rest on cold stones . . .' Rayda's sulky voice rehearsed her litany of grievances. Destry caught her arm and gave her a shake to be silent as he pulled her out of the main cavern. Malenda, blankets bundled in her arms, scurried after them.

Perhaps, thought Chloe in malicious hope, the bear might still be in the gooseberries and hungry enough to take a few well-placed nibbles out of Rayda.

She heard the crackling of fire consuming dry wood and looked around approvingly as Dorcas set the kettle tripod in place over the hearth. Too bad the woman had got herself with child and Chloe had not known soon enough to remedy the condition. The docile Dorcas was an excellent, undemanding servant, but not exactly the sort of companion who wore well in the long run, especially if lumbered with an infant.

'I will fetch meal for johnnycake, Dorcas, and herbs while thee pares vegetables. Carrots and onions will probably suit whatever flesh the men snare.'

Not a woman to waste breath with unnecessary words,

Dorcas nodded acknowledgment and went to the sand-box where the root vegetables were stored.

As Chloe moved down the short corridor to the stores cave, she reached into her copious skirt pocket for the heavy keys.

'It's ridiculous to have locks and keys in this place,' Douglas had protested to Chloe when she requested them of him.

'Thee has not yet been through sufficient time shifts to know how the privations can affect the weak in character. I deem it wisest to keep our stores close guarded.'

'What would happen if you didn't make it back to the cave . . .'

'Ah, but, my dear Douglas, I always shall!'

Chloe had seen no point in explaining to a man of Douglas's time the true significance of the keys. She had received her first set from her father's hand at the age of fifteen and proved herself a careful chatelaine despite the inefficient, slovenly colonial indentured servants. How well that training had stood her through these parlous times.

She selected the heavy key that Douglas had scoffingly forged and slipped it into the heavy lock, hearing the tumblers snick. She supposed that Douglas was much in her thoughts because she was, as ever, grateful for his doors, bolts, locks, and keys. If only the man had been as honest in his dealings as he had been as an artisan.

Chloe turned on the diffuse-lamp, noting that its illumination was as bright as ever, and measured meal into the pannikin. She selected herbs from their bags, her fingers pausing over the satisfactory plumpness. Sufficient unto the day! Especially when the demands on her supplies would soon be reduced.

She turned off the lamp, closing and locking the grille behind her. Edward had returned from his first trip to the brook with the big kettle. One glance at Chloe and he made haste to get on with his chore. Dorcas had already set the sheet on the fire for the johnnycake, so Chloe handed her the supplies silently.

Dorcas was carefully mixing water into the meal under Chloe's watchful eye when they both heard the hubble-bubble of excited voices. Michael burst into view, Destry running close behind him.

'The rifle, Chloe! The rifle, quickly! A bear has treed Rayda!'

'A bear?'

'I'd've thought you'd've heard her yelling all the way up here,' Michael gasped out. 'The rifle!'

Chloe hesitated. The winter-thin bear and his mangy coat were really not worth the powder and shot.

'Or did you know there was a bear when you sent Rayda for berries?'

'I picked there myself a scant hour ago!' Chloe pointed contemptuously at the full pail.

'That tree ain't very big nor strong,' Destry added, having caught enough breath to add his argument to Michael's.

Chloe saw Dorcas watching her, hands suspended over the meal bowl. She recognized the anger in Michael's eyes and the anxiety in Destry's. She mustn't seem as if she was eager to be rid of Rayda or she would experience difficulty in discarding any of them at the appropriate moment.

Chloe moved swiftly then, selecting the proper key as she made her way to the gun case. She handed Michael the heaviest of the rifles and two rounds of shot. He gestured impatiently for her to give him more.

'Let thy vaunted skill make the first shot count. The noise will likely frighten the creature away.'

Michael gave her a searing look before he turned and pelted out of the cave, Destry behind him. Chloe followed more slowly to the entrance and saw the underbrush flipping back into place after their passage. She sighed with exasperation. That wretched bear! There'd be far too little work got out of any of them today. Perdition take Rayda! Chloe saw that she'd have to contrive cunningly to get the woman out of the cave at all after this 'unnerving' experience. All the more reason to see the last of the overtimid Rayda.

Chloe retraced her steps, pausing to be sure Dorcas was busy, the only honest worker of the lot. Both women heard the resounding echo of a shot. Dorcas's hand quickened in the meal, anticipating meat for her stewpot.

'I shouldn't count too heavily on Michael's ability, Dorcas.' And her skepticism was punctuated by the second shot.

As she waited to learn the outcome, Chloe turned all the sleeping bags, furs, and blankets on their branches. Malenda led the way, holding back branches as Michael staggered under the burden of a limp Rayda.

'She fainted,' Michael said as he laid the unconscious woman down by the fire. 'She managed to stay conscious and hang on to the branches until I shot the bear.' His eyes met Chloe's in mutually felt contempt.

'Two shots?'

'It did take two. Tough old bugger,' said Michael. 'Fensu and Destry are dressing the carcass.' He unslung the rifle and extended it to Chloe.

'The rifle must now be cleaned,' Chloe said, gesturing Michael to that task as she bent to examine Rayda.

Dorcas was already beside the woman, sponging away blood.

'Nothing deep. Nothing to swoon over,' said Dorcas.

'She's had a terrible shock,' murmured Malenda.

Dorcas made one of her noncommittal sounds.

'Thee surely sustained the same shock, I think,' Chloe remarked dryly as she began to smooth comfrey paste into the scratches. Blood drops formed on the deeper punctures but most of the gore was due to shallow scratches where Rayda had scrambled through briars and up the tree.

'The bear didn't come straight *at* me,' Malenda said in Rayda's defense.

'Did thee manage to pick any berries before this tragic occurrence?'

'Yes, we did,' and then Malenda faltered, looking warily at Chloe.

'Then thee may return to that labor and be sure to return also with Rayda's pail as well. Full, if at all possible. There are several more hours of daylight.'

'Oh, you're impossible, Chloe!'

'If I truly were, then all this,' and Chloe's sweeping gesture included the cave, its shelter and supplies, 'would have been unavailable in Rayda's hour of crisis.' Rayda groaned. 'It will take Fensu and Destry time to dress the bear carcass. You will have their company in the berry patch. Gooseberries will go well with bear stew. Away with thee now!'

In fact, the gooseberries and johnnycake were the better parts of the evening meal. The bear had broken its winter's fast on a diet of fish, and its stringy meat was so tainted by that flavor that even Dorcas's fine hand with seasoning could not disguise the taste. Rayda, her hands bandaged and her legs smeared with comfrey paste, moaned from her sleeping bag that she couldn't possibly eat the flesh of the beast that had nearly killed her. A solicitous Malenda fed her pieces of the johnnycake and ripe berries. Fensu was the only one who had eaten heartily of the stew, smacking his lips with a courtesy that Chloe would have preferred he did not practice.

When the men set to scraping the bear hide, Chloe settled herself on her stool outside the cave with the latest patchwork. Sewing did much to tranquilize her after the day's frustrations. Nor did she relish sitting inside on such a bright evening, particularly if she had to listen to Rayda's moans and Malenda's compassionate chirpings.

The current quilt Chloe was working in the Flock of Geese pattern, its patches cut from garments of former occupants of the cave. She had noticed over the years that blues, grays, and browns were the predominant shades of the rural past, while the vivid lighter primaries and curious virulent pastels seemed rampant in most city-futures. Chloe began a new square; the last of Issaro's red tunic triangles and Douglas's plaid patterned shirt were offset by Fanel's gray shirt. The gray was the finer material, to be sure, but of a similar weight to Douglas's and Issaro's. She did have to take care to match textures. She would have preferred good stout linsey-woolsey or calcicoes, for the artificial fabrics of the futures puckered and stretched, thus ruining the look of the finished quilt. Still, one had to make do with whatever was to hand. No one complained about the look of the patchworks when they warmed a body during the intense and bitter cold of time storms.

They had been so lucky these past five shifts, like the goose triangles, all headed in the same direction – spring. The gray intervals had alternated between intense heat and dreadful cold.

Chloe set the final stitch into the square, but now she stopped, looking intently at the pattern, remembering with a sudden clarity the people whose discarded garments had been set to this new purpose. And she discerned an astonishing *order* in that purpose. There was, in truth, a pattern to the time shifts that had nothing to do with the varying intervals of storm and lull: it had to do with having *been* at each point, of remembering *when* it had been in past or future. She didn't need Issaro's calculations: all she had ever needed was her own recollections, placed in an orderly fashion, like the patchwork pieces, to see the pattern of shifts.

Suppressing her internal excitement, Chloe began to sort through the completed squares, identifying the fabrics, the people who had worn then, the cultures that had produced them. Time was like an enormous circular well. The planet Earth was a plumb weight suspended from a long cord, jerked up and down the well, hitting first one side of the well and then another, jounced up and down by the irresponsible hand that had initiated the time fracture. She was mixing her similes and metaphors but she knew what she meant. And she knew where she was.

First light tomorrow, she could in all conscience send Michael, Destry, and Fensu on a trip down the south river. They would find, she was now certain, a small but not primitive settlement where the south river joined the mightier torrent that flowed southeast to the sea. She would give Michael sufficient ammunition to reassure him. He'd never know. In this time there were few animals left: that poor specimen of a bear proved that to her. There would, however, be those skilled in medical treatments and she could, in conscience, dispatch Rayda to them, once Michael and Destry had returned. She rather thought that Fensu would find this time to his liking and disappear. Savage the man was, but not without cunning and perception. Malenda would go with Rayda. That would seem eminently logical and not the least bit unnatural in Chloe. Michael and Destry could stay on if they behaved but she could forgo their company. Edward might stay on another shift or two. Physically he had limited usefulness but his mind was sharp and she had not yet learned all the wisdom he had spent so much time storing in his head. Dorcas could abide. The babe would not be born for another four months. Chloe smoothed the next patch with careful fingers. The next time shift would bring them closer to Dorcas's original time. The woman would be more content there and undoubtedly find another husband.

Well pleased with these dispositions, Chloe sorted through the patches in her basket, four colors that would combine well in the next Flock of Geese square!

THE GREATEST LOVE

written in 1956

'You certainly don't live up to your name, Dr Craft,' Lousie Baxter said, acidly emphasizing my name. 'I trust your degree is from a legitimate medical college. Or was it the mail-order variety?'

I didn't dignify the taunt with a reply. Being a young woman, I held my Cornell Medical School diploma too valuable to debase it in argument with a psychotic.

She continued in the sweetly acerbic voice that must have made her subordinates cringe, 'In the fashion industry, you quickly learn how to tell the "looker" from the "putter." It's very easy to classify your sort.'

I refrained from saying that her sort – Cold Calculating Female posing as Concerned Mother – was just as easy for me to classify. Her motive for this interview with her daughter's obstetrician was not only specious but despicable. Her opening remark of surprise that I was a woman had set the tone of insults for the past fifteen minutes.

'I have told you the exact truth, Mrs Baxter. The pregnancy is proceeding normally and satisfactorily. You may interpret the facts any way you see fit.' I was hoping to wind up this distasteful interview quickly. 'In another five months, the truth will out.'

Her exclamation of disgust at my pun was no more than I'd expected. 'And you have the gall to set yourself up against the best gynecologists of Harkness Pavilion?'

'It's not difficult to keep abreast of improved techniques in uterine surgery,' I said calmly.

'Ha! Quack!'

I suppressed my own anger at her insult by observing that her anger brought out all the age-lines in her face despite her artful makeup.

'I checked with Harkness before I came here,' she said, trying to overwhelm me with her research. 'There are no new techniques which could correct a bicornuate womb!'

'So?'

'So, don't try to con me, you charlatan,' and the elegant accent faltered into a flat midwestern twang. 'My daughter can't carry to term. And you know it!'

'I'll remind you of that in another five months, Mrs Baxter.' I rose to indicate that the interview was at an end.

'Ach! You women's libbers are all alike! Setting yourselves up above the best men in the country on every count!'

Although I'm not an ardent feminist, such egregious remarks are likely to change my mind, particularly when thrown in without relevance and more for spite than for sense.

'I fail to see what Women's Liberation has to do with your daughter, who is so obviously anxious to fulfill woman's basic role.'

The angry color now suffused Louse Baxter's well-preserved face down to the collar of her ultrasmart man-tailored suit. She rose majestically to her feet.

'I'll have you indicted for malpractice, you quack!' She had control of her voice again and deliberately packed all the psychotic venom she could into her threats. 'I'll sue you within an inch of your life if Cecily's sanity is threatened by your callous stupidity.'

At that point the door opened to admit Esther, my office nurse, in her most aggressive attitude.

'If Mrs Baxter is quite finished, Doctor,' she said, stressing the title just enough to irritate the woman further, 'your next patient is waiting.'

'Of all the—'

'This way, Mrs Baxter,' Esther said firmly as she shepherded the angry woman toward the door.

Mrs Baxter stalked out, slamming the street door so hard I winced, waiting for the glass to come shattering down.

'How did that virago ever produce a sweet girl like Cecily?' I mused.

'I assume that Cecily was conceived in the normal manner,' said Esther.

I sat down wearily. I'd been going since four-thirty a.m. and I didn't need a distasteful interview with Baxter's sort at five p.m. 'And I assume that you heard everything on the intercom?'

'For some parts, I didn't need amplification,' said my faithful office nurse at her drollest. 'Since this affair started, I don't dare leave the intercom hook up. Someone's got to keep your best interests at heart.'

I smiled at her ruefully. 'It'll be worth it—'

'You keep telling yourself—'

'—to see that girl get a baby.'

'Not to mention the kudos accruing to one Dr Allison S. Craft, OB-GYN?'

I gave her a quelling look, which she blithely ignored. 'Well,' I said, somewhat deflated, 'there must be something more to life than babies who insist on predawn entrances.'

'Have a few yourself, then,' Esther suggested with a snort, then flipped my coat off the hook and gestured for me to take off the office whites. 'I'm closing up and I'm turning you out, Doctor.'

I went.

I had a lonely restaurant supper, though Elsie, who ran the place, tried to cheer me up. Once I got home, I couldn't settle down. I wanted someone to talk to. All right, someone to gripe to. Sometimes, like now, I regretted my bachelor-girl status. Even if I had had a man in mind, I really couldn't see much family life, the kind I wanted to enjoy, until I had a large enough practice to bring in an associate. On a twenty-four-hour off-and-on schedule that such an arrangement provided, I could hardly see marriage. Not now. Especially not now.

I poured myself a drink for its medicinal value and sat on my back porch in the late spring twilight.

So – Louise Baxter would sue me if her daughter miscarried. I wondered if she'd sue me if her daughter didn't. I'd bet a thousand bucks, and my already jeopardized professional standing, that the impeccable, youthful-looking Louise Baxter was shriveling from the mere thoughts of being made a 'grandmother.' Maybe it would affect her business reputation – or crack the secret of her actual age. Could she be fighting retirement? I laughed to myself at the whimsy. Cecily Baxter Kellogg was twenty-seven, and no way was Louise Baxter in her sixties.

However, I had told Mrs Baxter the truth, the exact truth: the pregnancy *was* well started, and the condition of the mother *was* excellent, and everything pointed to a full-term, living child.

But I hadn't told the whole truth, for Cecily Baxter Kellogg was not carrying her own child.

Another medical 'impossibility' trembled on the brink of the possible. A man may have no greater love than to lay down his life for a friend, but it's a far, far greater love that causes one woman to carry another's baby: a baby with whom she has nothing, absolutely nothing, in common, except nine months of intimacy. I amended that: this baby would have a relationship, for its proxy mother was its paternal aunt.

The memory of the extraordinary beginning of this great experiment was as vivid to me as the afternoon's interview with Mrs Baxter. And far more heartwarming.

It was almost a year ago to this day that my appointment schedule had indicated a 2.30 patient named Miss Patricia Kellogg. Esther had underscored the 'Miss' with red and also the abbreviation 'p.n.' for prenatal. I was known to be sympathetic to unwed mothers and had performed a great many abortions – legally, too.

There was nothing abashed about Patricia Kellogg as she walked confidently into my office, carrying a briefcase.

'I'd better explain, Dr Craft, that I am not yet pregnant. I want to be.'

'Then you need a premarital examination for conception?'

'I'm not contemplating marriage.'

'That . . . ah . . . used to be the usual prelude to pregnancy.'

She smiled and then casually said, 'Actually, I wish to have my brother's child.'

'That sort of thing is frowned on by the Bible, you know,' I replied with, I thought, great equanimity. 'Besides presenting rather drastic genetic risks. I'd suggest you consult a psychologist, not an obstetrician.'

Again that smile, tinged with mischief now. 'I wish to have the child of my brother *and* his wife!'

'Ah, that hasn't been done.'

She patted the briefcase. 'On a human.'

'Oh, I assume you've read up on those experiments with sheep and cows. They're all very well, Miss Kellogg, but obstetrically it's not the same thing. The difficulties involved . . .'

'As nearly as I can ascertain, the real difficulty involved is *doing* it.'

I rose to sit on the edge of the desk. Miss Kellogg was exactly my height seated, and I needed the difference in levels. Scarcely an unattractive woman, Patricia Kellogg would be classified by men as 'wholesome,' 'girl-next-door,' rather than the sexy bird their dreams featured. She was also not at all the type to make the preposterous statements and request she had. Recently, however, I had come to appreciate that the most unlikely women would stand up and vigorously demand their civil and human rights.

Miss Kellogg was one to keep you off balance, for as she began doling out the contents of her briefcase, she explained that her sister-in-law had a bicorunuate uterus. During my internship in Cornell Medical, I had encountered such a condition. The uterus develops imperfectly, with fertile ovaries but double Fallopian tubes. The victim conceives easily enough but usually aborts within six weeks. A full-term pregnancy would be a miracle. I glanced through the clinical reports from prominent New York and Michigan hospitals, bearing out Miss Kellogg's statements and detailing five separate spontaneous abortions.

'The last time, Cecily carried to three months before aborting,' Pat Kellogg said. 'She nearly lost her mind with grief.

'You see, she was an only child. All her girlhood she'd dreamed of having a large family. Her mother is a very successful businesswoman, and I'd say that Cecily was a mistake as far as Louise Baxter is concerned. I remember how radiantly happy Cecily and Peter, my brother, were when she started her first pregnancy six years ago. And how undaunted she was after the first miss. You've no idea how she's suffered since. I'm sorry; maybe you do, being a woman.'

I nodded, but it was obvious to me, from the intensity of her expression, that she had empathized deeply with the sister-in-law's disappointments.

'To have a child has become an obsession with her.'

'Why not adoption?'

'My brother was blinded in the Vietnam War.'

'Yes, I see.' Now that abortions were legal, there were fewer babies to be adopted, and consequently the handicapped parent was a very poor second choice.

'Children mean a lot to Peter, too. There were just two of us: our mother died at our births. Peter and I are twins, you see. But Cecily has magnified her inability all out of proportion, especially because of Peter's blindness. She feels that . . .'

'I do understand the situation,' I said sympathetically as she faltered for adequate words.

'Since I got this idea,' she went on more briskly, 'I've been keeping very careful charts on my temperature and menstrual cycle,' and she thrust sheets at me. 'I've got Cecily's for the past six years. I stole them. She's always kept them up to date.' She gave me an unrepentant grin. 'We're just two days apart.'

I smiled at that. 'If matching estrous cycles were the only problem involved . . .'

'I *know* there're many, many problems, but there is so much at stake. Really, Dr Craft, I fear for Cecily's sanity. Oh, no, I haven't breathed a word of this to Peter or Cece . . .'

'I should hope not. I'm even wondering why you're mentioning it to me.'

'Chuck Henderson said you'd be interested.'

No name was less expected.

'Where did you meet Dr Henderson?' I asked, with far more calm than I felt.

'I've been following the medical journals, and I read an article he wrote on research to correct immature uteruses

. . . uteri? . . . and new methods to correct certain tendencies to abort.'

I'd read the same article, written with Chuck's usual meticulous care, complete with diagrams and graphic photos of uterine operations. Not the usual reading matter for a young woman.

'Well, then, why come to me?'

'Dr Henderson said that he hadn't done any research on implantation, but he knew someone who was interested in exogenesis and who lived right in my own town. He said there was no reason for me to traipse all the way to New York to find the brave soul I needed, and he told me to ask you how the cats were doing.' She looked inquiringly at me.

The name, the question, brought back memories I had been blocking for nine years: memories (I tried to convice myself again) which were the usual sophomoric enthusiasms and dreams of changing mediocre worlds into better ones with the expert flip of a miracle scalpel.

Chuck Henderson had helped me catch the cats I had used for my early attempts at exogenesis. Cats were easy to acquire in Ithaca and a lot easier to explain to an apartment superintendent than cows or sheep. I had had, I thought, good success in my early experiments, but the outcome was thwarted by some antivivisectionists who were convinced that I was using the cats for cruel, devious pranks, and the two females that I thought I had impregnated disappeared forever beyond my control. Chuck had been a real pal throughout the stages of my doomed research, all the while caustically reminding me that good old-fashioned methods of impregnation did not arouse vivisectionists.

'He said some pretty glowing things about you, Dr Craft, and by the time he finished talking, I *knew* you were the one person who would help me.'

'I'm obliged to him.'

'You should be,' she replied with equal dryness. 'He has the highest opinion of you as a physician and as . . . as a person.'

'Flattery will get you nowhere,' I said evasively and turned toward the window, aware of a variety of conflicting emotions.

'Will you at least examine our medical records?' she asked softly after respecting my silence for a long moment. 'I beg you to believe my sincerity when I say that I will do anything . . . painful, tedious, disagreeable . . . anything to provide my brother and sister-in-law with a child of their own flesh and blood.'

She might be right, I was thinking, when she said the real difficulty was in *doing* it. Here was the magnificent opportunity I'd once yearned for, thrust at me on an afternoon as dull as my predictable future. The adventurousness, the enthusiasm of that sophomore could now be combined with the maturity and experience of the practicing physician. I'd be a fool not to try: to be content with the unwonderful.

'From the moment you stepped into this room,' I said slowly to the waiting girl, 'I've had no thought of questioning either your sincerity or your perseverance, Miss Kellogg.'

'You'll do it?' And she began to blush suddenly and irrelevantly.

'Would you mind not boxing me into a corner quite that quickly?'

She laughed by way of apology.

'Let's say, Miss Kellogg, that I will examine the problem in the light of present-day techniques. Which have only been partially successful, mind, on animals.'

She rose and stretched out her hand to me. I took it and held it briefly, hoping only to express sympathy and respect, not a binding agreement.

'I haven't said yes,' I reminded her, alarmed by the look of triumph in her eyes.

'No, but I'm damned sure you will, once you've read all this.' And she transferred half a dozen Department of Agriculture pamphlets and other miscellaneous printed documents from her briefcase to my desk. At the door, she turned back, looking contrite.

'I'm sorry about the shocking phraseology I used to attract your attention. I mean, about wanting my brother's child.'

I had to laugh. 'There's a bit of the showman in the most sedate of us. I'll call you in a few days.'

'Grand! I won't call you,' and with a warm smile she left.

I heard the street door close, and then Esther had whisked in, staring at me as if I'd changed sex or something. It was obvious that she'd had the intercom key up again.

'You're crazy if you do it, Allison,' she said, her large brown eyes very wide.

'I quite agree with you, Esther.'

'Of course, you're crazy if you don't at least *try*,' she said, less vehemently, and with a breathiness of enthusiasm that surprised me in my levelheaded nurse.

'I quite agree with you.'

'Oh, be quiet, Allison Craft. Have you the least idea of the problems you're going to encounter, or are that Nobel Prize and the AMA citation already blinding you to reality? Women aren't cats . . . at least not gynecologically.'

'Well, in a brief spontaneous thesis or two, I'd say the main problem would be . . .'

'Be practical, not medical,' she snapped.

Esther was herself again. She keeps me out of debt, weasels the income tax down to the last fraction permissible, gets my bills paid on time, copes with hysterical primiparas, new fathers, and doting grand-parents, and she's a damned good R.N., too.

'And what are *your* visible monkey wrenches?' I asked her.

She held up her left hand and counted by the fingers. 'Have you considered the moral issue if someone finds out she's giving birth to her brother's child?'

'A different hospital, in another town or state.'

'Great time traveling was had by all. Or had you planned to transfer the fertilized egg right here in the cottage hospital before God and his little brother?'

'That's easy to wangle. At night. On an emergency basis. Everyone knows Cecily Kellogg keeps aborting, and keeps trying.'

I couldn't let Esther see that she was making me find answers to contingencies I hadn't got around to consider-ing yet. I was still trying to figure out how to flush the fertilized ovum from the womb. Fortunately, Esther doesn't second-guess me as much as she believes she does.

'You have flipped your ever-loving wig,' she said, exhibiting an appreciation for current slang that I hadn't known she possessed, 'but I'm awfully glad it's the Kelloggs.'

'You know them?' I asked, mildly surprised.

'And so you do,' she replied, exasperated. 'I thought that's why you even considered such a sugar-mad scheme. Peter Kellogg? Professor Peter Kellogg?'

Recognition came: I certainly did know Peter Kellogg. The shock technique Patricia had employed had suc-ceeded in keeping me from associating the name with a face or character. I had heard the campus chatter about Peter Kellogg's brilliant dissertations on English poets of the eighteenth century, and I'd enjoyed his own exquisite verse. As with another notable poet, blindness was only a physical condition, not necessarily a limitation, because

Peter Kellogg refused to consider sightlessness a handicap. Although I had never met the man, he and his German shepherd, Wizard, were campus familiars. I had often seen the tall dogged figure as he strode the town streets or college paths. It now occurred to me that I had also seen his wife, Cecily, walking beside him. The picture of the tall couple I had all but decided to help, heaven helping me, was a very pleasurable one in my mind's eye, and I felt a surge of altruistic euphoria. Yes, I could appreciate why the sister was so determined that they should have a child. Surely here was a man who deserved progeny, if only a minor part of his brilliance could be passed along. A thought flitted through my head, causing me a spasm of mirth.

'Well?' demanded Esther, who hates missing a joke.

'The Catholic Church won't like it at all, at all.'

'Like what?'

'Usurping the prerogatives of one of the Trinity.'

'Okay, Doctor, what's the first step?'

In the following weeks, I should have seen the psychologist, not Patricia Kellogg. But, as Esther became too fond of remarking, I was so happy butting my stone wall. Except I was certain I'd found the keystone. I augmented the pamphlets and treatises left me by Pat Kellogg with as much material as I could find on all the allied fields – endocrinology, hormones, uterine surgical techniques – and a very interesting study about successful exogenesis in rabbits.

I also went kitty-catching again, having exhumed the notes I'd made on my ill-fated college experiment. Coincident with the shadows of that disappointment was the mocking face of Chuck Henderson. I exorcised that ghost when I successfully transplanted the fertilized ova from a white pedigreed Angora to as nondescript a tabby as I could find. The other three attempts didn't fertilize properly, so I'll pass them without mention. As soon as I was assured the tabby's pregnancy was well advanced, I did a Caesarian and checked the fetuses. They were unarguably those of the Angora, and all five were perfectly formed.

There are, however, more than minor differences between the procreative apparatus of the feline and that of the human female, so that my experiments were merely reruns that proved exogenesis was possible in cats. The successful exogenetic births of sheep and cows in Texas were encouraging, but in the final analysis only added two more species in which this delicate interference with normal conception and pregnancy was possible. One minor physiological variation between humans and cows or sheep was very significant for my purposes: In human females the length of the oviducts before they unite to form the corpus uteri is short, leaving less time and space to catch the fertilized egg before it reaches the endometrium and undergoes impregnation there: at which point there can be no hope of transplantation.

This lack of time and space would prove one of the real barriers to success. It takes approximately twenty-four hours for the fertilized ova to drop from the ovaries through the Fallopian tubes into the suitably stimulated endometrium of the uterus. The sticky bit would be to catch one of Cecily's fertilized ova before it could reach her uterus and put the captured ovum into the equally stimulated uterus of her sister-in-law.

The fertile ova of cows, sheep, and cats had been relatively easy to flush out. To overcome the disadvantage in the human, I planned to use one of the new gossamer-fine plastic films, in the form of a fish-trap-like contrivance (which nearly drove me crazy to fashion). This would fit at the end of the Fallopian tubes and, I hoped, would catch the fertilized ovum. By surgically removing the bag, I could empty its contents into the other womb, unscientifically cross my fingers, and hope!

With the use of a new estrogen compound, it would be relatively simple to synchronize the estrous cycles of the two women. Standard dilation and curettage on both uteri would prepare the areas for the best possible results and allow me to place the plastic film at the end of Cecily's tubes. The first D&Cs could be legitimately performed without questions asked. The second and subsequent dilations would, as Esther had remarked, require a little more doing, since both girls would have to be in the same room, under anesthesia, at the same time. This meant the connivance of an amenable anesthsiologist as well as Esther and myself.

That's how Chuck Henderson got to sneak into the act. He was Pat's suggestion, not mine. He already knew of the Plan, she argued. He would be acceptable as an emergency anesthetist at those times when I had to dispense with the regular man. (That also took finagling, but Esther managed it: she never would tell me how.) The moment we contacted Chuck, he was delighted: too delighted, it seemed to me; as if he'd been waiting – breathlessly – to be asked. I was of several minds about including him again, mostly for my own peace of mind, but all reasonable arguments led to his active participation.

The day that Pat and I were able to approach the Kelloggs with a plan of action will remain one of the most stirring memories of my life. I had called Pat, some two and a half weeks after her first visit to me, to say that I had researched sufficiently to approach the principals. I had already confirmed to her my willingness to try. I stressed the 'try.'

Pat arranged an evening meeting, and we arrived together at the Kelloggs' apartment, myself laden with a heavy briefcase containing twice as much material as Pat had given me. Pat was so nervous that I wondered if she feared that she might be unable to persuade the other two members of the cast to go through with the attempt.

I had to pass an entrance exam myself, executed by Wizard, Peter Kellogg's guide dog, an exceedingly beautiful tan and black specimen with beauty marks at the corners of his intelligent eyes. He stood at the door, sniffed the hand I judiciously extended, gave a sneeze as Pat told him I was a friend, and then retired to lie under the dining room table. I was awed by the inherent power in the apparently docile beast. I was glad I was considered a friend by that 125-pound fellow.

Peter Kellogg had risen as Pat drew me into the room, and Peter introduced me to his tall, too slender brunette wife.

We put off the important announcement with some chitchat, my appreciative congratulations on his latest verses in *The New Yorker*, our attempts to find mutual acquaintances. Finally, unable to endure further inanities, Pat blurted out:

'How would you like to be parents?'

Even the dog came alert in the sudden pulsing silence.

'Pat . . .' began Peter in gentle admonishment, but Cecily overrode him with a sharp, nearly hysterical 'How?'

'Exogenesis,' Pat said, expelling the word on a breath.

Peter and Cecily looked at me. I include Peter, because he never did fail to turn his lifeless eyes in the direction of the speaker, a habit most blind people never acquire but one that is very reassuring to the sighted. Peter always tried to avoid embarrassing people.

'I take it that you have arrived at some method of accomplishing exogenesis, Doctor?' Peter asked.

'Dr Craft *believes* it can be done.' Pat was careful, as I'd insisted she should be, not to present the plan as an established procedure. 'There are problems,' she said, in a masterpiece of understatement; 'much to be discussed . . .'

'Who's the other mother?' asked Cecily, jumping a giant step ahead.

Peter turned unerringly toward his sister. At Cecily's gasping sob, Wizard gave a low whine. Peter quietly reassured him.

'I had a suspicion you'd been up to something, Pat,' he said dryly. 'I hardly anticipated something as momentous as this. Smacks of the incestuous, I'd say, doesn't it, Doctor?'

'Peter! How can you even mention such a thing in connection with your sister after she's suggested this . . . incredible sacrifice?' Cecily's voice quavered, partly from outrage, partly from tears.

'What else can it be called when your own sister proposes to have your child . . .' he said, smiling slightly as he patted his wife's hand.

My respect for Peter Kellogg's perception rose several notches. He had unerringly touched one of the difficulties, taken it out, laughed at it and let it be put in its place.

'It'll by *my* child,' Cecily said fervently. The terrible child-hunger in her face vividly confirmed all that Pat had told me about Cecily's obsession for a child of her own conception. I had seen that look before, in other eyes, and had been unable to bring hope. What if I could bring hope now? And what would happen to Cecily if we failed?

'It won't, of course, draw anything but prenatal nourishment from its host-mother,' I said, resorting to the clinical to hide my emotions. 'That is – and I cannot stress this strongly enough, Mrs Kellogg – *if* transplantation is possible. You do realize that's a very big if.'

Cecily gave a sigh and then smiled impishly at me. 'I know, Dr Craft. I must not permit myself to hope. But don't you see, hope is so vital an ingredient.'

I saw Peter's fingers tighten around her hand, and then he turned to me. 'What are the chances?'

'Would you believe one out of four cats?' I couldn't bear the tautness of Cecily's face. 'Actually, it works out four to one in rabbits, and with livestock experiments in Texas, a ninety-five percent success with cows and sheep.'

'Baaaaa,' said Cecily, and again she grinned impishly to show that she was in complete control of herself.

'I've prepared some diagrams, and I've a plan of action to propose,' I said, and dug into the bulging briefcase.

Several hours later, we had discussed procedure, probabilities, problems from as many angles as four minds could find. I had explained all the relevant medical procedures, some of which seemed brutal, in the apartment of the prospective parents. My eyes were drawn again and again, unwillingly, to Cecily's oval, delicately flushed face. Despite her continued lightness of word and expression, the hope rekindled was heartbreakingly apparent.

Pat moved to sit beside her brother on the couch. As Peter relied on the verbal descriptions, he leaned back so that the two women could crowd over the diagrams and charts spread over the coffee table. Occasionally he seized his wife's hand to calm her; once, as I explained Pat's role, his other hand gripped his sister's shoulder so tightly that she winced a little. His immense patience and incredible perception made him a good focal point for me, and it was easier to speak to his calm, attentive face than to Cecily's.

He and his wife must have already examined the possibility of exogenesis, or had a superior knowledge of biology, for they showed their familiarity with the principles involved.

'Yes, I can see why cats – maybe; sheep and cows, yes.

Let's hope there's more of the bovine in you, darling, than the feline,' Peter said, summing up.

'Ha! We'll just blanket the target areas until we succeed. And try and try and try,' said Cecily staunchly. 'I'm more than willing.'

'And that, my darling, is exactly what we have to guard against in you.'

'Can you endure the disappointments we're likely to encounter, Cecily?' I asked her bluntly. 'In view of your previous medical history,' and they all knew I meant psychological, 'you will have the hardest task.'

'Trust the men to have the easy one,' said Cecily, lightly giving a mock angry buffet to Peter's arm.

'That's why we're the superior sex,' he said, laughing and pretending to duck from expected blows.

'Even if transplantation is successful,' I went on, 'you must restrain yourself until such time as you actually hold the child . . .'

'My child . . .'

'In your arms.'

'Hey, don't hold your breath,' Pat piped up, for that was what Cecily was doing. She laughed sheepishly with the rest of us.

I left Pat with them after making arrangements with Cecily to come to my office for a preliminary pelvic. Then I'd schedule the initial D&Cs for both women.

The warmth of the relationship among the three people, along with Pat's extraordinary willingness to attempt this improbability, warmed me all my cold way home in the frigid car. I still didn't quite fathom myself caught up in an event as momentous as this, my abandoned sophomoric dream, might be. No matter: my routine existence took on a hidden relish as I became drawn closer and closer to the three amazing people. Cecily's fervent, oft-repeated 'We will! We must!' became my credo, too.

Those memories were as strong and vivid as the acid interview with Cecily's fashion-plate mother. Night had fallen now, and my drink was stale. I had another one, stiffer, for courage.

The preliminary steps had gone without a hitch: by a miracle I didn't wish – yet – to subject to too much scientific dissection, the successful transplantation of the fertilized ovum had been accomplished by the third attempt. I had fervently believed that the little plastic film trap would be superior to any form of flushing, but if it hadn't done the trick the third time, I would've been forced by Chuck's arguments to try flushing. Three times he had made the trip across the state to act as anesthetist at odd early hours in our cottage hospital.

'To think I'm being dictated to by a thermometer's variations,' he'd growl.

We were lucky, too, in that there were no questions in the minds of the hospital administration. Cecily Kellogg had had three spontaneous abortions within those walls: if she was willing to keep trying to carry to term, the hospital couldn't care less – so long as her bills were paid. Pat showed up in the record as a blood donor. Chuck and I would take Pat home each time directly she came out of the anesthesia to preserve the fiction, while Cecily rested on in the ward. At Chuck's insistence, we both kept complete, chronological records of our procedures, and, for added veracity, punched them in on the staff time clock.

'Remember,' he cautioned me more than once, 'we will definitely not be able, or want, to keep this a secret. Let's just hope there's no premature slipup.'

I recall groaning at this choice of phrase.

'Sorry about that, Ali. I just shudder to think of the holy medical hell that's going to break loose when this gets out.'

'We're not doing anything illegal.'

He gave me a patient, forbearing look. 'No, we're not, Allison, love. But we are doing something that hasn't been done before, and that is always suspect. I grant you the techniques and theories are pretty well known and understood, but no . . . one . . . has . . . done . . . it on, of all sanctities, the human body.' He reverently folded his hands and assumed a pious attitude for a split second. 'May I remind you that exogenesis smacks marvelously of the blasphemous?'

'I never considered you to be particularly religious, Chuck.'

'Heaven forbid!' He was in one of those contrary moods, which could be allowed a man who'd worked a solid day, driven speedily for 250 miles of wearing highway, assisted at some very tricky surgery, and, at three-thirty in the morning, had to face a return trip of 250 miles. 'You're no longer naive, Ali, but for God's sake just equate the State Senate debates on legalized abortion with what we're doing, and think what will fall on our humbled heads.'

'Ah, but we're giving life, not taking it.'

'A distinction, but you've got asses who balk at heart massage, resuscitation; you know the furor heart and organ transplants made, to save lives.'

'I'm thinking of the hundreds of women who are dying to have kids, who could, by proxy, if this works.'

'Great! Great! I'm almost glad you've retained your altruism after – how many years in a small town?' He was disgusted with me. 'At least I'm here to set your feet on solid earth once in a while. Now I must into my iron chariot and wend my homeward way. I left my poor overworked partner with the probability of three to five deliveries, one of them almost certainly bass-ackward. Before he has a spasm, I hope number three of the G.E. takes. Let me know the minute there's any clinical proof.

I will even put you on the short list of those who are permitted to break my slumbers.'

He thumped me a little too soundly on the back and departed with a wicked 'Fare thee well.'

Pat had been a twenty-eight-day regular, almost to the hour, so fifteen days after the third implantation, we held our collective breaths. The next ten days reduced even me to taking tranquilizers. I had to give Cecily the strongest I dared, and I was about to prescribe some for Peter and Wizard. At slightly under four weeks, I gave in and did a pelvic on Pat. The change was definitely apparent. I phoned Chuck. He was in the delivery room, but the nurse promised faithfully to have him call me.

When he rang back, I blurted out the glad news and was taken aback by his total lack of response.

'Sorry, Ali, to sour your big moment,' he said so wearily I could almost picture the slump of his lanky body. 'Perhaps I'm not as irreligious as I thought. Or perhaps it's just because I delivered a hydrocephalic half an hour ago.'

I could sympathize. I'd delivered one as an intern, and it took a long time for me to shake off the shock of that particular abnormality and the illogical sense of guilt I felt, that I had been instrumental in bringing such grief to two perfectly normal, healthy people. Every practicing obstetrician holds his breath as he delivers the child from the womb and unconsciously prays to see the healthy form and condition of a normal baby.

'Maybe we have no right to tamper with conception,' Chuck said bitterly. 'God knows what we might inadvertently have helped to propagate.'

'You know the percentage of spontaneous abortions for damaged or imperfect fetuses . . .'

'Yeah, yeah. I know. But what about damaged cells, blurred chromosomes . . . And for Christ's sake, Ali, how can we be sure that Pete's sperm fertilizes only

Cecily's ovum? I mean, artificial insemination is not as risky as letting those little fellas find their own route up. It could be Pat's that took . . . and then we've got a charming case of consanguinity and a real nasty new batch of genetic problems.'

I couldn't say that I hadn't spent some anxious moments worrying about just that. Now I limited my remarks to reminding him that from what we had on Cecily's records of her previous abortions, the fetuses had been in normal growth, with no sign of abnormalities, at the time of abortion; that it was her peculiar uterine construction that interrupted the pregnancies, and not faulty ova. We'd done chromosome checks on all three: never a sign of blurred or damaged cells. But I couldn't argue with him about the virility of Peter's spermatozoa.

'Chuck, you need a stiff drink.'

'Sorry to be a wet blanket, Ali, but I guess you do know how I feel, and what I worry about.'

'I do. Now get that drink and climb into bed.'

'Damned thing's always cold!'

'A condition you ought to have no trouble remedying, Casanova. What about that dulcet-toned nurse of yours?'

'Dulcet tones, yes, but oh, the face!' He was speaking with more of his usual brashness. 'I'll spin up there and see the little mother myself soon . . . in the role of consultant, of course.' That's what he said, but his laugh put a different interpretation on the words.

After I hung up, I got to wondering if the Big Time Obstetrician might be interested in Guinea Pig Kellogg. But the idea of Chuck Henderson courting a pregnant virgin overrode my sense of proportion, and I only wished that I could call him back and tease him. I didn't, but I did laugh.

After the initial exultation simmered down, things progressed normally, almost boringly, with Pat's proxy pregnancy. I began to appreciate for the first time why some of my patients bemoaned three-quarters of a year of waiting. Nine months was no longer a matter of ten appointments with one fetal heartbeat, but a damn long stretch.

Peter told me one evening that Cecily was in a constant state of anoxia; she came to me for relief from dizzy fits. It was not sympathetic-pregnancy symptoms with Pat: it was pure and simple anoxia. Mutual friends had begun to remark how radiant Cecily was: one armchair psychiatrist pontificated the opinion that she had finally accepted her childlessness. Then she took up knitting. And took up wearing bulky sweaters and fabrics and bought maternity slacks and skirts.

Pat continued her job as a mathematics teacher in the local high school. Our plan for her to have a sudden emergency leave in the spring did not have to be put into action. She carried almost unnoticeably until the end of the school year, when she was a scant six months. The prevailing fashion of blousy dresses came to our aid, so that her thickening waistline and abdominal bulge were fashionably concealed. One or two unkind friends remarked that she was putting on a little weight, to which she blithely replied that she'd lose it in the summer, before Labor Day. Even if Mrs Baxter had seen Pat during her brief explosive visit, the pregnancy was barely discernible. But Cecily, when her mother had phoned her from the railway station, had thickened her middle with carefully folded toweling.

Louise Baxter's violent negative reaction shocked both Peter and Cecily – who had been so happy to tell her mother the good news. When Peter called me to give warning of my impending collision with the reluctant grandmother-to-be, I could hear Cecily sobbing in the background.

There is little point in recounting that explosive

interview from beginning to end. Suffice it to say that Louise Baxter left me with the distinct impression that her daughter's dearest wish was an abomination to her. Her agitation was not for my supposed hoaxing but a genuine – I'll say it – psychotic fear of ultimate success.

I made a mental note to learn more about the woman from either Pat or Peter. The one time Pat had made a mildly derogatory remark about Louise, Cecily had retorted with an angry defense. I'd encountered such misplaced loyalty once before when the mother sweetly dominated her fatherless son into a psychiatric ward in a catatonic state. With Cecily's emotional balance under severe stress already, I didn't like to see her loyalties torn.

Pat's gestation was calculated to end by August 25. No baby is late, but even with the date of conception known, there are possibilities for error. The habits of the Kelloggs suited our needs to keep the birth unremarkable. They always spent their vacation months together, usually traveling, and occasionally, when Peter was working on a book, sequestering themselves in a quite upstate village. We hoped for a punctual delivery so that Pat would be recovered and able to return to school. That would make fewer waves.

Chuck suggested a small town in the Finger Lake district which boasted not only a well-equipped hospital but a chief of staff who had been a classmate of ours: Arnold Avery.

Everything was going splendidly, except that Pat did put on more weight than I liked. I didn't suspect a thing, and I can still kick myself that, for all my experience in the field, I could blithely ignore so obvious a clue. Perhaps it was an unwitting desire to discount Chuck's gloomy misgivings. Still, the fetal position was good, the heartbeat strong, about 150. Pat's condition was excellent, and, if she was heavy, she was a fair-sized girl with a good pelvic arch, and a big baby was not unlikely.

However, what was to be known as the Transplantation Split came into existence early the morning of August 15. I'd managed to blackmail a colleague to cover my practice the last three weeks of August and was actually having a nonworking vacation in the pleasant company of the Kelloggs. So when Pat woke with abdominal contractions, she roused me to time them. They were a businesslike three minutes apart. It's not unheard of for a primipara to deliver quickly, so I hospitalized her and phoned Chuck to get the hell up there.

If he'd driven instead of hiring that damned helicopter, I'd have been all right. I tell myself, and him when he brings the matter up, as he often does, that I wasn't hogging all the glory for myself. He had a right to some.

At any rate, the helicopter set him down on the hospital grounds just as Pat went into second-stage labor, and he assisted me in the delivery room along with the regular nurse. I hadn't been able to wangle Esther in there, but she was more valuable in the waiting room keeping the parents from exploding.

Chuck and I couldn't restrain our shout of triumph as, at 8.02 a.m., I delivered the six-pound, seven-ounce, perfectly normal, bright red daughter of Peter and Cecily Kellogg from the womb of another woman. I brushed aside the nurse who reached for the newborn and made my own breathless examination of her squalling wrinkled person. I left Chuck to deliver the afterbirth and suture the episiotomy.

'Hey, Doc,' Chuck drawled with infuriating irreverence, disrupting my delighted examination, 'you forgot something.'

Half-angry at his aspersions about my competence, I turned to see him delivering the butt end of another girl child, as healthy as her preciptious sister. I stared transfixed as he eased the head through with deft hands and slapped breath into the mite, who weighed in at a scant five pounds, three ounces.

'You didn't tell me about this,' said Chuck, all innocence.

If I'd thought more quickly, I could have told him that I felt he deserved something for all his help.

'I didn't know,' I admitted instead.

'God bless you, but I love an honest woman, Ali. It's such a relief.'

Then he went over the new girl as carefully as I'd done her sister.

I do feel obliged to add to this account that the heartbeats of identical twins are often synchronized. My mistake lay in assuming a single birth and in not taking a precautionary X ray, as I ordinarily did when the mother appeared to gain more weight than normal or was carrying a large fetus.

My oversight is a family joke, but the most felicitous kind for the Kelloggs. The Transplantation Split is now a familiar medical fact: some minute change in temperature (perhaps moving Pat to my house after the implantation) caused the egg to split, yielding twins. It doesn't always occur in exogenetic pregnancies, but the incidence is proportionately higher than with regular pregnancies.

We were hard put to explain our jubilation to the delivery-room nurse. We made sure that Pat had delivered the afterbirth and would rouse satisfactorily from the anesthesia. Then we literally burst into the waiting room, simultaneously yelling:

'It's a girl!'

'No, it's—'

'What?' demanded Esther, irritated.

I remember that Cecily looked as if she were about to faint, but Peter caught on quickly.

'Twins?'

'Ali outdid herself. It's twins!' cried Chuck. 'She delivered your first daughter, a spanking six pounds, seven ounces . . .'

'And I gave Chuck the honour of ushering your second daughter into the world.'

'A very dainty miss at five pounds, three ounces. As healthy a pair as any parents could wish.'

'Pat's all right?' asked Cecily, tears streaming down her cheeks.

'Right as rain.'

'When can we see the children?' asked Peter.

I know I stopped talking and stared at Peter, stunned with the sad realization that he would never see his children, and wishing that another miracle would occur for him.

Chuck covered my gaffe. 'They'll be in the nursery by now. Go see the modern product of a virgin birth.'

'Dr Henderson, you ought to be ashamed of yourself,' said Esther, but she wasn't really angry and was far too eager to see the twins to argue with him.

Champagne is not recommended by any dietitian to break a night's fast, but we were all back at the vacation cottage, getting pleasantly polluted with toasts to Pat, the parents, Esther, ourselves, never for a minute suspecting that the hardest part was just beginning. Not even when the phone rang.

Esther, being nearest, answered it. I just happened to be looking in her direction, so I saw the abrupt change in her expression and realized that something was wrong. My first thought was for the children, then for Pat. Was she hemorrhaging . . . ?

Esther only listened, openmouthed and sheet-white, and then dazedly put the receiver down.

'Mrs Baxter's in town,' she said, which was sufficient to silence everyone. 'A friend of hers saw Peter and

Cecily in the supermarket last week and told her. I don't know how she found out about the births . . .'

'We weren't exactly closemouthed about twins,' Chuck said, remembering our hilarity when we bought champagne in the town at ten o'clock.

'Well, she went to the hospital, she saw Pat, she saw the twins. She's crazy, the things she said. She told the whole blooming hospital. But it isn't the truth. It isn't the truth at all.'

I've never sobered faster in my life. Cecily dashed to the kitchen sink to be ill.

It was a good thing I had medical license plates, because we passed three cops on the way to the hospital at a speed that was unwise even for doctors.

Chuck went for Avery, who was already trying to explain the situation to the village-sheet's reporter who had been informed of this tidbit of malicious gossip. Esther and I dashed to the maternity wing. I could hear Pat's sobbing voice as we turned the corner. I snapped an order for a sedative to the floor supervisor, who made the mistake of not concealing her snide expression.

'Crafty, Crafty,' cried Pat as she saw me enter the room. Her two roommates had poisonous expressions on their faces. She was trying to get out of the bed, clutching her tummy. I pushed her back, shoved her legs horizontal and yelled at the nurse to get the hell in there with the hypo.

'Crafty,' sobbed Pat in weeping distress, 'you can't imagine the horrible things she said. She didn't give me a chance to say anything. I don't think she wanted a logical explanation. She hates Peter! She hates him! She hates Cecily for being so happy with him. And she despises you for giving Cecily her children. I've never seen anyone so full of hate. She must know the children aren't mine and Peter's, but that's what she said. And she kept on saying it, and saying it' – Pat was covering her ears to shut out the sound of that vengeful slander – 'and everybody heard it. It's ghastly, Crafty. Oh, Crafty, what will Cecily do?'

I swabbed her arm and gave her the sedative as she was talking – rather, babbling. I also gave orders for her to be moved to a private room. Pat's words became incoherent as the drug took effect. Even as I was pushing her bed toward the private room, I thought of how very characteristic of Pat to worry about Cecily rather than the equivocal position into which Cecily's mother had put herself and her brother. I do not recall ever before being so consumed with anger as I was at that hour in my life. Had I known where Louise Baxter could be found, I think I would have strangled her with my bare hands.

Talk of feathers in the wind, there was no way of stopping the slander. It was obviously all over the hospital and would undoubtedly precede us back into town. I was in such a state of impotent wrath that it was all I could do to keep from lashing out at the floor nurse and the orderly, to wipe the smug expressions from their faces as we shifted Pat.

Pat was mumbling herself into a drugged slumber, and the floor nurse was fussing unnecessarily about the room, when Chuck came stalking through the hall.

'All that fuss because Pat's brother and his wife are helping the girl cover an indiscretion,' he said with commendable poise. 'What some people will think!' He shook his head over the frailties of mankind and then imperiously gestured the nurse out of the room.

When she'd left he indulged himself in a spate of curses as inventive as they were satisfying, and all relative to the slow and painful demise of one Louise Baxter.

'You've sedated her?' he asked, feeling for Pat's pulse and then stroking her disordered hair back from her face. 'Let her sleep.'

He turned from the bed and perched his rump against

the windowsill, trying to light a cigarette with shaking hands. He finally got it lit and inhaled deeply.

'Is that what you told Avery? That Pat was indiscreet?'

'No, I told him the truth. I've a hunch it might be important later. I can't say he believed me,' and Chuck let out a harsh snort of laughter, 'but I've convinced him that the charge of – ha! – incestuous fornication is the accusation of a psychotic. He's quite ready to believe that, judging from the way Her Ladyship Baxter carried on. He does think, and he subscribes to making it informally the truth, that we're covering up an illegitimate birth and that Peter and Cecily are going to adopt the children. He's a good man, Avery, but I'm afraid our revolutionary and irreligious fact is beyond his comprehension.'

'Illegitimacy is a lot more palatable than' – I couldn't even say it – 'the other.'

'Our public fiction depends on a cooperative grandmother, and I can't see the likes of her cooperating with you or me, or the Kelloggs. Christ, how I'd love to get my hands on her. I'd have her committed so fast . . . But Avery will handle matters here – neurotic grandmother, hates to admit her age – he's smooth as silk. He's having a *long* talk with that floor supervisor – one for letting Baxter in, two for not shutting her up the moment she started, and three for half believing her.' He walked back to Pat, feeling her abdomen.

'No, it's hard,' I said.

'I'd like to move her out of here, quickly.'

'Will Avery let Esther stay on as special?' I asked.

'You just bet he will,' said Esther from the door, grim-lipped. She was in her whites, starched and ready for action. I was inordinately relieved. 'What else do you expect from provincial hospitals?' She checked Pat, smoothed the bedclothes unnecessarily, and began checking the room's equipment, as if she hoped to find fault with it. 'They don't have rooming in or I'd bring the babies right here. But she's all right with me. You'd better get back to the cottage. Oh, and Dr Craft, I administered a strong sedative to Cecily before I came out. You look as if you need one, too, Allison,' she added and then settled herself on the chair by the sleeping Pat.

As we passed Avery's office on the way out, we heard him administering quite a lecture to some unfortunate person.

Wizard's angry barking alerted us before we turned off the main road into the lane that led to the cottage. Two of the group hovering by the path evidently had urgent business somewhere else.

'My God! People! I hate 'em,' muttered Chuck, staring belligerently back at the four hangers-on as we parked the car.

'Don't go in there,' one of the men told Chuck. 'That dog's dangerous!'

'Is he?' asked Chuck with innocent mildness, and we walked right past the snarling dog.

'Howd'ya like that?' someone muttered.

Peter was in the shadows of the small screened porch.

'Esther gave Cecily something. She'd made herself ill with weeping,' he said. 'Is Pat all right?'

'Esther's with her. Avery's handling the hospital staff.' Chuck wearily combed his hair back from his forehead. 'He doesn't believe in exogenesis, but the notion that you and Cecily are going to adopt your sister's indiscretion is acceptable.'

'What?'

Perhaps it was a trick of the sun, but I thought I saw a glint of anger in Peter's dead eyes.

'How long do Pat and the babies have to stay here?'

'We'll leave as soon as Pat can stand the trip,' I said, sagging against the wall.

Chuck sort of maneuvered me into the nearest chair, but it faced the pathway and the curious faces parading by. I tried to tell myself it was reaction to the whole nasty scene, but I was depressed by the notion that if Louise Baxter had spread her filth this fast in a small vacation village, she'd sure as hell go on to pollute the more rewarding atmosphere of our university town. Though what she stood to gain by such slander, I couldn't understand.

Before we all got very drunk, Chuck sat me down at the dining-room table, and we wrote up our notes on the delivery. I could see that they were going to be very important documents, but the clinical reportage sure as hell took the glamour out of the achievement, just as surely as Louise Baxter had tarnished the greatest gift of love.

The third day after her delivery, we took Pat and the babies home downstate in an ambulance. As I was still nominally on my vacation and I certainly didn't want Pat alone in her apartment in her psychological condition, I insisted that she stay in my house. So Chuck, who was following the ambulance in my station wagon, turned off to go to Pat's apartment to pick up a list of unmaternity clothing for her. Peter, Cecily, Wizard, and the babies dropped out of the cavalcade for their place.

Esther and I had suitably settled Pat when first Chuck, brakes squealing viciously, then Cecily and company pulled up in my driveway.

I had thought in the hospital three days earlier that Chuck had a superb vocabulary of invective, but he had evidently kept a supply in reserve, which he now employed as he helped Peter out of the car with the babies.

'What happened?' I asked, rather inanely, because it took little guessing.

'That blankety-blank female is not going to have an incestuous woman living in her respectable house. And to think that she had once admired her. And to think that all along that adulterous woman had been poisoning the minds of helpless youngsters and— Do I really need to read further from that script?' asked Chuck, now at the top of his strong baritone voice. He woke young Anne Kellogg.

'Mrs Baxter's got to town?'

'*Quod erat demonstrandum!* Only I'd say that the bitch has *gone* to town!' Incongruously, Chuck was deftly soothing the frightened baby before he passed her on to Esther.

Peter's usually calm face was etched with grief as he helped Cecily up the steps. Wizard, head down, tail limp, followed them to the steps, then turned and settled himself on the paving, watching the front gate.

'We are no longer welcomed by the management of the apartment house,' was all Peter said.

'Good Lord,' said Esther, 'did she use a bullhorn?'

Then the phone rang. Jiggling Anne, Esther answered it. She listened for a moment, then with grave pleasure firmly replaced the handset.

'I think it would be better to have the phone disconnected or the number changed immediately, Dr Craft. Shall I put in the request?'

I nodded numbly.

Wizard uttered a warning bark, and Chuck peered out the window.

'Who're they?' he asked me, and I glanced out at three militant figures about to enter the yard.

I shook my head.

'Peter, is Wizard on the guard?'

Peter nodded sadly. So we watched as the trio opened the gate. Wizard advanced menacingly, slowly, but his intention was quite plain. The visitors hesitated, conferred together, withdrew. Wizard took up a new position, twenty yards from the gate.

In the next few hours I would not have traded Wizard's presence for a cordon of unpolluted police. An irate mob might charge a police line (I don't say we had the quantities of a mob), but our visitors had not the courage to face 125 pounds of belligerent unleashed German shepherd. It was incredible to me, or maybe just naive of me, that so many people could believe such a thing of Pat and Peter Kellogg, but the traffic past my house was inordinately heavy. I like to think that those who paused and were not growled at by Wizard had friendly intentions, but they were very few. I still can't figure out why people have to descend in such mobs on the unusual.

At any rate, the only one who entered the house until the police came was the telephone man, and he wouldn't pass the gate until Peter had snapped the choke-chain lead on Wizard.

I frankly don't remember much of the next few hours. I think we all sat around in a semi-stupor, with the exception of the practical Esther. We had brought some of the food left over in the cottage, but it wasn't enough, and more formula mixture was needed, so Esther went out . . . the back way. She returned shortly afterward and grumbled angrily under her breath the entire time she cooked lunch, though I don't know what it was she served us. Fortunately there were lusty, hungry, healthy babies to care for, and I think they saved our sanity. If I heard Chuck mutter it once, I heard it fifty times:

'We got the kids!'

With Wizard to guard the house, none of us paid any attention to our whilom visitors or hecklers until we heard the police siren whine down to inaudibility right outside the house.

'Well, they took their time,' said Esther with righteous indignation.

Innocently we all filed out onto the porch. Wizard was impartial enough to resent police intrusion.

'Call off the dog. We're on official business,' the first man ordered.

Wizard obediently retreated to Peter's side at command.

'You certainly took your time coming,' Esther said acidly. 'We've been plagued by . . .'

'Which one of you is Peter Kellogg?' the policeman interrupted her arrogantly.

Peter raised his hand.

'I have a warrant for your arrest. Incestuous fornication and adultery is a crime in this state, buddy.' There was no doubt of his private opinion of such an offense. 'Which of you women is Patricia Kellogg? I've got a warrant for her arrest on the same charge.'

Chuck snatched the second warrant out of the cop's hand. When the policeman stepped forward to retrieve it, Wizard gave a warning snarl. Chuck read the document hastily.

'Christ! It is in order, Peter.' Chuck had been angry before; now he looked defeated.

'Can't he read his own, mister?' sneered one of the cops. The other man jabbed him in the ribs and pointed to the dog.

'As you perfectly well know, Joseph Craig,' Esther replied, her fury so plain that Policeman Joseph Craig stepped back, 'Professor Kellogg was blinded in Vietnam.'

'I'm Dr Henderson, Miss Kellogg's physician. I cannot permit her to answer this summons in person. She's under heavy sedation and incapable of supporting any additional strain.'

'You can come with me then, Doctor, and tell it to the judge.' Then the man informed Peter of his rights and gestured him off the porch.

Chuck turned to me. 'Call' – he gave me a number – 'and ask for Jasper Johnson and get him to work immediately.'

'Hey, that dog can't come,' the arresting officer complained, backing hurriedly away from Wizard's path.

'He's Professor Kellogg's Seeing Eye dog, and he . . .'

'Hell, he won't need any eyes where he's going!'

'Wizard had better stay here, Chuck,' Peter said with quiet meaning. He bent down and cradled the dog's head in his hands. Wizard whined quizzically as if he already understood. Hard not to, with the atmosphere crackling with suppressed emotions.

'Wizard, guard Cecily. Guard the babies. Obey Crafty. Understand?'

Wizard whined, sneezed, and bowed his head but made no move to follow Peter, Chuck, and the policemen. But the moment some of the bystanders tried to crowd in at the gate, he renewed his vigilance with savage growls and risen hackles.

It seemed to take forever to get Johnson's number, and then they must have done an office-to-office search for this Jasper Johnson before his brisk voice came on the line. I explained the situation as tersely as possible.

'For this I joined a fraternity ten years ago?' was his cryptic comment; then I heard him mmm-ing to himself for a moment or two. 'For such extraordinary charges I'd better get up there. They have to accept bail, but I can do that by phone. I should be able to make it to your place in about two hours at this time of day.' Then he groaned. 'But my wife's going to hate me again.'

His flippancy was oddly reassuring, and as I cradled the phone, the awful depression began to lift.

Chuck and Peter came home in a taxi about an hour later.

'Under the circumstances, I'm sure the neighbors

would have preferred another four-alarm fanfare,' Chuck said snidely as they came up the walk.

'You're forgetting what Sergeant Weyman said,' Peter remarked.

'Yeah,' and Chuck's expression brightened.

'George Weyman better be on our side,' said Esther, her eyes blazing. 'After all Allison did to save his wife and baby. So what did George say?'

'That this was the biggest load of shit he'd ever seen made official,' said Peter with a grin.

'He read the riot act to Craig and his cohort and treated us with more courtesy than is customary in police routines. However, I can't be as charitable about His Honor.'

'Who?' asked Esther.

'Colston.'

That didn't surprise either of us.

'I assume by virtue of our speedy release on bail that you contacted Jasper. Is he coming up?'

'He gave himself two hours.'

'Two hours? Well, I suppose he has to obey speed limits. He's only got a Mercury, poor deprived lad.' Chuck gave one of his wicked laughs. 'His last three babies paid for my Lincoln.' His amusement faded, and he barged toward the kitchen. 'I need a drink. We all need a drink to celebrate this third day P.P.E.'

'P.P.E.?' asked Peter.

'Yeah,' Chuck called from the kitchen, where he was rattling bottles and glasses. He came back in with a laden tray. 'Postpartum exogenesis.'

Conversation lagged, and Peter, Chuck, Esther, and I sipped our drinks fairly meditatively. I knew I was trying to numb my perceptions even while I knew that drinking at this pace wouldn't do the trick. Then one of the babies started crying and just as suddenly stopped. Pat wandered in from the kitchen with Carla and a bottle.

215

'Hey,' Chuck said, ushering her to a seat, 'you shouldn't be awake yet.'

Pat shrugged indifferently and settled the baby in the crook of her arm, smiling as her hungry wail was cut off by the nipple.

'I see that my job doesn't end with producing them,' she said. 'Funny thing. You know, Crafty, I miss their kicking. I waited for it as I was waking up, and I got a little panicky when I didn't feel it, and then I remembered I'd had the babies.' Her tender reminiscent smile faded abruptly. 'Ah, well. Good thing I'm their aunt, I can tell you. I'd just hate to have to give up all title to them.'

Chuck and I exchanged worried frowns over her bent head. In all the unpleasantness I'd forgotten about the emotional impact of maternity on Pat. She was a mother, and she wasn't. She had had all the emotional, biological, and psychological distortion of pregnancy, and if the problem was not handled carefully, her involvement could become critical. In the ill-wind department perhaps this flap would provide sufficient, if salacious, distraction, and she might be damned glad – both psychologically and emotionally – to be relieved of any relationship with the two kids she'd borne.

'Let me hear you say that in another week of sleep-torn nights, m'dear,' said Chuck wryly. The twins had different internal clocks.

'Ha,' Pat said with some disgust. 'With all the professional help around here, you have to have a priority rating to get close to one of them.'

Peter moved over to the couch to sit beside her. He touched the child's head where it rested on her arm, cupping the downy scalp in his big hand, his thumb hovering over the fontanel and its gentle pulse. With fingertips, he 'read' Carla's face and one waggling arm.

'There are advantages to being blind. I can truthfully

say to Cecily that she grows not a day older.' Peter smiled gently. 'She's truthful, too, and tells me of her wrinkles and graying hair, but I don't see them, any more than I can see the changes they say have occurred all around me. Visual time has stopped forever for me, and I "see" only my memories.' His hand cupped the warm little head. 'I've seen a lot of babies. I know what one usually looks like . . .' What he didn't say was palpable in the room. Esther wasn't the only one who made hurried use of a Kleenex.

Chuck cleared his throat and remarked with a broad professional pomposity, 'I assure you, sir, your daughter is most beautiful for one so newly born, which, truth-fully, isn't very beautiful. She *is* losing the lobster shade of red, her chin *has* come forward, the head bones are gradually assuming a normal . . .'

'Charles Henderson, how can you?' cried Pat, out-raged. 'Carla is a perfectly beautiful child. Ignore this clinical lout, Peter. He's just plain jealous.'

'Truer word was never spoken,' Chuck said in a doleful tone.

'Couldn't you have made an honest woman out of any of them,' I asked, plaintively, 'and acknowledged a child or two?'

Chuck negligently waved aside my suggestion of whole-sale philandering. 'A baby for A, a baby for B, but never, oh never, a baby for me,' he warbled slightly off pitch.

'Oh, you mean, "always the deliverer, never the delivered"?' asked Pat, all innocence as she deftly burped Carla over one shoulder.

'You can say that about Ali here, not me,' said Chuck with simulated indignation.

'Thank heavens you're here,' said a voice at the door. 'I got home only half an hour ago, and your number doesn't seem to ring.'

We all turned.

'Dr Dickson!' cried Peter, rising to his feet, since he had identified the voice before we could turn to see who could possibly have got past Wizard. 'Trust that dog to know our friends.'

'Indeed, indeed. Wizard and I are the best of good friends. Such a magnificent beast, such intelligence, such sympathy. I wish I could get along as well with some of the human members of my congregation as I do with Wiz.'

Peregrine Dickson, the minister of my Presbyterian church, entered the room, simultaneously mopping a perspiring face and shaking each of our hands with a warm but firm grip. He was a medium-sized, middle-aged, slightly overweight, slightly balding man, but only his physical appearance was mediocre or slight. His whole personality exuded inexhaustible good humor, patience, and empathy, and his kindly face, with alert twinkling eyes, was well wrinkled with laugh lines.

'My dear Peter, how happy I am for you! Allison, my dear girl, but I'd expect you to help!' He shook my hand, passed on to Esther, and grasped Chuck's hand so that I had to make an introduction instead of an explanation. Then Perry Dickson was bending over Carla. 'What a remarkably handsome baby! Her sister sleeps? Twins! Well, my word, my smart Pat never does things by halves, does she? I always like to baptize twins. I feel it puts me ahead two steps in the Good Book instead of the usual one. But what an extraordinary resemblance,' and he paused, backing off slightly from Carla and narrowing his eyes much as a painter does for perspective. He looked at Pat with an expression akin to awe. 'However did you manage that, Pat? But bless you for carrying through with it and giving Peter and Cecily the children. Is Cecily resting?' He looked about hopefully and then collapsed beside Pat on the sofa, mopping his sweating face with his limp handkerchief. 'I shouldn't wonder. Such a hot, close day.'

At that point Esther appeared with a glass of lemonade for him.

'Thank you, Esther. You are always beforehand. Really, it seems as if I've been hurrying for hours. It's a relief to get here and sit!' Dr Dickson took a sip or two and then put his glass down to continue his monologue. 'I was overcome with joy for you, Peter, when I heard the news. After all, I did baptize you, did confirm you, did marry you, and now I shall be able to start that comforting cycle with the new generation . . .'

Perry Dickson could rattle on so engagingly that you didn't have time to organize your own thoughts or rebuttals. I was beginning to realize that Perry was telling Peter that the irregularity of the children's births would be no bar to their admission in church.

'Perry,' I tried to get a word in edgewise, 'I don't think you've heard what . . .'

'Tut, Allison, I hear everything, you know. Someone always tells *me*. As I'm a minister, there is always something they think I should hear. That may be one reason why I am impelled to talk so much, so no one else will have a chance to tell me something they *think* I ought to know.

'In this instance, a kind parishioner – she is very charitable . . . with her purse – actually telephoned me at the Retreat House with such an exceptional interpretation of a really unexceptional occurrence,' and he smiled sweetly at Pat, 'that I realized I had better return forthwith. I was already packed when Father Ryan phoned.'

'Father Ryan?' Peter and I exclaimed together.

Beside me, Chuck shuddered, groaned, and covered his eyes with his hand. 'We're in trouble with the ecclesiastical as well as the secular?'

'Oh, I hardly think so. I assure you, Father Ryan gave

me no details, but he was so emphatic that I return because of the . . . tone . . . of the gossip . . .' And now Perry Dickson faltered, as though in the rush the truth had not had a chance to catch up with him. He looked blankly at me, only I didn't know how to start.

'Then you do not believe, Dr Dickson,' Peter asked deliberately, 'that the children are mine and Pat's?'

'Good heavens, no!' Perry Dickson lifted voice, eyes and hands upward in horrified repudiation of the thought. Then he gave Pat the kindest possible smile. 'I can only hope, Patricia, that you were indiscreet just to give Peter and Cecily the child they've longed for.'

'He simply hasn't tumbled,' said Chuck to the rest of us, almost annoyed.

'I haven't what?' and Perry looked at the solid sofa as if it were expected to collapse under him.

'Pat was not indiscreet, Dr Dickson,' said Peter in his quietly emphatic way. 'She is not an illegitimate mother. She acted as the host-mother for Cecily's and my progeny.' And he gestured toward Chuck and me.

'She was . . . the . . . host? Mother?' Perry's face was absolutely still. He held his breath while the words made sense to him. He blinked his eyes once, twice, and then gave such a triumphant crow that Carla jerked partially awake and whimpered. 'Exogenesis?' His eyes went so wide that his brows joined his receding hairline. 'Exogenesis!' He grabbed at Chuck for reassurance, and, grinning, Chuck nodded vigorously.

'Exogenesis documented and done!'

'Exogenesis! Exogenesis!' Perry said in wild excitement. 'Oh, absolutely magnificent. Patricia! My dear girl, greater love hath no woman! My dear child!' He was embracing her in an excess of emotion. He pumped Chuck's hand, grabbed Peter in an exultant hug, all the while mumbling 'exogenesis' in every sort of tone, from excited, incredulous, and relieved to prayerful.

While we were still grinning delightedly at the effect of our revelation on the good doctor, he collapsed again on the sofa, fanning himself with the soaked handkerchief. 'Oh, my dear people, my dear, dear friends . . .' Then he clapped his hands together and stared down at Carla. 'Well, that would, of course, explain it. Wouldn't it?' Then another thought struck his reeling brain. 'Oh, good heavens, poor Father Ryan!' At that exclamation, Chuck started to howl with laughter. 'Whatever will *he* say? Oh, my word!' There was, however, an unholy look of gleeful anticipation in Perry's eyes despite the humble dismay in his voice. 'This is going to strike him at a very fundamental point in his dogma. How ever is he going to explain this away? Oh, my dear friends, how could you?' As if we'd achieved only to discomfort Father Ryan.

'I'd be glad to provide you with the records,' Chuck said, and then took a wild look at Pat but obviously could not restrain himself, 'because they prove that it's an undisputable virgin birth! My dear Patricia, I could not resist!'

We all pounced on Chuck for that, while he kept demanding what was wrong with the guys in this burg and begging Pat's forgiveness. She was so torn between laughter and embarrassment that she couldn't say a thing, but the general confusion roused the baby in her arms. She made that an excuse to leave the room, saying that the conversation had taken a damned crude turn for her virgin ears and it was not fit talk for her niece's impressionable mind.

When we had calmed down, wiping the tears of mirth from our cheeks – we had needed that laugh – Perry pressed us for details. We had no hesitation in being candid with him: it was to our advantage.

'To go back a bit,' he suggested when he'd absorbed the important facts and points of the exogenetic technique, 'you said something about being in trouble with the ecclesiastical as well as the secular. Now, exactly what did you mean?'

'Your kind parishioners didn't have all the news, Dr Dickson,' said Chuck. 'Warrants were served on Peter and Pat about two hours ago for incestuous fornication and adultery.'

Perry's eyes went out of focus, and his jaw dropped.

'Oh, my word! How terrible! I mean, who would possibly . . .'

'My mother,' said Cecily from the hall door. She was pale but composed. Pat came in behind her.

Dr Dickson was on his feet instantly, and after giving her the gentlest, most affectionate of embraces, he drew her and Pat back to the couch to sit on either side of him. He was patting their hands consolingly.

'My dear child, are you *positive* it was Louise?'

'Oh, yes.' Pat answered. 'Mrs Baxter visited the cottage hospital where I was registered as Cecily Kellogg . . . so the birth certificate would show the real parents. It was Louise.'

'I have never understood your mother's antagonism toward Peter,' Perry said to Cecily, 'particularly since he is so like your own dear father, but for her to . . . to scandalize her own daughter . . . I shudder!'

Cecily was doing just that, and then Wizard's warning bark caught her and us up short.

'Hey, call off this dog before I have to shoot him!' yelled an irate male voice.

We looked out the front windows. A police car, without sirens, had pulled up to the curb behind an equally official-looking white station wagon. I couldn't see the emblem on its side, but there was a uniformed nurse sitting on the passenger side. The policemen were in their car, just watching the perspiring seersucker-suited man held at bay by Wizard.

'You oughta tie up a vicious animal like that,' he said

to me as Peter and I got to the porch ahead of the others.

'The shepherd is here to keep off trespassers,' I told the man.

'Well, I ain't trespassing. I'm on official business.'

'What kind?' asked Chuck, solidly planting himself in the doorway.

'Call off that dog first.'

'Only after you state your business.'

Dr Dickson tugged at Chuck's sleeve but kept back in the shadow of the doorway.

'He's a process server,' Perry whispered. 'I don't usually interfere with the grinding of legal wheels, but stall him!'

'Why?' Pat asked in an urgent low voice.

Perry pulled her back into the house, and out of the corner of my eye I saw Cecily join them and disappear down the hall. Then my attention was engaged by this latest emissary of law and order.

'Look, call off that dog. I got a court order here to take into protective custody the infants' – he turned the paper right-side up so he could read it – 'Carla and Anne Kellogg.'

Peter groaned, his shoulders sagging hopelessly. Chuck threw a protecting arm about him.

'You'll never take those children from me,' Peter said in low but distinct tones.

'Buddy, you gonna be in contempt of court, too?' He beckoned toward the police car, and the officers got out and ranged themselves behind him.

'Mr Kellogg, you better give up those kids, unless you want to be in more trouble than you already are,' one of them advised. 'I'd hate like hell to shoot Wizard, but you're resisting a court order.'

'Issued by whom?' demanded Peter.

'That don't matter, Mr Kellogg. We got a writ for the kids, and we're gonna have to take 'em.'

'Oh, really?' asked a suave voice cheerfully.

'Jasper, thank God,' cried Chuck, leaping off the porch to greet the tall, excessively thin man turning in at the gate. We had been so engrossed with the threat of the process server that we hadn't noticed the sleek black Mercury convertible pull up to the curb. 'Legal eagle, do you stuff, now if ever!'

Jasper held out an array of long white bones and snapped them negligently for the warrant, which he examined very closely, whistling as he handed it back.

''Fraid it's all too legal and binding, folks,' he said dolefully, and, grabbing Chuck by the arm, he propelled him past Wizard to gather us into a conference group on the porch.

The process server tried to follow, only to stare at bared teeth. The policeman stepped forward, too, his hand on his revolver butt.

'For God's sake, man, I must confer with my clients,' said Jasper, waving peremptorily at them to keep their distance.

'Let them proceed. Let them search the house,' he told us in a low voice. 'Oh, it's all right. I know what I'm doing,' he said at our shocked reactions. 'Someone control that dog, huh?'

Reluctantly, Peter called Wizard to him. The dog's whining protest echoed my feelings precisely as we numbly watched the odious little man enter the house and trudge toward the hall.

'You've some powerful enemies, to get that kind of writ served so damned quick,' Jasper said to us sotto voce.

'Goddammit, Johnson,' Chuck said, but at that moment the process server came storming back into the living room, holding up an empty carry cot.

'Where are they? I saw a woman holding a baby when I drove up here. Now where are they?'

'Where are who?' asked Pat as she and Cecily came in

from the kitchen. 'Who's this? What's he doing storming around here?' Pat sounded quite indignant.

'Where are those babies? I got a writ!'

'There are no babies in this house,' said Cecily quietly. 'Go ahead, look!'

'There were babies!' The empty carry cot was brandished and then flung onto the couch.

'How the hell did you do that?' Chuck muttered to Jasper, and then all of us had to keep our questions and our emotions to ourselves, for the process server came charging back into the room.

'I want those kids. Where are they?'

'You'll have a stroke, rushing around like this in all the heat,' Chuck said dispassionately.

'Mr Kellogg, you're in enough trouble,' one of the cops said.

'I'll get those kids, you incestuous bast—'

Peter's fist was cocked, but Chuck was quicker. His punch landed with a satisfactory crunch that sent the process server toppling over the sofa arm, onto the edge of the carry cot, which tipped onto his head, smothering him briefly in, I hoped, smelly sheeting.

'That's assault, mister,' one of the cops said severely, and started for Chuck. Wizard crouched, growling.

'With four impartial witnesses to testify to undue provocation?' asked Jasper. 'I think not.' The crispness and authority in Jasper's manner cooled the situation. He gestured to the policeman to help the groaning man to his feet, at which point Jasper relieved him of the piece of paper he was still clutching. 'You are only required to serve the court's warrants, summonses, and writs, in a manner befitting the dignity of your position, which does not include slanderous remarks. As there are no babies, infants, kids on these premises, Officer, I suggest you search elsewhere.' He handed back the summons.

The two policemen and the server conferred briefly

and, after hovering for a few minutes indecisively, finally left, Wizard hurrying their gateward way.

The moment they were out of earshot, we turned on the girls for an explanation. Pat was grinning triumphantly, but Cecily was gravely sad.

'Peregrine Dickson spirited them out the back door, muttering something about the instruments of the Lord, divine timing, the FBI, and his conscience,' Pat told us. 'If you could have seen him, trailing receiving blankets, the bag of formula bounding on his hip, ducking through the garden . . .' and she covered her mouth to smother her laughter.

'That was the sight I caught as I drove around the corner,' said Jasper, smiling as broadly.

'I apologize for all my recent foul thoughts, Jasper,' said Chuck earnestly. 'I was afraid that when Ed cured you of your last ulcer, he'd also removed the milk of human kindness from your scrawny breast.'

Jasper shuddered. 'For God's sake, Chuck, don't mention milk again,' and he made a show of retching. 'Now, which is which of you two charming ladies? I can't tell the real mother without an introduction, and, frankly, you both look like death warmed over.'

'Best lawyer in the world!' said Chuck. 'Always tells the truth!'

'I'm Cecily Kellogg,' Cecily said, shaking Jasper's hand warmly, 'and if you can do anything to keep them from taking my children away from me . . .'

'I've already made myself an accessory after the fact, my dear Mrs Kellogg, though I must confess I never suspected they'd move that far this fast. It's a rare instance that the children are removed from the care of their parents until actual guilt is established. Even then, the state hesitates. The worst parent is considered preferable to none at all. I'd say that whoever's after you has some very influential friends.'

'It's Mother, then,' said Cecily, sinking to the sofa as if her legs had given way. Peter reached for and found her hands and held them firmly.

'Your mother?' Jasper's urbane manner was briefly shattered.

'Mother has always managed to have influential friends, and she's always used them whenever necessary.'

'She's ruthless,' Chuck said.

'Ra-ther,' replied Jasper.

'And psychotic as all hell.'

'Obviously. Therefore twice as dangerous.' Jasper spun on his heel, one hand shoved into his pocket, the other absently smoothing down the hair across the back of his head as he paced. 'Dr Craft gave me a splendid outline, but now I want full details, please.'

While we recounted the events of the last year, he continuously paced, apologizing at one point by saying the walking helped him concentrate. I was later to be amazed at the accuracy of his total recall. When we had given him the whole story, he made one more complete circuit and halted in front of the couch, looking down at Peter and Cecily.

'The action against you revolves around a morality charge.'

'"Incestuous fornication is against the law in this state, buddy,"' repeated Chuck.

'Yes, it is,' Jasper said, 'but d'you know, I had to look it up?' He smoothed his hair again. 'You sure picked a dilly. Did you have to be related to him?' he asked Pat in a petulant tone.

'It's not at all the thing you do for total strangers,' she replied blandly.

'So we disprove the moral issue, also the consanguinity – although how they hoped to remedy *that* by depriving you of the children, I can't guess, and the charge must, by definition, be dropped.'

'The *charge*, yes,' said Pat gloomily. 'But how about the slander?' She gestured toward the front of the house.

'Yes.' Jasper heaved a sigh. 'I don't suppose you object to the procedures becoming public knowledge?' he asked me.

'Exogenesis will have to be admitted into the record – even though it will mean that hordes of childless women will descend on Ali,' Chuck replied before I could answer.

'Well, they'd be preferable to sensation-seekers,' I said.

'True, true. We shall have to bide our time,' Jasper said gently, apologetically, 'before we spring that explanation, so I'm afraid you all will remain under an unenviable cloud for a bit. Did you keep medical records of this medical tour de force?'

'By God, we did – every temperature drop, every milligram of medication,' said Chuck.

'They can be admitted as evidence.'

'Even from prejudiced sources?' I asked. 'I expect I'm considered one of your accessories to facts, too.'

'And me? Don't forget me,' said Chuck belligerently.

'Or me,' spoke up Esther, her jaw set as determinedly.

'Oh, you're all so wonderful,' said Cecily, and then dissolved into tears, apologizing through hiccuping sobs. Chuck exchanged looks with me, but Cecily refused sedation and pulled herself together.

'I'm sorry to seem callous or brutal, Mrs Kellogg, but I've always operated on a completely candid basis with my clients. I can, however, promise you that I can move for an emergency hearing on this. I'm not without a few influential friends myself. Now, to resume. Medical records, Dr Craft, no matter the source, are considered reliable information by the court. The hospital where the twins were born, your own institution here, will certainly have corroborative records?' We nodded, and he said he could subpoena them. 'Now, I'll need the blood types of the three principals and the children. That should prove conclusively whose children they are, shouldn't it?'

Chuck caught my dubious glance and shrugged.

'Well, won't it?' Jasper asked. 'In paternity cases, I know . . .'

'Man, this is a *ma*ternity case,' Chuck said.

'Yes, but . . .'

'Blood types only prove that the person could or could not be the parent, not that he or she *is*.'

'Yes, but . . .'

'In fact, since we are being brutally frank, and damn well have to be,' Chuck went on grimly, 'until we know what the twins' types are, we don't actually know that Pat couldn't be the mother.'

Pat gasped, and Cecily snuggled closer to Peter, hiding her head in his shoulder.

'You mean, that awful charge that I had my brother's children could be true?'

'Wait a minute, Pat.' Chuck reached across the coffee table to hold her down on the sofa. '*Not* by incestuous fornication, however. The medical records absolve you of the morality charge right there. But, God damn it, it is possible – not probable' – he paused to let his emphasis sink in – 'that the active sperm of the father could have fertilized ova of both the intended mother *and* the carrier.'

'The twins are *identical*,' I reminded Chuck as well as the others.

'True, so they both came from one fertilized ovum. Both Ali and I have worried about that *possibility* . . .'

'And I had twins . . .' breathed Pat, horrified.

'No, no, Pat, you've missed the point. You and Peter are fraternal twins, two eggs fertilized at the same time. This is an egg split, an entirely different process. And to keep you from turning neurotic, with such a close linkage, genetically speaking, it is unlikely you'd have had such healthy kids. Imbreeding multiplies defective and recessive genes, and an inbred child generally shows visible proof of the problem – frailness, sickliness. Those kids are beautiful, perfect, healthy.'

'Look,' began Jasper authoritatively, and something in his attitude gave Pat and Cecily reassurance, 'it doesn't take long to have blood types tested, so we can take you three off that particular tenterhook pretty quickly. Okay? So tell me how to get in touch with our clerical kidnapper. By the way, I'm sorry to have to advise you that it is better that you don't know where the children have been taken. I do promise that I'll do everything I can to see that you have them back in a very short time.'

I gave him Dr Dickson's home address, and he glanced around the room.

'I wish I had met you people under slightly happier circumstances, but let me say that it'll be my pleasure to represent you. By God, exogenesis!' His eyes held the same stunned, incredulous expression that Perry Dickson's had. 'Wait till the Catholic Church gets hold of this one.'

'In a sense, it has,' Dr Dickson said from the doorway. He had a new handkerchief, which he used as vigorously on his face as he had the other. 'When I returned . . . well, from where I went' – he smiled at Jasper as the lawyer quickly gestured to him not to be specific – 'Father Ryan had called. I haven't seen the poor man so distressed since the day we both arrived to preach a burial service over the same grave. It was a grisly joke, because the man had been an atheist of the most vehement sort . . . a fact we both knew. His relatives – tsk, tsk, terrible people; no wonder he was an atheist. I digress, a fault I cannot correct even when I'm not sermonizing . . .

'Father Ryan, yes. He had heard of the incredible

charges being made against the Kelloggs, and he wished to know if there was any way in which he could help . . .'

'Father Ryan?' Peter asked, surprised and, I could see, rather gratified.

'Oh, yes. Father Ryan has the highest regard for you, Peter. His exact words were, "There is nothing Byronic about that young man in his poems or his personality." So! There! He is quite willing to testify to your moral fiber if his presence would be of any help. Indeed, he insists on it.'

'Does he know about the exogenetic twist?' asked Peter with wry humor.

'Well, as to that, I'm afraid to . . . Peter, I just couldn't tell him yet.' It was the first time I'd known Perry Dickson to be at a loss for words. 'Just think, Peter, this renders a major, an essential, Catholic mystery a mere surgical technique. But you know, it has occurred to me that such a possibility merely enlarges the mystery rather than explodes it.' The handkerchief was flourished to provide the appropriate gestures. 'For was not our Lord Jesus remarkable because of the person He was, not just because of His holy origin? And surely, does not such a miraculous method of arousing our instincts for good give evidence to even the most confirmed unbeliever that there is an agency, a being – God, who *does* care and who directs our petty ways?

'Oh, my oh my, and this is only Tuesday. At all events, the babies are safely bestowed' – and his face was painfully earnest – 'where, I assure you, they will have the most loving and competent care, and,' he went on more briskly, mopping his forehead, 'complete anonymity.' He sighed. 'Poor Father Ryan. But I did do right in spiriting the children away, didn't I?'

'Morally, yes,' Jasper said. 'Legally, no. If you hadn't, I should have tried to snatch them myself.' He looked at us. 'I realized what was up when I saw the nurse in the

Red Cross wagon. And you know how I prefer to operate, Chuck: strictly on the up-and-up.'

'I sometimes suspect that the up-and-up has a little bit of down in it in the middle,' remarked the minister. 'Now what's to be done?'

Jasper explained about the necessity for blood tests.

'Oh, I don't see that that will matter,' Perry said. 'However, for the legal minds, one must produce documents. But it won't, in the final analysis, matter if the blood types *are* similar.'

'Why on earth not?' demanded Jasper, surprised.

'You doctors and lawyers consider legal and scientific proof the only essentials, but I fear you forget the power of human conceit. All those weighty clinical and notarized statements look most imposing on the record, and show that the lawyer has been worthy of his hire. Indeed, this sort of event needs all the documentation possible. But have no fears.' He rose to his feet, gesturing. 'All is resolved for the righteous. Vengeance is mine, saith the Lord. It's unchristian of me, I know, but such justice, such divine justice . . . No, I digress again. Mr Johnson, if you'll just come with me, we can settle the matter of blood types from the children, and then I shall have to be about other of my Father's business. Old Mrs Rothman, you know . . .'

He had bustled Jasper out of the house like a dinghy pushing a sleek yacht.

'I wonder how Father Ryan will take the news,' said Peter as he stroked Wizard's head.

Jasper was as good as his word about obtaining an emergency hearing with the Juvenile Court. He did remark that they had no opposition from the prosecution. He had commented again on the influence of our enemy's friends because the State of New York was the complainant, not an individual.

'Of course, the sovereign State of New York *is* the guardian of all children within its borders, but it's a neat piece of legal eagling.'

It was good to know that our ordeal had limits, because the atmosphere in town was, to use the so apt teenage phrase, 'hairy.'

'Sure takes a moral crisis to tell the sheep from the goats,' Esther remarked as she scratched off another patient from my books. 'Just as well; McCluskey, Derwent, Patterson, and Foster were all due the same day.'

'Whom does it leave me with?'

'Oddly enough, Patterson. You wouldn't think such a quiet little thing would buck the tide.'

'You've never heard her in the PTA meetings, have you? A strong libber, God bless her.'

Perry Dickson insisted we grace his church Sunday – that was his phrase. The ushers greeted us effusively, but some of their smiles were strained. Perry preached one of his most inspired, and shortest, sermons on prejudgment, prejudice, and persecution. That his words were taken to heart was noticeable by the numbers of our acquaintances who came up to speak to the Kelloggs, Esther, and me. I heard that Father Ryan took the same chapter and verse for his sermon. I promised that I would get to know that good man better in the very near future. If, after the exogenetic bit, he was still willing to speak to me.

The 'slander' had fractionated people into those who were willing to believe incest, those who thought Peter and Cecily were adopting Pat's indiscretions, and those who were for or against unwed mothers, for or against abortion, for or against women's right to have complete say in what they chose to do with their own bodies.

'By God,' Chuck said, for he insisted on coming up every Friday night, though it meant a mad streak down the Throughway on Monday mornings for his first appointments, 'you've wiped drugs, moon shots, the Middle East, not to mention elections, right out of conversations. And most of my colleagues tell me exogenesis is impossible.'

We all greeted the day of the hearing with more relief than anxiety; such is the power of the easy conscience.

Since this was a hearing involving minors, it had to be held in camera. I would have preferred a public coverage so that when we were exonerated, as many people as possible would know. Because of the number of principals involved, we were assigned to one of the larger chambers. Unusual for such hearings, there were police officers, a bailiff, and a court secretary. Louise Baxter was conspicuous by her absence, which was as welcome to us as it was puzzling. Nor had all Jasper's probings elicited the name of the original complainant.

Judge Robert Forsyth was presiding, and he entered the chamber scowling – not a good sign, but he hated anything that smacked of the sensational, particularly when it involved children. He was, however, extremely perceptive and commonsensical.

'Oyez, oyez,' rang the bailiff's cry as we got to our feet at Judge Forsyth's entrance. The rest of the initial proceedings were spewed out in a bored mumble. I noticed, cringing a bit, that when he cited the charge of 'incestuous fornication and adultery,' his enunciation promptly clarified and his delivery was strong.

'Yes, yes,' said Judge Forsyth, waving him aside. 'How do you plead?' he demanded of Pat and Peter.

'Not guilty, Your Honor,' they said quietly.

'Is the presence of that animal in this courtroom necessary?' he asked, testily pointing to Wizard, who was sitting by Peter's side.

'Yes, Your Honor,' said Jasper, rising. 'Wizard is Mr Kellogg's guide dog.'

'Oh, indeed.' It was obvious that Peter's deficiency had not been mentioned, nor had he heard the sly jibe circulating in town that Wizard had escorted Peter to the wrong bed one night.

The county prosecutor, Emmett Hasbrough, was an average-looking man with an above-average reputation for courtroom fireworks and results. His prefacing remarks were few, as he merely stated that he could easily prove that the charges were true and would like to proceed by calling the first witness. The judge waved assent and settled back in his chair, apparently far more engrossed in the water damage on the ceiling.

The delivery-room nurse, looking both frightened and important, took the stand and gave the oath, her name, her occupation, and her current place of employment.

'On the morning of August 15, 1976, at 8.02 a.m., did you assist at the birth of twin girls?'

She nodded.

'To whom were these children born? Will you identify the mother if she is in the courtroom?'

'She is. She's sitting right there,' said the nurse, pointing to Patricia.

'Now, is the father of the children in the courtroom?' Hasbrough glanced sideways at Jasper as if he expected an objection.

'Yes,' said the nurse, and pointed at Peter.

'How do you know he is the father of the children?'

'I was still in the nursery where I had taken the children after their birth when he, and the other woman there, came to see them. He said he was their father.'

'Thank you.'

Smiling broadly, Hasbrough excused her and asked the admissions clerk of the hospital to take the stand.

'Were you on the admissions desk the morning of August 15, 1976, at the Mount Pleasant Hospital?'

'Yes, sir.'

'Did you admit as maternity patient any woman seated in this court?'

Pat was duly pointed out.

'By what name was she admitted?'

'As Mrs Cecily Kellogg.'

Hasbrough shrugged as if to underscore his point and gestured toward Jasper that the clerk was his to cross-examine. Jasper rose, his pose thoughtful.

'Sir, I don't believe that you have reported that incident truthfully.'

'Huh?' The clerk, clearly startled, glanced toward the prosecutor. Hasbrough shrugged again.

'Did this woman answer the questions herself?'

'Oh, well, no. Not actually. Uh, she was in labor, you see . . .

'Come to think of it' – the clerk was embarrassed – 'Mr Kellogg did all the talking.'

'Think carefully, now. When you asked him the patient's name, what precisely was his answer?'

The clerk thought a moment, confused. 'But she's *listed* as Cecily Kellogg.'

The judge advised him to answer the question to the best of his ability.

'It was some time ago . . .' Then his face brightened. 'Yeah. He said, "My wife's name is Cecily Kellogg," but I thought he meant *her*!' And again the man pointed to Pat.

'So Mr Kellogg did not actually say that the woman he brought to you was Cecily Kellogg? Nor did she?'

'Well, no, put like that, I guess he didn't. But who else would I expect it to be?'

Jasper was finished making that point. Other members of the hospital staff were called, all substantiating the fact that Pat had been delivered of twins, and that Peter had openly admitted to being the father of the twins.

'That, Your Honor, is the case for the prosecution,' said Hasbrough, not particularly bothered by the clerk's recital.

Judge Forsyth sighed, pursed his lips, and then turned inquiringly to Jasper. Beside me Cecily had torn the border from her handkerchief and was knotting it so tightly around her index finger that it was nearly cutting off the circulation. I carefully released it, and she smiled wanly at me.

'Your Honor, I move for a directed verdict,' Jasper said, and Hasbrough gave a start of amazement.

'On what grounds, Counselor?' demanded the judge, frowning.

'On the grounds that no incestuous fornication or adultery has yet been proved by the prosecution,' replied Jasper, all innocence at the judge's reaction.

Judge Forsyth leaned toward him. 'You have heard the testimony of several witnesses that Patricia Kellogg was delivered of two children whose paternity her brother, Peter, has not denied – in fact, has openly and unashamedly admitted. And you have the unutterable gall to tell me that no incest or adultery took place? I'm all ears, Counselor,' he said.

'I claim, Your Honor, that no incestuous fornication has been proved by these statements. The witnesses have confirmed that Patricia Kellogg gave birth to twins, the father of whom is Peter Kellogg. No one has proved that Peter Kellogg fornicated and committed adultery with his sister.'

'If you can give me another logical explanation that satisfies my credulity, I wish you'd proceed. However, I will point out that consanguinity is also a felony in this state,' and while the judge leaned back he was challenging Jasper to prove there was no inbreeding.

'Very well, Your Honor. I will now prove, irrevocably, that there was no act of fornication or adultery, nor are they guilty of producing children within the criminal degrees of consanguinity.'

'Proceed, by all means,' said the judge, steepling his fingers.

Jasper called Patricia to the stand. She took the oath with quiet dignity.

'Were you delivered of twin children on the morning of August 15, Miss Kellogg?'

'I was,' Pat answered bravely and unashamedly.

'Who was the father of these children?'

'Peter Kellogg.' The quiet answer fell on the silent room.

'Who was the mother?'

'Cecily Kellogg.'

There was an audible reaction of disbelief from the prosecution's side.

'You, can, of course,' the judge drawled slowly, 'substantiate that second statement?'

Jasper went on. 'These are the separately kept records of Drs Allison Seymour Craft, obstetrician of this town, and Charles Irving Henderson, consultant obstetrician of New York City. They have all been time-stamped, you will notice, on the hospital's time clock.'

The judge made a moue of appreciation for that point and gestured for them to be brought to him. He leafed through several pages in each, frowning at the clinical details.

'The initial chapter,' Jasper said, 'in both accounts describes the process of exogenesis by which this birth was made possible. The actual propagation took place in the hospital operating room with both women under anesthesia and the father of the children in an anteroom, scarcely in a position to commit fornication and adultery with his sister. Even with the help of a guide dog.'

'I beg your pardon, Mr Johnson,' the judge admonished him sternly, closing the record books with some force.

'Your Honor, I must object to the way this court's patience is being tried by the inclusion of these alleged records as proof of the innocence of the defendants. It's a preposterous alibi for an incredibly obscene act,' said Emmett Hasbrough, on his feet with indignation.

'I shall admit the evidence. However, Mr Johnson, I'm afraid this court is by no means convinced.'

'I'll proceed with further evidence, Your Honor. Will Dr Samuel Parker take the stand?'

Jasper quickly established Dr Parker as the serologist of the University Medical School Hospital, thoroughly qualified to testify on his specialty. Dr Parker admitted taking blood samples from Patricia, Cecily, and Peter Kellogg, as well as from twin girls, four days old, whose footprints corresponded with those taken at the births of the Kellogg children. Dr Parker admitted that he had been asked by Mr Johnson to type these blood samples.

'Will you please tell the court the results of your tests?'

'Briefly, the man, Peter Kellogg, is a Type B negative, with a Pe factor. Cecily Kellogg is a Type B positive with a C factor, and Patricia Kellogg is a Type O negative with a Pa factor.'

'You make a point of the difference in the additional factors?' asked the judge.

'Yes, I do, sir. We are able to type blood in more detail now than just A, AB, B, and O. These additional "factors," as we call them, are every bit as important as the different types.'

'I see. And what type were the children you examined?' asked Jasper.

'Both of them were Type B positive.'

'Well, then, from her blood type, would *Miss* Kellogg possibly be the mother of the two children she delivered?' asked Jasper.

'I'm afraid to say it – but she *couldn't* be their mother,' answered the serologist, puzzled by his own conclusion.

'Do you mean to tell me that the children *could* be *Mrs* Kellogg's?' asked the judge, sitting bolt upright.

'I couldn't swear to that,' the man admitted. 'But I do most emphatically know that Miss Kellogg, that one, the defendant, could *not* be the mother of those children in spite of what I've heard today.'

'How do you arrive at that conclusion?'

'Without getting too technical, although there are several substantiating factors besides the prime one, all children of a C and Pe blood factor *must* be Rh positive or heterozygous. All children of Pa and Pe factors *must* be Rh negative, which is homozygous, a recessive trait. So that Miss Kellogg, who is Pa, could not have had children with a positive Rh factor from Mr Kellogg, who is Pe. So, while the blood types don't prove that *Mrs* Kellogg is the mother from a serological standpoint, they prove that it is absolutely impossible for the babies' mother to have been *Miss* Kellogg. But that, of course, is itself impossible.'

'Is there any chance the blood types were mixed, or that the infants differed from those in question?' asked the judge.

Instead of taking offense, Dr Parker sighed.

'No, Your Honor. I checked my findings thoroughly – the children's footprints, everything involved. I had my assistant and one of the lab technicians check my findings and run two more complete serologies. Our results were identical.'

'You may retire.'

'Your Honor,' said Jasper in the silence that ensued while the bench pondered the evidence, 'I admit that the scientific proof is perhaps indigestible to the court. I would like to present one final piece of incontrovertible, and easily accepted, proof.' Judge Forsyth gave a curt wave of his hand to indicate permission. 'Bailiff, will you call Mrs Louise Baxter to the stand?'

Cecily gasped and clutched at me. I could only stare at the unperturbed Jasper. None of us had had any notion that he'd call her as a witness for us.

Louise Baxter walked down the center aisle, staring straight in front of us, two angry spots of red on her cheeks, her mouth firmly closed, her eyes flashing with suppressed emotion, and every inch of her trim, elegantly attired body protesting the indignity. When she took the stand, she refused to look at anyone. Her voice when she gave the oath and her name trembled with anger and was so low the judge asked her to repeat her name.

'You have one child, Mrs Baxter, a daughter named Cecily Baxter Kellogg, is that correct?'

Her lips pursed firmly as if she were about to repudiate Cecily.

'Answer the counselor, if you please, Mrs Baxter,' said the judge.

'Yes!' One tight word, and she spat it.

'Bailiff, please direct the attendants to bring in the persons of Carla and Anne Kellogg.'

Cecily half rose as a nun (and I now remembered Dr Dickson's enigmatic reference to the church's help) and the woman warden brought in the babies. Jasper had got around Dr Dickson's kidnapping by saying that the parents, when they realized what a furor was being caused, had arranged for the girls to be placed in an institution, where they were being anonymously cared for by qualified people. This was the first time Cecily had seen her children in almost three weeks, and she was perilously close to a complete emotional breakdown.

'Easy,' I told her, putting my arm about her. 'It's only a few moments more.'

As the attendants reached the front of the chamber, Wizard rose and placed himself between the babies and Mrs Baxter. I hadn't seen a hand signal from Peter.

Fortunately, the judge was too preoccupied to notice the dog's insubordination.

'Your Honor,' said Jasper, 'it has been said by wise men that all the scientific proof in the world on paper is not worth one second's visual proof. Will you and Mr Hasbrough please take a careful look at the two infants, and then at Mrs Baxter?'

The judge peered over the high bench at the babies, who were held up toward him. They were just beginning to rouse from sleep. He glanced at Mrs Baxter, sitting rigid on the witness stand. He looked quickly back at the twins, muttering something inaudible to me, although the startled bailiff and Hasbrough both stepped closer to the babies. I craned my neck to try to see what they could be looking at.

'Oh, what is it?' breathed Cecily. 'Why did Jasper bring Mother here?'

'Your Honor, I renew my motion for a directed verdict,' said Jasper, with none of the inner satisfaction he must have been feeling.

The judge leaned back, staring with considerable respect at Jasper's tall, lean figure.

'You have made your point, Counselor, and your motion is granted. As a matter of law, I hold that the evidence adduced by the defense is admirably sufficient to dismiss any hint of incestuous fornication or adultery, or consanguinity, that may have arisen from the evidence produced by the prosecution. Therefore, there is in fact no issue for determination. The defendants are not guilty as charged!'

He banged his gavel, Wizard barked twice, and we were all on our feet, yelling and crying, and I wasn't the only one weeping for joy.

Cecily scrambled to the babies. She all but grabbed Carla from the nun's arms and then turned with astonishment toward her mother. By that time, Chuck,

Esther, and I were beside her. And we all saw what the judge had seen.

Dr Dickson's mutterings hadn't registered with me on that frantic day, and I realized now that he had immediately seen that the twins were the spit and image of their maternal grandmother. From eyebrow tilt to the slight cleft in their little chins, they were miniatures of Louise Baxter. All the scientific documentation in the world was unnecessary in the face (I should say, faces) of such a strong familial resemblance. What a trick of fate!

Cecily suddenly moved forward toward her mother, sitting motionless on the stand.

'Look well, Mrs Baxter,' she said in a low voice, rich with the accumulated bitterness and uncertainty of the past weeks. 'So help me God, it is the only time you will ever look on your granddaughters.'

The only indication Mrs Baxter gave that she had heard her daughter was to turn her head away.

Pat took Anne from the arms of the warden, and it was a measure of her acquitted innocence that she received a warm smile from the woman. The nun was assuring Cecily that the children had gained weight at a most satisfactory rate and she'd be glad to discuss their 'vacation,' as she sweetly put it, with Cecily at any time.

Chuck gave up pounding Jasper on the back and started shooing us all toward the door. 'Back home where we belong,' he said.

No one had left the courtroom, so I don't know how word had reached the reporters, but when the officer at the door opened it, the hall outside was crowded, and the flashbulbs and the noise woke the startled babies.

'Miss Kellogg, will you do this again – for your brother and his wife?'

'Will you be a proxy mother for other deserving childless women?'

'Mr Kellogg, how do you feel about . . .'

Jasper pushed his way to the front as Chuck protectingly put himself between Pat and the surging crowd.

'Now, now, boys,' Jasper said, loudly but amiably. 'We got some small girls here who need to get fed. Just let us through.'

He and Chuck bowled their way past while Esther and I rear-guarded Cecily and Pat, my arm linked into Peter's.

'Please, now, this has been a trying experience for my clients. Later, fellas, later.'

'Aw, come on, Mr Johnson!' Several of the more aggressive were keeping pace with us, the others swarming in behind.

We were only to the cross-corridors when someone stepped on Wizard's paw, and he let out a hurt yipe, effectively halting our getaway.

'Esther, you take the babies to the car,' said Pat, handing over Anne. 'Let's get this over with, and they'll leave us alone.'

'I didn't mean to step on the dog,' the offender said earnestly, but he ruined the apology by getting a full-face shot of Pat in a very angry pose.

'Yes, let's,' said Cecily, and handed Carla over to Esther, who hurried away, unhindered.

'No, I don't think my brother and sister-in-law would allow me to help them again,' said Pat. 'Once is enough. No, the next child I have will be my own. It's a lot easier socially to *be* the mother of the child you bear.' She was grimly humorous.

'Do you think other women will consent to being host-mothers?'

'I wouldn't presume to say. But if people can be bought to take life, I expect there are some who can be paid to give life.'

She was making a terrific impression on the reporters.

'How did you feel about having these babies?'

'It's not the most comfortable way to spend nine months,' Pat said dryly.

'I mean,' said the reporter insistently, 'how *you* feel? Psychologically.'

'My psychological reactions are my own.'

'Oh, c'mon, Miss Kellogg, be a sport. There are millions of people waiting for the personal story behind this exogenesis.'

'You forget,' she reminded the reporter acidly, her eyebrows raising, 'I have been a sport' – one of the group laughed at her double entendre – 'and the personal story is much too personal. The facts are all I'll give. My brother's wife couldn't carry a child to term. There was no reason to suppose I couldn't. There was only one way in which that end could be achieved. I did it – with the medical help of Dr Craft and Dr Henderson. That's all.'

She turned purposefully away, but one of the women reporters grabbed her arm.

'Do you support Women's Lib?'

Pat let out a forbearing sigh. 'My philosophy is also private,' and she broke through the group and went down the corridor as fast as she could. We tried to follow, with some success, but we were still being bombarded with questions.

'Will you set up in practice as an exogenic specialist, Dr Craft?'

'I haven't had time to think about it.'

'Had any offers from clinics and laboratories?'

'No comment,' Chuck said grimly, and pushed Cecily and me on, while Jasper helped Peter.

'Do you plan to have children by exogenesis, Dr Craft?'

'She won't have to,' said Chuck, gripping my arm firmly as he hurried Cecily and me down the steps to my station wagon.

That was as much of a proposal as I ever did get from

Charles Irving Henderson, but later, in private, he made his intentions so abundantly clear that I finally realized that his faithfulness had been prompted by an attachment to me, not to Pat or the Kelloggs.

Wizard made an excellent rear guard. He turned, darted, and snapped, and everyone fell back so that we got into the car without further harassment. Then Wizard daintily jumped into the open back window, his tongue hanging on one side of his mouth in a canine laugh.

'Home, O noble Ali,' Chuck said to me, settling his arm around my shoulders as I turned the ignition key.

As we pulled away from the curb, Pat took young Anne from Esther, at which point the baby let out a squall of protest.

'Good heavens,' exclaimed Patricia Kellogg with mock pique, 'is that gratitude to the woman who gave you birth?'

A QUIET ONE

'Have you never ridden a live horse?'

'I achieved the maximum level . . .'

'*Have* you ever ridden a live horse?' the Interviewing Representative had repeated.

Remembering her hours on the mechanical surrogate where she'd learned the basic equitational skills, Peri said, 'I haven't had the opportunity . . .'

'Yes, quite. Well, I suppose that can't be helped.

'There will be a trial period, you realize?' He kept scrolling through her file on the recessed screen, which she could not see.

'Yes, I do.'

'Well, then, that's all now, young Peri. You'll receive notification of the decision in two weeks.' The Interviewer stood, gave her one of those formal little rictus smiles that Interviewers seemed to cultivate, and she had left with the sense that she had not quite won the last argument.

But Peri felt that she had won another major battle in her long, private, quiet struggle to have the career of her choice. Modern parents as well as modern educational systems had, as their aim, fitted young people to rewarding, fulfilling careers in the widest variety of professions in a space-traveling society.

Class trips constantly introduced students to possible career opportunities, taking them to aquaculture farms, space stations, laboratories, hydroponic installations.

From the day that ten-year-old Peri had visited the Working Farm, her ambition had been to work with horses, whose very existence had recently been under threat. The others on the class trip had fussed and complained about the 'smells,' the 'stinks,' the 'stenches,' but Peri had rapturously inhaled them . . . especially the lovely odor of the horses. She'd always liked watching them move in the training films or the oldie movies. They were so proud, so regal, so wild.

Alone of her class, she had asked to touch a horse, which had responded to her tentative caresses with a soft nicker that had somehow thrilled her. The feel of the warm muscles under the skin, the bright and intelligent eye of the animal on her, its response to her tentative caress when it snuffled in her hand, its velvet nose nuzzling her palm: *that* had been the single most enthralling experience in her life.

Through the ensuing years that sudden fascination did not fade. Indeed, she accessed all the information about the equine species that the data banks in her Linear Residence Complex possessed. She even found ancient books about horses, read all available disks by the currently acknowledged experts, like T. King-Sangster-Mahmood III, and, with avid eyes, watched every tape of equestrian sports available.

When Peri discovered that their Residential exercise facility included simulated horseback riding, she had asked permission from her mother to attend regularly. Peri, in her quiet way, simply hadn't mentioned that she had concentrated on one activity. The *construct* was subtly disappointing – like all things mechanical – although it performed as a living horse would. On it she had learned the basic equitational skills, had gone on to show jump on an advanced model. At least her instructor had recognized her enthusiasm and encouraged her to achieve the maximum skills available on the surrogate. But the simulations were just that, and she was constantly frustrated by the sense that she was ineluctably missing the most important facet.

So, with her goal in mind, she had tailored all her courses, even her special assignments, toward the end of qualifying for the Idaho Preserve. In zoology she had done an extensive survey into the propagation of breed animals. She had studied the stresses now attacking both equines and bovines, and was fully cognizant of the perilous future that needed no probability curve to trace. She had joined the lobby that wished to send specimens of the endangered species out to new worlds where they could flourish and regain the strengths and numbers they had once enjoyed.

When her acceptance to the Idaho Preserve had arrived, complete with hotel travel voucher, Peri was ecstatic. Her mother was horrified that her daughter had applied for a career in such a bizarre occupation.

'What on earth made you choose an-i-mals?' her mother demanded, syllabifying the word to express her disgust.

'You brought me up to think for myself, Mother,' Peri said, hoping for a kinder farewell, 'and I have done so. If you can be proud of my brother terraforming worlds, please be proud of me for breeding the animals meant to inhabit terraformed places.'

'But to do so without discussing it with me at all! And you're leaving today? I suppose I shouldn't be surprised. You've always been a quiet, self-contained child.' With that, her mother had left the room, not quite slamming the door.

Peri resumed her task of emptying her cabinets and drawers, realizing that there was very little in them that would be useful in her new life. On the Idaho Preserve, where would she need the gauzes of social life: the platformed heels, the decorative face patches, the baubles and bangles, even the security belt? *That* might deter a grown man, but it would be useless riding a horse!

Her few real treasures of booktapes, holograms of her family, and her comfortable riding gear were all that she packed. Her mother had left a note on the fax – 'Do write! Do right!' Her mother had a slogan for everything. But Peri sensed both the outrage and the disappointment in those crisp injunctions.

The journey to the Idaho Preserve was not direct, since the nearest station was relatively unfrequented, and she had to change twice to feeder lines. She arrived at the Preserve in full dark, annoyed at being deprived of her first view – said to be spectacular – of the natural mountains and valleys. The station was also small, dirty, and unoccupied. No one was there to meet her.

The dispenser refused to supply a beverage and the slots for sandwich or snack bar were empty. Disgusted, she blew away enough dust to settle herself on one of the hard benches – wooden? – and ran through a meditation exercise. It wouldn't do to appear disgruntled in her first contact with her new life.

'Yoo-o!' The loud call roused her from a light doze and Peri shot upright, disoriented. 'You the tenderfoot?' The tall man in dusty clothes, hat shading his face in the dimly lit station, hauled a scrap of – could it be real paper? – from under his belt. 'Peri Schon-Danver-Keyes? Man, that's a lot of name for a li'l thing like you.'

Stiffly Peri rose and, discarding other reactions to his unexpected approach, smiled. 'Peri's enough!' She extended her hand and had it engulfed in a worn leather glove and a moment of viselike grip. No one in polite society ever did more than press fingers. Her hand was numb.

'Monty! That all your gear?' He pushed his hat back and she saw that his face was seamed with lines, tanned a leathery brown, which made his very blue eyes startling. His slight grin somehow told her that she had surprised him.

'Yes.' Peri had never been particularly talkative, but her laconic answer surprised even her.

'Wal, how 'bout that!' Unexpectedly he swooped the pak up and started for the door. 'C'mon! Time's awasting. Got a long drive.' He stopped, one hand on the door. 'You *can* ride a horse, can't you?' Peri nodded, not trusting herself to words as the memory of that interview bobbed up. His expression was slightly skeptical and she psyched herself up for that moment of truth. 'Last one couldn't!' He sounded both amused and sour. 'Great on theory, lousy in practice.'

He went on through the door and she followed into a night the like of which she had never seen. She stood for a moment, face turned up to the starry sky, inhaling the crisp chill air, gasping as a breeze actually flowed across her face and body. She coughed.

'Gotta take it easy, city girl.' Monty's voice came out of the darkness and suddenly lights came on, showing the aged ground-effects machine. It was something out of a Vehicular Museum – a straight-sided rectangle with funny windows, great wheels all muddy, and flip-up side seats in the back half. There was even a spare wheel on the front of it, a long narrow package tied to its roof rack. And not a horse in sight.

Peri felt an intense deflation. So his question had been idle curiosity.

'C'mon, Peri. I don't have all night. Morning comes early in these parts. And we'll both be rising and shining with the others.'

She hiked herself awkwardly into the high seat and pulled the door shut. A slight shower of dust settled to her clothing and she was halfway to brushing it off when she realized he was watching her out of the corner of his eye. She saw the seat harness and managed to secure it without too much fumbling. He already worked the foot pedals and the vehicle jumped forward with a belch and a roar.

Peri scrabbled for something to hang on to as the vehicle jolted them from side to side. Assuming that the ground-effects machine was operating properly, since the driver seemed unconcerned with its antics, she realized that she must relax. When she felt secure enough among handhold, seat belt, and braced feet, she looked out the dusty window, trying to pick out landmarks in the headlights.

Dark shadows loomed and things seem to arch over the roadway – if you could call it that, all ruts and stones and untreated surface. It was quite the eeriest experience Peri had ever had.

Suddenly two huge orange orbs loomed out of the darkness and the vehicle swerved violently away from them.

'Damned critter!' Monty muttered. 'We'll have to do some fence riding, that's fer sure!'

'You permit your animals out at night?' Peri was astounded.

'You betcha. Now don't tell me you're one of the bleeding hearts? Wrap 'em up in cotton wool and doan let 'em so much as sneeze or stale on their own-i-os.'

'No, I am not a bleeding heart,' Peri said firmly. 'Animals thrive in their proper natural environment. It is mankind who has restricted them to artificial habitats, not always suitable for the species.'

'Lordee, those are mighty big words for a li'l girl.'

'I wish you would stop with such affectations, Monty, or whatever your name really is,' Peri said in a caustic tone. 'If you are employed by the Idhao Preserve, then you have to have received an education and training that allows you to deal with its complexity and problems. Don't patronize me.'

'Just a touch of local color. Most appreciate it.' This time his speech was uncolored by drawl and sloppy emunciation. He almost sounded contrite.

She could think of nothing to say so she continued to peer out the window, trying to identify the natural landscape they passed. Monty did something with what she now realized were antiquated gears, and the engine of the vehicle changed pitch to a deeper tone. The vehicle began to climb. The roadway was narrow, dirt and gravel, pitted with ruts and holes that caused the vehicle to bounce and sway. To her right there seemed to be nothing but black space. To her left the slope of a mountain.

'Rather a spectacular view by day,' Monty said in an agreeable tone. 'Unless you're agoraphobic.'

'I'm not.'

Peri wondered if the journey would ever end, for having gone up the side of the mountain, they came down on the other, around a second and third. She was also incredibly relieved that she had not been required to make such a long trip her first time on a real horse.

'Is there a reason the station is so far from your headquarters?' Peri asked.

'It's not if we have the heli in service, but one of the vanes has crazed. I picked up the replacement from the cargo bay.' He pumped a thumb toward the roof. 'The primitive contributes to the sophisticated from time to time.' He grinned at her and pointed to a bright tangle of lights some distance ahead of them. 'We're nearly there.'

As they neared their destination, the orange of the main illumination surrounding the crippled heli also lit up some of the other buildings in the complex. Several were familiar to her from her reading – large barns, feedstores, the stark rails and posts of pastures, and long low buildings, some showing lighted windows.

'I'll drop you off first,' Monty said as if conferring a favor.

Peri did not take offense. If the Preserve had only the one airborne vehicle, naturally its repair would take priority over a lowly recruit.

But she was pleasantly surprised when the vehicle stopped at the door of what was obviously a row of individual accommodations.

'We may work rough and hard, but you got your own pad and the chow's top quality,' Monty said. 'Get your sleep. You'll rise and shine with the rest of us in the morning.'

Peri unbuckled the safety harness and got out stiffly, grabbing her pak. Reaching across her vacated seat, Monty hauled the door shut, leaving her standing in the roadway, coughing in the dust the tires churned up. She walked up the three steps onto the long covered porch and felt around for the door's thumb plate. She couldn't find one in the dark and was beginning to be irritated when she noticed a knob on the left-hand side of the door. With nothing to lose, she turned it and the door swung in.

To her surprise, lights came up immediately. Compared to her family's quarters in Jerhattan, this was palatial. Two *big* rooms, three by four meters each, separated by a small food dispensary and a sanitary unit. The first room was clearly a living space, complete with a communications center in one wall, and the second was for sleeping with all its amenities clearly displayed. No wall units here. The bed looked terribly inviting. Peri made short work of her necessary ablutions, removed her footgear, pulled up the covering, and laid herself down with a grateful sigh on the bed.

                              *   *   *

In what seemed the shortest possible space of time, a klaxon startled her into full wakefulness.

'Wakey-wakey-wakey! All hands ready at oh-six-thirty at the barn.' The voice was inescapable and shock had Peri stumbling out of the bed, pawing through her pak to find work clothing.

An odd noise and appetizing odor made her inspect the food dispenser to discover a mug of dark brown liquid. The liquid was scaldingly hot and rather bitter, but she recognized and welcomed the caffeine jolt it contained.

As she stepped out of her quarters, she was even more surprised to see only the faintest tinge of light in the eastern sky. Lights were on all over the complex, figures purposefully heading toward the biggest barn. The air chilled her through the light fabric of her shirt. Why had she not realized this place would not be element-protected? Shivering, she took time to retrieve the only outer garment she possessed and then ran, for the warmth, slightly out of breath as she joined the others.

'Okay, folks,' said a big man, jumping to a crate, holding up his hands. 'Monty says there's fencin' down on the station road and there's buffaloes loose. Josh, take a team an' check it out. Main job today is rounding up beef stock for the Centauri shipment. We'll work the north two hundred. Before the heli vane cracked, Barty spotted most of what we need in Crooked Canyon.' A groan rippled through the twenty or so facing him. 'Tam, Peri arrived last night so she's yours. You others can meet the pretty li'l gal later. Right now, roll 'em.'

To Peri's shock, no one went into the barn for a horse. They moved to the right as lights came up over extensive parking racks for two- and three-wheeled vehicles, some with sidecars already loaded with fencing and other equipment. Helmets and goggles were donned and the vehicles revved up, spoiling the air with exhaust fumes as the bikes – yes, the archaic name popped into Peri's mind – crisscrossed each other's paths with seeming disregard for safety before they split into two groups: one going down the right-hand road and the other straight across the grassy land that headed north.

'I'm Tambor,' a voice said beside her, and a hand, gloved as they all seemed to be on this Preserve, was jutted at her.

She took the hand, steeling herself for another viselike grip, and gave as good as she received. Tambor was a wizened man, his face grooved with lines so that his age could not be determined. He wore the same worn workgarb as the others, the broad-brimmed hat, and the gloves.

'You look a strong young 'un,' he said, appraising her with shrewd if bloodshot eyes. 'Let's see if you're worth your salt.'

Did everyone use ungrammatic speech, well sprinkled with archaic idioms? Considering the strong scientific background required by the Preserve, she had not expected the vernacular to be so conspicuous.

'You're lucky,' he added, gesturing for her to accompany him to the barn. 'We've only one more passel of mares to ship out. Just got this one lot left to be conditioned for their ride to Centauri. Cattle are put in coldsleep, but the hosses ride first class. With a li'l help from us.'

They entered the barn now by the inset door. Simultaneously lights came up along the aisle and the odor, long remembered, of horse and manure assailed Peri's olfactory senses. Then she stared, for her recollection of stabling facilities from textbooks did not match with those she now beheld.

There were fifteen very narrow straight stalls on either side of the main aisle, which was not more than a meter wide. She had assumed that the Preserve would follow the traditional ways of stable management: big loose boxes filled with straw, high ceilings, and wide corridors. In confusion, she turned to Tambor, who had been waiting for some reaction from her.

'This is a conditioning barn, gal,' he said. 'So we gotta get these critters used to the shipboard facilities, hygiene, and exercise. This is where they larn how. C'mon.'

He beckoned for her to follow him up a narrow steel ladder to an open control facility. There was one chair at the console and a stool, which he motioned for her to pull up beside him. Below, the horses were nickering.

'They know what's up. Okay down there, gals? Time for your dance step.'

He initiated a program and as Peri watched, astounded, jets of water sprayed over the rubber matting under the animals. Then from the front of each stall a bar began a slow passage to the aisle, pausing briefly as it touched the front hooves, which the horses dutifully lifted – just like a dance step, in fact. The bars continued sweeping toward the aisle where flaps suddenly opened to receive both droppings and soiled water. The bars retracted, the horses politely lifting their feet over it. The flaps closed and Peri could hear the faint rumbling of conveyor belts.

'On the ship the muck is processed, moisture recycled and the roughage compressed into cubes about so big' – he encompassed the appropriate space between thumb and forefinger – 'and stored to introduce Terran bacteria into the new soil. We just compress it and use it as fertilizer in the spring. Now,' he went on as the nickering below became insistent, 'they get their reward.'

His gnarled fingers ran over the keys and initiated another rumbling, this time over the horses' heads. They looked up expectantly. Feed cascaded into mangers and the horses began eating with stampings of pleasure and much shifting of their haunches.

'Now we gotta do the same in the sheep and goat house. Then, by the time we're finished, it'll be time for a snack fer us. After that, we exercise 'em.'

'We do?' Peri caught her breath at the prospect of riding a real live horse. She also began to psych herself up again, to prove that her surrogate training would suffice.

However, after she nearly gagged on the concentrated stench of goat and sheep in their conditioning barn, Tambor marched her back to the horse barn and up the steps, where he dialed for the snack of more hot coffee and hot muffins, which must have been freshly baked. No programmed breadstuff matched this light texture or enticing odor.

'Now we exercise our beauties. Where d'you think you're going, li'l gal?' Tambor demanded when she jumped to her feet. 'We exercise them' – and his gloved forefinger emphatically indicated the mares below them – 'just where they stand. Watch!' He tapped out a sequence, folded his arms across his chest, and followed his own advice.

To her amazement, each of the horses was beginning to move, first at a walk, then gradually into trot, and finally, into the canter gait . . . all in place on the rubber floor mats, which were also treadmills.

Peri sat down, totally deflated. How naive of her to assume that horses would be exercised by humans. If fencing was done from bikes, and stock was rounded up by heli, why did anyone need to ride the poor beasts just to conform to historical precedents!

'Now, doan look so glum, li'l gal,' Tambor said, reaching across to pat her hand. 'This is special conditioning for this extra-special shipment. The mares gotta get used to this sort of carry-on until they finally get to the meadows of Centauri. We want them, and the foals they carry, to come through the long journey fit as a fiddle and rarin' to go. This lot is about ready to graduate. They done real good. They won't suffer from a long period of inactivity. They won't spook from the sounds of a spaceship or go bananas. If you'll notice, the halters give accurate readings of their vital signs.' He pointed to the display on the monitor, which she'd been too stunned to notice. 'Now they got twenty minutes on the treadmill. *Then*' – and he presented this option as a reward to her – 'we go down and give each mare a lot of TLC.'

'TLC?'

'Tender loving care: a lot of stroking, petting, making much of 'em, and just generally making them feel pretty good. Horses like human contact. The grooms going along will do that, two-three times a day to keep 'em jollied along. Machines don't do all the work that's necessary to keep a horse happy. Not by a long shot, they don't.'

That part of the morning routine Peri really did like, once she got over feeling sorry for the horses stuck in such cramped conditions. They had, as Tambor pointed out, enough space to lie down if the urge took them.

'Horses spend a lot of time on their feet. They don't really need to take the weight off 'em, but they'll want a change of position now and again and we've allowed for it. Mind you, we had to reject some of the bigger-boned mares.' He chuckled. 'Can't have 'em castin' themselves in outer space, now can we? Did yer books tell ya how to groom a hoss?' Tambor abruptly became more rustic. 'They did? Well, here's your kit. Give 'em a good grooming. You take one side of the barn, and I'll take the other. Slap 'em on the rump and tell 'em you're coming in. They like to hear voices.'

Dutifully Peri slapped a rusty red rump.

'Nah, gal, not like that. These ain't fragile shrinking violets. They's hosses, with thick hides that won't feel no fly tap!' He demonstrated with a hearty whack and the brown mare moved to one side.

Perri slapped with more vigor and now the chestnut took notice of her. But knowing *how* to groom a horse properly did not explain how tiring the process was. By the second side of the chestnut, Peri was panting with her exertions. By the fourth mare, she was dripping with sweat and her shoulders, back, and ribs ached. Her strokes got slower and slower until she saw that she was three horses behind Tambor.

'I'll just lend you a hand this morning, being as how you're new at all this,' he said, moving in beside the gray mare.

She redoubled her efforts and finished two in the same time it took him to do two. But by then she was exhausted.

Just then the noon bell rang and Tambor guided her to the quaintly named mess hall. There was a cuttingly cold wind sweeping down from the mountains and she hugged her arms around her.

'Just you, me, and Cookie t'day,' Tambor said with obvious satisfaction as they burst into the big room, a huge fireplace throwing out additional warmth. 'Admin crew eat up at the main house noontimes, stallion barn crew are busy up there today, and everyone else is out. Cookie knows what *I* like so you're in for a treat, gal.'

Cookie was an incredibly thin tall man with a hooked nose (which, Peri thought in surprise, anyone else in this world would have had modified), a wide smile, and a cheerful disposition.

'Stew and dumplings, as ordered, Tan ol' buddy,' he said as they entered. 'Hi there, Peri, glad to meetcha. Just belly up to the table and pitch in!'

'Apple pie too?' Tambor asked, his expression like an expectant juvenile's.

'You got it.' Then Cookie affected a solemn expression.

'Poor gal. Havin' to eat what this here human disposal unit wants.'

'The aroma is very appetizing,' Peri remarked politely, determined not to judge the food by its color and lumpy texture. She could not recall ever having eaten 'stew and dumplings' or anything that resembled *this*.

'Hey, gal, yore hands is sure in a state!' Cookie said, grabbing her right hand halfway to her mouth with her first forkful. 'Git over there and put 'em into that there box! Why'nt you say somethin' 'bout 'em? Tambor, you ain't takin' good care of the help!'

'Lordee, I plumb forgot she'd need skinning. She didn't say a thing.' That last was added in a tone of approval.

Tambor dragged her off the bench and propelled her into the small treatment room off the kitchen facility. He flicked a switch as he entered and then hauled Peri by her shirtsleeve to the familiar sight of an extremities-treatment rectangle. He shoved her hands in, glaring at her so fiercely that she grinned, recognizing his look as paternal. She rotated her hands and felt the healing vibrations rejuvenating the abused tissue, smoothing away the blisters raised by the grooming tools.

'Yore hands'll toughen but you better get yoreself some gloves right smart. Come to think of it, gal, you need a few more clothes. You ain't ever lived outside a weather-regulated facility, have you?'

When Peri sat down again to eat, the stew had cooled sufficiently and, even if the textures were unfamiliar to tongue and tooth, she found it delicious. The apple pie – and she had eaten fresh apples as a special treat from time to time – was an experience for her. She expressed her pleasure to Cookie, who beamed with fatuous pride.

Tambor ate two more slices of pie before he left the table. He gestured for her to follow him to the appropriate slot that would cleanse their dishes. Evidently one did not take a long luncheon respite, but the meal had revived Peri. Tambor then took her to the Commissary outlet, just off the mess hall, where she was outfitted with real leather gloves ('nothin's better than real leather') and fleece-lined waist-length jacket ('we grow our own, y'know'), and a long weatherized coat, with straps to secure her legs ('we get all kinds of weather up here; you'll need this soon enough').

'That about takes care of your first week's wage,' Tambor said as they left the Commissary booth. 'Lib'ry, rec facilities, lounge are down this hall. You can meander down there later. Now we gotta get those animals tested, hoof, blood, and hide! They're serial tested until the day we lead 'em on board.'

While Peri was familiar with the necessary laboratory tests required for any animals to be shipped off planet, she found it odd to be working at this task with Tambor. When he was discussing the procedures and going over the results of blood, skin, saliva, feces, and urine tests with her, he seemed to slip into another personality entirely: methodical, precise, and quite professional. He gave her a satisfied nod when she had finished her lab work.

Then they went back to the conditioning barn for another session of mucking out and TLCing the mares. This time she asked Tambor for their names.

'Doan get too fond of these, gal. We spin 'em out in job lots. You could break your heart getting fond o' one or another.'

'But you said "tender loving care" . . .'

'Of the objective kind, gal. Be objective with this bunch.'

By the end of the day, when the fencing and roundup crews returned, she was so tired, it required an effort to respond to the pleasantries. She counted about forty people seated at the rough tables in the mess hall – all dressed in utilitarian gear, with weathered faces and jaunty, self-confident attitudes. Her immediate neighbors asked her to join them in some of the recreational activities, but she was too tired to accept.

'First day's the roughest,' the long-legged brunette, Chelsea, agreed. ''Specially if you're working with Tam. He's fair but he's tough.'

Chelsea was correct on all counts. Tam was tough, he kept moving every minute of the day, and never mind if she had to run to keep up. She would or die trying. Her hands hardened, she grew to enjoy that early-morning grooming, as much for the olfactory gratification that had lured her into this in the first place. The unique fragrance of horse, the tactile sensations of warm flesh under her hands, her growing realization of the individual personalities of the various animals was the reward she had anticipated. And yet . . . she became increasingly dissatisfied. Horses, horses all around, and not a one for *her* to ride.

The hands were sent here and there, on the bikes, in the big trucks, on horseback to perform the necessary tasks of the Preserve. She began to resent her very basic duties and was mollified only by the fact that Tambor was treated with great respect by everyone, including the administrators. Not even that trio were called by any titles that she ever heard in the relaxed and informal atmosphere that pervaded the Preserve. Even the exercise facilities in her Residential, where everyone worked to achieve the same goal of physical fitness, were not as casual.

By the first week, Peri had had a chance to orient herself, calling up the Preserve 'spread' on the computer in her quarters and memorizing the various areas and the twists and turns of the access roads and track. The

Preserve extended over an impressive sector of mountain range and valleys, a bastion of the natural, three hundred square kilometers that were not quite squared, having to take into account the vagaries of mountain contours. She noticed where the base camps and forestry stations and the educational farm were located, separate from the headquarters so that ponderous tour-helis did not disrupt the daily routine or disturb the animals in pasture. She was amazed that some ten thousand horses, cows, sheep, goats, and a small herd of buffalo were resident on the Preserve as well as other small animals and fowl whose natural habitat was this mountainous area.

The main base had once been a dude ranch, Tambor told her, where people would vacation in natural beauty and ride out on long treks. Her quarters had originally been one of the guest accommodations. The mess hall was original, and the barn by the corral as well as the paddock complex. The conditioning barns, the stallion quarters, lab, storage and garage facilities, heli hangar, and the other smaller buildings had been added as need arose.

She had been there two weeks when Monty borrowed her from Tam and started to teach her the fundamentals of bike riding, an experience she found wildly exhilarating and unnerving. Imagine a vehicle that was *not* voice-activated! Why, it could be dangerous with no single command safeguards for speed, direction, and braking.

'Wal, it's true hosses listen to you, and you tell 'em a lot with your tone of voice,' Monty agreed, 'but all your experience is closer to mechanical things. Learn to ride this bucking bronco first. You can't do *it* much harm.'

She fell off the mechanical thing several times, stalling, forgetting to shift gears, forgetting to brake in time, although she caught on to steering easily enough. She scraped her elbows and the calves of her legs but she finally managed to put the bike around the obstacle course behind the garage.

'Not bad,' Monty said with faint praise as she stripped off the protective helmet and mopped her sweaty face. 'Larn the tracks and roads now from the main map. You gotta be able to get anywhere on the spread in an emergency.'

She was borrowed frequently then, generally about the time she should have been having a brief respite from her work with Tambor. One day she took some tools to one base camp; another, additional lab supplies to the men up at Crooked Canyon who were scoping this year's crop of calves. She fell off twice on the rough roads until she got the knack of watching the terrain ahead of her. She boxed herself when she got back and so no one noticed her new bruises or scrapes.

But her greatest desire – to ride a live horse – seemed as distant as ever.

Whenever she could, she would spend a few moments, hanging over the corral rail, watching the mounts used by the teams: Monty's big Appie, with its spectacular blanket of cream and roan splotches; Chelsea's paint; Barty's dun; Pedro's dappled blue roan. It occurred to her that most of the hands had chosen the sport colors. There were three palominos, two pintos, a leopard spot, three grays – flea-specked, dappled, and iron – two more roans, and the very elegant bright sorrel chestnut she'd seen Tambor on from time to time. Was there some kind of competition to choose the unusual from the breeding herd? They were cetainly easily identifiable as they grazed. It was then she noticed that they moved among animals with the more traditional colors, bay, chestnut, brown . . . and one so dark it was nearly black. She liked it best – for no reason she could have explained.

* * *

'Does anyone ever ride these mares?' she asked Tambor as casually as she could when she had been two weeks at the Preserve. She hoped the little quaver in her voice was not too obvious.

'Yup. We break 'em all in case they'd be needed where they're going. Reckon we say *hasta la vista* to this lot tomorrow!'

'Tomorrow?' She couldn't suppress her surprised and regretful tone.

'Told ya not to get attached to the critters.'

Peri swallowed the lump in her throat, patting the neck of the bay mare she'd been grooming.

'There'll be another set in here soon's they rig the stalls,' he added. 'Git used to it. This's what we're here to do, and do well.' Somehow Tambor implied that she, too, had done well, and that eased the pang. 'We'll just give 'em a bath 's afternoon on account there won't be no water available fer such nonsense on board.' Then he snorted. 'Not that they'll like it much 'cause we gotta use debuggers and that stuff stinks.'

It did. Halfway through washing twenty mares, Peri could no longer bear the stench and put on a filter mask. Tambor didn't say anything but she felt she had lost his good opinion. She couldn't quite rid herself of the odor even after a long shower and much lather.

'Pugh! Stink! Goldurnit, Tambor, you and Peri sit down at the far end' was the order from the other diners.

'If that's the way you feel about it, we'll raise you one,' Tambor said and, with a broad wink for Peri to join him, they moved to the bar to eat their dinner.

'We really do stink,' Peri said as she settled herself with her back to the dining room. 'I washed real good and I can still smell myself.'

'Doesn't last long but I gotta admit it is a powerful stench. But then, it's efficient. Most colonies prefer to leave the parasites back here. Ever think of shipping out?'

'You mean, as a groom?' Peri glanced at him but his expression gave no hint of any ulterior motive for the question.

'Nah, as a settler. Purty li'l gal like you'd do well out there.'

'If there were horses,' she began tentatively.

Tambor grinned at her. 'Yore shore gone on horseflesh, ain't you?'

Peri nodded slowly, not able to confide the depth of that fascination to anyone, even to someone like Tambor, who had evidently spent his life with the creatures.

The next day, while Peri did feel the wrench of watching animals she had cared for and grown fond of being shipped out, she was also fascinated by the process. The entire unit of stalls, complete with treadmill and cleansing bars (which would be reattached to appropriate outlets in the cargo hold of the spaceship), were slipped out on well-oiled runners into the maw of the transport.

She, Tambor, and the three handlers who would be traveling with the mares to their new world stood on the center aisle, ready to go to any animal that showed distress. But the mechanical noises had been part of the conditioning and the transfer was so smoothly made that none of the horses demonstrated any strong reaction.

'A nice healthy bunch, Tambor,' the head groom said, passing over the consignment note for his signature. 'You do yourself proud. This your new offsider?' Peri was given a broad grin.

'This is Peri. Good li'l worker.'

Peri felt herself blush with pride at Tambor's unexpected praise. She had an errant urge to wave good-bye as the immense cargo-heli lifted. She did watch it until it was out of sight over the foothills, and only then realized that Tambor had, too. He gave a sigh but she didn't hear exactly what he muttered under his breath.

'Yore on the main workforce tomorrow, Peri. Take the rest of the day off.' Tambor strode quickly away, followed by her burble of thanks. His shoulders were slumped and his head down; he kicked a rock out of his way and suddenly Peri realized that Tambor should listen to his own advice.

Behind her was the empty shell of the conditioning barn, all cables and rollers, a strangely gutted organism. With aimless steps she wandered over to the pasture where stock were having a rest day. Her little blackie was racing, head up and tail carried high, with two bays. She'd never seen anyone riding the little black, but maybe it hadn't been broken yet. She'd heard enough now to know that horses were broken and backed at four or five, depending on the need for them. Most of the animals used by the teams were mares expected to breed foals at some time in their lives. Sperm from stallions of all breeds had been preserved against need, and only if a colony required an entire horse was one bred.

Working so closely with the stalled animals had given Peri confidence. Now, prompted by that still-unsatisfied desire to *ride* a horse, she ducked in between the rails and walked down to the nearest group. They lifted their heads, eyeing her. Monty's big Appie softly nickered what she translated as a query.

'No, you're not needed, Splodge,' she replied, and moved on a zigzag course toward the black mare who was standing hipshot, head to tail with one of the yearlings, each tail whisking flies from the other's head. 'Easy there, gal,' Peri said as she approached, holding one hand out, palm up.

Sleepily the mare raised one eyelid. Peri moved closer, being careful to move toward her left side, as Tambor had instructed her, keeping away from the yearling and its quick hind feet. The mare was not in a stable, was not haltered to a ring, could move away the moment she suspected danger.

'Hi, there, gal,' Peri continued not realizing that she was falling into the prevalent drawl, 'how're ya doin'? You're sure a pretty thing! All shiny black, like satin – dusty satin.'

Curious, the mare stretched out her neck, nostrils flaring slightly as she made identification of Peri. Her nose whiskers tickled and Peri took another cautious step forward. The yearling poked its head over the black's back to take notice of the intruder, but it also wasn't startled.

'Hello, there li'l gal,' Peri went on, close enough now to stroke the nose. Another slow step and she was at the mare's side, one hand still under her nose, the other stroking her neck and down her shoulder. The mare whuffled into her hand, then abruptly raised her head and pulled her lips back from her teeth, shaking her muzzle in the air.

'Don't tell me I still stink of disinfectant?'

The mare stamped but drew back when Peri attempted to stroke her again. Suddenly her ears pricked up, her head went erect, and she stared off to the foothills.

Faintly Peri heard the distant sound of an airborne vehicle and judiciously stepped away. While most of the horses on the Preserve were well accustomed to such noises, they could all spook, and she'd be smart to retreat.

By the time Peri reached the corral fence again, the aerial disturbance had passed off to the northwest. She stood for a long while, watching the little mare move, noting her conformation, everything about her. Then she went back to her quarters. Maybe a good long soak would eradicate the last of the medicinal stink. One good thing about the Preserve: There was no water rationing when artesian wells drew upon hidden reserves deep in the mountains.

After some desultory lounging about after her long shower, Peri realized how busy she had been: healthily tired at night in a way that was never possible in the Linear, no matter how hard one exercised or worked. She also didn't like doing nothing. In just three weeks she was attuned to the pulse of the Preserve in a way she had never been to the Residential rhythms. How odd!

She could put this time to better use than napping, so she dressed and went up to the mess hall. Since she hadn't even had time to explore the research library, she went right to its shelves of tapes on the history of the Preserve. She was in one corner when she heard the voices. Then a phrase stood out and, shamelessly, she listened.

'So far so good, but you know the percentage of failure, Steve.' Tambor was speaking and not in his drawl.

'Wouldn't much matter if she failed the last test,' she heard the other man say in a rueful tone, 'she's good enough on the practical. Seems to fit in.'

There was a snort. 'Who'd know? She doesn't say much – just sits there with those big eyes of hers watching. A real Residential graduate.'

'Hmm. What's wrong with being quiet? That's better than those motormouths you always complain about. All wind and no substance. You said she does whatever she's asked, does it well and no complaints. Not even when the bike pitched her off. Cookie saw her using the box, and from the reading it was a bad fall. Did the mares like her?'

Tambor laughed. 'Yes, and she really liked working with them. All but wept to see 'em loaded.'

'Isn't that your usual criterion, Tambor King-Sangster-Mahmood?' asked the other man ironically.

'I just wish she was a tad more outgoing. She's too

self-contained. The quiet ones can surprise you.'

'Are you talking horses or humans, Tam?'

The two men moved off down the corridor and Peri didn't hear Tam's response. She remained stock-still, one hand on the spine of a tape, the hairs risen on the nape of her neck and a sick sort of cold feeling in the pit of her stomach. There wasn't anyone else they could have been talking about but herself. Tambor had been testing her all along and she hadn't realized it?

A second shock jolted through her. Tambor King-Sangster-Mahmood? The tape she had been reaching for – one of the foundation tests, *Adaptation Techniques for Equine Types on Colonial Worlds* – had been compiled and taped by T. King-Sangster-Mahmood. She'd read every tape he'd produced before she got here. Drawl and all, that undistinguished man who had worked her butt off was the *real* boss of Idaho Preserve. She gulped.

'But he did say I was a good little worker.' She clutched at that praise as she crept back to her quarters. What was wrong with being quiet? If she had something to say, she said it . . . *except not to ask if you could ride a horse. You were afraid to ask that, weren't you? Maybe if you had* . . .

She couldn't just suddenly talk a blue streak at dinner; that would have been too out of character. Especially in the vicinity of Steve or Tambor. That'd be a real give-away.

And this final test? What could it be? If she'd been tested all along and hadn't realized it . . . Worry made her more silent than ever. She wished she could ask someone but, as she looked over those in the mess hall, she realized now that she'd had very little contact with anyone but – Tambor.

'That's a deep sigh for a li'l gal,' Monty said, slipping into the seat beside her.

She managed a genuine smile, frantically casting about

in her mind for something to add, for she couldn't just grin at him like a fool.

'The mares left today. I was sort of sorry to see the last of them.'

'Glutton for punishment, huh?' Monty grinned at her. 'Conditioning's not *my* favorite chore but we all gotta do it. Didn't I see you out in the pasture?'.

'I had a half day,' she said, almost apologetically. 'Splodge was friendly.'

'He likes pretty gals too.' Monty had a very winning smile. 'Saw you with that black mare. Didja like her?'

'I couldn't get near her,' Peri said ruefully. 'Do I still smell of debugger?' she asked him.

'Nope! Or I wouldn't be sitting this close to you!' His grin got broader. 'Say' – and he cocked his head at her – 'wouldja care to have a go at the big board?'

'With you?' She was astonished.

Monty was a formidable gamesplayer, the solo champion of the Preserve. She had watched his lightning reflexes often enough and admired his strategy, but the game board was a popular evening occupation and she hadn't wanted to put herself forward.

Monty grinned, full of devilment. 'Wal, I don't rightly think you'd want to go agin me, but I've a bet on with Pedro and Chelsea and you're the only partner they'll allow me.'

She exhaled with gusto. 'I think they're rigging it.'

'Could be. But I've a notion you aren't as slack a player as you make out.'

'I'll do my best!'

'S'all anyone can ask of you.'

She didn't disappoint him nor did she grin at the chagrin suffered by Pedro and Chelsea.

'We demand a rematch,' the two losers chanted.

'Late to start another one.' Tambor spoke up, having joined the audience about the board and players. 'We've got some ponies to break tomorrow an' you-all's gonna need your wits fer sure.'

'An' I sure as shootin' don't want no soreheads breakin' bones on me,' Monty added.

'Rematch tomorrow then, Monty!' Pedro eyed him with a stern eye.

'Sure. Right, pardner?' And Monty gave Peri a friendly clout on the shoulder.

'Sure!' she said, not at all certain.

She lay awake far too late, worrying about the final test and her incurable taciturnity, hearing owlhoot until the rhythmic sound finally lulled her to sleep

There was a buzz of excitement the next morning in the mess hall – an excitement to which Peri, despite her fretting, was not immune. Not everyone was to take part in the breaking, so those assigned elsewhere shouted cheerful encouragements and Peri heard wagers laid. There were evidently four in the breaking team, Monty, Pedro, the dark-haired Chelsea, and a lanky girl named Beth.

'You might as well come watch too,' Tambor told Peri, who hadn't been assigned to any duty. 'See how it's done.'

When she reached the smaller corral, Tambor gestured for her to take a seat on the rail as others were doing, but unlike them, she could think of no banter or jokes to exchange. She noticed her little black satin mare in the pen just beyond the corral with ten or twelve others that were milling about uneasily.

Then Monty entered the pen, gracefully swinging his lariat loop over his head, and the animals began to canter about, whinnying in alarm. She thought he was aiming to catch a sturdy piebald but, instead, at the last moment, the little black mare seemed to run into the noose.

'Change your mind, Monty?' someone yelled in a bantering tone.

'She'll do as well,' Tambor called.

The black had other ideas and valiantly tried to run away from this sudden restriction, head down and bucking, but Monty had snubbed the rope on a post. With his quarry captured, the others were let into the next pen.

'It's the old-fashioned way.' Tambor said, appearing beside Peri, arms draped over the top rail. 'She'll be a range horse. Doesn't have the quality for one of the advanced schooling saddle stock. Nice enough conformation, a shade too short in the back, a trifle more bone, but that's all to the good in these parts.'

Fascinated, Peri watched as Monty walked his hands up the rope to the rigidly straining mare. He stroked and talked to her and gradually slack appeared in the rope. The mare was still tense, head held high, nostrils flaring, but Monty persisted, stroking and then slapping her more casually – neck, shoulders, withers, rump – until she stood more easily.

Before either Peri or the mare was aware of what he intended, he had a blindfold on her. Chelsea and Pedro approached with breaking tackle and the little mare, trembling now, was saddled and a hackamore slipped over her head. Chelsea stood at her head, one hand on the blindfold. Pedro hovered on the same side, stroking the mare's shoulder.

'At my word,' Monty said, taking up the thick reins and springing lightly to her back, not quite putting his full weight in the saddle. The little mare tensed on her splayed legs. Peri held her breath. Then Monty sat down. 'Let 'er rip!'

Blindfold whipped off, Chelsea and Pedro spring back and the mare sprang up, all four feet off the ground. Head down between her knees, she bucked and twisted, turned and sunfished, trying to remove the weight on her back. Everyone along the corral was yelling, whistling, shouting. Peri wasn't sure whether they were encouraging the mare or Monty, who kept kicking her forward.

He looked far too big to ride that little mare, Peri thought. *It just wasn't fair.*

'Nope, it isn't,' Tambor said, and Peri was appalled that she had spoken out loud. 'But he's a great hand at riding 'em out. She's spunky but she's smart. See, she's had a chance to figure out that she can't buck him off. Now she'll start running.'

'I don't think so.' Some perversity made Peri say this just as the mare planted her feet and came to a jarring halt. And refused to move despite Monty's heels and the shouts and yells from the onlookers.

'Hmm. How'd you figure that one out?' Tambor asked.

She grinned at him. 'She's smart, too smart to wear herself out running around in circles.'

Monty, with Chelsea at the mare's head, dismounted. She snorted, sweat staining her neck and flanks, but her legs remained stiff, propped like an immovable scaffolding.

'G'wan down there, Peri,' Tambor said, and before she knew what he was about, he'd shoved her off the rail into the corral. 'G'wan! Monty's taken the buck out of her for you. Your turn now.'

Pedro was beside Peri, slapping a crash helmet on her head, propelling her inexorably to the mare, who was again blindfolded. Monty grabbed her by the leg and hoisted her toward the saddle. Reflex actions found her settling into the deepest part, finding the stirrups, responding to drills learned on inanimate surrogates. But there was a vast difference to the feel of the mare between her legs, the trembling under her buttocks, the acrid aroma of sweaty fear rising up to her nostrils. Mixed with her own.

'When you're ready, Peri. Now's the time to put theory into practice,' Monty said, his grin encouraging.

Gulping, Peri managed a short nod of her head and Chelsea whipped off the blindfold. The others stood back.

'Easy, girl. Easy now, girl!' Peri said, her voice trembling as much as the mare.

'G'wan there,' roared Pedro, and he must have swatted the mare with the rope end for she barged forward with an incredible surge.

This was totally unlike anything Peri had ever experienced, even when the surrogate had been programmed for random and violent movements. Peri's teeth jarred together and she felt the jolt through her entire body, but those long hours of practice saved her as her thighs tightened and she leaned back, against the forward motion of the bucking mare.

Buck! Buck! Switch! The mare was determined to relieve her back of its burden. *Rear!*

Unexpectedly the black neck came up and cracked Peri painfully across her nose. She grabbed for mane, feeling her leg grip loosen in surprise at the shock. Grimly she clung, one hand on the rein, the other on the mane, struggling to regain her seat, but she was off balance and the mare wasn't underneath her anymore but to one side of her and she was falling . . .

For a frantic moment Peri was afraid she'd never be able to breathe again. That ground, for all the sand, had been very hard. Much harder than occasional tosses to the matting around the surrogate had ever been. She was aware of the sudden silence from the onlookers, a congregate bated breath, waiting for her reaction to the fall. She elbowed herself to a sitting position, smearing blood and dust across her face as she looked around for her recent mount.

'Grab her, someone! Don't stand there eating flies!' She

climbed to her feet, aware that her shoulder ached, her ribs, that her nose was leaking blood. And very much aware that this was her final test. She rubbed her bloody face on her sleeve as she strode purposefully across the little corral to where the mare was backing away from Pedro as fast as she could. Peri intercepted her circuit, jammed her foot in the stirrup, and hauled herself back up into the saddle before the mare or Pedro realized what she had done. Before she herself realized what she had done. But no flesh-and-blood critter was going to get the better of her. Not when she had practiced and practiced and practiced. All that time and effort was not going to be wasted by one lucky buck of a range-bred mustang. Settling herself as deep as she could, Peri grabbed the rein from Pedro's hand and dug both heels in the mare's heaving flanks.

'C'mon, you mangy wall-eyed bangtail, show me your worst!'

'Kick her, Peri! Ride her, cowgirl! Yahooo! Keep her moving! Ride her out! Give her what for!'

Advice came from all sides and Peri, determined not to measure her length in the sand again in front of this audience, kept after the mare until she settled to a weary trot, her sides pumping with exertion, and finally reeled to a halt, head down.

She got a rousing cheer from her audience but, wiping her face in her sleeve, Peri swiveled to face Tambor.

'Well, now, Tambor King-Sangster-Mahmood, it appears to me that it isn't only the hosses you rough-break here. Do I pass muster now?'

There were a few hoots and good-natured hollers at her question. From the corner of her eye, she saw Monty grinning, sheer devilment in his eyes. Pedro had flung his hat to the ground in a sort of triumphant way. Chelsea was slapping her legs at her impudence. Obscurely encouraged by their demonstrations, Peri kept her eyes fixed on Tambor. He glanced around as if taking in the attitudes of the assembled, but Peri knew it was his verdict that mattered, that he'd been her examiner in all the skills she would need here at the Preserve. She couldn't stand it if she were rejected. She'd never felt more alive than at this moment, with a heaving mare between her legs, sweat and blood trickling down her face, the hot sun above and the mountains around. She waited, aware that her breath was no less ragged than the mare's.

'Wal, Tam, do I?' She'd never been so bold before in her life. But this time it mattered too much to remain silently, obediently waiting.

Deliberately he pushed the hat to the back of his head and slowly let a grin break over his weathered face. 'I reckon you do at that. For all you're a quiet li'l gal, you're full o'grit. I reckon we just better sign you on permanent.'

And Peri let fly with a wild yell that startled even the tired black mare.

'Did I say "quiet"?' Tam asked. 'Now you put that mare up and I doan wanta find a single sweaty hair left on her hide. Didn't I larn you nothing in that barn?'

IF MADAM
LIKES YOU . . .

'It's green for go, fellas,' said the Systems Engineer, his bony face wreathed with a weary but satisfied expression. He leaned back in the chair, arching his spine until all heard a muted *crack*.

Migonigal, the Portmaster, winced and grinned comically at his assistant, Sakerson; his shipmate, Ella Em; and Rando Cleem, who manned the suspect glitched mainframe.

'And?' Migonigal prompted.

'And what? You had a couple of sour chips, five worn circuits, a wonky board, and some faulty connections – according to my diagnostics. Nothing serious.'

'Nothing serious! Nothing serious?' Migonigal echoed himself as he turned a stunned expression to the others.

'But what caused the . . .' Sakerson began, but Migonigal cut him off with a sharp slice of his thick fist.

'Your basic system is jolly good,' the SysEng said, rising and stretching his arms over his head. This time a crick in his neck went *pop*. He patted the console affectionately. 'Well designed. However, I upgraded your mainframe with a couple of new programs. An internal systems check so this won't happen again. You know how cost-conscious the Space Station Services are,' he went on as he packed up his service kit. 'And I installed new holographics software to help you guys dock faster.'

'Docking isn't a problem,' Migonigal said, disgruntled,

but he signed the others not to pursue the matter. 'Look, need any fresh tucker from our hydro garden?' he asked ingratiatingly as the SysEng zipped himself into his space gear. 'We've got some beaut . . .'

The SysEng gave a scornful snort. 'I got better'n they issue you lot, and I don't have to share.' He beckoned closer to Migonigal in a conspiratorial fashion. 'The ghost I hear tell you guys got . . .' Migonigal leaned away from the man in denial. 'Just a sour chip in the visualization program. You won't have trouble now.'

'A sour chip?' Migonigal's bass voice traveled incredulously up an octave to end on a despairing note. Sakerson crossed his fingers behind his back and he noticed Rando making an odd warding gesture. Ella grunted her disgust with the SysEng.

'Hey, what's this?' The SysEng had picked up his helmet, in which now reposed a yellow banana. 'Hey, maybe you guys got something I haven't at that? Got any more where this came from?'

Migonigal stifled a groan and shrugged again, spreading his hands and grinning. 'Could be. But I'm hoping that is the last one.'

'Yeah, well, ta very,' and, peeling the fruit, the SysEng bit off a hunk, chewing with pleasure. 'Hey, just ripe too. Okay, I'm off. Check me out, will you, mate? I'm due at Wheel Four in two days. Gotta burn it!'

Migonigal signaled for Sakerson to escort the specialist to his vehicle, moored at Dock 4, which was nearest the control module.

'Anything we should know about the updates?' Sakerson asked as he followed the SysEng down the corridor, his felt slippers making no noise on the plasrub flooring.

'All I did was wipe the glitches and load the new programs. Same general format as the old . . .' A wicked grin over his shoulder at Sakerson. 'And exorcised your ghoulies and ghosties.' He chuckled his amusement.

'Fine. Thanks!' Sakerson could not keep the sarcasm out of his voice as he paused at the control module.

'Catch,' the SysEng added, flipping the empty banana skin at Sakerson. 'Biodegradable, you know! This station needs all it can get.' The portal closed on his healthy guffaw, and with Sakerson bereft of any suitable rejoinder.

It had been ignominious enough to have had to call in a systems engineer to check the mainframe, in the unlikely case that . . . recent developments were a systems malfunction. While all the stationers had examined their . . . inexplicable problem among themselves at great length . . . no one was bass-ackward enough to let a whisper of it off Three. Just like a SysEng to 'know' it all before he'd even docked.

With a sigh, Assistant Portmaster Sakerson threw the skin at the nearest disposal hatch on his way back to the control center, wishing it were something else that apparently wasn't biodegradable.

When Sakerson reentered the control room, Ella was on Console, completing the debarkation routines. The SysEng's flashy little FTL drifted down-away from Space Station Three's Wheel before ignition and the flare vanished quickly in the twinkle of star blaze. Sakerson registered, and appreciated, the Portmaster's sour expression.

'Well?' Migonigal asked his spacemate.

'Well,' Ella replied with a shrug, giving the console one more tap. 'Program sure ran smooth. But *it* always did. I just can't see how *she* could materialize, or whatever she does, in a mainframe built a hundred years after she breathed her last. It doesn't compute. It also doesn't make any sense.' She rose and gave the disconsolate Migonigal a hug and a kiss, winking over his shoulder at Sakerson. 'Little enough to titillate folks stuck out in the Void. Been kinda fun to have *something* to puzzle out.'

Migonigal gave her a wide-eyed look of dismay. 'But if that wag-winged SysEng spreads this around . . .'

'You're a good portmaster, sir, with a clean record,' Sakerson said stoutly. 'SS-Three's never had any effups, bleeds, crashes, or leaks. It's a good station and a good crew. Besides, we can always say it's just a new game.'

To relieve the boredom of off-duty, 'leisure' hours, Space Stations, Wheels, and Mining Platforms were immensely creative, given their limited recreational facilities. There was an ongoing informal competition to invent new 'games,' physical or mental! The good ones circulated.

'That's it, Sakersonboy, you tell him,' Ella said, grinning. 'He won't believe me and I've been his mate for yonks!' She glanced at the chrono. 'Your watch, Sakersonboy. C'mon, Miggy, Rando says his new war starts at twenty-one hundred, and I'm gonna whip that war-ace no matter how long it takes me.'

In self-defense, and to keep from thinking about their apparition – and 'her' habits – Rando Cleem had started a long drawn-out 'war,' winning battle after battle no matter who was his opponent.

'Us,' Migonigal corrected her, letting himself be drawn out of the control room. 'I figured out the tactics that had his forces retreating last watch . . .' The panel slid shut over the rest.

Sakerson grinned ruefully. He envied Migonigal for Ella. She was all that a fellow could want in a spacemate. Trouble was that, when Sakerson had been assigned to Space Station Three six months ago, everyone was paired off, one way or another, with the exception of Sigi Tang, who was near retirement, and Iko Mesmet, who never left the spin-chambers. Sakerson tried not to feel like the odd man out but his singleness was beginning to get to him.

He took the console seat, for it was now time for the routine station status check. When Sakerson began to log the results in, he really did see an improvement in the speed at which the data was reported. Once the report was finished, Sakerson altered his password. SysEngs were supposed to be discreet but no one liked to think that even the most closemouthed head in the galaxy had accessed personal data. There were fifty-nine minutes before any further routine, no scheduled arrivals, and his relief was not due for another two hours.

Rubbing his hands together, Sakerson ran a test check, to familiarize himself with the new internal systems check. That activity soon palled because, despite his proficiency and a half year's familiarity with SS-3's mainframe, he could not discern the subtle minor alterations. He had his hand halfway to the switch to looksee what was happening to Rando's war in the staff leisure facility, but he wasn't really that interested. Rando always won. He had reactions like the station's cat and must have been sleeping on military history and strategy tapes. Great man, Rando, even if he did see ghosts. Girl ghosts. Pretty girl ghosts. Cuddly girl ghosts! Sakerson hadn't seen a manifestation, though he'd found a lot of cherries in his bunkspace. Rando had pronounced her vivaciously attractive, which had annoyed his spacemate, Cliona, considerably.

Sakerson liked a calmer, dignified type of girl, but not as phlegmatic as Sinithia, the unflappable station medic. Tilda, who was Trev's mate, was aggressive and went in for tae kwon do with an enthusiasm only Rando matched. Trev usually watched. It didn't do, he'd told Sakerson privately, for two spacemates to get too physical with each other. (Having watched Tilda spar, Sakerson decided that she could deck Trev anytime she liked. It was shrewd of Trev to let her work steam off on Rando.) In any event, while there were some very good-looking female persons on board, not one had indicated they might prefer his company to that of their present attachment.

A green flashing light on the visual pad caught his attention. SPECIFY. Sakerson blinked. He didn't remember turning on the holography program but the amber-lit pad was on.

SPECIFY WHAT?

APPEARANCE.

Some had said that the Carmen Miranda ghost had been generated by the holography circuits. The SysEng had put paid to that theory. But Sakerson gulped because he hadn't, to his knowledge, accessed the pad.

Then he grinned. Well, he could check the new software out, and have a bit of fun. He'd program the girl of his dreams and see what came up. He wouldn't mind a ghost of his own creation. Preferably one that didn't leave bananas where a guy could slip on the mushy things.

He entered in the spirit of the exercise so completely that the bells of change of watch sounded before he had quite finished the holograph. He just had time to name the file, 'Chiquita,' thinking of the SysEng's banana skin, before he filed it away under his new password. He grinned as Rando arrived, certain that would be one of the first things the war-ace would also do.

'Did you win, Rando?'

'No contest,' Rando replied, slipping into the chair Sakerson vacated.

'How many does that make?'

'Hell, I lost count. Easily over the eighteen-hundred mark now.'

Which was nearly as many as the Station's previous war-ace had achieved.

'Have a quiet one,' Sakerson said in traditional exit fashion.

He had a light meal before going to his space, jetting himself clean before he netted down in his bunk. But sleep eluded him as his thoughts kept returning to the unfinished holograph. He had her a shade too short – he'd have to bend awkwardly to kiss her. Much more comfortable to just bend his head slightly. And the shape of her face should be oval, rather than round. He'd rather she had high cheekbones to give her face character, and a firmer jaw. The retroussé nose wouldn't fit the cheekbones: make it delicate and longer, and a broad higher brow. He'd got the hair just right, swinging in black waves to her shoulder blades. Sometimes she'd wear it up, the ends curling over the top of a headband. He'd seen some beautifully carved scrimshaws, plastic, but stained and polished like old ivory. One would go great against black hair.

The eyes proved a quandary. He vacillated between a medium green and a brilliant light blue. Then he compromised. One would be the green, the other the blue. He'd had a station mate on Alpha-2 with a blue eye and a brown eye. She said it was a genetic trait.

He hovered between a cheek dimple or a cleft in the chin – he'd seen a very beautiful pre-Silicon Age actress who'd had a fetching cleft. His mind made another tangent – would a cinema search break the monotony of Rando winning wars? Or better still, song titles!

'I'm Chiquita Banana and I'm here to say . . .'

Unbidden, the advertising jingle popped into his head. Old Rando wouldn't do well in that kind of game, now would he? All he ever read were strategy treatises and he only watched ancient war movies. Of course, that was all there were.

Having called up the silly tune, Sakerson found it hard to shake and ended up having to go through his Serenity Sequence to get to sleep.

★　　★　　★

'One thousand eight hundred and twelve wars is enough!' Trev yelled, enunciating carefully. 'That is all, Rando, *finito*! The wars are over.'

'Yeah, and what're we going to do now?'

'"The skin you love to touch,"' Sakerson said, grimacing ludicrously and smoothing the back of his left hand with his fingers, blinking his eyes coyly. '"Eighteen hour one."'

Rando stared at Sakerson. 'What's wrong with him!'

Trev shrugged.

'What's the reference?' Sakerson asked, snapping a finger at Rando. 'A new game – spot the product from the jingle!'

'"The skin you love to touch"?' Rando guffawed. Then he paused, rolling his eyes. Rando was a competitor: he hated to lose – anything. 'Okay, how much boning up time do we get?'

'Anytime you're off shift,' Sakerson replied, feeling generous. The brief scrolling he'd done in the history of advertising reassured him. Not even Rando's rattrap mind could encompass all the variations of the centuries. Hell, most big companies changed slogans three and four times a year. The Madison Space Platform was named for the industry that started on the famous Avenue, in honor of all the catchphrases that had generated enthusiasm for The Big Step. 'Warm-up game tomorrow thirteen hundred in the wardroom.'

By 1400 the next day, half the off-duty stationers were there, nearly forty players, and Trev had programmed a tank to display the distinctive logos and watchwords. Sakerson got a buzz watching the enthusiasm of the players. In another day, it had become a fad to log in and out with some catchy slogan or whistled tune. A lot of people spoke to Sakerson in the aisles and corridors who had never noticed him before and he was feeling pretty good with himself. Except that, he still occupied single space. He keenly felt a woman need and there was simply no match for him on SS-3.

Out of this sense of loneliness, he called up the Chiquita program again and made the alternations he had considered that first night. She was real pretty, his Chiquita, dark curls falling from the headband, a trim tall figure in her station togs. And he extended his daydream beyond physical appearance.

Chiquita had a quick mind, and a temper. She was a . . . medic? . . . teacher? . . . programmer . . . engineer . . . quartermaster . . . Yeah, quartermaster would fit in with his goal of Portmaster. Space required more and more stations as way-points, beacons in the deep Void, manned and ready to guide the merchantmen, cargo drones, and passenger cruisers as well as 'shore leave' for naval personnel. A good team complemented each other, like Migonigal and Ella, Cliona and Rando, and Tilda and Trev. Chiquita would have been asteroid-belt born, comfortable with life on a space station because too often the planet-born got to yearning for solid earth under their feet or wind in their face or some such foolishness. She'd maybe have done some solid-side time in university so she had polish. A spacer should have experienced the alternative so s/he'd know what s/he wasn't missing. Sakerson hadn't minded four years' study on Alpha Ceti but he'd been bloody damned glad to get posted to the Alpha-2 Platform, and on to Station Three . . . in spite of recent 'occurrences.'

Then, too, the job was getting too much for the present Quartermaster, old Sigi. On the one hand, everyone did their best to help the old guy – hell, he was Original Personnel – but there came a time when you couldn't cover up because it endangered the Station.

Sakerson turned back to the more pleasant pastime. He tried to imagine Chiquita's laugh: some girls looked great and had laughs like . . . like squeezed plastic. And she'd have a real sparkle in her eyes so you had a clue to her inner feelings. And she'd have them, too. Straight dealing, straight talking, so he wouldn't have to think up alternatives the way Trev did with his Tilda.

He heard someone beyond the panel and he fumbled across the keys to save Chiquita to his personal file before Migonigal entered to relieve him of duty.

'No problems?' the Portmaster asked him, looking at the main panel with raised eyebrows.

'None, sir. None at all. Quiet watch, all status reports logged in quiet, too,' Sakerson replied, staring the Portmaster right in the eye to prove his innocence.

'Hmmm, well, thought I saw a send flash. Personal correspondence has to go out in the public spurts, Sakerson.'

Sakerson now looked back at the terminal but the only color showing was the green of stability and order.

'I know that, sir. Have a quiet.'

Migonigal flashed him a quick look. 'Is that a slogan, too?'

'Up here, maybe,' Sakerson replied with a grin.

He left without unseeming haste and gave the matter no further thought. Until it was sleeptime and he had to slow himself down after a rousing game of Slogan, which he had won on points. Rando wasn't the fastest eidetic, on board, not by a long shot. In fact, it soon began to take all Sakerson's free time to keep ahead of Rando on the history tapes to air more and more esoteric slogans and score Rando down.

'"The world's finest bread"?'

'Silvercup!'

'"Let them eat cake"!'

'Not an advertising slogan! Disqualify!'

'"When it rains, it pours"!'

'What about "Never scratches"?'

'"Good to the last drop"?'

'"I'd walk a mile for a Camel."'

'What's a camel???'

'"Nestlé's makes the very best . . ." what?'

'Hey, does it have to be a product, Sakerson?'

'It has to be a slogan.'

'Gotcha this time, then,' Trev chortled. '"Only YOU can prevent forest fires."'

'Forest fires? That's prehistoric!'

'Yeah, but whose slogan was it?'

'I got one – "You'll wonder where the yellow went . . ."'

'Not fair, you gotta give the whole slogan. Give us a break!'

'"Call for Philip Morris!"'

'Who he?'

'You mean, what's he.'

'Keep it clean, gang, keep it clean.'

'That's not a slogan.'

'No, good advice!'

Everyone caught the fever and the station sizzled as much as it had when the ghost rumor started. They sent the game on with the crew of the freighter *Marigold*, the light cruiser *Fermi*, and the destroyer *Valhalla*. Space Station Four beamed for the rules and then Tilda had the bright idea of trading them with Mining Platform Tau Five for twenty cases of prime gin: a grand change from Cookie's raw rum. A passenger liner brought Slogan for three carcasses of authentic earth beef meat and the Mess voted Sakerson free drinks for a week. Which, since he didn't drink much anyhow, Sakerson thought was spurious, but he took it as being a gesture of good will.

Of course, Chiquita wouldn't mind a drink or two, and she'd be very good at Slogan: nearly as quick as he was.

'"99 and 44/100% pure – it floats."'

'Let's not mess up the Station now, gang!'

'"Damn the torpedoes!"'

'Not applicable!'

'Well, it became a warcry.'

'Warcries are not slogans!'

'I don't see why not! A slogan's a slogan. It stands for something!'

'What does "damn the torpedoes" stand for?'

'Not surrendering when faced with invincible odds!'

'"Nuts to you!"' Rando shouted, finally getting a chance to play.

The Police Vehicle hailed Space Station Three while Sakerson was on duty and protocol required that the Portmaster be summoned for such official arrivals. The PV came from Alpha, priority mission, coded urgent.

'I dunno,' the Portmaster said, scrubbing his short-cropped gray hair. 'What's the priority, Captain?' he asked the PV.

'Urgent personnel orders, Portmaster Migonigal! Just let us nose in. I've got the requisition and travel papers. Shipshape and Bristol fashion, highest priority. I'm putting them in the scan now. Hear you've got some good gin aboard for a change.'

'Commencing docking procedures, Captain,' Migonigal replied stiffly. 'Sakerson, you have the conn. Dock this . . . (the pause said 'sodding so-and-so') vehicle. I've got to tell Sigmund to hide some of the gin.' The PVs had been known to drink a station dry, for hospitality decreed that the defenders of the Void should have un-limited access to Station consumables. 'He would know about the gin,' the Portmaster said with a rueful sigh. 'And what in hell is he bringing in? I don't remember requisitioning anything recently, certainly nothing high priority that requires police escort!'

'They might just have been first available space, sir,' Sakerson said, busy with hands and eyes on the delicate task of matching the three-dimensional speeds and shapes of a large space station and a very small, fast PV.

'Now, how the hell could this happen?' Migonigal demanded, watching the printout on the scanner. His question was not rhetorical but Sakerson could not spare a glance. 'You can ask and ask and ask for something essential, even critical, and you can't get them to shift ass below and send it up. I could have sworn I hadn't forwarded Sigi's transfer to Control. And here I've got a replacement.' Migonigal sounded totally mystified. 'Not a bad looker, either.' Migonigal snickered. 'Makes a nice change from old Sigi. Time he retired anyhow.'

'Ship's locked in, Portmaster,' Sakerson said, leaning back with a sigh. Big ships were a lot easier to dock. He glanced over at Migonigal's screen and nearly fell out of his chair.

'Yeah, pretty as a picture,' Migonigal went on, oblivious to the consternation of his assistant. 'Perez y Jones, Chiquita Maria Luisa Caterina, b. 2088, Mining Base 2047, educated Centauri, specialty, Quartermaster. Not that much experience for we only need someone who can remember to order what we need and where it's stored.'

Sakerson stared with panic-widened eyes at the ID scan. This had to be the weirdest coincidence in the galaxy. Granted that out of the trillions of physical possibilities, someone vaguely resembling his 'dream' girl was theoretically possible, but the probability . . . Sakerson's mind momentarily refused to function. HOW? The mainframe had just been vetted: all the boards, the circuits; there hadn't been so much as a tangerine or a cherry appearing for a week, nothing since the SysEng's banana.

'I'll go down and greet her, give Sigi the good news. He won't believe it either. Yeah, while I'm doing courtesy, you call Sigi and tell him to save some of the gin for his farewell blast.' Migonigal left Sakerson to stare at the visual realization of his imagined perfect woman.

After his watch, it took all Sakerson's courage to enter the wardroom. He could hear the laughter, the cheerful conversation, always stimulated by the arrival of new personnel. Everyone would be getting to know her, getting to know *his* Chiquita! Rando might horn in, he and Cliona had had that brawl over slogans . . . Sakerson resolutely entered the cabin.

'You gotta avoid this guy, Chiquita,' Rando exclaimed, seeing him first. 'He's the weightless wit responsible for Slogan!'

As she turned to look at him, Sakerson's throat closed and he couldn't even gargle a greeting. She was *his* holo, from the slight cleft in her chin, to the way her hair was dressed, curling over a band, green eye/blue eye and sparkling, with a grin of real welcome on her sweetly curved lips. She held out a hand and even her nails were as he had imagined, long ovals, naturally pink. Dreamily, he shook her hand, reminding himself to release it when he heard a titter.

'I'm pleased to meet the man who invented Slogan,' she said, her eyes sparkling candidly. How come he hadn't realized that her voice would be a clear alto?

He slid into the free chair and grinned, hoping it didn't look as foolish as it felt, plastered from ear to ear, because he couldn't speak, couldn't even stop grinning.

'Slogan's all you hear about Station Three these days,' she went on, not dropping eye contact, although her left hand strayed briefly to her hair.

'That makes a nice change,' Sakerson managed to say, making his grin rueful. He knew from the tilted smile on her lips and the sparkle in her eyes that she had heard the ghost rumor.

'Now,' Rando said, breaking in, 'war games are far more a test of intelligence and foresight.'

'Oh, war games,' she said, dismissing them with a

wave of her hand and further entrancing Sakerson. 'I played every war game there is when I was growing up on the MP. And won!' Deftly she depressed Rando's bid. 'Now Slogan stimulates the brain cells, not adrenaline.' She wasn't coy, she wasn't arch, but the way she looked sideways at him made Sakerson's heart leap. 'Say, didn't you dock the PV?'

'I did.'

'You're smooth!'

'Watch it, Chiquita,' Rando warned. 'This guy's dangerous. He's single-spaced.'

Ignoring Rando's thinly veiled leer, Chiquita tilted her head up to Sakerson and just smiled.

'Give over, lout,' Cliona told her mate, elbowing him playfully out of the way. 'Say, Chiquita, how'd you snaffle a posting like Three?'

Chiquita lifted both hands and shrugged. 'I don't really know. I didn't think I was very high on the short list. And then suddenly I was handed orders, shoved toward the PV as the first available vehicle coming this way.' She flashed a charming smile around the wardroom. 'But it's great to be in such good space!'

'Why waste space?' Sakerson demanded, winking at her.

Even in the free and easy atmosphere of a space station, where personnel have little privacy and every new association is public knowledge, Sakerson did not rush Chiquita. She had indicated a preference for the way his mind worked, and more directly, that she liked his physical appearance. He let her get settled into the routine and waited until the next day before he asked her to the hydroponic garden. She smiled softly and winked at him before turning back to her supply texts. Like any space-bred girl, she knew perfectly well what generally happened in such facilities.

'This is a splendid hydro,' she said, and paused as the

path took them to the banana palm. 'Well now,' and she flushed delicately so that Sakerson knew she was aware of the Slogan for her name. 'How . . . how very unusual.'

'That's tactful of you,' Sakerson said before he realized that his words were tantamount to an admission of the truth of the scuttlebutt.

'I think you're tactful, too,' she replied and stood right in front of him. It would have taken a much more restrained man than Sakerson to resist the urge to see if he only had to bend his head. So he did.

Then, just after they had thoroughly kissed one another, easily, gracefully, with no stretching or straining, Sakerson distinctly heard a soft smug sung sound.

'What's the matter?' Chiquita asked, sensing his distraction.

'I could have sworn . . . no, it couldn't be . . .'

'We're not to have secrets from each other.'

He could sense that he'd better think quickly or lose the best thing that had happened to him. Then it occurred to him that when it came time to tell her the truth, he'd have the logged-on holo program to prove it. Right now was not the appropriate moment for that. He answered the immediate question.

'Part of a slogan, I guess.' But Chiquita tilted her head, prompting him. 'Something like . . . "the lessons are free."'

ZULEI, GRACE, NIMSHI,
AND THE DAMNYANKEES

I remember very clearly the day Zulei and her son, Nimshi, arrived at Majpoor Plantation. Papa had just finished giving me a sidesaddle jumping lesson on Dido when Mr James, our overseer, arrived with the new slaves. Despite Mama's best efforts, there had been some deaths among the field hands from an outbreak of measles. So, when Papa heard of the auction of prime bucks being sold off in Greensboro, he'd sent the overseer, Mr James.

'And if you should chance to find a likely lad to exercise the 'chasers . . .' I'd also heard Papa say, when Mr James stopped by the office on his way out of the place. Petey, a wizened little black who looked more like the monkey Mrs LaTouche owned, had been broken up by a bad fall at the Greensboro 'Chase, and no other black boy could measure up to Papa's high standards to ride our 'chasers.

I wasn't supposed to know that, but I did. Being the youngest of six, and the only daughter, I knew a lot more of what went on than Mama would have thought proper for a girl. She had been plain scandalized when I had informed Papa that I was perfectly willing to ride our entry in the next 'Chase. Hadn't he said I had the lightest hands and the best seat on Majpoor? My brothers had howled with laughter and I'm sure that even Papa smiled a bit behind his full beard but Mama had made me leave the table for such pertness.

'I declare, Captain Langhorn, I just don't know how I'm going to raise Grace properly if you, and your sons, encourage her improper behavior.'

Mama was a Womack of Virginia and had standards of behavior from her strict upbringing that sometimes clashed with Papa's. Most of the time she laid that to his being English and having lived so long in India, fighting for Queen Victoria among pagan heathens. He even treated our slaves as if they had minds of their own and opinions to be heard.

'He never has understood how to treat darkies and I don't think he ever will,' she would often complain, usually when someone had made allusions to the comforts and latitude Papa allowed our people.

'Why, lands, Euphemia,' Mrs Fairclough said to Mama once during a visit I'd had to attend, though of course I said nothing at the time (that much I had learned from Mama), 'I do declare that her father treats your nigras like they was human.'

'Captain Langhorn believes that it's only good husbandry to keep stock in healthy surroundings.' Mama had inclined toward Mrs Fairclough in sweet reproof. I knew she agreed completely with Mrs Fairclough, but she wouldn't be disloyal to Papa. 'I do believe, Samantha, that his methods have genuine results. Majpoor certainly gets more cotton and cane per acre than most anyone else in Orange County.'

But that day, as the farm wagon brought the new purchases into the yard, I saw Zulei and Nimshi arrive.

'Ah found ya that rider, Captain' were Mr James's first words. 'Stannup thar, you Nimshi boy.'

As Nimshi rose to his feet, he was facing in my direction and caught my astonished look. I knew all about high yallers, quadroons, and those sorts of distinctions among the blacks, but I'd never before seen a boy with coloring like Nimshi. His hair was red, curled

296

close to his scalp but not in kinky curls: his eyes were blue and his skin a light coffee color. He was slender, with fine bones and a face that I thought far too beautiful for any boy to have. More than that, he held himself with a casual dignity that no slave should display.

'D'you ride, Nimshi?' Papa asked, looking him straight in the eye and not as if he were a piece of merchandise. (Nimshi told me much later that that was the first reason he had to be grateful to Papa.)

'Yessir.'

'Who'd you ride for?'

'Most lately, Mr Bainbridge of Haw River.'

'Why'd he sell you down?'

'He died and Mrs Bainbridge sold up all the racers.'

Nimshi did not speak in the pidgin speech most blacks used. He spoke as well as one of my brothers and much better than most house slaves. I'd heard Papa say once at a race meet that Mr Bainbridge had some very unorthodox notions, coming as he did from Massachusetts. Mr Bainbridge also had curly red hair, but I wasn't supposed to notice such things.

'What sort of a character was Nimshi given?' Papa asked Mr James.

'Good 'un, Captain, or you kin bet yore bottom dollar I wouldn't've bought him. A well-grown fifteen years and not liable to grow too much taller. Not a mark on his back nor a word agin 'im.'

Even then I was sensitive to what wasn't said, and so I looked at the others in the wagon, to see which ones did have marks on their backs or words against them. That's when I noticed Zulei. And realized that she had to be Nimshi's mammy for, despite the terrible gauntness of her face, her features were unusually fine, like Nimshi's. Her nose was particularly aquiline, unusually so for a Negress. Her hair was brown and straight, showing a few reddy glints, not blue-black ones; her eyes were gray, and she wore an expression of strange detachment that reminded me of the English porcelain doll Papa had given me for my birthday. She sat, hands limp and palm-up in her lap, unaware of her surroundings. Her wrists were badly bruised and bloody.

I don't remember what else Papa and Mr James discussed but on such occasions it was their habit to learn the names of every new slave and what he or she had done for their previous owner. I kept trying to catch Zulei's gaze and reassure her that she would never wear fetters at Majpoor, for Papa did not believe in such measures.

Then our head man, Big Josie, a gentle man for all he was twice the size of most field hands and very black, gestured for the new slaves to get down out of the wagon. I saw Nimshi go to her assistance, his expression full of concern. Papa saw the deference, too, and saw the telltale marks on her slender wrists.

'You, there,' Papa said, gruff because he couldn't abide what he called sadistic treatment. He frowned, too, because he couldn't help noticing, as I did, that the bones of her shoulders poked through the flimsy fabric of a dress that seemed too ample for the slight figure it covered. 'What's your name?'

'Zuleika,' Nimshi replied.

Papa frowned at the boy, for he didn't tolerate impudence even if he was lenient. Then he gave Zulei an intent scrutiny.

'She can speak for herself, can't she? Your name, woman?' Papa spoke gently. Even though Nimshi was tenderly assisting her, she also had to hang on to the wagon side to descend.

'I am called Zulei, Captain Langhorn,' she said in a firm, low voice.

'James, she's no field hand,' he said to the overseer in a testy voice. He stared long and hard at her, puzzled.

Abruptly, but still kindly, he asked, 'Zulei, why were you chained? You run away from Mr Bainbridge?'

She lifted her head, the gesture denying that suspicion. Nimshi said a single phrase to her but it didn't sound like geechee to me, much less English. She gave her head a tiny shake.

'No, Captain Langhorn, I did not run away.' Her voice was still low and even, but the way she said 'run' struck me as odd, for the *r* was guttural, the way Mrs LaTouche said her *r*'s.

Mr James cleared his throat. 'Now, Cap'n, Ah did deal on this female 'cos I figgered you an' Mrs Langhorn might find a place for her now Miss Grace is growing up, like. She was trained as a lady's maid and she's well spoken, like. Then, too, Cap'n, seeing as how you never like to split up families, she's Nimshi's mammy. I didn't get no character for her, no character at all. Seems like she'd been some troublesome.'

'Are you troublesome, Zulei?' Papa looked her squarely in the eye, at his most military. No one lied to my Papa when he gave them that look.

'I have never studied trouble, Captain Langhorn. Sometimes it comes where it's not wanted.'

I remember Papa *hmmm*ed deep in his throat as he does when he won't commit himself. I was then much too young to appreciate what sort of trouble might be meant: much too young to realize that Zulei's 'trouble' was generated by her appearance.

'We will contrive to see it doesn't come to you here. Now, Josie' – and now Papa beckoned to him – 'take Zulei up to the big house. Her injuries are to be treated. She looks half-starved. Ask Dulcie to fix her something nourishing. You are Nimshi's mother?' When she gave a brief nod, he added to Mr James, 'Then see that she is quartered with him in the mews.'

The horseboys lived in quarters right in the stableyard

to be close to their charges at all times, in case one got cast or became colicky at night.

'You will not regret this, Captain,' Zulei said and made the oddest curtsy, clasping her hands palms together, their tips touching her forehead as she bowed her head. Papa gave her the strangest look, but when she dropped her hands she shook her head just once in a curious denial. Papa brought his riding crop down hard on his boot, then used it to point at Nimshi.

'Nimshi, you may take the pony from Miss Grace. Down you get, my dear,' Papa said, and turned back to hear the rest of Mr James's report.

I didn't wait for Nimshi to come to Dido's head but unhooked my leg from the sidesaddle horn and slipped to the ground, patting Dido's shoulder in appreciation. Nimshi was not much taller than I in those days but what recommended him to me was the way he held out his hand to my pony for her to get the smell of him before he so much as put a hand on her bridle. She was a spirited pony and didn't like unfamiliar hands on her.

Nimshi smiled as she blew into his hand, then, taking the reins from me, he ran the stirrup up the leather and loosened the girth expertly. I smiled in approval for he had done exactly what I was going to tell him to do. Sometimes even Bennie, who was head groom, would forget to loosen the girth of a horse that had been worked hard. Nimshi gave me a look that suggested I should never doubt his competence.

'I hope you'll be happy here at Majpoor, Nimshi. You must ride my Papa's horses to win.'

'I always mean to ride winners, Miss Grace.' And then he gave me a timid smile.

'That'll suit Papa down to the ground,' I said, and then I decided it was time I got back to the house. Mama didn't like me lingering in the stableyard, even if that was the best part of Majpoor in my estimation and especially when new slaves were brought in. She always worried about the diseases they might have on them until they'd all had a lye bath, had their hides scrubbed with good yellow soap, and been flea-powdered.

So I had a very clear recollection of the day Zulei and Nimshi came to Majpoor. Mama wasn't as easily reconciled to Zulei's arrival ('That female's going to cause trouble, Captain, you mark my words' – which Papa did not), but somehow there never was any trouble about Zulei. Nimshi proved to be every bit as good a rider as he'd been touted. He truly loved horses and they responded to him as if they knew they could trust him.

My brothers, Kenneth, David, Lachlan, Evelyn, and Robert, might complain that Papa said Nimshi this and Nimshi that, but they didn't object when Nimshi won race after race, and they collected sizable wagers from everyone in the county.

Mama reluctantly admitted that Zulei was more use than trouble, for the quadroon (that's what Mama said she was with her light skin, straight brown hair, and gray eyes) had a knowledge of herbs and remedies that was nothing short of miraculous – Mama's phrase. There were some murmurs about voodoo and obeah and conjure, superstitious twaddle like that which Mama wouldn't abide, not mutters that Zulei was different. My mammy said that Zulei wasn't one of them, not no way no how, but as Zulei was a slave, I didn't know what mammy meant. A slave was a slave. I asked Mama and she thought I was worried about all the superstitious talk. She made it quite clear to me that Zulei's understanding of simple remedies was quite unexceptional, nothing to do with black magic; only common sense.

Any resistance from the other slaves ended soon after Zulei concocted a potion that cleared up Daisy's rash and a poultice that eased old Remy's arthritis. She had a salve that made burns disappear, even those from splashings of boiling lye soap. She was a dab hand at lying-ins, though I wasn't supposed to know such things. I also heard – from Lachlan – about how Zulei's clever hands had turned the foal inside Joyra, Papa's expensive new thoroughbred mare, when it wasn't lying right to be born. Bennie had given up, but she'd brought the colt live into the world.

Zulei also made creams, which the other county ladies begged of Mama for they reduced freckles like nothing else could. She had all sorts of other female potions that Mama loved to dispense to her friends who didn't have anyone half so clever as Zulei. I do remember that Mrs Fairclough wondered how Mama could stand to have such a frowsy slave attending her. Even Mama was surprised by that comment. Dulcie's feeding had put weight on Zulei's bones and Mama had given her one or two of her old gowns to wear, so Zulei couldn't be called 'frowsy.' Mama privately thought that Zulei was a shade too fastidious.

Zulei had a knack of refurbishing Mama's dresses or pinching in a bodice, altering a sleeve so that somehow the gown looked twice as elegant as it had new. She was deft at dressing Mama's lovely blond hair into the most intricate and fetching styles.

And when I was old enough to put my hair up, it was Zulei who curled it so fashionably and flatteringly.

In fact, that was one of the few times she had occasion to dress me for a ball. The year I was sixteen, the Confederacy declared war on the North. All the young men in the county, and some of those old enough to know better – like Papa – decided to teach the damn-yankees a thing or two and rode off to war.

I thought it was all very exciting, with six Langhorn men stomping about in their fine gray-and-gold uniforms: Papa had had so much experience in the British army, even if that had all been in India, that he was immediately made a colonel in the county regiment. Kenneth and David became captains and Lachlan, Evelyn, and Robert were lieutenants. And most of our beautiful horses became war steeds.

Our men rode off, handsome in their broad-brimmed hats, gold sashes around their waists and sabers and pistols on their hips. Everyone was on the front steps to wave them to victory. For it wouldn't take long for Southern gentlemen to teach those damnyankees what-for.

Mr James was left in charge of Majpoor, but no one minded that, for he was a fair man: even Zulei said so. Josie supervised the field hands, and Bennie, with Nimshi as his right hand, took care of Brass Sultan, Majpoor's stallion, and his mares and foals. I had let Lachlan, my favorite brother, have my very own Cotton as his remount so I was reduced to Dido again. That is, until Nimshi had backed a promising three-year-old flea-specked gray that Papa had promised me to replace Cotton.

Mama fretted from the moment she lost sight of Papa and the boys until the day she died of typhus three years later, despite all Zulei tried to do to break the fever. We all knew Mama wanted to die anyway once she heard that Papa had been killed in one of Jeb Stuart's cavalry charges against that damnyankee Mead, so it wasn't Zulei's fault. Though, by then, we all knew why she had had no character from the Bainbridges at Haw River.

'I know my medications, Miss Euphemia,' Zulei had told Mama one time in my hearing. 'I know how to reduce fevers, set broken bones, and help a woman in labor, but there was nothing I could do with snake venom. When they finally got Mr Bainbridge home, the poison was all through him. What could I do then?' She had a very elegant way of shrugging her shoulders.

There was another reason why the Bainbridge overseer

had chained Zulei up, but Nimshi told me that later, when I was much older and understood such matters better. It had had nothing to do with her nursing skills but a lot to do with why Zulei looked frowsy to some people.

When Zulei had confided in Mama, we all trusted her, having seen the near miracles she could work. But there are no miracles, near or true, to mend a heart broken by the deaths of her husband and three of her sons, and weakened by the privations that the war visited on all southern families. Zulei and I nursed Mama together and made her as comfortable as we could with what limited medicines we could find or Zulei could concoct.

We were luckier than most, I suppose, due to Majpoor's location. We suffered from the lack of supplies and things we had previously taken for granted. While battles raged in Virginia and up and down the coast of both North and South Carolina, we were not in the path of the combat nor near enough to benefit from blockade-run goods. We had trouble enough with deserters or, worse still, the cavalries of both armies that came hunting horses from Majpoor's acres.

It was Nimshi who devised the means to hide what few good horses we had reared, including my flea-specked gray gelding, Jupiter. And especially our precious stallion, Brass Sultan. He was old, twenty-five years now, brought from England by Papa to be Majpoor's foundation stud. He neither looked nor acted his age and, with the Confederacy three years into the war, any horse that could walk and trot went into the cavalry. Loyal though we were to the Confederate cause, Brass Sultan was far too valuable to be wasted as a remount.

Mind you, Sultan, a fine seventeen hands high, was not an easy horse to manage. Nimshi had an understanding with Sultan that was almost magical, and the stallion would follow Nimshi wherever he led. This became tremendously important when we had to hide Sultan.

Mr James had pickaninnies stationed on every road and track to Majpoor, to watch for 'visitors' and warn us, particularly of mounted men. When their whistle alarm was relayed cross the fields to the big house, Nimshi would take Sultan and Jupiter down into the now empty wine cellar and swing a door covered by old trunks to cover the entrance.

As the war continued, Mr James enlarged the hidey-hole to include whatever young stock we had and any barren mares. With Nimshi there to calm them, they stayed as quiet as mice no matter how fractious they'd be at other times.

That ruse worked very well for us until that morning when, with no warning at all, Yankee raiders came out of the woods from the mountains behind us. Sultan was actually covering a mare at the time. Six good strong two-year-olds were grazing in the front field, where they could be rounded up easily. The pregnant mares and those with foals at foot in the far paddocks were not vulnerable – yet – at least not to the Confederacy. You'd never know what damnyankees would do and our mares were proud, strong ones, with plenty of bone and spirit. Damnyankees might shoot the foals and take the mares although Mr James didn't think that likely.

But this morning, we had no chance to hide Brass Sultan, or Jupiter or the two-year-olds. We could only watch in horror as the troops trotted up from the back fields, their uniforms so dusty that at first we thought they were our soldiers.

'Morning, ma'am,' the captain said, saluting me as I stood on the veranda, terrified by his arrival. Zulei was at my side, for we'd just come up from the smokehouse, turning the few hams we had from this year's slaughtering. 'Sorry to trouble you,' he added, which was as untrue as anything any Yankee ever said. His eyes lingered briefly on Zulei, behind me, before they ranged down to the paddock and the young horses.

To my horror, Sultan bugled his success, an unmistakable sound so that, even before he swung off his tired horse, the captain signed several troopers to go investigate.

I prayed for Mr James to come to my assistance. I felt so vulnerable with just Zulei beside me to confront such unwelcome visitors. I remembered how Mama had acted when she faced down damnyankees and I tried to emulate her calm disdain. But my knees were shaking and I felt sorely inadequate at that moment.

As the captain trudged up the veranda steps, Zulei flashed me one of her piercing looks. Usually I knew what Zulei meant but this time I couldn't interpret it. So I just stared through the captain, wondering how in God's name we were going to save my precious Jupiter and the young stock this time.

'We're looking for remounts, miss. We need 'em badly,' the captain said, slapping the dust from his dark blue trousers with worn leather gauntlets.

'You Yankees have been here before,' I said as inhospitably as I could.

He turned his head, squinting at the youngsters in the field. Jupiter was lying down in the shadows of the live oak. Maybe he wasn't visible. There was a queer look on the captain's face as he turned back to me.

'I'll just take a gander at those in the paddock, ma'am,' he said, blinking suddenly at me as if I had changed shape. 'We might find something we can exchange for our lame ones.'

'They're only . . .' Zulei pinched my arm sharply and I faltered. '. . . the only ones we have left,' I finished lamely when he shot me another odd glance.

Zulei gave me a shove, so we followed him down to the paddock, a corporal and a private falling in behind us.

My heart squeezed with fear. Surely they'd see that these horses were too young to be backed. Usually the young stock would come charging up to me, hopeful of some tidbit from my pocket, but today they stayed where they were, picking at the grass or standing hipshot and half-asleep. Jupiter hadn't moved from his shady spot.

Halfway across the field to the nearest two-year-old, a fine bay by Sultan out of one of the best 'chaser mares remaining to us, the captain stopped, pushing his hat back off his brow. He turned to his corporal, shaking his head.

'Those all you got, ma'am?'

'That's all we have left,' I said, trying not to hope that they were going to leave us the two-year-olds: that for once a Yankee would leave empty-handed. Surely any horseman worth his salt could see that these youngsters hadn't grown into themselves, hindquarters higher than their withers, knees still open.

'Cap'n, what we got's better'n those crowbaits,' the corporal said, giving me a sympathetic glance.

I blinked, astonished, for there was no way you could call the two-year-olds 'crowbait.' Out of pride, I started to protest when again Zulei nipped the soft part of my arm.

'They're what the last troop left behind for us,' Zulei said with bitter dignity, and I contained my surprise. 'Took all the chickens and the last cow.' Somehow she sounded exactly like Mama just then.

'Sorry, ma'am,' the captain said and, gesturing to his men, started back to where the rest of his small troop were watering their horses in the fishpond.

The two troopers who had been sent to the stableyard had returned, shaking their heads, grinning slightly.

'Nothin' there, sir,' the sergeant said, 'but a rack of bones with big ideas.'

While I was relieved beyond measure, for Sultan's loss

would have meant disaster for Majpoor, I was surprised. No one could call Sultan a rack of bones! He might be a bit stiff but his coat gleamed and he held condition.

Another pair of troopers swung into the yard, their tired mounts at a shambling trot.

'Just mares and foals, Captain, and none of the mares worth bothering about' was their report.

I didn't protest, quite willing for their opinion to stand, though none of those mares were poor, either. One shouldn't question minor miracles. Majpoor might not have much grain to give its horses, but the grass was lush even with only manure to fertilize it in the spring and every animal we owned had a fine glossy coat and good condition on it.

'Captain.' A grizzled sergeant came around the corner, our hams looped over his neck and draped down his pommel. He was grinning, all white teeth in a dirty face. 'Got us some prime eating for tonight.'

'Captain, those are our last hams!' I cried in considerable anguish. The pigs had not been as fat as in previous years, but they would add sustenance to hominy and beans and give the field hands some strength.

'Sorry, ma'am. My men haven't had a decent meal in weeks. Horsemeat's not so bad if you're real hungry. I know,' he said grimly, and then waved a gloved hand at the paddock. 'Not that there's much meat on that lot, but it's all they'd be good for now anyhow. My compliments.'

And, while I stood there with my mouth hanging open, he gestured for his troop to move out, down the wide avenue to the main road.

Although the two-year-olds were forever racing up and down their paddock, especially if any horses were on the avenue, they stood where they were, like statues.

'Yankees! It's like them to suggest that we eat our horses,' I muttered in outrage when they were far enough away. 'Mind you, I regret those hams like the dickens, Zulei. I'm so tired of rabbit and pigeon I could scream. That captain can't know much about horses, nor those troopers of his. Strange, though, that the two-year-olds didn't run about like they . . .' I broke off for, as I swung around to Zulei, I saw how pale she had become. Her eyes went back in her head and she sort of folded up. I just caught her in my arms before she fell to the veranda floor. 'Zulei? Zulei?'

I still carried a vinaigrette in my pocket, despite the fact that Mama was no longer alive to need it. So I held it to Zulei's nose. Feebly she batted it away but didn't open her eyes.

'I'll be all right, Miss Grace. It takes so much strength.'

I stared down at her for a long moment, trying to absorb the significance of her words. Then Nimshi came racing around the corner of the house and up the steps, dropping to his knees at his mother's side.

'Mother?' He looked at me in alarm.

Her eyelids fluttered but she managed to lift one hand to his arm, reassuring him. I was anxiously feeling her pulse and her forehead, fearful that she had been stricken down with some fever.

'It's not a fever, Miss Grace. Mother must have done the biggest working ever to save the horses from the Yankees.' Nimshi grinned proudly at me. 'She's just weak. I'll just put her to bed. She'll be right as rain in the morning.'

I stumbled to my feet as he picked up his mother's slender body, all limp in his arms, her lashes long against her cheeks.

'A big working? What do you mean, Nimshi?' I was frightened again. I remembered then the murmur of 'voodoo, obeah, conjure' that had flickered through the slave quarters when she and Nimshi first arrived. 'What happened in the stableyard? They didn't take a single horse. Said they weren't worth taking.'

Nimshi smiled at me. 'What *they* saw sure wasn't. Mother made sure of that, Miss Grace. Now, if you'll excuse me . . .' He carried her off the veranda, leaving me staring after him, trying to make sense of his words.

Just then Mr James came running around the side of the house, breathless and perspiring. He'd been in the top field, and that was a long way for an old man like him to run. The expression on his face told me that he had feared the worst. Now he stared in astonishment at the foals cavorting about in the paddock, Jupiter leading the pack in their racing, and at the Yankee dust cloud barely visible down the Greensboro road. I decided then and there not to tell him what had happened. I didn't *quite* understand it but I thought I did. But this could not be classed as silly voodoo or obeah or conjure, which always dealt with black magic and death and evil things. What Zulei had done was good. Just as her salves and potions and poultices had been good, helping people. She had just helped us save the only valuable items left to Majpoor, our horses. I wasn't about to question this major miracle.

Considering that the Yankees found Sultan too poor to steal from us, it was gratifying when the colt foal that service produced was one of the best ever born at Majpoor. He was his sire's spit and image, a deep liver chestnut that was very like the dull brass of Sultan's hide, with three white socks, a well-placed white blaze on his forehead, and superb conformation. He was up and nursing his dam fifteen minutes after his birth, strong and energetic enough to kick anyone trying to come near and dry off his fuzzy foal coat.

Nimshi called him Wazir and the name was so appropriate that it stuck. It was a splendid homecoming surprise for Lachlan, though he had a sad surprise for us: he lacked half an arm and was deeply embittered by all he had seen of North Carolina as he made his way home. Amazingly enough, Lachlan still had my own dear Cotton, who was very much indeed a rack of bones, walking short from a saber slice on his left rear, with hooves split from lack of care and a hole on his once full neck where a Yankee minié ball had plowed through it. Lachlan had only a blanket for a saddle but their return was a minor miracle for me.

I saved my tears until my exhausted brother had been fed and tucked in his bed. Then I cried my heart out in the stable, while Zulei comforted me and Nimshi hand-fed old Cotton.

'You've been brave so long, Miss Grace,' Zulei said, stroking my hair. 'Major Lachlan needs only rest here at Majpoor.'

'He needs good nourishing food, beef broth, meat, butter, cream, and we haven't so much as a chicken or an egg for him.' I wept afresh at my inability to care for my dearest and only brother now that he had finally come home.

'Rabbit's good eating,' Nimshi said, 'and there're deer in the woods if you know where to look. Don't you worry.'

I saw the look that passed between mother and son, but they often exchanged speaking glances and I was too woebegone to pay much heed.

The next day I rode Dido while Lachlan took my Jupiter about the place. He was amazed that we had saved anything, much less the bales of cotton we had hidden in the woods.

'That was Zulei's idea. We couldn't sell it, she said, but we could save it. Wars don't last forever and the English would buy Majpoor cotton.'

Lachlan regarded me as if I'd turned green. 'Zulei's

idea? How could Mr James allow a slave to . . .'

'Mr James can't keep two thoughts together in his head, Lachie,' I said, for I'd've thought my brother would have seen how vague the old overseer was. 'Nimshi figured out where to hide Sultan and the others, and he and Big Josie see to what planting we've done. Majpoor would be a ruin if it hadn't been for Zulei and Nimshi.'

Lachlan didn't reply to my heated defense but I knew it gave him much to think about, and I lost no opportunity to point out other ruses, contrived by either Zulei or Nimshi – like the kitchen garden hidden behind used banks of old manure on one side and thorn thickets on the other. Zulei's idea. I've often thought that the sight of the three-year-olds in the paddock were all that saved his sanity. By the time we walked back into the stable-yard, Nimshi had finished gutting a fine stag.

That night, Lachlan made a fine meal of the venison, washing it down with moonshine, procured by Big Josie from who knew where. After that, Lachlan seemed to drink rather more than I thought a gentleman should. Every morning Zulei had to force one of her remedies down his throat.

'He feels the phantom pain,' Zulei told me, 'of the hand they amputated. That happens.'

'Can't you make it go away, Zulei?' It was wrong of me, I know, to wish for another miracle from her, but how could I have known then just how much these years had cost her in strength; how often she had clouded the avenue so that deserters didn't find their way to our house or cavalry see the true form of Majpoor's horses, or even see me young, innocent, and vulnerable.

As I clutched at her arm, Zulei gave me a long piercing look, the expression in her eyes going from anguish, to deep sorrow, to such resolution that I was ashamed of my momentary weakness.

'I'm sorry, Zulei,' I said. 'How could you have a salve to heal a hand that's not there. And I know we've no laudanum left so that corn liquor will have to do to cut the pain.' We used the last of Mama's supply when one of the field hands had nearly severed the calf of his leg with a cane knife.

Lachlan tried, though, with white lips and pain-racked eyes, to take up plantation duties. He told me how brave and resourceful I had been to keep everything going as well as I had. I repeated that I'd had help from Zulei and Nimshi and he gave me an odd look. But it was so good to have my brother back that I scarcely noticed anything other than my joy at having one Langhorn spared by the terrible conflict. As a mark of that joy, I willingly gave him Jupiter to ride – until Cotton was restored, I told him with a laugh, though we both knew Cotton's working days were over. But having a fine horse between his legs did Lachlan the world of good. Until darkness fell and he had to wrestle with the phantom pain again.

Often I would see Nimshi supporting my brother up the stairs to his room in the small hours of the night. I would see Zulei ascending them in the morning with the tisane to cure his hangover. She looked as worn as Lachlan.

Then those occasions dwindled and, at my tentative inquiry, Lachlan muttered something about an itch being an improvement over an ache. He began to take a real hold of the management, consulting with Nimshi and Big Josie. Mr James was relegated to sitting on his porch and swinging, seeming not to notice the passing hours. I assigned one of our older women to tend to his needs and see he ate.

Many of our people had drifted off once conditions at Majpoor deteriorated, but, some months, we could barely feed those who remained. Lachlan organized the loyal ones who had stayed with us, and planted what seed we had. He and Nimshi took two geldings into Greensboro to sell, and although there were few people able to buy anything, he did get some gold, though most of the sale price was our Confederate legal tender, which few of the Greensboro merchants would accept. The gold bought flour, mealy though it was, and machine oil and other things we could not make ourselves.

The next week we found Sultan dead in his box. Three days later the news of Robert's death reached us. The following week we learned of Appomattox. Lachlan sat in Papa's study and drank himself stupid.

He apologized to me the next day – once Zulei had got one of her remedies down his throat. He looked awful, even worse than the day he'd come home.

'I understand, dear Lachlan, really I do,' I said, and inadvertently glanced down at his arm.

'No, it's not my arm that made me want to get drunk, Grace, and it's not losing the war. It's what will happen now that the North has won.'

'What more could those damnyankees do to us?'

Lachlan eyed me pityingly. 'We're the losers. Papa used to fret a lot about what would happen after the war. Spoils are always divided after a war. And taxes raised to pay for it.'

'How could we possibly pay taxes, Lachlan?' I cried, fear rising in my throat. I thought of the wads of now worthless Confederacy notes that we had so loyally accepted.

'Thanks to Nimshi, Majpoor's horses will provide us gold . . .' Lachlan said, and then grimaced, 'if we can find buyers with any.'

Buyers appeared, if not the sort we cared to sell our Majpoor horses to: dreadful encroaching people with smug smiles and loud voices and no manners whatever; carpetbaggers, scalawags, poor white trash pouring down from the North to pick what flesh remained on the defeated Confederate bones. At that we were once again luckier than many of our neighbors. For when horrific taxes were levied on the struggling impoverished South, many of the county families were reduced to penury, having to sell their family homes for a pittance. Majpoor's horses, so cherished during the war years, paid the crippling ones we were charged.

I know it grieved Lachlan to see them led away, tied to Yankee carriages or ridden by sniggering Yankee grooms, but it saved us Majpoor's acres, and put chickens in the yard, two cows in the barn, pigs in the pen, and new clothes on our backs.

It was then that I realized that Zulei was nearly as thin as she'd been the day she arrived at Majpoor. I picked her out a gown myself, even before I bought material for my own, but when I made her unwrap the tattered shawl from her shoulders, I saw how the war years had eaten into the very fiber of the woman. And when I pinned up the sleeve of Lachlan's new coat, I could have sworn that I'd mistaken how much of his arm had been amputated. No, not arm, for he had forearm to the wrist.

He looked at it, too, surprise on his face. He'd long since got over people staring at his injury but that didn't mean he, or I, looked at it often.

'Does it still itch?' I asked him, not thinking of anything but surprise at my faulty recollection.

'No, it doesn't itch,' he said in such a short tone that I regretted my question and stood back to admire my fine-looking brother. He had lost the haunting in his eyes and filled out much of the flesh the war had burned from him. His hair was glossy and his skin tanned right to the place where his hat covered his brow. 'At least we won't disgrace the crowd at the 'Chase tomorrow.'

For Wazir was old enough to race and the event had been scheduled – by Yankees, to please all the Yankees who had bought plantations and now lived in our area, though of course they weren't received at Majpoor.

Then Nimshi, slimly splendid in silks Zulei and I had sewn him, rode Wazir to win, against Yankee horses, which made their owners mad. And some offered Lachlan paltry sums for the stallion, thinking we were poor enough to take what gold was offered and be grateful.

I was just coming to see if Nimshi had Wazir ready for the trip home when I heard one man offering Nimshi a job, telling him how much better off he'd be in a *grand* big Northern stable with many fine horses to ride, and proper quarters and money in his pocket. I admit I wanted to hear what Nimshi would say to such an offer. Loyal though Nimshi was to Majpoor, every man has his price, or so Lachlan said. We certainly hadn't been able to put much money in Nimshi's hand, even if he was emancipated.

'I ride for Major Langhorn,' I heard Nimshi say with quiet pride.

'You can go where you want to now, boy,' the Yankee said, his face flushed at the refusal. He clapped Nimshi on the arm, unaware of how Nimshi moved away from such familiarity. 'You're not a slave anymore. You don't have to take orders from Southerners anymore.'

'I have no wish to leave my employment with Major Langhorn,' Nimshi replied.

'If you will excuse us,' I said, sweeping in from the aisle between the stables, brimming with pride and relief over Nimshi's reply. 'Lachlan's waiting for us, Nimshi,' I said, and, making a great show of not letting my skirts touch the damnyankee, I put a hand on Wazir's halter and together we led our winner away.

'Well, I'll be damned! Did you see that? And she looked like a real Southern belle, too. One of them high yallers, I 'spect.'

'See how she looked at him? I heard some of them

Southern ladies got mighty fed up with all their menfolk away in the war.'

I nearly choked at such insult and Nimshi began to trot Wazir firmly away.

'Don't you take offense, Miss Grace,' he said, but there was something so fierce in his tone and his expression that I feared what he might do. And I was far more worried about that than any loose-mouthed talk from an ill-bred damnyankee.

'"I have no wish to leave my employment with Major Langhorn,"' I said, mimicking him. 'Nimshi, that was priceless. Wait till I tell Lachlan how you answered that damnyankee.' Then I stopped, appalled at my selfishness. 'Oh, Nimshi, maybe you should take that offer. We certainly can't pay you what you're really worth . . .'

Nimshi hauled Wazir to a stop and glared at me. 'You will say nothing about that incident to the Major. He has enough to worry about.'

'But, Nimshi . . .'

He fixed me with the sort of haughty stare that Zulei used effectively, his eyes glittering dangerously. 'My mother and I owe you more than any Yankee could pay us.'

'We barely pay you at all,' I began, painfully aware of that.

'You paid us in a coin few people in our position ever receive, Miss Grace, respect and appreciation.' I had never heard such fervor in Nimshi's voice before. 'Your papa and your brothers left my mother alone. Your papa let me ride his best horses. Your mama never belittled us in front of her friends and you gave us back our pride. And we've been free from the moment Colonel Langhorn went to war. Mr James gave Mother the papers.'

I hadn't known that, and I had to run to catch up to Nimshi as he rushed Wazir onward.

'We've always been proud to work at Majpoor, Miss

Grace, and do what we can to repay your parents for all their considerations.'

'Oh, Nimshi!'

'Just for the record' – and Nimshi smiled around Wazir's head at me – 'I'm not high yaller, though I am half-white. The other half of me and all of my mother is Arabian. But Mother was sold into slavery. In spite of that, I'm the grandson of an emir, so you can't be insulted for being in my company. I'm better born than any of that Yankee white trash.'

By then we had reached the wagon that Lachlan used to transport Wazir to the 'Chase. Once the tired stallion was loaded up, we all climbed to the high seat for the long trip back to Majpoor.

Our affairs began to improve with Wazir's win, for it was not only the purse but also the publicity about his speed and scope that helped us. Mares arrived for him to cover, Southern as well as Northern. Stud feeds brought us money to restore the big house and the stables, to repair the quarters for those blacks who still lived on Majpoor, and to pay them a wage, and those we needed to hire to get the repair work done.

So I was surprised when Lachlan began to drink again – brandy this time – and suffered his hangovers without benefit of Zulei's tisanes. At first I thought that Lachlan was being considerate because she seemed to be wasting away. I had her moved to the room next to me, for she often had bad dreams at night and needed to be roused to sanity. But when I took pity on him and made a potion, he wouldn't take anything Zulei had concocted, despite the fact that they had always done him good. Then he began to avoid Nimshi instead of spending every minute of the day working side by side with him in Majpoor's management and the breeding operation. I thought at first it was because Lachlan was handicapped in helping Nimshi break and school the youngsters. That it was painful for him to watch someone else do what he had been so good at before the war. When I did notice the estrangement, and the hurt it caused Nimshi, I confronted Lachlan.

'I don't know why you're angry with Nimshi, Lachlan, after all he's done for us . . .'

'It's not the all, Grace, but the how' was Lachlan's cryptic response. We were having dinner and Lachlan was drinking brandy with the meal.

'Whatever do you mean?'

Lachlan gave me a blank stare. 'I wish they'd both go!' he blurted out, giving me a look that made me shudder.

'Both? Zulei . . .' My protest was simultaneous to his denial.

'No, no, I don't really mean that, Grace. I just . . . don't know . . . I'm afraid, Grace. I don't understand what's been happening. Or how!'

I hadn't really noticed until then that he had been keeping his stump in his coat pocket. Now he brought it out and laid back the cuff.

I gaped at what I saw – a tiny hand, growing out of the renewed wrist. The regenerated portion of his arm was healthy firm flesh and the little hand complete despite it being miniature.

'It's growing, too. Noticeably,' Lachlan said, frowning at the grotesquerie. 'I spotted the fingers coming out of the wrist before the 'Chase. I didn't think about it then because I didn't believe my eyes. I . . . don't know whether I want it or not.'

'Not want your hand back? But you could ride and write your name instead of that scribble, and dance,' I heard myself say, for I wanted nothing now so much as my favorite brother a whole man.

Lachlan stared at me and made an odd strangled sound. 'You amaze me, Grace. You really do,' he said, and looked down at his budding hand. Carefully he pulled down the cuff and shoved his arm back into the pocket.

'Does it hurt?'

'No, and it doesn't itch,' he replied; then he went on in a different tone, pouring more brandy into his glass. 'Tell me what else happened at Majpoor during the war, Grace. Tell me what else Zulei did with her black magic.'

I shook my head. 'She doesn't use black magic, Lachlan.'

'Then what the hell is that?' he demanded roughly, jerking his chin at his pocketed limb.

'I don't know what art she uses but I do know that black magic is evil. Zulei isn't evil. Whatever . . .' I remembered the word Nimshi had used the day Zulei fooled the Yankees. '. . . working she does is not evil, for with it she protected me, and Majpoor. Restoring what you lost is not evil either. And she's not a Negro, so it's not conjure or voodoo or obeah that she's using.'

'Not a nigra?' That surprised Lachlan so completely that I grinned at the effect.

'She's an emir's daughter and was sold into slavery,' I said, willing to startle him into belief of Zulei's goodness. 'Nimshi wouldn't explain why.'

Lachlan gave a snort of disbelief. 'And don't try to tell me Nimshi's not get of old man Bainbridge with that hair and those eyes.'

'We're not discussing Nimshi's parentage,' I said as primly as I could, recalling that Mama would have been scandalized to hear my brother mention such a topic in my presence, 'which shouldn't matter a hill of beans when we owe everything we have at Majpoor to Zulei's help during the war.'

'Exactly what form did this help actually take, Grace?'

I'd never heard my brother use quite that sort of tone before and, because I remembered the incident with that Yankee captain and Sultan, I related that and what

Nimshi had said – that his mother had made the horses look different. And me.

'When they left, Zulei fainted . . .' I broke off because at that moment I realized why Zulei was so ill. I stared at Lachlan, at his pocketed arm, and nearly fainted myself. 'Oh, no . . .' The chair toppled, I sprang from it so abruptly. I picked up my skirts and ran up the stairs, Lachlan calling for me to stop, to explain 'She's working herself to death for you!'

I burst into the room, not surprised to find Nimshi there; he often sat with his mother in the evenings. I fell on my knees at her bedside, staring down at her face, all bones and nearly skull-like in a deterioration that was rapidly seeping her life away.

'Oh, Zulei, you must leave off the working . . . you must! You and Nimshi have done enough!'

A wan smile curved on her lips, and I remembered how lovely she had been in the days before the war, and wept to see her so wasted now, as wasted as the South was.

'Nimshi, how could you let your mother . . .' I cried, turning on him in my anger.

He shook his head and then I felt Zulei's fingers on my arm.

'It is not this working, Miss Grace, but the other which has drained me, as evil will.'

'What other? You're not evil.'

'The man who sold me into slavery,' she said, and her eyes glittered feverishly, 'has taken a long time to die. He could never get far enough away to shake the Curse I put on him, though it has taken my lifetime to do it. And my life. Evil takes its toll and the good I have done has not been enough to balance the vengeance exacted, rightful though it is. War is not the only way to waste the breath of life, Major Langhorn.' She looked beyond me to Lachlan standing in the doorway. 'For the kindness of your father and your mother, I used the Great Arts I was taught to heal the sick and injured, and to veil Majpoor's wealth and goodness from its enemies, hoping that that would expiate the other harm I did. *Inshallah!* May God now have mercy on me!'

Her breath fluttered and ceased. We were all so stunned by her death that we stared at her, incredulous, for many long moments. Then I closed her eyes and, marveling at the look of peace on her ravaged face, slowly covered it.

We buried Zuleika bint Nasrullah in the family cemetery with her real name on the headstone. You can see it there if your heart is pure enough to find Majpoor, for even now, Lachlan says that some folk still can't find the avenue, though it is plainly marked.

His hand grew, although it was never quite the same size as his left one. But he could now break and train the horses we bred. I was bridesmaid at his wedding to the daughter of a Northern lawyer who'd been sent south to see about claims of misappropriation of funds and carpetbagger chicanery.

Nimshi did go north, but for himself, with a son of Wazir and enough mares to found his own stable. And I, I went north, too. Where I could marry a red-haired emir's grandson who bred horses that always won their races.

CINDERELLA SWITCH

Deagan, Fenn, and Cordane were standing on the top level of the broad terraced steps above the ballroom of Fomalhaut V's Official Residence, commenting on the costumed dancers swirling to the exotic music of the android musicians. Having identified everyone there, they were bored. But their location and mood put them in an excellent position to see the girl sweep in through the open garden doors. Her sparkling mist of a gown scintillated against the darkness behind her.

'Fardles! What a party crasher!' Cordane exclaimed, his eyes widening appreciatively.

'What a costume!' said Deagan, wondering just how that shifting mist of pastel light was generated. The new arrival was covered from neck to ankle, shoulder to wrist, with a haze hiding all but her eyes and her streaming black hair. Furthermore, whatever the mechanism, it was quite sophisticated. As the shades shifted from opacity to transparency in a tantalizing random fashion, even the most casual observer realized she wore absolutely nothing under her hazy attire.

Before the three observers could move toward her, a tall man in the garb of an ancient Terran diplomat – his black-and-white an excellent foil for her pale shimmers – bowed formally and led her to the center of the dance in progress.

'Wouldn't you know Walteron would be on the prowl and in the right place?' Cordane was disgusted. 'He's the only one ever wears such a confining rig, isn't he, Deagan?'

'But what's he doing here?' Fenn asked. Then, without giving Deagan a chance to answer, Fenn went on. 'I heard he had trouble at his mines: cave-ins and a massive displacement.'

'He came in to apply to Father,' said Deagan, son of the planetary manager, 'for permission to import a soil-mechanics expert from Aldebaran.'

'And nabs the only interesting female here? Usually he takes to the Streets as soon as he's done his duty dance with your mother.'

'He's always had good timing,' Deagan said, sounding amused.

'And bad intentions.' Cordane glowered. 'If he tries to Street her . . .'

This was Touch-Down Time, when the citizens of the bustling, propserous planet of Fomalhaut V – rich in the transuranics, the actinides, so vital as the energy fuels needed to extend the surge of colonization to every habitable planet in the spiral of the Milky Way – relaxed industry and inhibitions in a three-day spectacular of day-long contests, night-long dancing, and eating and carousing.

The Official Residence, a sprawling complex of domes, residential, diplomatic, and business, was the traditional site of the special festivities to which the descendants of the original First Landing Families congregated from their distant domains. The more important off-world visitors and city and spaceport officials were added to this exclusive gathering. Conducted as it was along rather sedate lines, the festival held little glamour for those wanting to sample exotic and erotic pleasures available in the Streets' celebrations. Occasionally a brash young male newcomer, hoping to impress a Domain Family daughter favorably, took advantage of the Celebration's license and appeared at the Residence. As long as the person behaved with propriety acceptable to the Residence, he was permitted to stay. A few nights' dancing was hardy sufficient time in which to form a lasting alliance with the shrewdly raised young women of Fomalhaut. Even so, it was rare indeed for a young woman to put herself in such an equivocal position.

'Could she be from one of the newer Domains? They work so hard there, they don't usually attend Touch-Down,' said Fenn.

'Newcomer?' Cordane suggested, turning to Deagan, who was studying the girl as she and her partner moved past them.

Deagan was the highly trained security manager for all imports, exports, and applicants seeking short or permanent residence. 'I could check again, but she doesn't match my recollections of any of the three female IDs we processed last week.'

'She couldn't be a newcomer,' said Cordane, now flatly contradicting himself. 'How would she know there's only a minimal guard at the Residence tonight? And that she could scale the garden wall because it's no longer powered?'

'She's no Streetie, or Walteron would have tried to ooze her off the floor by now,' said Deagan. 'I wonder how she's operating that haze she wears in place of a gown. Fascinating use of refracted light for those random opaques and transparencies.' He jiggled his hand as if the movement would generate the answer. 'Must be a net, but where does she get so much power?'

'We're not going to let old Walteron get her, are we? Lovely creature like that,' Cordane asked in a tone that made his friends regard him with some amusement.

'If Deagan's right and she's in a circuit-protected dress, what could Walteron do?' asked Fenn.

'Short the circuits in a dark corner,' Deagan replied.

'If he can. I'd like a dance with her if only to see how the haze is engineered.'

The other two glared at him whereupon Deagan chuckled and gestured toward other parts of the vast room where the majority did seem to be staring at Walteron and his shimmering partner.

'You've got to admit it's a bloody clever costume. Pure hatred gleams from half the female eyes. Just look at your mother's disapproving glare, Fenn. And you know that your sister Marla spent all year dreaming up that rather fetching concoction of Verulean lace she's wearing. But it doesn't compare with our crasher's effort.'

'If she's from Outback, she might not know she's at risk with old Walteron,' said Cordane, sounding a bit anxious. He was a considerate and responsible young man. 'The gavotte's not easy to master. She's obviously danced it before and often. They don't do that sort of thing in the Streets!'

'Dance with her next then, Cordane. You know the Street accents,' urged Deagan. Before his friends could vacillate, he took them both by the elbows and propelled them through the onlookers to the point where the girl and Walteron were likely to finish the gavotte. 'If she's not Street, you take the next dance, Fenn. You range enough in the Outback to identify their twang.'

'Then you'll dance with her and short out her dress,' said Cordane, indignantly pulling his arm from his friend's grasp.

'Short her dress? Here in the Residence?' Deagan grinned sardonically and jerked his head toward his father, who was laughing affably with some ranking outworld guests. The PM's moods could change to implacable sternness when necessary, and all three young men knew it. 'Besides, shorting would burn her between the contact points. My interest is purely theoretical. The creation is ingenious.'

'Expensive, too, I'd say,' added Fenn. 'She's like a lovely double-moon mist.'

Cordane blinked in surprise, for the young Domainer was not usually given to metaphors.

'Under that face veil, she could be ugly as a roake, but right now, what a fillip to a dull dance,' said Deagan. 'Quickly, Corrie. The dance is ending!' He gave his friend a push forward onto the dance area so that the slick surface all but catapulted Cordane against Walteron.

'Look, the old lecher won't relinquish,' said Deagan, irritated, as he and Fenn watched the exchange between the two would-be partners. 'Let's reinforce before Corrie muffs it.' Deagan, clutching Fenn unobtrusively at the elbow, strode quickly over to the trio. 'Oh, lovely maiden of the double-moon mists,' he opened, with a click of his heels and a smart salute in keeping with his elegant formal Space uniform, 'my friend here' – he gestured to Fenn, since names were never exchanged at a costumed Touch-Down dance – 'is a shy and gentle youth who, like myself, is all admiration for your raiment. My sincerest compliments on your originality.'

'Accepted, good sir,' the girl said with such composure and in such pure Standard accents that Deagan knew that she was neither Streetie, newcomer, nor Outback Domainer.

'Since he is so shy, may I request that you favor him with the next dance?' Deagan continued, subtly changing his position to form, with his two friends, a circle in front of the girl that excluded Walteron.

'The dance *after* the one I am claiming by right of first request,' said Cordane, with a smart clap of his boot heels and a mock glare at Deagan and Fenn.

One could just perceive her smile through the coruscating mist of her face veil, but her eyes, a clear, intelligent green emphasized by the shifting shades of her

327

attire, glamed with amusement. A flick of her green gaze told Deagan that she was aware of Walteron, fuming at the deft exclusion and the man's obvious keen intention to extend his acquaintance with her.

'I put in my most humble bid for the third dance, lovely lady,' said Deagan, 'and each third one afterward.'

'You mean to monopolize my dances?' She looked from one importuning costumed officer to the next, avoiding Walteron's attempts to reclaim her attention.

'Three doesn't constitute a monopoly,' said Fenn, who tended to be literal.

'But assuredly offers protection,' added Deagan.

'Mutual protection?' She tilted her head sideways just slightly in Walteron's direction. Her eyes lingered on Deagan's face, and he knew she had taken the warning.

'Please say yes,' Cordane urged, with just the right note of petition in his voice so that she could be swayed to compliance without appearing to offend the other whilom partners. She nodded assent to Cordane.

'May I have the dance after his?' Fenn asked eagerly, inspired by Cordane's success. The two were oblivious, as Deagan was not, to Walteron's set mouth and angry eyes.

Fortunately the music began just at that moment and Cordane triumphantly swung the girl onto the floor, taking their position in one of the faststeps at which Cordane was very adept.

'Didn't think you'd be able to join us tonight, Walteron,' said Deagan politely as he, Fenn, and the older man left the dance floor.

'Sorry about that subsidence, Walteron. Trust no one was killed,' Fenn added ingenuously. 'That Aldebaran specialist'll soon sort it out, they've had so much experience in the same sort of thing.'

Walteron's eyes blazed at Deagan, and with a disgusted

snort toward Fenn, he stalked away to the refreshment room.

'What did I say to put him in such a temper?' Perplexed, the young Domainer peered at the departing man.

'Don't worry about it.' They both turned to spot Cordane and the girl twirling amid the other enthusiastic dancers.

She could, Deagan thought, be a trained mimic or actress, contracted for the Celebrations, but she hadn't faltered in her pure accent of the well-bred and highly educated. She had been quick to take advantage of their protection from someone like Walteron, who would have been the obvious choice of a Streetie. Of more interest to Deagan were the tiny sparkling green nodes she wore like jewels as ear, finger, and toe rings. Two slightly larger ones were attached as pendants on the fine circlet about her neck and on her browband. Earring and browband set up the circuit for the face veil and the gown was generated between the other nodes. The resultant haze of light refraction was more of an engineering feat than a fabric maker's.

When Cordane's dance ended, Deagan and Fenn quickly joined the trio, edging out two new contenders for her company. They chatted with her on inconsequential topics until the music of a slow patterned dance started, whereupon Fenn had the privilege of handing the girl in to a space in the decorous circle.

'She's got style,' Cordane said enthusiastically as he and Deagan watched from the sidelines. 'She's not a Streetie or a new-come Outbacker. Say, could she be one of that new lot of technicians landed a few months back?'

'I thought of that possibility, too, but I handle all identity programming, and I'd swear she couldn't be one of them.'

'Oh!' Cordane sounded deflated. 'Private adventurer here on a visit? Lots of 'em come for Touch-Down.'

'If she had any planetary standing elsewhere, she'd've been on the official list.'

'We don't know that she isn't, do we? I only assumed she was party-crashing because we first saw her near the garden entrance.'

'A good point. I'll check the guard console.'

Deagan's progress around the perimeter was hampered by envious questions, subtle or blatant, about the identity of the lovely girl in gauze.

The nearest console, located in the men's room, provided him with a list of all official invitations as well as a quick view-through of the costumed figures as they arrived, passing the guard-eye at the main door of the Residence. As he suspected, she had not entered formally.

He returned to the ballroom just as the music came to its stately climax, with dancers bowing or curtsying to their partners.

'During my dance with her,' Deagan told Cordane, 'you and Fenn check the garden. She didn't come in past the guard-eye. But keep your ear on the music. We don't want them in on our time,' he added, flicking his fingers at other young men poised at the edge of the dance floor, just waiting a chance to cut in on the mystery girl. Then, turning his glance back to the girl, he noticed that, as she rose from her deep curtsy, she glanced at the crystal timepiece suspended above the main entrance to the dancing hall. An odd concern for a girl enjoying enviable popularity.

He tried, during that interval, to turn the conversation to her arrival at Fomalhaut City, or her family, or anything that would give clues to her identity, but she deftly avoided answering him by flirting with Cordane and Fenn. As the strains of the next dance emanated from the android musicians, Cordane gave a disgusted laugh. 'You timed that well, Deagan,' he said, for his pavane had not allowed much contact and Deagan would obviously make the most of this waltz.

Even as Deagan laughed at Cordane's discomfort, his phrase lingered oddly. Deagan had almost made the connection as he offered his arms to the misty maiden. Then he forgot the half-formed thought as he placed his right hand about her waist, grasped her right hand firmly in his, and swept her out in perfect rhythm to the lovely ancient melody. She also knew the waltz exceedingly well.

Holding her close, he could not miss the delicate scent she wore, but it wasn't the sort used by a woman wishing to seduce a susceptible male. Her body, under the silky envelope of the generated haze, was lithe and fit and her hand grip in his firm – this was no indolent social lass. Her left hand, traditionally placed on the peak of his shoulder, did not, as he had half expected, curl provocatively toward his neck.

'It's an interesting game you play, lovely lady! My compliments on your campaign.'

'Campaign, Captain?' Her teasing tone was half reproof.

'A clever penetration of the sacred precincts of the Residence, and its most prestigious gathering.'

'Penetration, sir? But all restrictions are lifted during Touch-Down.' Her eyes danced up at him, offering challenge, then slid, fleetingly, once again toward the timepiece as they glided past it.

That action confirmed Deagan's previously half-formed notion. But she was regarding him again and her eyes widened inquiringly, so he masked his expression and casually smiled down at her. 'True enough, and a costume as magnificent as yours would be wasted on the Streets – though that is where the true adventurer would seek excitement.'

'In the Streets?' Haughty amusement rippled in her

voice as well as dislike for his suggestion. '"Adventurer" could be apt. So is the adjective, for merit accomplished on one's own resources is infinitely more satisfying. Don't you agree?'

He chuckled appreciatively, for that clever shaft was aimed at his inherited position in Fomalhaut society, although she would not know that his particular job was no sinecure. 'Life can be a true adventure in many ways, my lovely lady, and you've made this night adventurous for me . . . and my friends,' he added generously. But then he pulled her closer to him and heard her laugh in his ear as her cheek touched his lightly.

'Close tactics will avail you nothing, Captain. My costume is foolproof.'

'Mysterious one' – his tone was indignant – 'I wouldn't breach your security. I enjoy too much the come-and-go of your dazzlement.'

He loosened his tight hold because he was half afraid she would sense his growing excitement. Then he swung her in the wide circles of the dance, enjoying himself as he had never expected to do this Touch-Down night. When he courteously surrendered her to Cordane for his next dance, Fenn told him that they had found nothing to indicate that she had scaled the four-meter wall.

Deagan left Fenn to watch and did a few rapid calculations on the men's-room console, checked the time, and smiled. An hour to go at the most – nor would she leave the way she'd arrived. She'd surely have noticed the position of the side gates. Getting into the Residence was more of a problem than leaving it on Touch-Down night. He made his plans.

But first he would enjoy his other dance with her, enjoy sparring in conversation, for she had a lively wit as well as a keen intelligence. Fenn and Cordane were utterly smitten and were hard to convince that she intended to leave the ball as unexpectedly as she had arrived. He finally did convince them that, should she excuse herself from their company on any pretext, they'd never see her again. They were to let her go with good grace and then dash into the gardens to prevent her escaping that way.

At that, Deagan nearly missed his chance. But she gave herself away, her eyes betraying a faint apprehension as she glanced with apparent negligence toward the crystal chronometer.

Deagan excused himself, saying that his father had beckoned. He was careful to pause by the PM.

'Not fair of you to pull rank and monopolize that lovely creature, Deagan,' his father said.

'I haven't. Fenn and Cordane dance with her, too.'

The planetary manager gave a derisive snort. 'Do we know her?'

'We will!'

'Oh?' The PM raised his eyebrows in surprise at so emphatic a reply from his generally unimpressionable son.

Deagan left the hall as if on an urgent errand. He was – he wanted to program all gates on inner lock. The action ought not to discommode anyone for the short time he'd require. As he slipped out the main door, he caught a glimpse of shimmer entering the women's room. He also saw Fenn and Cordane striding out the garden doors.

From where he stood by the main gate in the shadows, Deagan could see the slope of the dome and the misty glow of her gown as she eased herself over the sill of the women's-room window. Just as he had guessed. She moved quickly for the side gate in a half crouch, so he gave her full marks for caution. As she pulled vainly at the locked gate, he heard not only a frustrated moan but a concerned note in her low exclamation. He glanced at his wrist chrono – she'd precious little time to try other side gates: she'd have to chance that the main one remained open.

At one instant she was a swiftly moving mist, the next a slender, white-bodied nymph trailing motes of sparkling fire that wafted to the garden sand behind her. She stumbled with a cry of pain, then uttered a round space oath just as he emerged from the shadow of the bushes. Courteously keeping his eyes on hers, he flung the cloak he had brought with him about her body. She did not resist as he encircled her with his arms.

'My apologies. I computed the possible energy in your jewel generators and . . . here I am.'

'Fair enough.' Her body did not yield.

'Is it unfair to outthink a true adventurer?'

He had meant to tease her further but something in her proud look made him forbear. Without a veil, her face had character, and the fine features of a noble background. Nor had her manner lost its innate self-confidence. He liked her even more as her true self than as a mysterious mist. So he kissed her lips lightly. After the briefest hesitation, she responded and her body relaxed in his grip. He did not press his advantage but stepped back.

'Suppose we find another costume for you for the remainder of the evening, if you'll do us the honor, my lady . . . ?'

'Darcia Cormel of Aldebaran IV,' she said, filling in the blank.

'The soil-mechanics engineer?' His doubled surprise made her laugh. 'But you weren't due to arrive for another week or more.' Deagan had never thought to check anticipated visitors and couldn't express the ruefulness he felt at that oversight. But it was no wonder she could create such a costume. 'Fardles, do you realize that it was Walteron who danced with you first?'

'I do now, but he'll never connect that me with his precious specialist. Let's go. I've clothes outside the gate you locked on me.' She bent suddenly, feeling with both hands about the dark garden sand. 'But first, help me find my other slipper?'

HABIT IS AN OLD
HORSE

As the Sussex cock summoned morning, the old gray horse woke. He lifted his muzzle from the ground and, blinking to clear his eyes, gazed about the twelve-acre field. The donkeys were, as usual, already grazing at the road end of the pasture. The two hunters were sprawled out flat, taking every advantage of their summer's rest. The yearlings were behind old Knock; he heard them stamping.

He shook his head. He must get up. He positioned his front legs, heaved his hindquarters under him. One more effort and he was standing. As he sauntered over to the water trough set between this field and the one that contained the broodmares and new foals, his off-hind leg dragged stiffly. He ignored the discomfort, knowing the stiffness would ease with exercise.

The yearlings suddenly acquired thirst, too, and frolicked about him as he made his stately way, ignoring their antics. The brown came a bit too near him and the old gray horse extended his neck, teeth bared, to put the brown in mind of his manners.

Knock blew across the surface of the trough, rippling away dust and leaves. He touched the water, cool on his lips, and then plunged his nose in to suck deeply. The first water of the day was best and he took his fill.

The younger stock, donkeys included, crowded in to the trough. The old horse backed carefully away and began to search, head down, sniffing out any sweet blades of grass that he might have missed in yesterday's grazing.

He had filled his stomach for the first time that morning before he heard any activity in the farmyard. As was his habit these past seasons, he wandered toward the house, to breast the fence that separated the fields from the gardens and the orchards about the neat bungalow. The fence, so neatly painted that spring, showed grimy patches where he leaned into it, opposite the window where she often appeared. The window was black, curtains drawn.

He gazed toward the barnyard now, to the figures carrying the morning feeds to the whickering horses in the stable row. He neighed softly, hopefully, but no one turned to wave at him. He looked back at the window: sometimes after he called, he could see movement – a hand or a white face as the edge of the curtain was pulled aside. Sometimes the blankness lifted completely and he could see the outline of her familiar figure. He hadn't seen her in some time; not since the hard weather eased into a wet spring. He snorted with disappointment and stamped the ground. He stamped again, tossing his head, and noticed long grass stems just on the other side of the fence. By a careful angling of his long head, he could just reach the grass. He contented himself with nibbling all along the fence by the house yard. She might just still come out to him with a carrot, or an apple, or even a slice of bread if he stayed by the fence long enough.

The flurry of activity in the horse yard ended as the three men went back into the house, leaving the stabled horses to finish their feed.

Philosophically old Knock finished cropping the far side of the fence and then moved off. If she didn't visit him in the morning, she often came out with the others in the evening when all the field horses were checked.

He was half-asleep in the sun, the hip of the stiff leg

cocked, when shouts and a scrabble of shod hooves on stone brought his head up and ears pricking toward the stableyard. A big bay mare was dancing about, eluding the rider who wished to mount her. The old horse wondered why she bothered: she only delayed the inevitable. He heaved a sigh.

It had been a long time since he'd felt a rider's weight. She hadn't ridden him, even gently about the fields, since last summer. No one else had backed him since that day. He looked again at her window and it was still blank.

The mare was still trying to have her way, rearing and prancing, the men shouting in the hard determined way he remembered. He heard the splat of crop on flesh: the mare hesitated and her rider vaulted into the saddle. Another splat brought an abrupt end to the contest. She had never had to use a stick on him, he remembered complacently. Always he had been ready to do as she asked, for she'd a light hand, a firm seat, and a kind voice. They'd gone like the wind together across field and through forest. Those had been the good days: when he'd breath and will to run, when his muscles moved easily, when he couldn't wait to see what the next field brought, ditch or fence or bank, the baying of the hounds ahead of them and most of the other, slower horses stretched out behind them. She'd been a light and gracious burden for him to carry, her hands along his neck encouraging him, her affectionate pulling of his ears (an indignity that he had permitted only from her), the slaps of approval on his neck when the day's hunting had ended. And the tidbits from her hand as she saw him safely bedded for the night inside a warm, deep-strawed box.

He'd had other riders from time to time: some he'd carried with no protest. There had been the odd one or two he hadn't wanted on his back. He had developed simple tricks, dropping his shoulder or going under a low branch at speed. Those times were few because, mostly, she rode him. He could take pride in the knowledge that he had never failed her, nor faltered no matter what she had asked him to jump or do.

The bay's rider had now guided the mare into the practice ring where the old gray horse had so often been worked with her on his back. The rider put the mare into the old remembered drill of walk, trot, canter, cross the arena, walk, trot, stop, back, job, canter, which was so familiar to the old horse that the skin across his withers twitched. He could almost feel the pressure of the saddle on his withers, the girth firm under his belly. He watched, head up and ears pricked, as the schooling continued. Then the rider turned the mare toward the jumps set in the training field.

As he watched the mare, the old horse could almost hear her voice in his ears, encouraging him, praising him as they careered about the field and over the obstacles. She'd steady him with her voice when the excitement of performance overcame his normal calm. She'd laugh when he'd buck out over the last fence, as if she knew how glad he was to have gone clear. He remembered, and the skin of his chest rippled, how he'd be jarred to his poll sometimes by the hardness of the ground as he landed after a big fence. But he was clever on his feet, and never once had he slipped on muddy ground whether they put studs in his shoes or not. Best of all, he had liked the spreads, for then he had seemed to be suspended between ground and sky. That sensation he had liked above all, spurning the ground in those scant seconds as if he might one day leap with her to the sun itself had he the right ground for takeoff.

Best of all were the times he'd stood with other horses and permitted ribbons to be attached to his browband. He could sense her pride and joy along the reins to his bit. And he never spooked, as others might, when bands banged and hooted close by him.

The *bruff-bruff* high blowing of the mare brought him out of his dreaming. She'd been checked for the second spread: he could hear the rattling tattoo of her hooves as she pulled to be free, the silence following her takeoff and the grunt of her landing as she cantered on.

'Ross!' he heard someone shouting from the front of the house. He pricked his ears forward, straining as the call was repeated: it sounded like her voice, but it wasn't. He stamped, disappointed. She used to watch them jump other horses. He knew she was in the house, behind the blank window. Why didn't she come and see him?

The mare and her rider had turned, cantering back to the gate into the stableyard, where the other woman waited. The man jumped from the mare's back.

'Ross, she wouldn't even take her tea this morning. I've called the doctor, and he's coming right over.'

The urgency, the ripple of fear in the woman's voice, so like the voice he longed to hear, made the old horse whicker hopefully. He whuffled again, when he saw them turn their heads in his direction. 'Oh, Ross, how could old Knock know?'

'Don't be silly, Mairead. He couldn't know. He's always at the fence in the morning. Mam used to feed him when she was still able. It's just habit, that's all.'

'It isn't as if we weren't expecting it, Ross, but somehow . . .'

'Just let me put the mare up.'

Knock watched as the two parted, the man leading the bay mare back to her stable. As the woman slowly walked toward him, he nickered softly.

'Do you know, Knock? Mam always said you were smart for a horse.' She extended her hand to his questing lips. 'Do you know Mam's dying?'

Her hand was empty but she stroked his nose. He

sensed her unhappiness and stood quietly as she leaned her forehead against his neck. She'd done that sometimes, standing with her head against him, hands quiescent on his nose and shoulder: sometimes, too, as this woman did now, she'd made funny sounds and left his shoulder wet.

'Oh, Knock, when I think of how she used to be . . . and then to see her now, in pain, so weak . . .'

Knock heard the man's footsteps but he didn't move.

'If Knock were in such pain, we could put him down so he needn't suffer . . .'

'Ross, how could you say such a thing . . .'

'It'd be kinder, wouldn't it?' The man sounded angry. 'Wouldn't it, Mairead? D'you think I don't realize what Mam's going through? It's a dirty rotten trick to pull on a gallant old lady but at least she can die in her own bed with her own family about her and . . .'

'Knock waiting for her at the fence.'

The woman whirled from Knock, crying with emotion the old horse could smell so acutely that he blew softly in reaction. The man had his arms about the woman, comforting her with small pats on her shoulders and soft words. As he stood that way, his eyes caught the old horse's, almost accusingly.

The horse heard the car first, lifting his head, seeing the bright flash of its blue paint through the trees that bordered the drive. The woman broke from the comforting arms and ran across the grass toward the front of the house to intercept the car.

'It would be kinder,' the man said in a low voice, staring at the horse, 'but we can't, can we? You'll miss her, too, won't you, old boy?' He slapped Knock affectionately on the neck before he walked quickly after the woman.

The first car heralded the arrival of many others; some discharging passengers and leaving, while others parked on the front lawn and the tarmacadam. Pleased by the unusual activity to entertain him, the old horse wondered what was to happen. So many cars generally meant a sale of animals or a show in the big jumping field. Today, however, no teams of people bustled about setting up jumps and roping off areas for rings. The uneasy aura about the house made him restless and he couldn't settle to grazing with the yearlings.

Obscurely troubled, the old horse stamped his off-fore. As if his action were some sort of cue, he heard the faint sounds of distressed cries, of loud weeping. The curtains now bounced with agitation and he thought for a brief moment that they would at last be pulled aside and he'd see her. The movement ceased but the noises, muffled though they were by the walls of the house, carried clearly to his ears. He didn't like the sounds and pawed the ground with nervousness. He wanted to leave the fence side but some unheard restraint compelled him to remain in vigil. Abruptly the compulsion ceased. Free to move, he did not. He waited by the fence.

Full of grass and bored of sportive play, the yearlings came over for a while midafternoon. They made a great show of fear and galloped off when a car came round the house to park on the tarmacadam in the rear. Knock maintained his dignified vigil.

'Mick, surely that's not Maeve's old Knock still alive?'

The sound of this woman's voice, slightly familiar to him, made the old horse turn his head, ears moving. He whuffled softly as she came over to him. She dug a sugar lump from one pocket and held out her hand flatly, so politely he extended his neck to accept her offering.

'You never supposed Maeve would sell this fella to the factory, did you?' asked the man with a lightly derisive laugh. He ran a practised hand from Knock's shoulder to his neck and gave him an admiring slap. 'Not after all the winnings she collected jumping him.'

'But Mick, he's surely over thirty?'

'Suspect he is. In grand shape for all of that.' The man's tone changed abruptly. 'C'mon. We'd better go in. Get it over with.'

'A minute, Mick. I've found another bit of sugar.' She fumbled in her pocket and held the battered offering under Knock's nose. He gave a sniff but lipped it up willingly. She patted his cheek. 'Poor old fella. No one's had time for you today, I'll bet.' Her voice quavered and Knock tensed, catching the note of unfamiliar emotion.

'Now, Sally . . .'

'I know, Mick' – and the woman gave a convulsive sob – 'it was just seeing old Knock waiting by her window and no way to tell him . . .'

No sooner had the two hurried around to the front of the house than another car arrived in the rear. Knock regarded the new arrivals with keen interest as they emerged from the car. There might be more sugar lumps.

'D'Gawd, he's there. Tol'ya he'd be,' said a thickened voice, which Knock associated with the man who used to shoe his feet. 'You and your notions that the one would die with the other!' He scoffed loudly and was ordered to hush by his companions. He glanced at the curtained window and hunched his shoulders up to his neck, feigning repentance. 'B'Gawd, though, he'd fetch a fine price at Straffan, now wouldn't he, Joe?'

The men were close enough to Knock now for him to smell the sourness he distrusted. He had always associated that odor with trouble and a groom he'd hated. He blew out in distress and backed away from the fence.

'Jaysus, if the old horse didn't understand ya!' The other two men pulled the farrier along with them to the front of the house. 'Mind your mush inside t'house, fer Gawd's sake.'

Warily observing their progress away from him,

Knock noticed that the windows of the big room overlooking the field were not blank. He could see the faces turned in his direction and, ears wagging at the muted sounds of voices, he watched the watchers until the next car came around. He stepped back to his position at the fence, head up, ears inquiringly forward. But the people were too occupied with conveying bowls, trays, and crates, though he caught the unmistakable odor of the food they carried briskly through the kitchen door.

The skies were darkening now and a chill wind blew raggedly up from the sea, an unusual direction at this time of year. The young horses joined Knock, pressing against his bulk to share his warmth. The hunters, aloof, chose a place along the fence nearer the stables.

There was a lot of bustle and calling and banging in the stableyard as volunteers coped with the arrangements of a strange barn as they fed the stabled horses.

'Hey, get a scoop for old Knock, too. He deserves a feed at this wake if anyone does!'

A man approached the old horse, a scoop held at waist level. The smell of nuts reassured Knock more than the man's soothing words. The scoop was only half-full but Knock was grateful. The yearlings, naturally, came to see what was happening. Laughing softly, the man gave them the odd few so they wouldn't steal from Knock's pile.

Sunset was obscured by a mizzling rain, following the rise of bluster in that sea-borne wind. Knock maintained his hopeful position at the fence, but no more cars came round to the rear, although there were enough coming and going down the drive to the main road. When the dampness soaked through to chill his back, Knock sought shelter with the others against the hedgerow where the trees lining the driveway gave some protection. The yearlings pressed around him for comfort and warmth.

Not only did the weather deteriorate but the headlights and noise of cars constantly up and down the drive kept rousing the horses from the little rest they could get. There had been a time when she would have brought him under cover on such a night as this.

Toward morning, the wind dropped and the rain eased off. The yearlings moved away, grazing to comfort their cold bellies, but Knock was too stiff to move. He longed for the sun to warm and ease his cold back and stiff hind leg. Knock was resentful as well as miserable and, acting from habit, he haltingly moved toward her window and, lifting his head, whinnied sharply. Abruptly the curtain was pulled back from the window. He blinked against the sudden sharp brightness. He whinnied again. The curtain dropped back into place, though a thin edge of light showed at one side. Then the kitchen door opened and three figures came out.

'Knock? Is that you, fella? How did you know, old boy? How did you know?'

Knock recognized the voice of the bay's rider and whickered again as the three men approached him. Then the window brought to his nostrils the sour smell he hated and, despite the kindness and sorrow in the blurred voice, he backed away.

'He was cold, that's all it is, Ross,' said the thick-voiced farrier. He bent to climb through the fence rails. 'I'll just catch him up and put him in the barn.'

Knock threw up his head, whinnying both fear and warning. He wanted no part of someone smelling like that. He wheeled sharply on his hindquarters, though his stiff leg nearly buckled, as he ran from the smell and the men. When he felt safely out of their reach, he turned to see if they intended to follow him. They were silhouetted now, for someone had thrown back the curtains of her window. He called once more. The curtains fell back and then even the edge of light went out.

He tossed his head, blowing, whinnying sharp and high in his distress. She did not even come to the window. He didn't understand his abandonment. Disconsolately, he plodded off to join the yearlings. They were better than no company on this disturbing cold night when she no longer heard him.

LADY-IN-WAITING

'Mummie, Sally wants to play dress-up,' said Frances, her pointed little face contorted with the obligation to accommodate her first guest in the new house.

'I do, too,' said six-year-old Marjorie, pouting her plump cheeks in anticipation of refusal.

Sally Merrion just stood in the loose semicircle about Amy Landon's kitchen table, her dubious but polite expression challenging her hostess.

'Dressing up seems a very good idea for such a drizzling day,' Amy replied calmly. To give herself a moment to think what she could possibly find for them to play in, she finished pouring the steaming bramble jelly into the jar.

Fran caught her breath as a gobbet on the lip of the saucepan splashed and instantly dissolved, coloring pink the hot water in which the jars were steeped.

'What had you planned to dress up as?'

'Ladies-in-waiting,' said Sally, recovering from the initial surprise of agreement but still determined to put her hostesses to the blush.

There was such an appeal in Fran's soft eyes that Amy was rather certain that the notion of this particular costume was all Sally's.

'Wadies-in-waiting,' Marjorie said, frowning and pouting as if to force her mother to accept.

'We'd be very careful,' Fran said in her solemn way.

'I know you would, pet,' Amy replied, smiling gentle reassurance.

Not for the first time, Amy wondered how long it would take the sensitive Frances to recover from the shock of her father's death: his brutal murder, Amy amended in the deepest part of her mind. Peter had been a victim of a bomb thrown without warning into a London pub.

She disciplined her thoughts sternly back to the tasks at hand: pouring the bramble jelly and figuring out how to comply with her daughters' needs.

'Werry careful,' Marjorie said, bobbing her head up and down while Sally Merrion waited to be surprised.

'Of course you would, love,' Amy assured the child, knowing that Fran could be depended upon to make certain that her younger sister was careful.

'Frances is a real dote,' Amy's mother often said with pride, since the child resembled her in feature and coloring, 'and more help than the twins, I'm sure, despite their being older. The poor wee fatherless lambkins,' she'd recently taken to adding in a tone that stiffened Amy's resolve to make the move that had indirectly caused Peter's death.

During the first days of her bereavement, the hideous irony of his dying had given her a passionate dislike for Tower Cottage. The only reason Peter had been in that pub at that critical moment was to phone her the good news that he'd signed the mortgage contract for a house that would take them away from the increasingly dangerous city streets: a house in the gray-stoned hills of Dorset, with its own orchard and gardens, and a paddock for a pony; the kind of rural, self-sufficient life that Amy and he had known as children.

Her parents, and his, had urged her to repudiate the contract, so stay close to them so they could give her the comfort, protection, and aid that a young widow with four growing children would undeniably need.

Stubbornly and contrary to her prejudice toward Tower Cottage, Amy Landon had honored that agreement, citing to her parents that the life-insurance policy required by the mortgage company now gave her the house free and clear.

'You could say that Peter died to secure Tower Cottage,' Amy had told the parental conclave. 'It *is* far away from London and I want to *get* far away from London. I want to abide by the plans my Peter and I made. I'm well able for the life. It isn't as if I weren't country-bred . . . Just because *you* wanted to retire to the city . . .'

'But, all alone . . . so far from a village . . . and neighbors,' her father and Peter's had argued.

'I'm hardly alone with four children. Young Peter's as tall as I and much stronger. We're scarcely *far* from a village when there're shops, a post office, *and* a pub a half mile down the lane. As for neighbors . . . I'll have too much to do to worry about neighbors.'

And the fewer the better, she'd amended to herself. She abhorred the pity, even the compassion, accorded her for her loss. She was weary of publicity, of people staring blur-eyed at herself and her children. They'd all be spoiled if this social sympathy continued much longer: spoiled into thinking that the world owed them something because politics . . . or was it madness? . . . had deprived them of their father.

'My mother keeps a special box,' Sally Merrion was saying to draw Amy's thought back to the present, to the low-beam kitchen redolent of bubbling bramble berries, sealing wax, and the casserole baking in the old Aga cooker. 'It's got clothes my grandma and great-gran wore.'

Amy wondered if she'd ever use those maxiskirts again. 'I've some things in the blanket chest . . .' She hesitated. She couldn't leave the jelly half-poured and she resisted the notion, once again, that there was something about the box room that made her loathe to enter it.

'Don't worry, Mother. I wouldn't touch anything *good*,' Fran said, patently relieved that her mother had risen to the need. 'And you daren't leave the jelly.'

'Wadies-in-waiting?' asked Marjorie in a quavering voice.

'Yes, yes, love. Go along then, girls. I really must finish the jelly. Fran, you can use those long skirts of mine. And there're old sheets in the blanket chest . . .' Why on earth be afraid of a blanket chest? But a frisson caught her between her shoulders. 'They'd make lovely flowing robes . . .'

From the scornful expression on Sally's face, Amy wondered what on earth the child was permitted to use in her own home. Cheeky girl.

Amy concentrated on the jelly, finishing the first pan of jars and getting the next ready before her maternal instinct flared. Back in the kitchen, separated from the main section of the cottage by the pantry, and thick walls, she could hear nothing. She'd better check. She pushed open the pantry door and the high happy voices of the girls, affecting adult accents, carried quite audibly down the stairwell. They were obviously playing there on the landing in front of the box room. Satisfied, Amy returned to her jelly.

She found unexpected satisfaction, she mused, in these homely preparations against the winter. Atavistic, Peter would have called her. The summer had not been kind to the land and its bounty was reduced, or so the villagers had said, but Amy Landon had no fault to find. The apple and pear trees of Tower Cottage were well laden when you considered that there'd been no one to prune, spray, or fertilize them: and how there came to be beetroot, potatoes, cabbage, carrots, and swedes in the kitchen garden, Amy didn't know. The villagers had rolled their eyes and each suggested someone else as the Good Samaritan. Her circumstances were known in the village, so she concluded that some kindhearted soul did not wish her to feel under obligation. Nonetheless, the abundance of the garden meant that she could manage better on the spartan budget she allowed herself. (She would make no unnecessary inroads on savings that were earmarked to see young Peter through secondary school and college. And she refused to think in terms of compensation money.) With the cost of all commodities rising, she must grow or raise as much as possible on her property.

Mr Suttle, who ran the tiny shop at the crossroads, had told her that old Mrs Mallett had kept chickens: she had owned Tower Cottage before the Alderdyces bought it. (The Alderdyces, now, they hadn't lived there very long: come into money sudden like, and bought a grand house nearer London only they didn't get to live in their new house because they died of a motor accident before ever they reached it.) While Mr Suttle hadn't heard of chickens living wild like that for two years or more, then returning to their own run, there was no other explanation for the flock that now pecked contentedly around the barn behind Tower Cottage, and obediently laid their eggs for Patricia to find.

To her father's amusement, and young Peter's delight, Amy had purchased a Guernsey cow, for what was the sense of having a four-acre meadow and a barn unexpectedly full of hay if one didn't use them. Mr Suttle had knowledgeably inspected the same stable and hay, pronounced the one fit to house cattle and the other well enough saved to be eaten by the cow, and applauded little Mrs Landon's sense.

Old Mrs Mallett, who'd been spry to the day of her

peaceful death, had kept chickens, cow, and pig (Mr Suttle thought he might be able to find Mrs Landon a piglet to fatten for Christmas) and lived quite well off her land, and kept warm and comfortable in Tower Cottage.

Amy assured Mr Suttle that this was also her intention, and she thanked him for his advice, but she rather felt the piglet could wait until she was accustomed to managing cow, chickens, and children.

Actually, it was young Peter who managed the cow, after instructions from the farmer who'd sold them the beast. And Patricia, Peter's twin, cared for the chickens. The two vied with each other to prove their charges in that curiously intense competition reserved to twins.

Amy sealed the bramble jelly and began to stick on the labels that Fran had laboriously printed for her. All of them had picked the berries the day before, a warm, sunny Sunday, and made a game of the work, arriving home in the early September dusk, berry-full and berry-stained, with buckets of the rich dark fruit. The only deterrent to complete happiness for Amy had been the absence of her husband: this was what he had wanted for his family and he wasn't alive to share it. In poignant moments like this, her longing for him became a physical illness.

She must continue to force such negative thoughts from her mind: the children had had enough gloom, enough insecurity. She must find contentment in the fact that they were indeed living as Peter had so earnestly desired.

Young Peter came in with the milk pail, the contents frothy and warm. Patricia was just behind him with eggs from her hens.

'I think Molly likes me,' Peter announced as he usually did when the Guernsey had let down her milk for him with no fuss.

'Another dozen eggs, Mummie,' said Patricia, taking

her basket into the larder and carefully arranging the freshest in the front of the molded cardboard.

Peter heaved the bucket up to the counter and got out the big kettle, whereupon he began to measure the milk before heating it. He was keeping a record of Molly's output as against her intake, so that they would have accurate figures on how much their milk and butter were costing them. He was all for trying to make soft cheese, too, since there were herbs along the garden path for seasoning.

High on the wall by the pantry door, the old bell tinkled in its desultory fashion, announcing a caller at the front door.

Wondering who that could be since the few people with whom she was acquainted would know that she'd be in the kitchen this time of day, Amy half ran to the front hall, wiping her hands as she went and pulling fussily at her jumper, aware that it was jelly-sticky. She gave the door the hefty yank it required and discovered Sally's mother about to use the huge clumsy knocker.

'Good heavens, Mrs Landon . . .'

'I'm terribly sorry to keep you standing on the stoop, Mrs Merrion . . .'

'I can't thank you enough for minding Sally . . .'

'No bother. Such a nasty day, the girls have been playing dress-up.'

In mutual accord, the two women crossed the square front hall to the stairs. Above them some charade was in progress: they could hear Sally announcing dire news in a loud and affected voice.

'Sally dear, it's Mummie come to collect you.'

'Oh, Mummie, did you have to come just now?'

Amy and Mrs Merrion exchanged amused glances at the distressed wail of protest. As they looked up, Sally was leaning over the upper balustrade, her face framed by a gauzy blue, the folds of heavy blue sleeves falling to cover her hands on the railing.

'I'm just denouncing the traitor in our midst who was de . . . dee . . . what did you say he was doing to us, Fran?' Sally turned her head and nearly lost the heavy headdress.

'Sally love' – Mrs Merrion's voice was patient and level – 'I've got to pick up the meat for tea and your father from the station. There's only just time to get to Mr Suttle's before . . .'

'Oh, Mummie . . .' Sally's tone was piteous, and undoubtedly tears were being repressed.

Amy heard Fran's soothing voice, to which she added her own assurance that Sally could return very soon and continue the game.

'It just won't be the same . . .' Sally's voice ended on a petulant high note.

The women saw a swish of royal blue shirts, which told them that Sally was submitting to the inevitable.

'Fran love, would you put the things away for Sally since she has to leave now?'

'Yes, Mummie. Come *on* now, Marjorie, you can help . . .'

Marjorie blubbered a protest, evoking her privilege as the youngest in the family.

'If you're big enough to *be* a lady-in-waiting, you're big enough to help,' Fran said in such an imitation of an adult that Amy and Mrs Merrion grinned at each other.

Sally's stiff-legged descent of the stairs reminded them of that young lady's disgruntlement well before they could see her scowling face. Amy gathered up Sally's school mac and book bag, quickly deciding that the dirtier of the two school scarves was not Fran's, and prepared to speed the parting guest.

Sally allowed herself to be helped into her coat, but her seething resentment dissipated as she babbled to her mother that Mrs Landon had smashing things to play dress-up in, Mummie, and when could she come again please, and thank you Mrs Landon for the tea and Mummie didn't you have to go to the dentist again soon?

Mrs Merrion, amused by her daughter's effusiveness, smiled and said all the properly courteous things as she hurried Sally across the square hall and out the door. As Amy waited politely on the steps while the Merrions' green shooting brake was bucking down the pebbled drive, she began to wonder at Sally's unexpected enthusiasm. What on earth had the girls managed to find in the 'smashing' category in that blanket chest? What else was in it? Suits of Peter's that she'd put by for his son, the odd blanket or two, a few drapes, some out-grown things of Patricia's, party dresses of hers that she would be unlikely to wear in Dorset, several lengths of fabric. Nothing royal blue in the lot! And she'd never had any occasion to use gauze. Nor headdresses. As far as she could remember, there'd been nothing left behind in the box room by the previous owners, the unfortunate Alderdyces.

'Mum, the milk!' Peter shouted through the pantry door.

'Do put everything back, Fran, won't you?' Amy paused long enough in the stairwell to hear her daughter's assurance before she returned to the kitchen and an urgent affair of pasteurization.

At supper that night, when Marjorie was safely in bed, Amy remembered the royal blue puzzle.

'Fran, pet, how did you get on as ladies-in-waiting?'

'Oh, Mummie,' and Fran's face glowed unexpectedly, 'we had a super time. Marjorie was in the red wool though we had to pull the skirt up over the belt so she wouldn't trip. She was the junior lady-in-waiting and carried Sally's train. Sally was queen because she was guest, so she had the blue because blue is a royal color.

Isn't it?' Peter had guffawed so Fran turned wide serious eyes on her brother. 'Sally said it was . . .' ('To be sure, it is, Fran pet,' Amy reassured her, glaring at Peter.) '. . . So that left the green for me. But I think the green was for a man . . . because it only came to my knees. Marjorie's and Sally's dresses dragged on the floor . . .'

'Red? Green? What green?' Amy was mystified.

'Green . . . sort of velvet stuff, I think, and it went from here to here' – Fran measured the length on her small body – 'and there was fur along the collar and no buttons so I used another belt . . .'

'I don't recall putting away any belts . . .'

'The fancy dress ones, Mummie, with the belt buckles and sparkly stones . . .'

Fran's pleasure was fading fast in the face of possible maternal disapproval, and her voice wavered as her eyes sought her mother's.

'Oh, those!' Amy said as if her memory had been at fault. 'Those old things. I'd forgotten about them.'

'I don't remember you and Father going to costume do's,' Peter said, gathering his brows just the way his father had.

'You could scarcely remember everything your father and I did, Peter,' Amy said placidly. Peter tended to act the expert. 'There's more Horricks.' She reached for Peter's glass, smiling to clear the anxiety from her daughter's face. 'Molly's making more and we have to keep up with her production. Peter, time for you to check her while we girls do the supper dishes. Then all of you, off to bed . . .'

She made the school lunches and checked the doors before she could no longer defer the mystery of the fancy clothes. Resolutely she climbed the stairs, looking down into the square hall, as she came to the first landing. The oldest part of the house, the estate agent had said, probably was an old Norman keep, though the stone-work was in astonishingly good condition for a structure so old. Doubtless that was why the fifteenth-century architects had incorporated the keep when the cottage was built. Certainly, thought Amy, the house was a continuous production: all periods, rather than one, now combined into a hodgepodgery that had appealed to Peter's sense of the ridiculous.

The heterogeneity had also fascinated the engineer who had examined the house for Peter and Amy prior to the contract signing. On the way down to Dorset, the man had been frankly suspicious at the asking price and warned Peter and Amy to be forearmed for disappoint-ment in its state of repair. Surprisingly, the engineer had discovered very few problems, most of which could be put right with a judicious slap of mortar, plaster, or paint, and the odd dab of putty or sealer. The cellar was dry, the thick sound walls oozed no damp, the floors were remarkably level, the chimneys, of which there were nine in all, drew, the drains were recent and in good order, the slate roof was undamaged by the storms of the previous winter. And not a sign of woodworm or dry rot. The engineer reluctantly concluded that the Tower Cottage had been so reasonably priced because, as advertised, it was genuinely to be sold quickly to settle the Alderdyce estate.

Still, there was a palpable aura in the square hall, which Peter had chalked up to antiquity. And something almost expectant in the atmosphere in the box room immediately above the hall, those two rooms comprising what was left of the old Norman keep. Amy was not a fanciful person, certainly not superstitious, or she would never have moved into Tower Cottage at all after Peter's death. Yet she avoided the box room, sending the children either to retrieve objects stored there or consign others to its capacious shelving or the huge, heavy wooden chest that dominated the front wall under the two slit windows. 'Flemish work,' the engineer had called the chest, with the modern addition of a thin veneer of cedarwood on the inside to make its purpose clear. He had wondered if the chest had been built *in situ*, for he could not see how it would otherwise have got through the doorway.

Peter had sat on the chest that day, Amy recalled: he'd thumped the wood, laughing at the hollow echo of the empty chest, remarking that it would be a good place to hide the body . . . several bodies by the size of it. Amy had felt the frisson then, running up her spine to seize her head and jerk it on the neck with an involuntary force that had astonished her. The engineer noticed and solicitously remarked that un-lived-in houses always chilled him.

Since they'd moved in, she'd made one concession to the distressing atmosphere of the box room: she'd put the brightest possible bulb on the landing and had Peter put an equally strong one in the box room's single socket. (Oddly enough, the children loved playing in the box room.) Tonight she turned on both lights and stood for a moment on the threshold, staring at the dark bulk of the carved wooden chest.

It did not move. The carvings did not writhe or gesture. A faint odor of lavender and cinnamon was detectable, mingling with old leather, wool, and camphor: homey smells, compatible with the room's use. Not a shadow stirred.

With swift steps, Amy crossed the room and tugged up the lid of the chest. Just as she'd thought. The two torn sheets, rough-dried, were neatly folded on top, her maxiskirts just below. But one was a check and the other black. Where was royal blue, or red, or green with a fur-trimmed collar? She sat on the edge of the chest and lifted one stack of garments, Patricia's outgrown jumpers and skirts, Peter's shirts and underclothes, socks. She turned in the other direction and sorted through business suits, vests, more jumpers, her crepe and wool party dresses. At the bottom were two pairs of old drapes and some glass curtains, white. Nothing gauzy blue. No ornate headdresses. No costume belts. She delved to the wood of the chest's floor and found only the mundane things she expected.

Fran was a literal child: if she'd said she'd dressed in green with no buttons and a fur collar, she had.

Puzzled, Amy ran her eyes over the contents of the shelves: nothing there surely but Christmas ornaments, boxed games, lampshades, empty jars, young Peter's tenting and backpack frame, oddments of china set aside for a jumble. On the other side of the door, the tea chests containing Peter's business papers, books, the family's suitcases as neatly stacked as they'd been since the day after removal from London.

Yet Sally Merrion had been dressed in royal blue . . . a queen's color . . . and gauzes!

A flash of color caught her eye and she turned toward the chest, blinking. She could have sworn that the topmost sheet had been, however fleetingly, a brilliant blue. To reassure herself, she smoothed the sheet, but her fingers told her that it wasn't velvet, just worn linen. She stood up, closing the lid of the chest, almost dropping it the final few inches as the full weight of the wood tore the lid from her fingers' inadequate grasp.

She'd ask Fran in the morning where she'd found those dress-up clothes. Possibly she'd misunderstood.

The frisson caught her by the back of the neck before she'd reached the safety of the door. It was like a hand on the scruff of her neck, pulling her back to the scene of some childhood crime: an injunction against a cowardly retreat.

In spite of herself, Amy turned back into the room and

stared around her. The scent of lavender and cinnamon was cut by a sharper smell, vinegarish. Then a sweetish odor, familiar but unnameable, assailed her, an odor as sharp as the previous intangible command to stay. Stiffly, Amy walked back to the chest, set her hand on the lid, imagining, as Sally might have, wondrous costumes in which to be medieval ladies-in-waiting . . . and a queen.

No torn sheets, no dull woolen jumpers now lay exposed, but royal blue velvet, a deep red wool dress, a green surcoat fur-trimmed, and belts, encrusted with rough-cut bright stones set in the dull gleam of gold links.

She let the lid drop and the compressed air smelled of sweat, human and horse, of stale food and spilled, soured wine, heavy perfumed musk mixed with camphor. Weakly, Amy sank to the cold stone floor, impervious to that chill.

'The Alderdyces came into money . . .' Mr Suttle's words came to mind.

Had some Alderdyce child, or adult, dreamed of hidden treasure in the old keep? And found it in the chest?

Amy shook her head, fighting to think rationally. Did the chest grant wishes, then? Pray God it was only one wish and Fran had had the chest's quota for them all, and that was the end of the matter.

She thought of gold and jewels, rich fabrics, Oriental silks, and gauzes, of ornate Arabian leather slippers. And opened the chest. Her heart pounded as she dropped the lid on those same imagined riches.

Mrs Mallett? She'd lived in Tower Cottage for years, spry till the day of her death. Hadn't Mr Suttle said so? Wanting for nothing, the house and grounds supplying her requirements.

Amy laughed, a single sound, hard and strained, like

her credulity. What had the widowed Mrs Mallett lifted the lid to find? A body? As Peter had whimsically suggested.

The sweetish odor, familiar but unidentifiable, pervaded the box room.

Amy screamed, a soft tortured cry, her hands stifling it to a whisper, lest Peter or Patricia hear her. That same sweetish odor had filled her nostrils as she'd knelt before Peter's coffin in the church. How could the house have killed her Peter in that bombed-out public house. It couldn't have . . . Illusions! Her longing for him that day!

'NO!' The single negative was as low as it was firm. She spread her hands, fingers flat on the lid of the chest, denying what could be if she so desired. 'No!'

She spread her arms across the chest in repression, in supplication, in prayer. This was just a chest with old clothes in it, two torn sheets and some dresses waiting for parties, for children to grow up to fill. This was just an ancient tower, used as part of an old house, a house where children could grow up in healthy country air, on fresh vegetables and milk, and where they could pick apples and pears in an orchard and bramble berries from hedges. Just an old house that had served many families in the same way.

The nauseating sweetness dispersed: lavender and cinnamon returned, and the smell of night and rain.

Slowly Amy pulled her arms together, rose to her knees before the chest. She placed the heels of her hands under the lid and, swallowing against the dryness of her throat, pushed upward. Her body blocked some of the light from the overlight bulb, but she saw the comforting white of old cotton sheeting, caught a whiff of her favorite cologne, impregnated in the dresses stored in the chest, a hint of the cedarwood. It was as she'd wished. She let the lid down gently and leaned her forehead weakly against the edge.

It took her a few moments to gather enough strength to rise. Really, she told herself as she walked toward the door, she ought not to attempt to do so much in one day, though they'd enough bramble jelly to last years, even with the amount Peter slathered on his toast.

She switched off the light and closed the box room door behind her. Her fingers hovered briefly over the key. No, she could not lock out what had apparently happened or lock in whatever it was. That would be superstitious as well as downright useless.

Nonetheless, when she flicked off the hall light, she said 'good night' just as if there were someone waiting to hear.

THE BONES DO LIE

They have pierced the wall of Time
And let the flood of centuries pour
Down in torrents of abused past
And future follies. Nor
Can the wit of man dam up
This foul stream, polluted
With History's excrement,
Channeled now in convoluted
Ways, cross-currented with tide,
Ebb and neap, with storm
From which only few can hide.

Vale was standing on Elric's shoulders, reaching for clumps of deep red cherries on the upper boughs when he thought he saw a wavering in the air. He went rigid with fear.

'Danger?' The Viking might speak bad English but he knew body language well.

'I thought I saw something! Something like a shift ripple.'

'Shift?' The Viking's fingers clenched Vale's knee so hard that he yipped in protest. 'Elric turn?'

'No. Just hold still.'

Vale parted the branches obscuring his view of the valley. It was so peaceful, with no suggestion of the ripple, like a flood of water on a glass pane, that preceded a shift. And Chloe was watching. Chloe was always on watch.

She wouldn't let anything happen to her people. That was the one constant for Vale since he had got caught in a time shift.

He had so hoped that there wouldn't be a shift for a long, long time. That they'd have the summer in the valley and he'd be able to leave the cellar all day long, to explore a region so familiar in contour, so differently habited in this kind shift by wood and meadow. He seemed to spend so much time gathering stuff to be synthesized. The Fooder was great but, after a while, everything you put in it tasted the same when it came out. To have fresh water whenever you wanted it would be great. It'd be good to clear his lungs of the fetid cellar air, which stank of damp stone, fear, and too many people. If he ever got back to his Born-time, he wouldn't complain about a Dorm again! There'd always been light and windows, and warmth and space. Space – that was the other chore that always faced them. He wished that the power cutters had lasted longer. It'd be so much easier, almost fun, to slice stone like fish – so hard to have to chip-chop it out sliver by sliver. But Chloe wouldn't let them go back out in that time. She'd said it was one of the most dangerous in spite of all the marvelous things they'd been able to plunder. She'd know. She'd watched the time stream for centuries and centuries. Chloe was old. As old as Time itself.

'See?' Elric asked, patient, but there was a hint of concern in the deep bass rumble.

'No. I don't see anything now,' Vale said grudgingly. The ripple *had* looked just like a shift. Vale narrowed his eyes and stared down the valley again, half-scared, half hoping the wavering would manifest itself.

Where the city sometimes was, or the little town, or the great sheet of glazed stone or, once, the orderly urban complex of his Born-time, there was only the convergence of the two rivers, peacefully flowing down to the sea. (Vale had been to the ocean once, on a Dorm trip.)

He couldn't be mistaken this time. The landscape leaked and swam. Maybe Chloe wasn't at the window slot. Maybe she'd fallen asleep. She'd been watching constantly since this shift had settled.

'My basket's full, Elric. Down please.' He tried to keep his voice calm, though he wanted to shriek out an alarm. If he scared everyone like the last time he thought he saw a shift starting, and it was only heat refractions, he'd get beaten by Steven when Chloe wasn't nearby.

'Mein alzo.' Elric grinned down at him, looking like something from a disturbed night, with his lip half sheared off from an old sword blow. Vale dutifully inspected the enormous can that the Viking had filled, his scoop-sized hands red-stained with bruised fruit – bloodlike juices dribbling down his beard.

'You're not supposed to eat half you pick, Elric,' Vale told him. 'We need all we can get for the Fooder. You eat more'n any of us and you get dam' uncongenial when you're hungry in a long shift.'

Elric understood the scolding tone and he looked away, just like a Dorm-mate avoiding the Mother's interrogation. Vale thrust that thought away.

'C'mon, Elric. Let's get these back to the cellar.'

He set as fast a pace as he could, swinging the heavy basket from one hip to the other. It was an awkward burden to lug up the steep slope, and he had to take care not to spill any. Elric, his big can balanced with negligent ease on one broad shoulder, strolled leisurely up the incline.

Vale glanced back over his shoulder, anxiously spotting the others. Would they have time to make it safely in if it really was a shift? Steve was working at the pool below the falls with Fateri, the breed. Teo-somoli, the squaw, was gutting twice as many fish as Jean. (Well, she was city-bred, from a time like his own.) Peter, Grace, and Samuel ranged the stream banks for herbs and cress. Down the valley, more figures were bobbing up and down, picking dandelion greens. They tasted bitter but Chloe made everyone eat them. Except Elric, who only grinned at anything besides meat, or Fooder slabs when he couldn't stand the hunger pains any longer.

Chloe had sent a crew into the woods, too, to trap and forage. She certainly wouldn't have done that if there'd been any sign of a shift. And she knew. She knew in her bones. Vale wondered what it felt like to have your bones know something . . .

It was a shift! And it was something you felt, like the most horrible, wrenching, vomit-causing, bone-moving, earth-shuddering, mind-grabbing terror!

Elric let out a roar and began charging up the slope, cherries pelting down on Vale. Mindlessly clutching his basket, Vale staggered and clambered on, keeping his eyes on the one thing not rotating, the threshold of the cellar. He heard the keen of the time-winds but if they buffeted him, he was too fear-ridden to notice in the total cataclysm. One minute it seemed he and Elric walked the sky, with the earth threatening to slam them on the head; the next, the grassy slope had turned to solid ice and they grabbed at burning-cold sheaves of dead grass, or lost their grip in mounds of snow-fluff. Chloe was in the threshold now, calling to them, her eyes wide, like blue beacons, her arms outstretched as if she could somehow stave off the fearsome currents that could lock them away for all eternity into that time stream.

As long as Vale could hear her, as long as he could see her tall figure, an orange wraith by the black basalt safety of the cellar, he was all right. As long as she remained there, they had not slipped into another current of time. They had not shifted.

Elric's can was knocked from his shoulders as he plunged through the doorway. Chloe grabbed the giant

Viking as if he were no more than Vale himself. The sight
of her making the blubbering warrior scoop up the now
doubly precious fruit gave Vale the steadying he needed.
He found his second wind, tightened the hold on his
basket, and forged on. It got harder, for the slope had
altered, a rocky face forming where the upland meadow
had been.

'Chloe!' Vale screamed, tortured with the knowledge
that she might not help him: that she rarely moved from
the cellar and he desperately wished that she would. For
him. She loved him best – she always said she did. He
was her boy, son of her heart. 'Chloe!'

'Throw the basket in,' someone yelled in his ear above
the shrieking wind. He was seized and thrown, arms
flailing in terror that the breathless winds of time might
blast him into another stream. Then Chloe's fingers
caught his and dragged him, wailing, across the grooved
basalt threshold. Someone else yanked him to his feet,
propelling him down the corridor until he fetched up
hard against the far wall and lay, sobbing, scarcely aware
of being kicked, of a heavy foot grinding his fingers into
the stone floor. He only knew he was safe, that Chloe had
pulled him through the door. The yelling and screaming,
the cries and angry shouts, even Elric's roar of outrage
and the splat of fist against flesh failed to penetrate his
hysterical relief as Vale pressed his cheek against the cold
damp stone. It was a bad shift but he was safe, safe, safe!

Suddenly the awful caterwauling of the shift lessened
as the iron-banded, studded door thudded into position.

'Boy saw. Boy saw!' Elric was shouting.

'If Vale saw something,' Steve's voice cut through
Elric's chant, 'then, by God, you must have, Chloe. You
must have! Who's missing? Who did you jettison this
time, you witch? Who did you dump?'

'Burleigh and Travers aren't here,' Jean cried, 'nor the
three new ones . . .'

'Burleigh and Travers?' Steve's echo hung, a scorn-laden accusation in the supercharged atmosphere.

Muffling his sobs of terror, Vale struggled to a sitting position, trying to focus through tears on the tense knot of dimly seen figures.

'What's bothering you now, Chloe?' Steve demanded in a harsh, bitter voice. 'Your magic slipping? Don't your spells work on Nuclear Age minds? Or is it that you can't run philters through a food synthesizer?'

'Thee had best leave off nattering, Steven, and get this fruit to the machine. Happen thee brought any of the fish?'

The icy fear in Vale's chest was dispelled by the calm unruffled tone of Chloe's voice. Why was Steve so angry with her? Even if Vale had cried alarm the moment he saw the first ripple, there would not have been enough time to save Burleigh and his work party. Sudden shifts had happened before. Why didn't Jean stop crying?

'Is food all you can think of, you . . . you black witch?'

'Shifts can be frightening times for us all. *I* am not without compassion and true understanding, Steven . . .'

'Don't try that crap on me anymore, Chloe!'

Vale gasped, for he could see that Steve had Chloe by the arm. Elric, who had slumped to his knees after getting the heavy door closed, stood up, growling. He had been uncongenial to Steve ever since Chloe had taken Steve into the front room.

'Unhand me, Steve!' For all she had neither changed tone or volume, Chloe was to be obeyed. 'Vale sweeting, compose thyself. Bring us light. We must salvage the fruit. Ah, Teo-somoli, we shall thank thee for the fish before this shift is over. 'Twill be a long one, I fear.'

As much to be out of the tension as to do Chloe's bidding. Vale ducked past Steve, into the front room. The shelf where the power beams were kept was to the right of the door. His hand unerringly closed on the smooth rectangles of plastic. He fumbled slightly for the notched edge of the switch. Light blinded him momentarily. He adjusted the strength down. You so often saw much more in less light. And learned more in total darkness.

Vale shivered. He didn't want to think about that now. He spotted a twig of three cherries and picked it up. There was bruised fruit all over the floor. Teo-somoli was waddling toward the Fooder room, her buckskin skirt gathered before her, showing her knock knees. Fascinated and hopeful, Vale stared until she turned the corner. He wondered what Chloe's . . .

'Yes, let's save the fruit and give thanks for the fish,' Steve was saying now. Of those in the chamber only he and Chloe did neither. 'We're one big happy family again, aren't we? Who else was with Burleigh and Travers? Did Grace make it back? She was farthest down the stream.'

'No, she stumbled and got pulled back,' Peter's choked voice said from the dark.

'We tried, but she was too soon pulled beyond our reach,' Samuel added.

'Neatly done, Chloe. Neatly done,' Steve said. 'All the dissidents have been sloughed. Well, nearly all.' Steve strode after Teo-somoli, his boot heels clacking on the stones.

It was a bad shift, a deep one, and Vale tried hard, very hard, not to listen to himself. Deep shifts were always preceded by many flickerings and waverings. Chloe had told him that time and time again, after she realized that he actually could see what only her eyes had been able to discern before. It was such a bad shift that even the cellar rocked under the impact of time distortions.

Elric chanted constantly, but that was better than the girls' hysteria. Couldn't they *try* to be congenial? Chloe finally dosed them. Vale half hoped that she'd offer him some of the cup, but he was relieved when she didn't.

She sat by him instead, which was infinitely preferable. And when he had to put his hands to his ears
against the high whines of time, she pulled his head to
her bosom. He wondered fleetingly why Burleigh had
called her a 'cold bitch.' She was so warm and there was
always a lingering spicy smell about her, so different
from a Mother's astringent purity.

The shift went on and on, with dead still periods that
were worse than the roaring currents. Reassured by
Chloe's soothing nearness, Vale tried to sleep during the
calms. But everyone talked then, trying to break that
horrible quiet with the sounds of humanness. Everyone,
except Steve and Jean, who had pointedly moved into the
unfinished back room: another fact the others tried to
ignore. Vale thought it was awfully brave of them, and
very uncongenial. Chloe was angry with them. He could
feel her body go hard though her hands remained gentle
as she stroked his head.

In such times, you ought to be congenial, even if you
didn't feel like it, Vale thought. It was your duty to the
Dorm in which you lived. And this cellar, with mixed
sexes and ages, was still a Dorm situation.

If only he'd been congenial that day, centuries back
and across time, he'd be a Guidance Aide by now. That
is, if he had turned fourteen. Subjective time was
impossible to measure but his body was manifesting
certain changes that marked the onset of puberty. At that
point of his Born-time, you could be a G.A. and have
access to the File Banks. He might even get lucky and
have a chance to find out who his dam and sire were from
the Dorm Files. Traffer had. Or said he had.

Then Vale, Dorm 143, M-82, had to pull an antisocial
and get caught up in a time shift – without even knowing
such a thing existed until it swooped him away from
everything familiar and known. But here, Chloe called

him 'her' boy, son of her heart, and she'd find the perfect time for him, the shift that gave him the best possible chance of making something of himself, instead of being pounded and chipped into a congenial mold. A time shift, Vale hoped wistfully, when he could have a family, a mother and a sister . . . Though he only thought such blasphemy, Vale shivered with delight. He might even have grandparents, whatever they were. But could they compare – ever – to a Chloe? Grace had said she had had grandparents, and aunts and uncles and cousins.

Well, all those relatives hadn't made her quick and clever. She'd been sobby and clumsy, silly nonconforming behavior. And that's why she'd got caught in the shift, not because Chloe hadn't warned . . .

The banshee wail of the time-winds rose to make even thought impossible.

They couldn't go out when the shift was completed. Not even to get water. Chloe removed the tiny plug set in the door and hastily bunged it up.

'Inferno,' she said in her calm voice and sat down, her hands folded in her lap, as she composed herself to wait again.

Vale had kept close to her when he felt that the shift was ending, just to be sure his hunch was accurate. He'd said nothing, of course, and hadn't looked at anyone, trying to keep his face expressionless, but pleasant, the way Chloe did, so no one would guess what he was thinking. And he'd known the shift ended badly. Even before Chloe announced it.

These were the times Vale hated most of all: the wait between shifts, with the water getting foul, the air fouler, and the Fooder slabs thinner and thinner . . . as well as people's tempers. This time, though, Chloe, didn't insist that they work on enlarging the back chamber. They didn't need it now, Vale reflected, not with so many gone. He fell to wondering what time stream had swirled away Burleigh and Travers and Grace and the others. A natural one, or a warring one? It was amazing how Chloe could tell from just looking into the valley. Maybe she'd meant to leave Burleigh and Travers, even Grace, in that lovely era, with cherries in the trees and fish in the stream, rabbits jumping about in the woods and singing birds.

Burleigh had been in the cellar when Vale arrived. He'd been in the front room with Chloe for a long time . . . until Steve had come, if Vale remembered rightly.

But Burleigh had been from a high-tech time. He hadn't been much good with his hands, being used to servo-mechs, until Chloe made Fateri teach him how to trap small game. Everyone had to help in the cellar. Particularly when they got to a good time with cherries and rabbits.

Some times there wasn't even any fish, just grass and trees, or rock, glazed and dead.

Why had Steve accused Chloe of ditching them? She never told anyone when she was going to leave them. She'd question everyone thoroughly when they first arrived. It was exciting to get a newcomer and listen to the weird tales they told about their times. Vale had often wondered if they were really telling the truth or just suffering from desynchronization. Some of the eras hadn't seemed too bad to Vale. Like Steve's. And some of the times they'd like to live in sounded far worse – to Vale – than what they'd come from. Maybe that's why Elric had stayed with them so long: he wanted a time of much battling and sailing, brawling and drinking. There wasn't any such asocial behaviour in Vale's time, what with drone sea-miners and a congenial society of nations. Still, Chloe said that, in the cellar, they crisscrossed the time sea, like a suspended weight, hitting different arcs of its circle as it swung back and forth, around and around.

Vale wondered what time Chloe had come from. She'd never say, only smile. And when would he make the final shift in to his proper time?

The second one did not seem to be as long a shift, fortunately, for Steve had turned very uncongenial, and Jean kept crying and wouldn't drink the sleep inducer that Chloe offered everyone.

And it was winter, cruel, cold, with snow clogging the cellar entrance. There was a settlement at the river, a good-sized one with buildings spread out in concentric circles. No vehicles were visible, no smoke. In fact, no activity at all could be seen in the field glasses and Steve turned them up to their highest power.

'There is life,' Chloe said. 'And we must have water and provender. We shall wait upon the darkness and then thee shall forage in the settlement, Steven.'

'Oh?'

At such an impudent rejoinder, Chloe gave Steve a sharp and penetrating look. Her large blue eyes were steady, with that inner fieriness that scared Vale more than her most icy voice.

'Thee will go, Steven, and, because thee does not trust me, thee may take Vale with thee. Bring the boy back safely! If harm befalls him . . .'

All Vale could understand was that he was going to be allowed to go on a search party, and he could barely contain his jubilation. He'd begged and begged to be able to go but Chloe had never permitted him beyond the range of her naked eye.

'We'd better use protective suits, Chloe,' Steve was saying. 'The layout down there, the buildings themselves suggest a high-level technology. Converted heat . . . which we could do with.'

'Our requirements are not technological, Steven,' Chloe interrupted sharply, her eyes locking with Steve's.

'Thee will remember that. We become far too dependent on the gimcracks and novelties of passing ages.'

'The food synthesizer? The air purifiers? The clothes we stand up in?' Steve mocked her.

'Aye, all of them,' she answered him in her steady voice, and she turned abruptly and reentered the cellar.

'I can really come, Steve?' Vale demanded.

'Oh, Steve, don't go!' On his other side, Jean was pulling urgently at his arm.

Steve laughed and hugged her. Vale wondered that he was so permissive with such a weepy girl. 'I'm in no danger as long as the heir apparent is with me.'

Jean stared at Vale so hard, so coldly, the oddest expression on her face, that Vale backed away. All the joy of the raiding was replaced by a distasteful confusion he couldn't understand.

'Yes, very apparent since this last change.'

Then Chloe returned to say that there was time before dark to trap, if they could, or gather evergreen limbs for a good sustaining meal before dark. Teo-somoli was sent to the pool. She chopped a hole in the ice and stolidly settled down to fish. Eric, using one of the big cans like a shovel, began to fill the cisterns with water.

'If you'd just let us get a pump, Chloe,' Peter argued again, 'we could always tap the stream.'

'Thee knows full well that only water kept safely in the cellar is free of the contaminations of time,' Chloe answered and in such a way that Peter did not persist.

But he could grumble as they plowed and slithered down the slope to the edge of the forest.

'What makes *her* the authority?'

'Her witch's bones,' Steve replied, his eyes gleaming.

'She is not a witch,' Vale said. 'The concept of a witch is the product of a superstitious, untutored society, ignorant of scientific lore, too primitive to relate cause and effect . . .'

'Out of the mouths of babes,' Steve laughed back at Vale, and tousled his hair in the teasing way the boy both resented and sought.

'He's a babe no longer,' Samuel said maliciously, 'for look you, there were many changes these past shifts.'

Vale shot Samuel a resentful look. The man had no right to be uncongenial just because he'd come upon Vale in the jakes when he was . . . Vale squirmed around to hide his fiery face.

'It happens to all of us, Vale,' Steve said, and, although his voice was kind, his eyes were very thoughtful. 'Chloe's not a witch. She does have some knowledge or skill denied us which enables her to perceive shifts. However, I defer to the rationale of your Born-time. There are no witches. But . . . Chloe . . .'

'I can see shifts.' Vale glared at Samuel and Jean.

Steve gave him another long deep look. 'Yes, you do. If . . .'

'If, if, *if!*' Peter muttered bitterly.

'If Vale really can,' Jean said, gasping the words out as she trudged through the snow, 'we could all get out in a good time.'

'What is your good time, Jean of the City?' Steve asked, extending a helping hand to her. His whole face had changed, Vale noticed, when he looked at Jean.

'My own time,' Jean said with such uncharacteristic firmness that they all stopped and stared at her. She glared back. 'And I know how good it was. Now!'

'By m'bones, the gel's a realist,' Samuel said. 'But, could we trust the lad to be captain of our fate, fellow voyagers? Vale, since you are rehearsed in one mystery, have you become versed enough in the others Chloe practices to recognize a truly congenial time?'

'Congenial time?' Vale repeated the phrase in astonishment. Samuel wasn't the least bit congenial.

'Young Vale . . . *vale*, that's Latin for farewell . . .

375

and farewell we ought to say to that bitch of time's hell, or is it hell's time? And we ought to take the lad with us when we run to save him his virginity. Otherwise he'll soon miss it. She hungers for a mate as she fishes in the sea of time, with chance her bait and arrant flattery her line.'

'Shut up, Samuel. Let's get this chore done!' Steve said, for they'd reached the forest now.

Samuel leaned against the nearest tree, panting from the double exertion of talk and walk. Samuel rarely said so much.

'Why fool with these?' he demanded, 'when there's a fine good town, with solid rib-clinging victuals . . .'

'We don't know that,' Steve interrupted him. 'We'd better be sure of some food first.'

'But if we're going to raid the town at dark,' Peter said, grumbling as he stripped off boughs, 'I don't see why we have to fool with vegetation. The synthesizer's still half-full. I checked it myself.'

Steve turned and frowned at Peter. 'Good point, boy. Good point.' He went right back to cutting but he didn't say anything, even after they got back to the cellar with their harvest. He said nothing until they were getting ready for the raid, when Chloe told them which buildings to investigate.

'Been shifted here before, Chloe?' he asked then, staring at her with hard eyes.

'I could not say,' Chloe replied without hesitation. 'The type of structure and the form of the settlement are familiar. But then all times begin to have similarities to one who has circled the present for centuries.'

'How long *have* you been here, Chloe? Who ensorcelled you?'

Chloe met Steve's hard glare.

'I chose my fate.'

'So you prefer us to think.'

376

'The shift may not hold long. Be sharp-eyed, Vale. Warn the others the instant thee sees a ripple. I'd not risk it but we must have more protein. I like not the patterns of these past few shifts. Try either the first or second building to the left of the center . . .'

'Shouldn't I remember to check for breaker boxes or eye circuits?' Steve asked mockingly.

Chloe gave him a long studied look. 'Thee knows well how to approach a strange place, Steven, else thee would not have returned so often.'

Samuel chuckled.

'Will I return from this one, Chloe?'

She gave him a longer stare. 'In the fullness of time.'

Then she stepped aside to let them pass. When Vale surreptitiously touched a fold of her dress for good luck, she caught his hand.

'Stay close to Elric and Fateri, Vale,' she whispered, and made as if to kiss his cheek. Then, as both realized their eyes were level, she drew in her breath with a hiss, and stepped back.

All the long trek down to the rivers, Fateri and Steve took turns checking on the settlement through the binoculars.

'How long ago was the snow, Fateri?' Steve asked once.

The breed jammed his fist through the crust, fingered the snow. 'Three-four days.'

'Any sign of people?'

Fateri shook his head slowly. Steve peered at the settlement for another long moment and then gestured the party on.

Full dark had fallen by the time they reached it, and Vale was tired. They huddled together, chafing cold faces and frost-clogged nostrils as Fateri crept around the outskirts. Vale wished they'd have time enough for

Fateri to teach him how to move so easily through snow, and creep around noiseless and unseen.

When the breed returned, shaking his head, Steve motioned to Peter and Samuel. They walked right up to the nearest building, then cautiously inspected it. Peter tossed twigs toward it but nothing happened. Finally Peter walked right up to one. Peered around its corner, disappeared behind it, and then reappeared on the other side. Just then lights began to appear on all the buildings like an advancing wave. Instinctively they all ducked down, to be roused by Peter's shout.

'It's automatic. C'mon, cowards.'

Cautious still, Steve rose, motioned the others toward Peter and Samuel.

'There's no one here. I tripped an automatic relay when I reached the front,' Peter said, grinning.

'What kind of place is this, then?' Samuel asked, peering closely at the doorway.

'Could be some kind of unmanned power station,' Steve said, but his tone was dubious. He stood squarely in front of the door now, examining the frame, the inset handle. He looked around at the other buildings in the same circle, their blank door-mouths indistinguishable from the one he faced.

He hunkered down, eyeing the doorframe until, with a grunt, he passed his hand over the threshold. Nothing happened. He rose and, using the handle of the power beam, touched the door handle. He gave another grunt and then, as if he expected no result, tried the door.

He dropped where he stood. So did Peter and Samuel. A huge hand grabbed Vale by the shoulder. He was pulled violently off his feet and propelled back the way they had come so fast that his head rocked on his neck. He had a kaleidoscopic jumbled impression of Peter, Samuel, and Steve sprawled in the snow by the door, of the circle of lights, of the dark slopes beyond the settlement, of Elric's staring eyes and gaping mouth on one side of him, of Fateri, plunging and lurching through the snow on the other.

This confused him, for he distinctly remembered seeing Fateri, flat on the snow, and Elric staggering and shouting. Now the three of them were racing away from the others as fast as they could. By the time they reached the safety of the darkness beyond the ring of automatic lights, Elric was gasping and groaning. Here Fateri stopped them, pushing Elric and Vale flat into the snow while he crouched, his attitude one of intense concentration. Vale made himself look back, where Peter, Samuel, and Steve lay, plainly visible and just as plainly motionless.

'Are they dead?' Vale asked, trying to keep his voice a whisper, only it came out in a broken rasp.

Fateri gestured abruptly, listening. Suddenly he whirled, his eyes so wide they seemed all whites. He pointed urgently up the slope, pulled at Elric, who was heaving for breath, and, taking Vale's arm in cruelly tight fingers, led the way up to the cellar.

'We can't just leave them,' Vale protested, trying to pull free. 'They may not be dead.'

'Bad sound,' Fateri said, jabbing a finger to the southern sky.

'We can't leave them!' Vale struggled harder.

'No! Chloe say you come. You safe!' Elric said, capturing Vale's other hand and yanking him along.

'Go!' the half-breed urged. 'Fast!'

There was no use resisting, so Vale tried to keep up with Elric's long stride and Fateri's jog trot. They did not relinquish their tight holds on him, though he reassured them he wouldn't be silly anymore. It was doubly humiliating: to be half helped along because his legs were shorter than Elric's and less powerful than Fateri's, and because they wouldn't trust him to walk . . . to run . . . alone.

They had reached a concealing slope when the bad sound Fateri had heard materialized into a stolplane. It circled the settlement twice at low altitude before squatting down, blocking from the watchers all sight of the fallen men, and of whoever emerged from the vehicle.

Fateri waited no longer but renewed his grasp on Vale's right hand and started to move. Elric did not, and Vale felt as if his other arm would come out of its socket. His cry of pain stopped Fateri, and both of them stood looking down at the fallen bulk of the Viking, his fingers seemingly welded to Vale's forearm. Fateri knelt down and began to slap the man's face.

'What's wrong?' Vale asked, his voice breaking again as he imagined himself forever locked to the giant.

Fateri grunted as he rose and began to pry the thick fingers loose.

'Is he dead?' Vale demanded, slapping at Fateri's hands.

'Not dead. Sleep. Not duck good.'

'Asleep? We can't leave him. He'd die in the snow.'

'He not die. They find. We go. Go fast.'

Fateri got Elric's fingers loose but their viselike grip was nothing to Fateri's claw-hold, nor the supple strength of the breed as he dragged the reluctant Vale onward.

'We can't leave them all. We can't, Fateri. I'll help you with Elric. We can't leave him.'

Fateri only grunted at his protests, jerking him roughly forward if he slowed so much as half a step behind. Suddenly Vale realized that Fateri was striking off to the lower end of the forest, where they had been garnering boughs scant hours before.

'That's not the way, Fateri. Where are you taking me?'

'They follow. No find track.'

Fateri was jogging faster now, because the thick evergreens had kept the ground remarkably clear of snow. Fateri came up against a huge trunk and stopped. He motioned for Vale to climb up into the tree and then roughly boosted the boy to the splintered end of the first limb.

'They'd find us here, Fateri,' he protested. His buttocks were sharply prodded to make him climb higher.

'Stop.' Fateri reached the same limb and then stepped around him. The breed took one of Vale's hands and fastened it around his wide leathern belt. Then guided the other to the limb directly below them. 'Hold. Follow.'

Scared, resentful, Vale did as he was told. At least Fateri moved cautiously, giving Vale time to find his own footing before moving on. Then suddenly, they were both in the air, a scream wrenched from Vale's mouth, to be cut off abruptly as he hit the ground. Or rather the thick myrtle bushes into which Fateri had launched them.

'Hurt?' Fateri asked with no sympathy in his voice.

'No!' Vale was too filled now with hate and anger to allow room for pain.

When he would have waded out of the thicket, Fateri directed him deeper into the growth, carefully moving the branches so as not to leave further evidence of their passage. Twice more, Fateri had them aloft and once, when they had to traverse a wide clearing, he pushed Vale on ahead, then brushed the snow with an evergreen branch to cover their footsteps.

Once Fateri was evidently satisfied that they had confused pursuers, he began to trot purposefully through the still dark forest. Shaken emotionally by the double desertion, Vale doggedly kept up.

Suddenly they emerged on a slope, the ridge that sheltered the cellar, black above them. Below, the settlement was still bathed in light. It was too far away for them to make out details such as bodies by an entryproof door, but the thud-whomp of the stolplane was audible on the thin cold night air. Fateri grunted, then pointed out the cluster of colored winkers that outlined the stol as it quartered the slope they had left.

'They'll find Elric!'

Fateri grunted and, taking Vale's hand, jerked him forward. Vale didn't take his eyes from the winking lights: red/green/blue/white, the blue delineating a narrow PVA as the stol went into hover.

Was Steve inside that? And Peter and Samuel? Wasn't it better for Elric to be found than for him to freeze to death? Why had they all so easily assumed that the people of this time were unfriendly? Surely property must be protected from asocial activities but that did not mean general inhumanity. The thought of the cellar without Steve, even without Peter and Samuel – with Fateri the only other male – was suddenly unbearable.

As if Fateri sensed Vale's thoughts, his grip tightened and he gave him an admonitory yank.

'Fast!'

They were nearly to the cellar. He could see the narrow line of light. Would Chloe be watching? Had she seen? Had she known what would happen? The thought burned Vale's mind so fiercely that he gave a cry and stumbled.

'Vale! Thou'rt not hurt?'

Chloe's voice was clearly audible. Audible, too, in Vale's mind was Steve's mistaken assurance. 'I'm in no danger as long as the heir apparent is along.'

Stunned by the realization of what Steve had meant, Vale did not resist as Fateri pulled him up the final snow-slick rise to the cellar.

'Elric, too, Fateri?' Chloe asked as the breed dragged Vale the last few feet.

'You knew!' Vale found his voice. And found strength enough to free his arm. 'You knew what would happen to Steve. And Peter and Samuel.'

'Vale, sweeting.' In Chloe's soothing voice was an oddly disturbing note. 'Vale, come in, dear heart. Come, we've hot fish stew to give thee strength.'

Chloe even took a step toward him . . . a step out of the cellar! She took another step and grabbed his hand, sweeping him into her arms and back into the cellar. As she pressed his cheek against hers, her hands were burning warm on his half-frozen flesh. They ran up and down his body before embracing him tightly again.

Chloe was glad he was home. She had hot food for him. She had actually stepped out of the cellar to greet him.

Then she held him from her and looked deeply into his eyes. Looked with an expression in their blue depths that made him very nervous somehow. And he was frightened. More frightened than he had been when the last shift started, or when Steve had fallen by the door, or Fateri had pushed him off the tree branch. Frightened to the very marrow of his bones. He had seen that look before, seen Chloe look at Steve that way, and Burleigh, and, once, even Elric.

And each of them had been shifted, with no warning. Shifted into a time not their own.

Before either Chloe or Fateri could stop him, he ducked out of the cellar, his feet skidding on the trampled snow. Even as he stumbled and slipped, sobbing, his only thought was that in a society that protected its belongings, there would be order and congeniality. There would still be a Mother for him somewhere.

THE END

A LIST OF OTHER ANNE McCAFFREY TITLES
AVAILABLE FROM CORGI BOOKS

THE PRICES SHOWN BELOW WERE CORRECT AT THE TIME OF GOING TO PRESS. HOWEVER TRANSWORLD PUBLISHERS RESERVE THE RIGHT TO SHOW NEW PRICES ON COVERS WHICH MAY DIFFER FROM THOSE PREVIOUSLY ADVERTISED IN THE TEXT OR ELSEWHERE.

☐	08453 0	**DRAGONFLIGHT**	£4.99
☐	11635 1	**DRAGONQUEST**	£5.99
☐	10661 5	**DRAGONSONG**	£4.99
☐	10881 2	**DRAGONSINGER: HARPER OF PERN**	£4.99
☐	11313 1	**THE WHITE DRAGON**	£5.99
☐	11804 4	**DRAGONDRUMS**	£4.99
☐	12499 0	**MORETA: DRAGONLADY OF PERN**	£5.99
☐	12817 1	**NERILKA'S STORY & THE COELURA**	£4.99
☐	13098 2	**DRAGONSDAWN**	£5.99
☐	13099 0	**THE RENEGADES OF PERN**	£5.99
☐	13729 4	**ALL THE WEYRS OF PERN**	£5.99
☐	13913 0	**THE CHRONICLES OF PERN: FIRST FALL**	£4.99
☐	14270 0	**THE DOLPHINS OF PERN**	£4.99
☐	12097 9	**THE CRYSTAL SINGER**	£5.99
☐	12556 3	**KILLASHANDRA**	£5.99
☐	13911 4	**CRYSTAL LINE**	£4.99
☐	14180 1	**TO RIDE PEGASUS**	£3.99
☐	13728 6	**PEGASUS IN FLIGHT**	£5.99
☐	13763 4	**THE ROWAN**	£5.99
☐	13764 2	**DAMIA**	£4.99
☐	13912 2	**DAMIA'S CHILDREN**	£4.99
☐	13914 9	**LYON'S PRIDE**	£4.99
☐	08344 5	**RESTOREE**	£4.99
☐	08661 4	**DECISION AT DOONA**	£4.99
☐	09115 4	**THE SHIP WHO SANG**	£4.99
☐	10965 7	**GET OFF THE UNICORN**	£4.99
☐	14098 8	**POWERS THAT BE** (with Elizabeth Ann Scarborough)	£4.99
☐	14099 6	**POWER LINES** (with Elizabeth Ann Scarborough)	£4.99
☐	14100 3	**POWER PLAY** (with Elizabeth Ann Scarborough)	£4.99
☐	14271 9	**FREEDOM'S LANDING**	£5.99

All Transworld titles are available by post from:

Book Service By Post, P.O. Box 29, Douglas, Isle of Man IM99 1BQ

Credit cards accepted. Please telephone 01624 675137, fax 01624 670923, Internet http://www.bookpost.co.uk or e-mail: bookshop@enterprise.net for details.

Free postage and packing in the UK. Overseas customers allow £1 per book (paperbacks) and £3 per book (hardbacks).